Aragon

Henri Matisse : a novel

I

But man is our subject . . .

I. – Henri Matisse, *Self-portrait* (1906).

Aragon

Henri Matisse a novel

Translated by Jean Stewart

I

Collins, St James's Place, London

The lines from Dante's *Divine Comedy* quoted on p. 55 are from the translation by Dorothy L. Sayers of *Book II: Purgatorio*, published by Penguin Books, Ltd.

KING ALFRED'S COLLEGE
WINCHESTER

759·4
MAT

54869

ISBN 0 00 211537-9

© Éditions Gallimard, 1971

© S.P.A.D.E.M. 1971 – Matisse

© 1972 in the English translation by
William Collins, Sons & Co., Ltd, London, and
Harcourt Brace Jovanovich, Inc., New York

TABLE OF CONTENTS OF VOLUME I

But man is our subject! And when will man ever come up for discussion?

Will anyone in the world raise his voice?

For man is our subject, in his human condition; and a widening of the eye upon the deepest inward seas.

SAINT-JOHN PERSE

(*Winds*)

The door, or the window, opens on to the past, uneasily. Feathers and dust of all sorts, insects caught in their own threads, memories, old scribbles, letters with illegible signatures, every sort of repentance and regret, tattered dreams, forgotten fragrances, rooms where the light has gone out, a nameless something that curbs the spirit, every sort of happening, the wind of life, digressions sprung from God knows where, the way paper and one's memory fade, the way everything blurs, the way fire itself flickers out, and there are no butterfly nets to catch words or the look of things, nothing is harder to hold than the music that once enraptured you, the illusion of words heard, lost, reinvented, with unintentional untruthfulness, and how can one retrace the thread of things said, or go backwards out of a swoon . . . the door, the door . . . everything is jamming it, and when it yields at last, when that cloud lifts, that dread, what will there be behind, what part of ourselves still there, what smoke? (For those who, once or many times, have experienced the blotting-out of the world, it's a pearl-grey smoke over everything, and nothing is left but one's head and one's pain . . .)

This book is like nothing but its own chaos. It straggles over twenty-seven years, twenty-seven years this Christmas, like a trail of scattered pins from an overturned box. It can't make sense, still less take shape. It goes rambling off, retraces its steps . . . At times you might think you're following it, and then you find yourself in some other place which you thought you had left long ago . . . Just as if we were in a theatre where the tickets have been wrongly numbered, confusing both spectators and ushers, so that nobody feels at ease in his seat, and there's a kind of tenseness when the orchestra in its pit softly strikes up the overture, the curtain quivers, but something stops it from rising (who? whose hand?) and if the play's to begin they should calm down, stop stirring uneasily in their creaking seats in dread of being turned out at any moment, they should . . . they should . . . and suppose the play were to start . . .

all the same before they calm down, they'd fall into their places like metal balls into their holes in those little round boxes that I'm always playing with, or perhaps . . . unless words are shattered before being spoken, who knows? Perhaps we are nearing the close of a calamity, men are flying round the moon, what is happening outside? We are living in the interrogative tense, as one might say the present or the future . . .

This book is as it is. I can't help it. It slipped out of my hands a long time ago, and I have been picking it up, page by page, ever since, in the confusion of years, retrieving it, rounding it up at every street corner, only to let it fall at the next bend in the road, fall and escape from me and scatter, and then I suddenly snatch back a page and wonder at it. What's this about? Where did this come from? In which chapter, which moment, of the book and of the world? At what point of time by my crazy watch? And yet from the depth of these sentences, through these awkward murmurings, there sounds a kind of calm, distant echo of a man; he seems to be sitting in the garden on a stone bench, and the evening is growing cool, he must pull over his shoulders some woollen garment that had slipped from them, something fawn-coloured perhaps, or whitish in this wintry light, just after dusk . . . This book is as it is. I can't help it. Perhaps because the man has fallen silent, because I can no longer hear the voice, because he has ceased to be a presence and has become a question. Questions. This book is nothing. Neither a story nor a speech. Forgive me. I have called it a novel, probably so that I'll be forgiven for it. I myself have reached the evening of life, that moment which is no longer day and is not yet night, and already doubt hangs over everything and over oneself–wasn't it in December '41 that I met the painter Henri Matisse at Cimiez, in the hills above Nice? I shall have to come back to that. Not so much for the sake of chronology as for my own sake, to understand myself at last, my hesitations, my delays, my sloth. Uncertainty on the threshold of oblivion. And then the fear, at the end of it all, that I'll have said *no more than that*.

And first, to get my bearings, I must go back to that article I had begun to write before I went up to Cimiez, indeed I thought I had really written it before I came to that palace of mirages where a great painter called Matisse was then living, a painter whom I had so often, all my life, hesitated to visit . . . Streams of rain were creeping like ants down the windows of the bus as it climbed uphill in that haze of December wetness that poured over everything, the pavements, the scattering of people, Queen Victoria, with her nose broken, standing at a crossroad, the cypresses, the houses, the winding road, my secret anxieties at the time, and somebody in that jolting box softly whistling a tune from other days, a song that made me prick up my ears . . .

(1968)

Matisse, or Greatness

(November–December 1941)

Poésie 42, No. 1
signed *B. d'Ambérieux*
(The pen-and-ink drawings illustrating this text were all chosen by Henri Matisse and given to the author for *Poésie 42*.)

Henri Matisse 29/3 39

After the storm has passed over a human home, after the waters have withdrawn, sweeping away a strange jumble of objects, old faded photographs, a cradle, the things of everyday along with souvenirs of that other war, the old war, after the stream of fugitives has flowed past along the road, with its crazy vehicles bearing a tragic load of high-piled mattresses and terrors, then in the devastated courtyard, in the empty spaces, here and there among sheds and squares, stations and hotels, children sit on the ground and count their broken toys.

I don't know why this image comes into my mind irresistibly, with the intensity of despair. We are those children, counting our precious fragments with a heavy heart; but they are not dolls or lead soldiers. For some nineteen months now,* all over France people have been ceaselessly scanning that inventory in search of reasons for going on living, for not weeping in front of mirrors, for looking at one another without contempt. And while some find a bitter and clamorous comfort in denouncing our weaknesses, others, and I feel I am one of these, sometimes silently assess our riches, our imperishable treasures, our incomparable sources of pride. The fresh air that cleanses our lungs. That which restores to us the sense of our greatness.

Our past mistakes may be scored up against us, our faults and our failures, yet nothing and nobody can rob us of that sense in front of French painting. And perhaps nothing in our painting can arouse it so keenly as that achievement which is its climax and its crown, the work of Henri Matisse.

In time to come, no one will think of dating a man or an idea or a discovery by saying: That was in Loubet's day, or in Deschanel's, or Lebrun's . . . They'll say: That was in Matisse's day. Which does the Renaissance mean to us – such and such a Pope or petty tyrant, or Michelangelo? There was the age of Louis XIV, and now, for the past half-century, there has been the age of Matisse, ranging from the wild blaze of Fauve painting that started at the time of the *style métro*, like a sudden leap forward, a repudiation of Impres-

* From June '40 to January '42 – here the author is already speculating on the interval between writing and being read, but I don't think *Poésie 42*, No. 1, can have appeared before February or March. In any case, the author had not written that to be read in 1969. He had not anticipated so long a delay in publication. He wrote in the present, which was the only tense one could believe in then. (*Note of 1968*)

And now, on reading the proofs, I see that the copyright is dated 1971 . . . two years will have elapsed, been wasted, and this won't have been read in 1969. (*September 1970*)

◀1. – Pen and ink.

sionism, up to these drawings in which the strokes sing and the line dances and which sum up, at this darkest hour of our history, the purest essence of French sensibility, that victory of the mind which does not depend on the number of aircraft or the speed of armoured cars.

I say that this belongs to us, to us alone, and that it's our duty to be consciously proud of it. I say that in those plains of Flanders and Artois, so often ploughed by foreign armies, an identical genius brought forth Watteau at Condé and Matisse at Le Cateau. And I cannot think without emotion of that gloomy, ill-kept museum at Lille, where the pictures are hung one above the other according to the curator's whim, under a ceiling of grimy glass, with no electric light, and where, of all the paintings, two – almost invisible – once caught the attention of the boy Matisse, Goya's *Old Women* and *Young Women*. Of all the paintings, those two; and he promised himself, in a manner of speaking, that he would paint like that, just as he might have promised himself that, since he could walk, he would reach a certain monument. Think of Matisse's sparkling work, that blaze of colours, the breadth of his draughtsmanship, and think of the young man making that choice. Let your thoughts dwell on that, and then switch them, following the Spanish painter of the *Disasters of War*, to the portrait of a woman with her dog that hung in Madrid in the palace of the Duke of Alba before war came to Spain* . . . And then switch back suddenly to Matisse, and the paradox will bring home to you the profound analogies that exist between great painters, in consequence of which if the young Matisse despaired of ever being able to paint like those academic race-horses in training for the Prix de Rome (whose dwelling he can see today, with a certain melancholy, from his windows at Cimiez, those glorious windows that open on to the finest painting in the world) – today, on the other hand, when, late in life, Henri Matisse casts his glance around his studio and that rich, peaceful and well-ordered landscape in which the Nouvelle Villa Médicis is merely a touch of ochre and bitumen in the evening light, he may think, with the Goyas at Lille still in his mind's eye: 'I have painted like that.' In a manner of speaking.

And we understand it in our own manner, we who failed to keep Le Cateau or its neighbour Caudry, where the factories make such splendid lace, which though it bears no relation to the Goyas at Lille yet has a mysterious kinship with those women, that ivy in an opaline glass, those succulent plants, that sketch of a marble statue, that white clematis, the whole kaleidoscope of the painter whose humble contemporaries we are.

The elegant coconut palms with their upswept hair, rustling in the trade winds that blow uninterruptedly, accompanying the murmur of the free sea over the reef against the quiet, unruffled water of the lagoon, at the mouth of the channel . . .

* It was still there in October 1936; I saw it when I visited the palace to advise on measures to be taken for the preservation of works of art. It was after this that everything transportable was removed (the wonderful Gobelin tapestries were left hanging, since they would have crumbled if they had been taken down, and they were destroyed soon afterwards by Franco's aircraft, commanded by the Duke of Alba himself, who bombarded his own house). I imagine the Goya in question must today be in the Prado, thanks to the Republicans. (*1967*)

2. – Drawing illustrating a letter to the author, which with Matisse's consent had been enlarged to fill two pages of *Poésie 42*.

I look at these notes, with all their crossings-out and interlinings, which Matisse allowed me to take from him, and on which he has tried to set down for me, to explain, what the Tahitian landscape means to him, that strange landscape that obsessed him to such an extent that he withdrew the selection of drawings he had originally made for *Poésie 42* and replaced it by a new group centred round the big drawing which this article accompanies, and which represents that obsession – so much so that he has chosen to surround it with this *Woman* and this *Shell*, because they suggest Tahiti although they are not in fact Tahitian, and also with the lovely *Woman Holding a Guitar*. I don't know whether, writing at the close of 1941, I shall have succeeded in conveying to you, reader, the strangeness of this preoccupation. I should have liked to.

The great painter sleeps badly in his Sleeping Beauty's palace high up in Cimiez, full of green plants and singing birds. At night, haunted by thoughts of those islands which he had visited some ten years previously, he got up to write down those sentences which, over and above his drawing, outline his obsession:

The lagoon – of the atoll of Apataki on the left, separated from its neighbour Apataka by the channel over which hangs a light, lovely white cloud which tells the natives that a boat will come within a week. The elegant coconut palms . . . etc., and he took up this phrase again to clarify it, on another sheet of paper, from which I have copied it. There are the things he has written and there are the other things he tells, about the wind for instance, which bends the palms, about the danger of life on that island rising less than a yard above the sea which sometimes sweeps over it so that everyone has to climb up into the trees and wait for it to withdraw, and about the desert island near by, to which the natives take their livestock, leaving them there and bringing them a little drinking water every week, and about the colour. But here I can decipher something more:

The water of the lagoon, a greyish jade-green, coloured by the bottom which lies very close, the branched corals and their variety of soft pastel tints, around which pass shoals of small fish, blue, yellow and striped with brown, looking as though they were enamelled. And dotted about everywhere the dark brown of the sea-cucumbers, torpid and almost inert . . .

(He is referring here to the lower part of the drawing, which is not a foreground, but the depth of the lagoon, whose surface occupies the centre of the drawing, as the following lines make clear.)

. . . This lagoon enables the painter on holiday, when he dives, to analyse the particular character of the light in the landscape, both beneath and above the water, by means of successive impressions, dipping his head in and withdrawing it suddenly, and seeking the relation between the pale gold light and the pale green light, which he . . .

This version of the text is unfinished, and I am obliged to refer to his first draft:

This lagoon, which enables the painter on holiday, when he dives, to analyse the particular qualities of the light at the same time as those of the vegetation, to stimulate his sensitive retina by successive impressions, by the quality of the light under the water and above the water seen alternately through the vegetation peculiar to each place . . .

A note has been added in the margin, written vertically, which seems mysteriously connected with this point in the painter's meditation. It reads:

. . . overwhelmed by a great sense of the loneliness which reigns over the whole scene (in spite of the intense light, as zestful as the light of Touraine), comparable to that which we experience in the great nave of a Gothic cathedral (Amiens), where the booming of the organ would replace that of the lagoon.

Here, directly expressed – and I have sought, amidst the network of crossings-out and interlineation, not to 'arrange' this transcript of a thought caught unawares – is everything connected with this mysterious drawing, in which a sudden remembrance of Tahiti has taken Matisse back ten years: Tahiti, which appears here and there in his work without apparent reason, as for instance in that other drawing, an illustration to Mallarmé's *Fenêtres*, where the window opens unexpectedly on to a landscape of that distant

3. – Pen and ink.

island. Lest I betray the text and impoverish the whole thing I must here transcribe the opening paragraph, which bears no relation to the lagoon itself nor to that cloud heralding a boat:

. . . Tahitian girl, with her satin skin, with her flowing, curling hair, the copper glow of her colouring combining sumptuously with the sombre greenery of the island. The rich scent of frangipani, the deep, substantial scent of the blossoming pandanus recalling the smell of good new bread coming out of the baker's oven, and the almost suffocating scent of tuberoses and of that Tahitian flower the tiari, tell the traveller he is nearing that isle of thoughtless indolence and pleasure, which brings oblivion and drives out all care for the future . . .

In fact the words had been written thus, but the end (*that isle of thoughtless indolence . . .*) had been inserted before *The rich scent . . .*, like a coda to the preceding phrase: *the sombre greenery of the island, that isle of thoughtless indolence* . . . etc. Thus in his sleepless mind this memory had twisted about, catching its own tail. And Matisse goes on to tell me that the coral was violet and pink, and he dwells on the gold of the landscape and on the excellence of the sea-cucumbers, those black things you can see between the corals, much sought after by the Chinese, who send them home to their own country. And he repeats the phrase: *Tahitian girl, with her satin skin . . .*, and shows me among his drawings women's heads with a look of that Tahitian girl, such as the head

* In *Poésie 42*. Here I have chosen rather to relate it to Matisse's text. (*1970*)

which stands at the beginning of this article* corresponding to the shell that stands at the end of it; the painter wants me to know, wants us to know that he looks at a woman when he is drawing her in the same way that he looks at a shell. To be accurate, he said: a plant. He thinks – and here is yet another mystery – that this will put me at my ease in talking about it.

And that's all there is to say about the lagoon.

The elegant coconut palms with their upswept hair, rustling in the trade winds that blow uninterruptedly . . .

4. – Shell (front view).

Surely this shell will bring me the sound of the sea!

The reader frowns: 'What's so strange about it?' he grumbles. 'The painter has sought a theme round which to group his drawings, a pretext for isolating them. There's nothing strange about that.' How wise you are, reader, you are like the sun: there's nothing strange about it. Nothing. Nothing strange. And yet . . . which is the harder task, to inscribe the thought of the present moment among things eternal, or on the contrary to seize hold of what is eternal and inscribe it in the passing moment? These women, these figures, these plants, which like a perfect thought unfolding adorn the walls of the painter's studio, seem at first sight as detached from the moment as Phèdre or Bérénice, or the Eastern Queens in the mosaics of Ravenna or Santa Sophia; glancing at them, you may think you have judged them rightly, but take care; note that they hold all the drama and the savour of their time. Note that the weight of a woman's chin against her wrist is heavier in the scale of things than many events, not because it has here been set down *for eternity* but because it was set down the day before yesterday, when the thing itself had its weight in the world.

There is thus nothing strange in the fact that, in this dying year[1] which is

1. 1941

just a date in the long sequence of dates, the great painter, in whom our native greatness is summed up, was seized (whether in hope or in despair) by the haunting memory of the Happy Isles, in his own fashion, neither deliberately seeking exile (since their light reminds him of Touraine and their loneliness stirs him like that of the peerless nave of Amiens Cathedral), nor moved by that escapist spirit which, from Rimbaud to Gauguin, has for the past seventy years governed our feeble dreams. Matisse, who is unthinkable outside France, carries on that great French interpretation of the world which remains our indefeasible right. There is nothing strange about it. Nothing but what is after all quite natural. We are, be it understood, in the realm of the eternal.

And then everything I should have liked to say is in that little cloud, so light, so dazzling, over the channel between the two islands. Don't you like reading the clouds? I could readily see in it a woman's head with loosened hair, or a great butterfly such as we don't see nowadays, or a fist clenched against the sky: the natives, more sensibly, see it as the herald of a boat that will come during the week. Come on, get your minds to work on that boat . . .

But follow the stroke that encircles the cloud, see how amazingly the artist's thought informs the slender line, which expresses all the yearning for the boat that will come. What Matisse teaches us, what we are told by this drawing with its immediate perfection, set in the margin of that urgent commentary written during a sleepless night, is the infinite expressive complexity of the pure line, of that seeming chance that guides the painter's hand, a written message at every point in its course and in every blank space that is left. This is badly said, but none the less important: drawing is a written message – that's something the academics have long forgotten, and that is what we learn anew, a lesson fraught with all the sweetness and greatness of French art, from the Master of Cimiez, Henri Matisse, our pride.

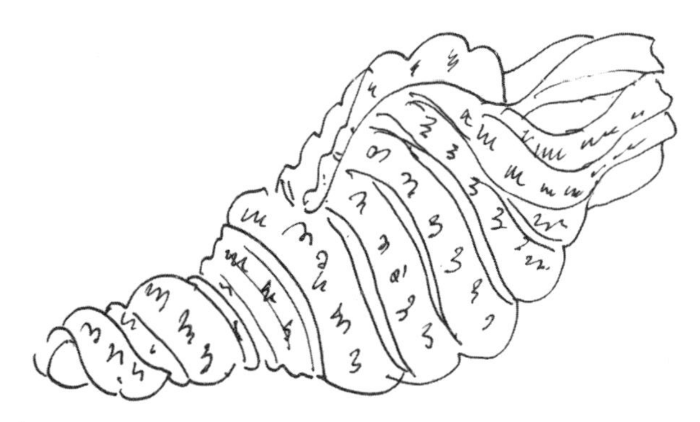

5. – Shell (back view).

To Be Inserted

(An explanatory note)

(1967–68)

Unpublished

To look back twenty-seven years, to turn and stare into that distant past, since when people and things have all lived out their individual destinies within the common fate. Words no longer have the same meaning, everything needs endless explaining. Henri Matisse, for example.

Should I not have done better to begin here – I mean, to put what I am now writing before what has preceded it, namely that article for *Poésie 42*, No. 1, which so strangely approached the unknown by way of the unknown? And in that case the article would have been in its right place in a sort of anthology of my prefaces, commentaries or what have you, about Matisse, its right chronological place, I mean. And yet if all this were, if it is, a novel, and not an anthology of articles, such a sequence would seem, would merely seem to have skipped its beginning and taken a sudden jump into history. If this were a novel.

The fact is that it is a novel: *the story of one of my follies*, I suppose (with apologies to Rimbaud), rather than an 'art book', as they call those works where the word 'art', used as an epithet, wrongly ascribes or at least pretends to ascribe to the author of the book a quality belonging to his subject, the protagonist of the 'novel'. This is a novel, that is to say a language invented to explain, apparently, the singular activity engaged in by a painter or a sculptor, if one is to give their common name to those adventurers in stone or on canvas whose art is precisely that which eludes verbal explanation. Assuming that the writer of this art book or novel has not used it as an expedient, a pretext for telling us about himself, about his knees or his bald crown, about his antique stele and the manifold difficulties of deciphering its hieroglyphics, which he finds as hard to understand as we do . . . Thus . . .

Thus when J.-P. Eckermann wishes to bring us close to Goethe, before beginning his *Conversations* (Weimar, June 10, 1823: *I arrived here a few days*

◀ 6. – . . . In 1939, in early summer . . . in the studio lent by an American sculptor, Mrs Callery, in the Villa Alésia . . . (p. 27).

ago, but did not see Goethe till today. He received me with great cordiality . . . etc.), he takes care to preface them with his own autobiography: *I was born at Winsen an der Luhe, a small town between Lüneburg and Hamburg, shortly after 1790. I first saw the light in a hut* . . . And so on.

(Oh, Lüneburg may mean nothing to you, but in 1813 the Prussians and the Russians beat the Saxons and the French before its walls, on those plains where they used to breed horses, and from which they extracted peat and salt. That was how Lüneburg, where they manufactured playing cards and wallpaper, lost the shame of being merely the chief town of a foreign department called the Lower Elbe . . .)

I might have copied this procedure, but I was not born in a hut, I never had a job in the tax office at Lüneburg, I never imitated Theodor Körner's *Lyre and Sword*, although like Eckermann and Körner *I harboured in my heart a hatred for those who for so many years had been our oppressors* . . . In short, I felt no desire to tell my own story, starting with my birth in the autumn of 1897 in the Esplanade des Invalides in Paris. I'll plunge straight into the deluge, and start in 1939 with France during the phony war. Then . . . '40, '41 . . .

When I had not yet begun to write *Aurélien* I had been tempted to resume the project, which I had dreamed of before even going to see the painter, of writing *Henri Matisse, a Novel*, and which explains that first approach of mine, a letter in the year 1941 and my hesitations later that year . . . To go up to somebody in the street and say: 'Monsieur, I'm thinking of writing a novel about you . . .' And what if he's not just the man in the street but a king, up there in his palace? For four months I had nursed the project, prepared apologies for my audacity, trying to prove my usefulness. Then the obsession of the 'novel' took shape, when I had just finished *Matisse-en-France* (actually, in the present book, what comes next), that is to say in April '42, so far as the letters written to me by Matisse enable me to date the thing. This preface to *Thèmes et Variations* had a secret significance for me, as being a kind of trial approach to *my* theme, a marginal commentary on Matisse's method, in order to justify the liberty taken with my subject, my own variations, the sort of detachment I aimed at, just as a painter, having started a portrait, finds his hand running away with him and becomes more concerned with his own activity than with seeking a likeness, forgets his model and eventually changes from a photographer into a novelist.

Let this be understood: under the impact of 1940 I felt like a mere supernumerary in some spectacular tragedy, a long, bitter insomnia, and the very idea of a novel, of any novel, seemed to me beyond the bounds of possibility – particularly as my last work of that odd species, *Les Voyageurs de l'Impériale*, had been completed amid the thunderclaps of the outbreak of war, and to resume *that sort* of work somehow presupposed that everything else, all the chaos in my mind and in my world, had been done away with, that the world was back in its place . . . Basically, this dream of a novel about Henri Matisse was a form of self-deception, one of those stories you tell yourself or tell a dying person (when my mother died, at the time I am speaking of or a little later, in March 1942, I whispered to her that I had just been listening to the London radio, that the Russians were advancing along the whole front and that the war would soon be over, and this was scarcely a lie . . . and I shall never forget that last look in my mother's eyes, *believing me*).

At the time when I visited Matisse at the end of 1941, hope was beginning to dawn for me, as something *improbable* took place beside me – Elsa* had embarked on what was to become *Le Cheval blanc*. Perhaps that was why my dream recurred. It faded quickly. Because my novel had become that preface . . . It had to be finished, so that Elsa's example could reassert its power, so that Aurélien could oust Matisse as my fictional hero.

* Elsa Triolet, Aragon's wife. and a poet and novelist in her own right.

But before I had yet begun *Aurélien*, the idea of a novel about Matisse haunted me for some days longer. How did I happen to give up this obsession, to set aside this temptation? A plausible reason might be found in contemporary historical events in 1942 and 1943 . . . And yet this seems to me inadequate to explain my renunciation. Perhaps, rather, the book *Thèmes et Variations*, to which Matisse had diverted my attention, expecting a preface from me at a time when my name was an embarrassment to any publisher, the to-do there was about my signature at the time, the sleight of hand by which the six wretched compromising letters of my name were banished from the cover to a shamefaced little subtitle inside, all that sort of thing must have killed any inclination for a casual approach so ill suited to the time. It was only in March '43, a year after those days I had spent with Matisse in the role of Eckermann, that I received a copy of *Thèmes et Variations*, from which I gathered that for the publisher it was an act of some generosity to let me play second fiddle in a corner of *Henri Matisse*, like some music student from the Conservatoire. I'm already skipping things; for I haven't yet talked about Nice in 1941–42, and now here we are, Elsa and myself, in 1943 at Lyons, in that Montchat attic where, having already lost our identity for the outside world, we received *Thèmes et Variations*. And as for writing a novel, I gave up trying to make Matisse imaginary in order to spend my stolen time with

Three states of the painting *The Rumanian Blouse*, photographed 7. – 13/12/39.

Bérénice and Aurélien Leurtillois, whom I had begun to describe at Nice without really believing in them, as soon as I had finished *Matisse-en-France*. Or thought I had finished it. Because nothing that one could undertake or do, in those days of which I won't talk, was ever finished, one was always at the mercy of some accident, of a ring at the door . . .

But all this, I am well aware, will seem very obscure to those of my present-day readers with whom I am chiefly concerned, I mean those who have just discovered the romance of being a man or a woman, who shock their elders by their way of dressing and then undress in the twinkling of an eye. For them, who know nothing about us – I don't mean only Elsa and myself, or Matisse and his dreams, but the whole world in which we lived – except what they happen to have been told, I shall have to go back a few months and set the whole thing in that strange atmosphere of Nice which is reflected in *Mille Regrets* (the opening story, Elsa, in your book of that name) and in a little

at the painter's request in course of execution.

8. – 20/12/39.

9. – 22/12/39.

decasyllabic poem in *Les Yeux d'Elsa*, published at Lausanne in March '42,[1] but written in '41 (I think towards the end of that winter, February or March), *Fêtes galantes*, out of which Francis Poulenc made a song the following year:

> *On voit des marquis sur des bicyclettes*
> *On voit des marlous en cheval-jupon*
> *On voit des morveux avec des voilettes*
> *On voit les pompiers brûler les pompons*

and so on, five verses of the same sort, giving Nice, 1941, somewhat the look of a modern drugstore.

In short, if readers in 1969 are to make anything of the book which has

1. In *La Revue de Belles-Lettres*, Vol. 78, No. 5.

10. – In 1939, Matisse leaves *The Rumanian Blouse* in this state, at Nice.

11. ▶
Work resumed on *The Rumanian Blouse* in 1940. (See p. 32 for the final version, reproduced in colour, of the painting now in the Musée d'Art Moderne in Paris.

All earlier versions are known only through photographs in black and white, since Matisse would wipe out and repaint on the same canvas.

grown up gradually, starting with the article I wrote at that time for Pierre Seghers's magazine in Avignon and including the little essay (*Le Ciel découpé*) from the last pages of *Les Collages*, published by Hermann in 1965 – what was I saying? if they are to understand these pages, whose only link is Matisse himself, covering some twenty-four years – indeed, as I write these words, between twenty-six and twenty-seven – some sort of curtain-raiser must be provided for those who are interested, to enable them to follow the play. And this ought presumably to be a kind of prelude, which would show the author, amid the silent chaos of defeat, turning up at Nice, or returning there, and the longing he felt to know a man by whom he had been obsessed for nearly

2-I-40

thirty years, without ever seeing him in the flesh,* and how that meeting took place, that is to say how the great man himself brought it about – Matisse with his pale blue eyes, the mysteries of his craftsmanship, its algebraic quality, that power of giving colour to ideas, at the end of that long story of twentieth-century painting which links our own time with the deep, dark past by way of Bonnard, Renoir, Monet . . . That visual France whose ancestry words can but feebly trace, and on whose future painters alone can throw open the window.

Perhaps that would be all that remained of the novel I had dreamed of, as you'll see, constantly interrupted by the scenes of my waking life, like a play in which the intermission is the real play and the novel the intermission. And when you go back into your dream nothing is where it was, people's names have changed and so have the colours of the scenery, everything's askew, and you lose your way in the streets, the lie of the land is unfamiliar . . . Life is utterly incoherent. Who knows? Perhaps only the beginning will be valid, that moment in December 1941 that marked, at any rate, the beginning of the plot. Racine, you know . . . Act I, scene 1:

Oui, puisque je retrouve un ami si fidèle . . .

But we two did not know one another and the time had not yet come, as you'll see, when I could say to that master of my youth:

Le dessein en est pris, je pars, cher Théramène,
Et quitte le séjour de l'aimable Trézène . . .

Because I had only just come there: to Nice, I mean. And I was not the son of Theseus. But when I went into that palace at Cimiez, with its pillars, its great empty halls, its staircases like mighty shoulders, in that emptiness of the *introit* everything seemed to begin as in *Bérénice*:

Arrêtons un moment: la pompe de ces lieux,
Je le vois bien, Arsace, est nouvelle à tes yeux.
Souvent ce cabinet, superbe et solitaire,
Des secrets de Titus est le dépositaire.
C'est ici quelquefois qu'il se cache à sa cour,
Lorsqu'il vient à la reine expliquer son amour . . .

Let us pause here . . . I am not the King of Commagene, and I have no confidant, and maybe Voltaire or somebody might criticize me, like Racine, for

* For instance, it must have been in 1913, or rather in 1914 since the picture was apparently painted in the autumn of 1913 at Issy-les-Moulineaux, that my mother caught me holding a photograph of the *Portrait of Madame Matisse*, seated in an armchair, with her scarf draped about her (a reproduction of this painting was later to be included in the selection of modern works which André Breton and I pinned up on the walls of our barrack-room, or at least of a little room adjoining it, in the Val-de-Grâce in September 1917), and exclaimed: 'If you care for things like that, wretched boy, you're done for . . . This photograph had been given me by the girl who appears in *Les Cloches de Bâle* as Catherine Simonidzé. (See p. 32.)

◄ II. – *Portrait of Madame Matisse* (1912–13). Hermitage Museum, Leningrad.

using such terms as *la pompe de ces lieux* or *ce cabinet superbe*, but I would reply that I am not 'a prince whom such splendour should not dazzle and who has other things on his mind than the ornaments in a study . . .' Never mind, put yourself in my place, I was far more dazzled by this deserted Grand Hotel than I should have been by any number of Louvres. Moreover, I had not yet found the lift, and had climbed the stairs in some haste, so that I was out of breath. Let us pause here . . . to begin all over again, as is fitting, starting with the hero of my novel himself.

Born on December 31, 1869, at Le Cateau-Cambrésis . . . That's a long way back to begin: Roger Martin du Gard, our neighbour at that time (living at Nice, I mean, at the time we were there, and Matisse), having come across some Colonel in the volume of *Les Thibaults* he was writing, in an effort to grasp the character felt bound to begin with the officer's parents and trace his career from the cradle onwards. At least so Jean Paulhan told us. So that he died (Roger, I mean) before his character had taken shape, or could be introduced by the author to his readers.* The fact remains that this officer prevented any further development of the proposed story.

* He keeps on intimating the arrival of this Colonel, but he seems to be on duty elsewhere.

And so, mindful of this example, we shall here assume (good Lord, what does that plural *we* mean, could this book have several authors without the author knowing it?) . . . we shall, *I* shall assume the reader to be familiar with the earlier history of our (my?) hero and only introduce Henri Matisse (of whom these pages contain no biography, strictly speaking) when he is nearing his seventy-first birthday, that is to say during the course of 1940; this slight flashback will entitle the so-called author to display a certain familiarity with the painter, such as is usually allowed only towards people of roughly one's own age. For otherwise – dare I, *dare we*, admit it? – few men have given me, and other people, such a sense of the unattainable, of an irreducible remoteness. So then . . .

So then, I take our painter at the moment when he left Paris in 1940. He was living at the Hôtel Vendôme. But . . . but . . . No, I can't start with the Hôtel Vendôme. Is it conceivable that anyone should live in the Hôtel Vendôme, on the right wrist of the square if you take the arms as stretching from the Caesar on the Column? I had learned from the bright confusion of certain women's lives what it was like to live in the small hotels of Montmartre or the Trocadéro district; I had myself stayed at the Gallia, the Ambassador, the Commodore (which might make you think I was rich, but it was only thanks to the complicity of my friend Marcel Duhamel, at the expense of his

8 13-9-46
12-22-7-42

N° 1
Naissance
Matisse
Henri Emile
Benoît

A contracté mariage à Paris (seizième arrondissement) le huit janvier mil huit cent quatre-vingt-dix-huit avec Amélie-Noémie-Alexandrine Parayre.
Le Maire

L'an mil huit cent soixante-dix, le trois du mois de janvier, onze heures du matin, par devant nous Jean Baptiste Thésin-Bonnaire, adjoint, remplissant par délégation spéciale les fonctions d'officier de l'état civil de la ville du Cateau, chef-lieu de canton, arrondissement de Cambrai, département du Nord, est comparu Emile Hippolyte Henri Matisse, âgé de vingt-neuf ans, commis négociant, domicilié à Paris, se trouvant momentanément au Cateau, lequel nous a présenté un enfant du sexe masculin, né le trente et un décembre dernier, à huit heures du soir, chez Benoît Gérard, rue du Chêne Arnaut, de lui déclarant et d'Anna Héloïse Gérard, âgée de vingt-six ans, modiste; et auquel il a déclaré vouloir donner les prénoms de Henri Emile Benoît. Lesdites déclaration et présentation faites en présence de Benoît Gérard, âgé de cinquante-neuf ans, cultivateur, aïeul maternel de l'enfant, domicilié au Cateau, et Constant Soufflet, âgé de trente-neuf ans, tailleur d'habits, oncle par alliance dudit enfant, domicilié au Cateau. Après lecture, le père et Benoît Gérard ont signé avec nous, Constant Soufflet a déclaré ne savoir le faire.

Henri Matisse Benoît Gerard

12. – Birth certificate of Henri Matisse (December 31, 1869), inscribed in the register of the Mairie of Le Cateau-Cambrésis, with a note in the margin referring to his marriage (January 8, 1898).

13. – Mme Émile Matisse and her son Henri (1889).

14. – Henri Matisse (centre) at the Académie Julian (1892 ?).

Henri Matisse
9/39

relatives who owned these splendid hotels); I had watched Oscar Kokoschka painting the Place de l'Opéra from a window of the Grand Hôtel; Éluard had introduced me to the Terrass Hôtel in the Rue Joseph-de-Maistre, above the Montparnasse cemetery, where one overlooked – where, I suppose, one still overlooks – Stendhal and Murger; I had been living in the Madison, behind Diderot on the Boulevard Saint-Germain, in 1927, when I joined the Communist Party . . . or soon after; what was the name of Ezra Pound's hotel, which I think was in the Rue de Beaune, and which has now disappeared? and that year or the next, in the Hôtel du Mont-Thabor, a room at the far side of the courtyard resounded to the strains of an allegedly Louis XIV dulcimer played by the celebrated Votichenko . . . Anything you like, even the Ritz, where that American lady . . . and I won't mention the Hôtel des Grands Hommes in the Place du Panthéon, or the Istria in the Rue Campagne-Première, which are too much part of my own life. But who the devil could I have known at the Vendôme to enable me to picture Matisse there, on the first page of my novel? Nobody thought of taking his photograph there. I have no documents; it was only after the war and the Liberation that Elsa and I happened to lunch there in the rooms of the then Ambassador to Canada, General Vanier, and his wife, in all innocence moreover, quite unaware that Matisse had lived there, which fact I only discovered quite recently. Besides, how could he have worked there, how could he have painted in those rooms where his wrist would not have had enough play for an arabesque? Actually he had rooms at the top of the hotel, from which there was a marvellous view over the square. Moreover, he had presumably chosen the Vendôme because of its position opposite Charvet's, his tailor's. And then, going over to the Right Bank meant being in a strange country, rather like a tourist visiting Paris.

Matisse, then, was living in the Hôtel Vendôme . . . But you must realize, too, that since 1938 he had had a great refuge at Nice, the Hôtel Régina at Cimiez, above Nice, which had been turned into flats, whence he had come to Paris in 1939, in early summer, to live in the Hôtel Lutétia and work in the studio lent him by an American sculptor, Mrs Mary Callery, in the Villa Alésia; he had left it just before the declaration of war, for a lightning trip to Geneva to see the exhibition of masterpieces from the Prado, he had returned to Paris on September 3 and had then spent two or three weeks away from the capital at Rochefort-en-Yvelines, in the Auberge Saint-Pierre, and less than a month later, some time in October, had gone back to Cimiez. In the atmosphere of the phony war, Henri Matisse, feeling a kind of nostalgia for the light and colours of distant lands, had wanted to return to Morocco, which he had visited in 1912, and to renew his acquaintance with its land-

◀15. – *Woman in a Hood*, pencil drawing dated 10/1939, made at the Auberge Saint-Pierre (Rochefort-en-Yvelines).

III. – The 'room on the ground floor giving on to the back garden, which the owners did not usually let', a painting usually referred to in this book in Matisse's own terms: *the picture in the Albi Museum* . . . (Ciboure, May–June 1940).

scapes, but administrative difficulties over visas, etc., had led him to plan, instead, a trip to Brazil. Back in Paris in April 1940, he had his ticket and his visa, and his passage booked on a boat sailing from Genoa on June 8. History was to ordain otherwise.

Let's pick him up, then, at the Vendôme, where in April '40 he had settled for reasons of convenience in those phony war days, and also because he needed suitable clothes for his proposed equatorial journey and intended to order them across the way; but things very quickly turned out otherwise, he had barely been there a month when the situation worsened, and what with air-raid warnings, and the need to go down into the cellars, which Matisse refused to do, being more afraid of cold than of bombs, he was obliged, after the invasion of Belgium, to resign himself to leaving Paris. The obvious thing was to return to Cimiez. But the painter's son, Pierre Matisse, who had for a long time been living in the United States, cabled to advise him against this, because of the rumours then current in New York of an imminent Italian invasion. In these circumstances, how could one reach Brazil by way of Genoa? Henri Matisse cancelled his passage on the Italian boat. He had been complaining of abdominal pains recently, while at the Vendôme, but his doctor had assured him it was nothing serious. He finally left for Bordeaux on May 19 with his secretary, Lydia Delectorskaya, taking the train, which was crowded enough but without the discomfort of the subsequent exodus, which he thus avoided.

However, Bordeaux was already over-full, stopping there was out of the question, and they resumed their journey after a couple of nights in a hotel. It was at Ciboure, a sort of suburb of Saint-Jean-de-Luz, on the further side of the Nivelle estuary, that Matisse eventually found several rooms in a private house, some on the first floor, overlooking the harbour, and one on the ground floor giving on to the back garden, which the owners did not usually let but which the painter persuaded them to give him as a studio. I refer to this elsewhere.* He stayed here about a month and a half, until after the armistice, when the Germans were expected to arrive at the frontier.†

It was at Ciboure that he received the first American offer of a visa for the United States. He refused it, for such a departure seemed to him like desertion. It is incorrect to say (as does Alfred H. Barr, Jr, in his *Matisse*, published in 1951 by the Museum of Modern Art in New York) that it was at this point that Matisse decided not to leave France. He had never had any such intention, and even the proposed visit to Brazil (which was to have lasted no more than one month from start to finish) had been envisaged not as an escape but simply as a way of turning the phony war period to good account. An erratum slip inserted in Mr Barr's book, after receipt of a letter from Lydia Delec-

* Page 91.

† And when, in view of the continuance of the war, he decided that his only course was to return to Nice.

16. – Claude Duthuit, the painter's grandson: 'The drawings of Claude made at Marseilles are dated between August 18 and 22 . . .'

torskaya, admits this fact, confirming it by reference to a letter to Pierre Matisse dated the following September which is included in the body of the book.

And so at the beginning of July 1940 our travellers loaded their belongings on to a taxi and made for Saint-Gaudens, where they had found temporary lodgings. Here Matisse suffered from a recurrence of the pains he had felt in Paris. He resumed his journey on August 8, stopping briefly at Carcassonne, where he had another attack of the same pains, and reached Marseilles on the 17th; here, quite by chance, he met his daughter, Mme Duthuit, who had come to send off her little son, Claude (in the care of Mrs Eugene Jolas, widow of the editor of the magazine *transition*), to join his father, Georges Duthuit, in the United States.*

The drawings of Claude made at Marseilles are dated between August 18 and 22. The precise dates are not vitally important here; the fact remains that Matisse was back in Nice before the end of the month. The doctor he consulted there also diagnosed his recurrent abdominal pains as merely symptoms of enteritis, and treated him for this until the end of the year. Thus for

* According to Mrs Jolas, she had come to Marseilles and was sitting at a café in the Canebière when she saw H.M. and his secretary walking by. She hailed the painter by name; he stopped in surprise, took a little time to recognize her and then came up to join her. Lydia D. moved away tactfully, without having the least idea what was happening. It was then that Matisse learned from Mrs Jolas that Mme Duthuit and her son Claude were in Marseilles. His journeys from Ciboure to Saint-Gaudens and beyond, and the state of the posts, accounted for his failure to receive his daughter's letters; he would have preferred his grandson to remain in France, as he himself had

17. – Henri Matisse working at *La Verdure* in his flat at the Régina at Cimiez (December 1940, photograph by Varian Fry).

a long time pain was relegated to a minor role in this part of his story.

Pierre Matisse had forwarded to his father a fresh American proposal: Mills College, California, offered him a chair. The painter replied at the beginning of October that he had not changed his mind about staying in France. About this time he completed, almost simultaneously, *Sleeping Woman* and *The Rumanian Blouse*, both similar in workmanship. The final version of the latter, now in the Musée d'Art Moderne in Paris, is dated October 1940.

In December, the head of the American Aid Committee in Marseilles, Varian Fry, went to see Henri Matisse and offered him asylum in the United States, as his committee had done for a number of intellectuals. Once again Matisse refused.

decided to do. But the question had been settled, and the child's father was now expecting him in the United States. This chance encounter, however, brought the painter into contact with his daughter, who remained in France, where she subsequently played a heroic role for which she would perhaps not have felt free if the child had still been in her care.

Meanwhile, however, his pains were growing worse, and the time he could devote to his work each day was diminishing. Finally he had to go into hospital to be treated for an obstruction of the bowels. And when X-rays revealed the existence of a tumour, Mme Duthuit was sent for and hurried to Nice to look after her father. On medical advice he was transferred to Lyons on January 7, 1941. Here he was operated on, soon after January 10, by Professor Santy, assisted by Professors Leriche and Wertheimer. I don't know what led A. H. Barr, Jr, to assert that the operation did not take place until March. This error was repeated in 1954 in Gaston Diehl's book. Presumably these are mere details for the art lover who is more interested in the date of a picture than in such particulars. But perhaps one should not rely on specialist historians, who, here and elsewhere, consider as facts what has been written and printed previously, and who for instance unquestioningly accept the date given for Matisse's operation by Mr Barr (*op. cit.*) and repeated by Gaston Diehl, in their serious and scholarly works.

Well then, at the beginning of January 1941 Matisse had said to the surgeon: 'Give me the three or four years I need to finish my work.' This is more characteristic of him than anything one could invent. In point of fact the surgeon was not very optimistic. Moreover, after the operation in the Lyons hospital, Matisse had two pulmonary embolisms. On each occasion, the resorption of the clot was awaited with great anxiety. The first embolism occurred six days after the operation, the second forty-six days after. Which brings us to the last days of February. Perhaps this explains the mistake made about the date of the operation; for in fact in March the wound began to suppurate and an incision was required.* This can hardly be called an operation, since it did not go beyond what is always liable to happen during the dressing of a wound. In any case, Matisse's stay in the Lyons hospital had not exceeded three months. However, he was kept two months longer at Lyons, in his hotel, under observation, which implies that his departure for Nice took place towards the end of May.†

The *novel* presupposes, at one moment or another, a grouping of the subsidiary characters around the chief protagonist. Allow me, then, to tell briefly how and where this might have begun in my own case: without going back to the *Indépendants* of 1913, to those pictures which André Breton and I

* The recent publication of the Bonnard–Matisse correspondence in the *Nouvelle Revue française* makes it clear that the operation did in fact take place about January 10. Writing to Bonnard on March 31, H.M. says that on March 2 he 'had a setback (the second since the operation) . . .' This is probably what gave rise to Mr Barr's mistake. Matisse makes it clear that on each occasion the trouble was due to an infarction.

† Confirmed by a letter to Bonnard, May 25, 1941, according to which H.M. returned to Nice on the previous Friday (i.e., May 23).

◀ IV. – *The Rumanian Blouse*, final state (October 1940).

fastened up with thumb tacks in a room next to our barracks dormitory at the Val-de-Grâce in 1917, or the obsession which in 1919 made me write *Madame à sa tour monte* in which I gave the name Matisse to a woman, etc. . . . But after all, Elsa, we were at Carcassonne when the painter passed through it in August 1940. I did not discover this until much later . . . We arrived at Nice on December 31; we were not to meet on this occasion, for Henri Matisse left the town early in January '41. Did I even know that he was back at Cimiez at the end of May? I don't believe so. And if I had known I should probably have thought of this as a stroke of fate. I was then expecting somebody whose arrival might have forced me to cancel any previous engagement . . . As a stroke of fate, just as once before, in 1918, on my last leave from the army, soon after the fall of Laon, André Breton had arranged through Pierre Reverdy for the two of us to meet Matisse, but it was too late, I had to go back to the front. And once again, I remember: this was no more than an impulse, in the spring of 1930. Elsa was suffering from the shock of Mayakovsky's death. I suddenly felt a longing to lift her spirits by taking her to see Matisse, as one might open a window to let in the sun. And then he had gone off to Tahiti (I don't remember who was going to help me approach him, probably someone from Montparnasse). I believe I have never mentioned this attempted, ill-contrived diversion, which Elsa will discover when she reads these lines. That Tahiti should have snatched him away seemed to me a decree of destiny – Tahiti, where ten years previously Elsa had nearly settled with somebody else, and then I should never have met her. After this, life had given me a distaste for such futile manœuvres.

The fact remains that at the beginning of June 1941 we were waiting with some impatience for news of Georges Dudach, my contact with Paris, who was to take us both there clandestinely, and I should not have dared (on what pretext? by what right?) to call on the great man, then convalescing at the Régina, in spite of my longing to know him at last, to realize a dream I had cherished so long, from childhood to the present tragic days. In any case, we left Nice. The demarcation line was beyond Loches, near La Haye-Descartes . . . We fell into the hands of the Germans and were both put in prison at Tours, in the cavalry quarters. When did we get out? After July 15, surely, for I remember how we celebrated the 14th with a band of tin cans played on by our companions in distress . . . All this is irrelevant, and so is the story of how we reached our Paris rendezvous, how we stayed at Édouard Pignon's and camped out in Lipchitz's studio, with Politzer and Danielle Casanova – and how we put Jacques Decour in touch with Jean Paulhan to found *Les Lettres françaises*. After all that, we thought it best not to go straight back to Nice; our landlady there believed we were still on holiday somewhere near

Avignon . . . We did in fact stay with Pierre Seghers at Villeneuve. Our purpose, after all, was to carry on the work that linked those in hiding with their fellows – writers, artists, all those concerned with the things of the mind – in the so-called free zone. But who had really given me Matisse's address? Someone in Paris? Or did Seghers have it? Surely not. Perhaps we got it through a letter from George Besson . . . Anyway, it was at Villeneuve-lès-Avignon that I took my courage in both hands, probably at the beginning of September.

On our arrival at Villeneuve I had picked up a little book which had touched me enough to make me write a poem about it: the whole thing is described in a postscript at the foot of this poem in the first issue of *Poésie 42* (you had to wait in those days to see yourself in print), which also contains the article by 'Blaise d'Ambérieux' of which I shall speak. The poem was entitled *Pour un chant national*, but in '42 it seemed wiser not to dot one's i's, and the magazine merely had the words *Pour un chant...* The note said, in parentheses: (*It seems that this poem, the author of which was obviously a contemporary of the Great Invasion, was written in '41, and presumably – to judge by its opening – towards the end of August or the beginning of September; this opinion is confirmed by the recent discovery of a book by the poet Alain Borne whose cover bears the title* Neige et 20 poèmes [Snow and Twenty Poems], *the only source mentioned being* Poésie 41. *This explains several obscurities in the text.*)

This lesson in contraband, which begins

Alain vous que tient en haleine
Neige qu'on voit en plein mois d'août
Neige qui naît je ne sais d'où
Comme aux moutons file la laine
Et le jet d'eau sur la baleine
Vous me faites penser à ce poète qui s'appelait
Bertrand de Born presque comme vous

Presque

comme

vous

is in fact (though I did not know it at the time) the start of another 'novel' that I've had in my mind for a long time, like the one about Matisse, and that I shall end by writing some day, the *Story of Alain Borne* . . . But the little note I have just reproduced here, somewhat oddly, was intended to point out, apart from the three dots in its title, that the man Aragon had ventured to fool the censor in this issue of a magazine where, in all innocence, the article here reprinted was published, with four drawings by the painter, under the title *Matisse, ou la grandeur* and signed B. d'Ambérieux. This meant little to its readers, who could have seen neither *Les Voyageurs de l'Impériale* nor *Aurélien* (the former, finished on September 1, 1939, had begun to appear in serial form in the *Nouvelle Revue française* before Drieu La Rochelle ousted Jean Paulhan, while the second had not yet been started) in which this name is that of a painter. But I had not wanted, at the time, to admit my relations with Henri Matisse for fear of compromising him if my underground activities should some day be discovered . . . I'll return to that later. For the time being I am only at the end of August or the beginning of September 1941, having written the poem for Alain but not yet the article by 'Blaise'.

All this had begun at Carcassonne, at the time when Matisse passed through there without my knowledge. We had sketched out, with Pierre Seghers, that first plan for a conspiracy of writers, under the ægis of *Poésie 40* or *41*, which, on my return from Paris, I had fresh motives for putting into effect. I urged my friend Pierre to widen the circle of his collaborators, to approach people he had hitherto considered unattainable. I offered to write to Henri Matisse to beg for some unpublished drawings which should make of *Poésie 41* something more than a regional review. He asked me to do so. I wrote, therefore, and thus began that 'novel' the first page of which (that letter from me) has in the meantime disappeared.*

* My letters to Matisse have been preserved, but the very first is not among them.

My request, which was not signed Ambérieux, reached Cimiez, and I promptly received an answer. But I needed the right to make use of Matisse's letter with its little drawing of the lagoon, enlarging this to four times its actual size so as to take up two pages of *Poésie 42*, and also adding my own commentary. I promised myself when I returned to Nice at the end of September to approach Matisse directly about this, taking this opportunity to conquer my shyness and to make contact with a painter I had dreamed about for so long. He encouraged me, moreover, with a pressing invitation. And yet when we got back to Nice I did not immediately pay my intended visit.

As it happened, unexpected difficulties had greeted us on our return. Our landlady, whose name was Célimène (while the lodging-house where we had one room with kitchenette was in the Rue de France!), turned us out without warning. She had had too many police inquiries about us, and she did not want to keep a note of all our visitors or listen to our telephone conversations as she was required to do. But finding lodgings at Nice in these circumstances . . . First we had a room in that hotel next to the Opéra where Bonaparte

V. – *Ivy, Flowers and Fruit* (1941).

apparently once lived, with baths on the ground floor. It was cold and uncomfortable, and we had a wretched October. I did not want to visit Matisse with detectives at my heels. Then on November 1, if I'm not mistaken, we found a new home: two rooms over a restaurant in Les Ponchettes, one looking out over the sky and the sea (underneath the very windows which had been Matisse's before he moved to the Régina), between the Quai des États-Unis and the Cité du Parc, with its courtyard full of fishmongers' stalls and the flower market beyond. Here Elsa, who had written *Mille Regrets* at Célimène's, wrote *Le Cheval blanc*, and here, encouraged by her example, I was that spring to begin *Aurélien*, in which the same Blaise d'Ambérieux who had already figured in *Les Voyageurs* was presently to reappear.

Were we mistaken in believing ourselves better hidden in the Cité du Parc than in the Rue de France? Surely not; Célimène, whom we met by chance on the beach, told us that the head of the local police, a notorious P.P.F.,* had said to her that he assumed we had left Nice, since he had had no report of our presence. Police supervision of lodging-houses seems to have been very efficient at Nice in 1941–42. (At the same period, in Paris, the policeman responsible for investigating the two editors of *Ce Soir*, Jean-Richard Bloch and myself, made a report, which was discovered at the Liberation, in which he said that on visiting the home of Jean-Richard Bloch he had been told that he had gone away without leaving an address (whereas in fact he was speaking on Radio Moscow every Tuesday under his own name), and as for Aragon, nobody knew where the devil he lived, perhaps indeed there was no such person; which leads one to suppose that the Montoire policy† did not enjoy the support of the whole police force, in Paris any more than at Nice).

* Parti Populaire Français.

† The policy of collaboration agreed on by Hitler and Pétain in their meeting at Montoire, October 24, 1940.

Henri Matisse had been back at the Régina for nearly six months. It was a place of such beauty, such calm, and even more astonishing was the calm of the man living there, knowing he had merely been granted a reprieve. The Ambérieux article is the reflection of those days of November and December '41: not of a single conversation but of three or four, including the remarks about the Lille museum and Goya, and one day when the weather was fine, looking out from his window over the palm-tree gardens below, his unfriendly comments on the Rome prize-winners . . . and so on. He wrote to me one Saturday (which Saturday?):

Cher Monsieur,

I have just received your book of poems[1] *which I look forward to enjoying, and I should like to thank you for it.*

Come and see me whenever you like, in the late afternoon; please ring me up first, the same day or the day before, when you feel like it, both of us being free to postpone the meeting if it proves impracticable.

Hoping to see you very soon.

Henri Matisse

I was to be *Cher Monsieur* for him only three times before that Christmas. 'You can't think how eagerly he expected you and how long he had been wondering, why doesn't Aragon come to see me?' a close acquaintance of his

1. *Le Crève-Cœur.*

told me later. If only I had known! It was like a novel in which a hero who has loved too late exclaims: Just think of it, twenty years! To begin with, we only discussed what I was to write to introduce three drawings, in connection with the letter I had received at Villeneuve in answer to mine, or at least how we were to reproduce them. But there were no decent photo-engravers at Avignon. What were we to do? If the photographs were entrusted to a specialist at Nice, Matisse could at least keep an eye on them; he suggested consulting a local artists' materials dealer. I had been to the Régina on a Saturday. We had talked about other things. Then, since that's the way I am, when he happened to say that he was preparing illustrations for an edition of Ronsard, it somehow seemed to me an unfortunate choice, considering my mental image of Matisse and, perhaps, the little time that was left him . . . I must have expressed myself strongly, because although I'm very fond of Ronsard I thought Mallarmé or Baudelaire . . . Henri Matisse asked me who else, in my opinion? He had never heard of Charles Cros, whose name sprang to my lips. And it's quite true that nothing is nearer to Matisse than Cros. To my mind. Even today. Then, on Sunday, I suppose, a note was left for me at 16 Cité du Parc:

Cher Monsieur,

I have found a quicker way than the one I suggested yesterday (the artists' materials dealer) to find out what can be done at Nice in the way of photogravure. So please don't bother about it – in a few days I will let you know what I've discovered.

I enjoyed our afternoon together yesterday, but I was rather tired by the end – we had talked for four hours – and my ideas were somewhat confused: that is why I was not able to explain why I was illustrating Ronsard. Do you think I could find any of Cros's poetry in Nice? I asked at the Librairie du XXe Siècle this morning what they had of his. They said I should have to look in the secondhand bookshops. Can you think of any other way?

Hoping to see you soon, cher Monsieur, with my best wishes,

Henri Matisse

It was on another occasion that Matisse referred once again to his obsession with the lagoon, with Tahiti. He had called up to ask me to come at once. He had slept badly; he had been thinking about it all, about my article. He had written a number of notes during the night. This formed the basis for the second part of the 'Blaise d'Ambérieux' article. But that day, when he let me take home his midnight jottings, Matisse had chosen some drawings for *Poésie 42* (since '41 was nearly over, Christmas was upon us). On the morning of Christmas Day a messenger brought me a note from him:

I1
Henri Matisse 1/42

December 25, 41

Cher Monsieur,

I am sorry to disturb your Christmas peace by telling you that I'm afraid I do not think the choice of photos we made yesterday for Poésie 40[1] *is right for me. When you have a moment, if you will be so kind, I think I can convince you of this. Since I am not working at the moment I am always free, even today. On the other hand tomorrow and the day after I shall not be free, I have visitors: a hectic week.*

I shall be happy to see Madame Aragon if you think that the meanders on my walls might interest her.

Please let me know your answer by telephone.

I wanted to give you prompt warning of the change before you got in touch with the editor of the magazine Poésie 40.

With all my apologies, and please believe me yours very sincerely,

Henri Matisse

Obviously, he wanted us both to come that very day. Matisse's delightful impatience was as yet unfamiliar to me; but I guessed at it. And so it happened that on Christmas Day 1941 *Madame Aragon* made the acquaintance of Henri Matisse at Cimiez. And it was the selection made that day that illustrated *Poésie 42*, No. 1, dated December '41–January '42, where my two imaginary novels, the story of Alain Borne and that of Henri Matisse, first met.

Why bring in the story of Alain Borne? you may ask. Why, indeed, except that this old association, this encounter in *Poésie 42* between Blaise d'Ambérieux's preoccupations and my own, *cannot* have been meaningless. It seems as if I then contracted two debts, one towards the painter, the other, a little later, towards the poet. One has not the right to think of something without carrying it through. I have waited ever since 1941 to come to this book, which is at last taking shape. Starting from the very first step (I mean *Matisse, or Greatness*), almost immediately Henri Matisse had offered me the opportunity to go further. The great irritation that he sometimes expressed at the terms in which art critics* spoke of him had impelled me to say several things which did not fall on deaf ears: that there is no spoken, written language of painting, that it's crazy to try to give the equivalent of what is painted when painting already means saying something, and that is why con-

*It's lucky for them I'm not treating them as minor characters in the novel about Matisse!

1. Matisse referred to the year of the first number he had seen.

◀ 18. – Charcoal drawing providing the 'theme' for the 'variations' of the series marked I, dated January 1, 1942.

temporary criticism – realizing no doubt that although one can produce the portrait of a person one cannot produce a portrait of the portrait – proceeds by means of a substitution of vocabulary, confusedly describing a painting in terms of music, the dance, perfume, more faithful in this respect to Baudelaire's poetic practice than to his criticism. I added that for my part if I wanted to speak of *The Night Watch* or *The Execution of Maximilian* I should not try to produce an equivalent in sound or a pictorial replica: I should simply try to picture to myself what was there *before* the painting for the painter, following him to the point where, being no painter myself, I can in no way vie with him.

I quickly saw how Matisse understood this, and the meaning of his blue hunter's gaze fixed on me. I immediately grasped the nature of the magnetism he exercised upon me. And to be aware of it meant yielding to it. One is as powerless before genius as before a snake. I should have remained silent, but Matisse drew me on, to the point where I could offer to practise my method upon him: as if I really could! I ought to have protested, refused, said that all this was purely conjectural, and of course it *was* all conjecture, I had no method really, it was pure imaginative chatter, I swear to you, but the demon, my own irresistible demon, possessed me. And so it was as if the painter had invited me to write just what he had not found in previous writings about him, what he evidently seemed to believe me capable of, and me alone – especially as an experiment in drawing on which he was just embarking could, if I watched him at work, give me the opportunity to follow him where nobody had as yet followed him. How could I refuse? I am naturally fascinated by danger; I have always loved a challenge. Everything told me that I was venturing on something in which I was bound to fail. But that was where the challenge lay, particularly as I now felt uncertain whether the proposal had really come from Matisse, or whether I had not in fact suggested it myself . . . I had been under this painter's spell for nearly thirty years, and now it was December '41 . . . At that point in the world's history, to have such an opportunity!

The whole month of January was spent on this project, which took no definite shape for either of us; at any rate, no acknowledged shape. I imagined a book, very beautiful, very long, very pure: the book *of* Matisse, in the sense of the Latin *de, De Sapientia.* I did not envisage a novel but just a book. Every time, or nearly every time, I came there were fresh drawings. Like temptations. A bait. And he watched me coming. So now he had made me his witness. Chosen me, I mean. A witness to these births. I had landed in the middle of them. The experiment, as far as I can see, had been begun – not strictly speaking begun, because before that . . . but begun systematically, with the drawings arranged in series and numbered within each series, and dated – in October or thereabouts. But all the same, it was when we had settled the problem of the magazine and chosen the drawings for it in connection with my little article, which now served merely as a pretext, that Matisse really made me the witness of what went on in his enchanted eyrie. This change took place between Christmas Day and New Year's Eve. The series marked I[1] inaugurates the year '42. Here the Christmas fairy tale assumes a different character for me: the novel begins. I had stopped being *Cher Monsieur* to Matisse. I was entrusted with the role conventionally described as *the author's*.

I kept putting off writing: how give face and form to that which, day by day, was being corrected within my own mind, as I learned more and as the painter, too, corrected himself, in words or in his drawing. To tell the truth, I felt relieved not to be dealing with painting, I mean with colour. And yet it was that which for so many long years had drawn me to him. But it was the side of him that still frightened me. Drawing seemed simpler, more familiar, easier of access. I only realized much later that this was an illusion. All the same it is clear from my devious approach in that article that I had not yet lost my timidity. My aim was twofold, no doubt: to do what Matisse expected of me, and to talk about those portfolios which, on each occasion, were awaiting me. I'd have had a phone call or a note brought by Lydia. As soon as I arrived, out came the drawings, one by one. Henri Matisse was watching to see what I would say about them. I was horribly afraid of looking like a fool to him: of his reading and understanding what I thought about myself. Above all, I must not write what I had invented on the spur of the moment just for something to say. The trouble was that Matisse sometimes fastened on words that had just slipped out and was surprised not to find them written down. And so I had adopted this way of skirting the subject, and I began to gauge our misunderstanding. For while I did not actually tell myself I was writing a novel, at least I thought I was sketching a portrait of Henri Matisse, no less! I would never have admitted it. He, on the other hand, wanted an opinion, not of himself but of his drawings, of drawing. Gradually, indeed, I understood where my mistake lay: Matisse was not concerned with *a book*, with the book. At one point he let slip the word, he said *the preface* or *your preface*, I'm not sure which. That put the thing in its place. That'll teach you, my lad. Matisse only wrote the word a good deal later, in April I believe, when he was growing impatient and wondering whether or not I was going to complete my task. By then the name no longer mattered. The *thing* had

1. In *Thèmes at Variations*, the series are marked from A to P, sixteen drawings.

taken shape. I thought I had been very cunning and brought off my *portrait* by indirect means. Now I only had to tie up loose ends . . .

All this does not explain Alain Borne. I might point out that that's not my subject here. It's not my subject here, and why linger over that remark of mine, a chance association? I've had to bring together these two men, so dissimilar in age and profession: not to talk about them, but about this book. About how this book came to be made. First an article for Seghers. Then the preface that Matisse expected. We were going through such times that we naturally felt the necessity for haste, anything might happen! It was just a preface, signed or unsigned, or signed, say, B. d'Ambérieux. All the same, for me, there were only the preface and the first chapter of the book which I thought I had completed in 1946 with *La Grande Songerie* and *L'Apologie du Luxe* . . . Then, for various reasons – the publisher, a different one, who had snapped it up, who had been dreaming of such a book, delayed putting it into shape, while Matisse was extremely exacting about the number and quality of the reproductions – we no longer confined ourselves to what was strictly necessary. Skira published the *Apologie* in their series *Trésors de la peinture française*, which necessitated another cover with *Henri Matisse* in capitals, and nothing else (no mention of myself). A set of circumstances led me to resume work on my portrait, if I may call it that: second thoughts, so to speak. Years passed. And so the manuscript grew. Prefaces to books and exhibition catalogues, which for me (if nobody else) meant another chapter each time. Thus the work took shape, with holes in the lace of time. Matisse some day . . . It had survived almost fourteen years. To end with, the brief note in *L'Humanité*. As though it were possible to close those eyes of his.

I took another thirteen or fourteen years deciding to give all this, which had no reason ever to become a book, the look of a framed portrait. Thirteen, fourteen years of feeling guilty towards Matisse, towards myself. You've got to carry through what you have thought of. This is where Alain Borne . . . For ever since Alain was killed in a car crash I've stopped wanting to do his portrait, write that novel. One can't remake oneself. And which is the digression, Matisse or Borne? When I have finished this *Matisse* I shall be left alone with Alain.* At this turning in the path of fate.

* O Lord, re-reading this at the end of summer 1970 . . . *left alone*, did I know what I was saying? (13/9/70) [the date of Elsa Triolet's death].

In 1967, when I was already deeply involved in the present novel and had just completed *Blanche*, I went to the theatre with Elsa again. A first night. The programme. I've grown a little deaf. Actually, the theatre, for me . . . Oh, I like it well enough, but I follow less and less. From the seventh row I

19. – *Variation* I_4 (pen and ink). ▶

can't hear anything they're saying. Mind you, that's not always necessary. But I do like to understand what's going on. It's a weakness of mine. That evening we were in the third row (people are beginning to know). Even from the third row I don't hear everything. I work it out for myself. I make things up. The oddest part is that my hearing is spatially disturbed: what is spoken on the right is heard by me on the left. So you see, to follow the dialogue . . . I correct it as best I can. In the end the play is partly by me. Imagine *Phèdre* with Hippolyte speaking Thésée's lines . . . or any other such example.

I try to get out of my difficulty by means of the programme. The problem is to snatch it from Elsa before the lights go out, and pounce on the argument of the play to find out what it's about, so as to follow it like a grown-up. Only the tiresome thing is that traditions are dying out. A novel has a

blurb on the cover in which the author (writing in the third person, as though he were somebody else) informs his readers and his critics what happens in the book; and then I say to myself that having read that, I don't need to know any more, and I put the thing away in the bookcase. But with programmes it's different: to begin with, the account of the play tells me nothing about the appearance of the actors or their performance, or the lighting, etc. Well, nowadays it's considered very boring to tell the story of the play. They think up all sorts of dodges to talk about something else. So I have to plunge in, and sink or swim. All the same, there are still a few authors who give you slight hints.

But not the ones we had that evening, at all events. Nothing. From the third row, nevertheless, I gradually gathered that we were in some odd sort of boarding-house. But what was happening there . . . Well, I could see what was happening there; the incomprehensible part, besides the meaningless

20. – *Variation* I_6 (charcoal).

sentences, was what was *not* happening there, the background, the past, where these people came from and why, where they were going . . . Pitiless programme. One tiny hint would have been enough, I'm not hard to please. Nothing. So I had to invent. Judging from what was being said in the intermission, my version was different from other people's. Elsa's too. It seems that deafness doesn't explain everything.

I shall be told that in the play, actually, the author does not explain everything, that he leaves scope for my imagination. How kind of him! And to be sure, if he hasn't written things down in his play he won't write them in the programme. I understand. All the same . . . Not everything. Furthermore, I shall be told that the theatre nowadays is like life. When you see someone you don't know come into a room, there's no speaker to inform you of his *curriculum vitae*. And so on. Because the less one understands the closer it is to real life. 'You who are a realist . . .' I smile feebly.

21. – *Variation* I_9 (pen and ink).

It's true that I've never understood much in real life. But at the theatre I can't ask (as I used to, long ago, at the Châtelet): 'Mother, who's the gentleman that makes everyone laugh?' before laughing myself.

But why am I telling you this? The play, the people, the programme, in a book about Henri Matisse! You'll start shouting: 'Keep to the point!' I've heard those words somewhere else already.

If I were consistent, this book would contain all the data that it demands from the reader, because the reader does not necessarily know that he's entitled to demand them from the book, that is to say from me; does he even know that such data exist? If I had not told him that Henri Matisse was born on December 31, 1869, at Le Cateau-Cambrésis, he would not have invented it, he's not deaf. Besides, he might have thought that the painter was not born on that day or on another, in that town or elsewhere. If I were consistent. But there you are, I'm not consistent.

After all, you can throw away the programme and look at the painting.

Let's be serious. This programme does not require biographical dates or a list of exhibitions or a register of the works, articles, catalogues, and art books devoted to Henri Matisse. This is not a scholarly work, but perhaps a gleam of light on *what happens*.

So at long last I had gone to see the painter in his palace. Somehow or other the thought had occurred to me that I might write a book about Matisse which would indirectly be a portrait of him. I had begun. I went almost daily to see my subject. I made him alter his pose, he consented. The lighting varied. Time passed. There was a sudden noisy white flutter of wings from the birds in the great aviary. I prowled round my model; I had to understand the shoulder, the way the branches grew out of the trunk . . . And then suddenly he began talking about his journey to Morocco, about a woman he had seen from a taxi, about a piece of stuff.* The difference between painters and myself is that they work towards a likeness by means of sketches and rough drafts, while in my case what I write winds about the subject like an endless tangled ribbon, I cut nothing, I throw away nothing, and finally the portrait is the sum of my thoughts, about my model and about countless other things when I raise my eyes to look out of the window or at the telephone . . . In short, what painters call a portrait is not what I call a portrait when I am writing.

* That piece of stuff might itself be the subject of a novel. It recurs throughout Matisse's life from the *Harmony in Red (La Desserte)* of 1908 to the very end.

Especially as on certain days, in spite of the bright sunshine, or even when dusk fell, a sudden star-shaped pucker would appear on Matisse's cheek and his lips would grow pale. He said nothing, and I pretended to have seen nothing. On one such occasion, noticing my hesitant speech, he asked me: 'What's the matter with you?' With me? Nothing. Once serenity was restored,

I had the sense of having myself experienced that furtive stab of pain. I looked into the shadows, behind Henri Matisse, imagining I had seen a blurred figure there, sneering. The fancies one has . . .

What happened next . . . the very thing that ought to appear in the programme, that which is incomprehensible unless the author stresses it, took place in the second act, the third if you prefer: I mean in March 1942. It was a sudden change of lead. One of those tricks you find in present-day novels (which would not have been clearly understood at that time). A shift of syntax. The nominative turns into the accusative and vice versa. Carrying the complicity that I asked of him beyond what I expected of him, the *subject* (as the *object* to be portrayed is called) involved me so deeply in his explanations about the current experiment, concerning the drawings he was showing me, that I imperceptibly found my role changing. For I, too, had to explain what I wrote from one visit to another, taking into account the comments and additions made by Matisse, who thus ceased to be primarily my model and became my corrector. Then, too, these corrections applied not only to facts but to ideas, to my ideas, to the man I am. So that one fine day I found myself, as a matter of course, occupying the position hitherto held by Matisse in relation to myself. Do you see? He wanted to learn something from me, by his own method, which indeed was different from mine: so that yesterday's untamed '*fauve*' had become the tamer, and in order to find out what he wanted to from me, he, whose portrait I had thought I was drawing, had started to draw mine. I was no longer *the author*.

If you fail to understand this you cannot hope to understand *the play*. This had to be put into the programme. As long as it was not there, the scattered scenes remained mere sketches, snapshots. There was no novel, no portrait, no comedy. One passage did not lead on to another, it was like those infuriating *de luxe* editions which are unbound, and which keep falling to pieces, which you put together as best you can (the latest fashion is to leave the pages unnumbered) like a pack of shuffled cards – find your way about if you can! Later on, I mean after *Matisse-en-France*,* I went on for a few years longer being scrupulous enough, or rash enough – it comes to the same thing – to show Henri Matisse the things I was writing about him. Thus the book, the novel, the portrait took its course. But when this had become impossible, however much I wanted to act as though Matisse were still alive, if I took out that disconnected manuscript that lay dormant in my desk, intending to give it all some coherence, to weave the pages together, it dropped from my hands, as depressing as a memory which is nothing but a memory. Ten times I announced that I was going to finish this book. It is very hard for me to be sole author of it. Today I am roughly the same age that Henri Matisse was at

* One of those unbound books I was describing: one spends one's life putting it straight.

the Hôtel Vendôme, and I feel my use of the nominative dwindling daily. I have already come to envisage so much of myself as a mere object. And I'm a prey to the uncertain chronology of things. I try, indeed, to date what I have written. But the images remain chaotic. That calendar can never be restored.

22. – *Variation* I_{15}, end of the series of January 1, 1942 (pen and ink).

Matisse-en-France

Preface to Henri Matisse, *Dessins: thèmes et variations*

(1942)

Thèmes et Variations
(1943)

'Don't you think it's rather too straightforward? Rather Manet-ish?' (p. 95)

VI. – *Woman with a Veil* (January 1942).

And in spite of twenty-seven years of the Peloponnesian War, indeed during those twenty-seven years of war, Sophocles, Euphorion and Euripides competed with their tragedies on *Medea*, Euripides winning the prize, while there were performances of *The Bacchae*, *The Phoenician Women*, *Oedipus*, *Antigone* and *Electra* which cost more than the Persian Wars had done, and finally Aristophanes produced his *Wasps*, *Clouds* and *Acharnians*.

And every branch of art advanced in the same way.

ALEXANDRE DUMAS

When the Portuguese painter Francisco de Hollanda went to Rome, four hundred years ago, he could not rest until he had fulfilled one of his dearest dreams, which was to see Michelangelo and talk with him about the mysteries of painting. The important point here is not that he succeeded thanks to the woman whom Michelangelo loved, Vittoria Colonna, widow of the Marqués de Pescara who defeated the French at Pavia, nor that the meeting took place in the Church of San Silvestro, where these strange lovers used to discuss St Paul's Epistles; nor indeed am I concerned with what the great man actually said. But when Michelangelo had enumerated the paintings which were to be seen in the churches and palaces of Italy, and which made his country's greatness, his visitor, not to be outdone, told Michelangelo which were the finest paintings to be seen in Spain and in France, where he had travelled. And as regards France, he spoke at length of a painting which then hung in Avignon in the Palace of the Popes, and which was said to be by King René, Duke of Anjou.

O vana gloria de l'umane posse!
Com' poco verde in su la cima dura,
Se non è giunta da l'etati grosse!

Credette Cimabue ne la pittura
Tener lo campo, e ora ha Giotto il grido,
Sì che la fama di colui e scura.

Così ha tolto l'uno a l'altro Guido
La gloria de la lingua; e forse è nato
Chi l'un e l'altro caccerà del nido.

(DANTE, *Purgatorio*, Canto XI)

O empty glory of man's frail ambition,
How soon its topmost boughs their green must yield;
If no Dark Age succeed, what short fruition!

Once, Cimabue thought to hold the field
In painting; Giotto's all the rage today;
The other's fame lies in the dust concealed.

Guido from Guido wrests our native bay,
And born, belike, already is that same
Shall chase both songsters from the nest away.

(Transl. Dorothy L. Sayers)

THE VANISHED PORTRAIT

I have often wondered about the tribute paid that day to French painting by this Portuguese, and even more about the work which, for a moment, was privileged to be introduced to Michelangelo as the glory of the French nation. Its hold over our imagination is all the greater today since its disappearance from Avignon, probably during the French Revolution, so that we know nothing about it except from hearsay. In fact, this singular work was possibly not very different from the picture painted, a hundred years after the scene in San Silvestro, by the Spaniard Valdés Leal, which was to be seen at Seville in the church of that convent where, according to legend and Barrès, Don Juan acted as storekeeper: it represented a King and a Bishop already half devoured by worms. I'll spare you the horrors; there was plenty there to thrill Barrès or Don Juan turned monk, just as a hundred years earlier Francisco de Hollanda had been excited by King René's picture, which represented a dead woman in a dress of magnificent brocade with the loveliest fair hair in the world. I am afraid painting, *qua* painting, was of secondary interest to the author of *Du Sang, de la Volupté et de la Mort*, and to the converted libertine. But as for Francisco de Hollanda, while the macabre element no doubt appealed to his Iberian taste, it should be remembered that he was a painter and that he was talking to Michelangelo. This really justifies the belief that King René's portrait of Lady Anne was somewhat different from that other painting, which I once saw at Seville* (where it was probably destroyed in the Civil War and which, in any case, had enjoyed a rather inflated reputation).

SISTER ANNE, SISTER ANNE . . .

In short, according to the legend, when King René came to Avignon his desire to see the Lady Anne, whose beauty had been so highly praised to him, was at least equal to Messer Francisco de Hollanda's wish to see Michelangelo. But this happened a hundred years before that meeting in the Church of San Silvestro, and five hundred years before our own time, and the fair Anne had long been dead and buried,

* In the autumn of 1927. It was a few days before I destroyed that manuscript to which I had devoted four years of my life (you will say there is no connection and it's true, there's no connection, except that sometimes flames achieve what the worms in the tomb or mere mice only attempt). However, even then, the picture was not mentioned in the 1924 edition of Bénézit. Did I, perhaps, after all, only dream I had seen it? And what about Barrès? I refer you to *Du Sang, de la Volupté et de la Mort*, and also to Seville, at any rate if you're one of those lucky people who can still go to Seville, where for the past forty-one years I have been forbidden to go.

I may add, speaking of mice, that in the first edition of this text, *Martin Fabiani, MCMXLIII*, the proofs of which I had not seen, for a very good reason, the final *l* of the Sevillian painter's name was nibbled away by the printers so that he became *Valdés Lea*. I had been unable to add, as I'd have liked, that this painter, oddly enough for us though not for the Spaniards, was also called Don Juan. *(Note of 1968)*

unbeknown to King René. He asked to see her none the less, and she was brought out of her tomb. In her fine array, with her hair so strangely framing her skeleton's face, she was still so lovely that René of Anjou insisted on painting her, and indeed, they say, would paint nothing else. Francisco de Hollanda declared that in his picture the Lady Anne, even fleshless, retained her human and superhuman beauty. As I have implied, this Portuguese art lover looked at French painting with very Spanish eyes. And yet there is no reason why we should not believe him, either about Anne's beauty or about the excellence of the artist's work. And I like to imagine the painter-king in front of the fair dead woman, inspired both by a sense of the beauty that she still retained in death and by those rich fabrics and that hair, and those bones which, it seems, were perfect – I like to imagine King René painting her, enraptured by her beauty and yet detached from it, because it had already shed all that was inessential, all mere *resemblance*, enabling him to rise above portraiture to attain something so pure and so lofty that no shadow of macabre delight still lingered there; and thus we can understand why Francisco de Hollanda assured Michelangelo that in France there was to be seen one picture above all which summed up all that was most intensely, most individually French at that time, the French concept of the beloved woman, the code of courtly love practised by that King, Duke of Anjou and Count of Provence, who was a poet as well as a painter and who wrote *Le Livre du cœur d'amour épris*.*

THERE'S NO SUCH THING AS *NATURE MORTE*

Towards the end of the first half of the twentieth century I entered the home of a kind of King René. You've no need to tell me that his models are living women, which they are, and that no art, perhaps, is more remote than his from that Baudelairean instinct for death which has come down to us through the

* *(Note, 1970.)* While this book was in the process of preparation, on our way back from Brittany on that sad last journey, we stopped at Angers, and there, at the entrance to *L'Apocalypse*, we saw for sale a number of *Verve* (Vol. VI, No. 23) which I did not know and the cover of which, obviously a Matisse, caught my eye. The magazine reproduced the illuminations to the manuscript of the *Livre du cœur d'amour épris*, of Vienna, the oldest known: the cover shows a red heart surrounded by the words *cœur d'amour épris* in blue pencil. In 1942, when I showed the painter the opening of *Matisse-en-France*, he knew nothing about King René and asked me questions about him. The number of *Verve* had been produced seven years later.

In 1942, moreover, it seemed quite natural to believe that no art was more remote than Matisse's from *that Baudelairean instinct for death*: if, many years earlier, there had been a link between H.M.'s painting and Baudelaire, this had only been in connection with the title *Luxe, calme et volupté*, which shows what I might call 'the Baudelairean instinct for happiness'. Matisse had not yet found the road to *Les Fleurs du Mal*, I mean *his* road to it . . . It was in the summer of 1944, at the time of the Liberation, that he made the lithographs the story of which I shall tell later, and which he gave me to publish in 1947, at least in the shape in which the accident of 1944 allowed them to survive.

ages; you've no need to tell me that, because it's not the real question. And whereas in that high bright room looking out over Nice and the sea and the palm trees and the birds, the drawings set out along the walls – some hundred drawings in which the white virginity of the paper is, as it were, confirmed by the artist's line, which is like a discovery – seem full of a light that precludes any thought of Anne of Avignon taken from her coffin, let me say that, for me (although I was immediately reminded of the story of René of Anjou and fair Anne), the question takes a very different form, and that after all, for instance, when Henri Matisse declares that his attitude towards these voluptuous models of flesh and blood is no different (and we must take his word for it) from his attitude to a plant, a vase, an inanimate object, we may likewise assume that what King René saw was not a dead woman but the starting-point of a reverie which words could not have expressed and which was the beauty he bore within himself. And this is true of Henri Matisse.

I may perhaps be held overbold to have dared show on the stage a prophet inspired by God, foretelling the future. But I have been careful to put into his mouth only expressions taken from the prophets themselves.

JEAN RACINE
(Preface to *Athalie*)

And there we may leave King René, the dead womar and her lovely golden hair.

THE MYSTERY OF THE *CAMERA LUCIDA*

This bright room, where in a labyrinthine palace on the heights of Cimiez the great French painter carries on an experiment quite as strange as that of René of Anjou, this *camera lucida* (to use a term from optics) contains at the very least a hundred samples of that experiment, like modulations of a single tune. Henri Matisse, amidst these *completed* images of that which can never be completed, seems himself to be seeking for the explanation of his enterprise while he pursues it.

We find here, indeed, the demonstration of two truths which have never yet been expressed either in drawing or in painting. These are that old saying of Buffon's: *Style is the man himself*, and Gustave Flaubert's wisecrack: *Madame Bovary is myself.*

23. – The '*camera lucida*' at Cimiez.

THESIS

Nothing in the world could be less like a cave than this bright room, and nobody is more different from Dr Faust than Henri Matisse.

ANTITHESIS

And as soon as I come into this room I am in a cave. In a different cave. But these drawings irresistibly reminded me of the picture-language of remote ages, when men traced on the walls of their cave dwellings the bison of early Europe. And this led my thoughts quite naturally to an Italian cave near Vespignano where a young shepherd, in about 1290, drew in charcoal or in chalk everything that he saw and *that he was not satisfied with seeing.* It was through these vanished drawings that Cimabue, passing by, discovered the child Giotto. And that work which revolutionized painting, ushering in its modern phase, was born from these drawings, which at the same time are akin to the primitive script of those who inaugurated written characters.

And here, at the further end of the long history of painting, I find something as bare and simple and pure as Giotto's drawings, a finishing-point as it were beyond that marvellous trajectory of forms and colours through the ages, something which is the crown of an artist's work, expressing a man's full mastery of himself and his world – the latest drawings of Henri Matisse, on these walls which suggest to me the walls of a cave dwelling, the counterpart of Vespignano, its equivalent in our minds.

While it is hard to imagine anything more remote from Dr Faust than Henri Matisse, surely it cannot be denied that between the boy Giotto and Matisse, as he now looks back over his whole life – which is his work – there is neither likeness nor unlikeness but a concord, a harmonic resolution which, just as well as or better than a dead woman, can give rise to a long, unending reverie.*

* Faust in reverse, the young Faust who cannot see himself as the future Doctor, Faust as a twenty-year-old rake running after girls. *(Note, May 1968)*

PARENTHESIS

(What I had meant to say, and did not say, is that the macabre element was for King René a factor analogous to voluptuousness for Matisse; a starting-point. But King René's feelings were not macabre, and Matisse's inspiration was not voluptuous. René's picture is macabre only to the spectator, for whom the corpse of a beautiful woman, devoured by worms, cannot be other than a macabre sight. In the same way, if I single out the drawing of a highly voluptuous woman who, with her arms clasped about herself, takes an intense delight in touching, in feeling herself, and whom Matisse has drawn solely for the sake of that enfolding movement, palpable to the senses yet eluding words,* I am almost sure that the spectator will bring to it an attitude which is his own and not that of the artist, which is chaste, just as King René's was devoid of any sort of necrophilia. And this takes me rather far for a parenthesis. But here's the point.

The macabre and the voluptuous elements, equally, here represent nature. Nature guides and inspires the painter, but it is merely his *object.* He reproduces, but is not, nature. His drawing is a curve which is an expression of nature, in particular of sensuous pleasure: it is not itself that pleasure. A parabola may thus be drawn to describe the movement of a projectile without having that projectile's destructive force; and the man who has drawn it is not necessarily a murderer. But he understands the thing that kills.

In front of his model, woman or flower, Henri Matisse's drawing has the vast chastity of intelligence.)

* Which drawing did I have in mind? Several of the *Variations*, probably . . . or perhaps, in particular, that of the Turkish princess (1941) on p. 69. I'm not very certain, my memory has retained a complex image in which several drawings are mingled. *(1969)*

AVIGNON IS NOT THE PORTRAIT OF ROME

Beyond portraiture :

Portraiture is a singular attainment of the human mind, a precious moment in art, but only a moment. It foretells photography. It played a decisive role in French art, of which it became an essential characteristic after a certain point in time. But only up to another point in time. Have we reached that point? I cannot judge.

Portraiture has become a discipline. It once had its social justification. It displayed on the walls of a house the continuity of the owner's family, its antiquity, its rights. At each new stage of society, when other men and their supporters attained power, they had to be portrayed in their turn, for lack of ancestors. The nineteenth century, being a century of revolutions, was also a century of portraiture. The future of the portrait depends on the history that is to be, and not on anyone's predictions of it. †

† For *portrait* read *novel*: you will find yourself involved in the campaign being waged against that art, which had not started in 1942. *(Note, 1967)*

24. – First variation of Series L (crayon).

But any art must some day meet the man who deliberately breaks its rules, thus paradoxically giving birth to a work which presupposes such defiance. Why should this not be the same with the generally accepted idea that a painting is always the portrait of somebody or something, a man or an apple?

I am not saying that the portrait has had its day. I am saying that some men have already moved on be-

25. – Fifth variation of Series L, marked L_5 (crayon).

yond portraiture. This is particularly evident in these Matisse drawings, where the inexperienced observer, seeing a highly individual woman, will always tend to see a portrait. And he will even convince himself, because of the distortion, the unusual draughtsmanship, that it is a close likeness of someone he does not know. It is indeed a close likeness; but of whom? Look at that series of drawings of the same head, of the same

What a pity! Gertrude Stein's maid remarked, seeing a nude by Matisse. *To have made* that *out of a pretty woman!*

And Gertrude Stein comments: 'So she'd seen it was a pretty woman!'

face, of the same woman. There is a likeness between them and yet they are not alike.[1] The woman, in five drawings, has five different noses. The likeness is elsewhere; it's in the style. In other words, their unity lies in the author. This might not have been noticed had he not precisely chosen a particular woman as *subject*. But that is what he has done. In the same way, there is between Corot's view of Avignon from Villeneuve and his view of Rome a *likeness* which is a very strange thing. Avignon is not the portrait of Rome . . . I don't know if I am making myself understood.

OF STYLE

Style is the man himself. We know, broadly speaking, what is meant by the style of a writer, the importance of style in written language, and nobody disputes Buffon's observation. A writer who has no style feels humiliated thereby. He might as well not exist.*

* This was André Breton's opinion of his own prose: 'I've got no style,' he would say. He was wrong: that sort of lack of style is Style: *Style is the man himself. (Note, 1968)*

But we hear very little about style in painting, about a painter's creation of his own style. And yet here even more than in writing the style is the artist himself. This style is what matters, and it is through this style that the artist expresses certain things, certain relations, which strike him powerfully at a particular moment but which are not guaranteed to remain striking for long or for everyone. The artist immortalizes this glimpse by setting it down in his own style.

An illustration from poetry: *Le Lac* by Lamartine seems to have been written at a moment when the author felt that the words used opened up a vista beyond their own meaning, and this seemed to him infinitely precious. He gave it permanence in his style. Otherwise, if you cast a cold eye over the poem: *O temps, suspends ton vol* . . . it's just a series of commonplaces on the flight of time. But there remains the man through whom these commonplaces have been transmitted. The man himself. His style.

1. See the later chapter *On Likeness. (Note, 1968)*

'So she'd seen it was a pretty woman!'

VII. – *The Blue Nude* belonging to Gertrude Stein, now in the Cone Collection in the Baltimore Museum of Art, entitled *Nu bleu (Souvenir de Biskra).*

There is a twofold mystery: the mystery of the man and that of the style.

What Matisse is seeking to express is his very self. His style is a means invented to express himself. And then the man will stand aside. The style will remain. A great style, which towers above his age, and in which you will perhaps find everything except that man himself, who is so unlike Dr Faust.

Nowadays, moreover, unless Dr Faust has been mobilized, he is day-dreaming somewhere at the other end of Europe, wondering whether he will ever suc-

Théophile Gautier on Poussin:

. . . although he spent most of his life in Rome and died there, he remained French, and with him ideas prevail over sensations. Nature does not affect him through her own special charm, and he sees forms only as means of expression.[1]

1. Matisse read this note and was surprised: 'Did Gautier say that?' He hadn't thought him capable of it. *(Note, 1961)*

ceed in imitating Matisse. Not indeed the man, who is so different from himself, but his style.

And yet the style is the man himself.

IF MADAME BOVARY'S NOSE HAD BEEN SHORTER . . .

We take Flaubert's remark: *Madame Bovary is myself* . . . for a mere wisecrack. Matisse does not assert, of those Oriental women who twist and twine in his drawings like the little branch of ivy with the translucent roots which he moves from one vase to another, that they are himself, yet they express him.

THERE ARE DIFFERENT KINDS OF PORTRAITS

He understands himself through them, and yet he obviously understands them too.

There's the story of the American woman whose portrait he was painting. He made one drawing after another of her. She insisted on keeping them all because she recognized her whole family in them, her mother, an uncle, a cousin . . . and I suppose unfamiliar glimpses of herself. She would some day become like a certain drawing, she had once been like another. Matisse had never seen her like that, any more than he knew her mother back home in Connecticut. He did better than that: he understood her. And through her, a lot of other things.

Beyond portraiture.

Yes, a man can trace the curve made when a stone is flung or a bullet is fired, and that is the nearest he will get to conveying their likeness in *human style*. And yet it is not the portrait of the bullet or of the stone. It is the sign that represents them. There is this difference between man and the other animals, that he can speak and write, can paint, can set down music. The difference lies in the invention and use of signs. The monkey imitates a man's gesture, the man gives a name to his gesture and a name to the monkey. The name is not a portrait. But such is man's intelligence that the

. . . the little branch of ivy with the translucent roots . . .
26. – Drawing H_3 of *Thèmes et Variations* (pen and ink). ▶

H 3
Henri Matisse 41

name resembles the thing, often in a language which is not that of the man in question.

Drawing is a language, in that miraculous sense. I repeat, it registers the curve of a bullet. This was never truer than of the drawings of Henri Matisse. Only the curve is expressed in terms of two coordinates, one of them this woman, this object, nature . . . the other Henri Matisse, the *x* axis, in abscissa.

This is the other way into the mystery. The mystery of the man. Henri Matisse, that stranger . . .

THE WRITER'S POINT OF VIEW

Matisse, moreover, has several handwritings but only one style. From time to time he puts pen to paper boldly, sergeant-major fashion; you see, there are some drawings consisting of a single line which stops only when it's finished, the paper left blank, almost confidentially, and there are some which are shadowed, whose life is in their shadows, and others where shade predominates, whose life is in their sparse lights. Everything depends on the medium used, and the writing may be cursive or upright or slanting . . . But the same hand can be recognized. The man. We're tired of art critics: let us have a graphologist instead. What would he say about Henri Matisse? That he is intellectually consistent, with an undeniable gift for evaluating the distance between objects, the relations between volumes, and the weight of a head. But that doesn't get us very far. The most mysterious thing about him is, perhaps, that he understands better than anyone else the way fabric lies against flesh, and how the straps and ribbons cross and slip in a woman's garments, how they wind about her waist or close to her armpit or under the curve of her breast: so many secrets which are not to be found in any dictionary.* Words are powerless; Matisse substitutes these discoveries of draughtsmanship. Each new drawing is like a letter added to the alphabet. Shall I be understood if I say that Matisse's genius reaches W, although he

* Secrets of the lover; or at least of the young man, for whom this year the wasp-waisted corset is something new. *(Note, 1958)*

. . . cross and slip in a woman's garments . . .

27. – Pen-and-ink drawing dated 1941, which seems to belong to Series F of *Thèmes et Variations*, and may be the one referred to in a note on p. 61.

Henri Matisse 41.

always seems to confine himself to the first three letters, the elementary ABC? That's the only way in which he deceives us, but he does so thoroughly. It's easy, he makes us say. This effect of ease is the greatest illusion about the whole thing. Matisse is a difficult artist. Not for nothing did he illustrate Mallarmé. But Mallarmé is far simpler in comparison, since his difficulty is obvious. If we want to find an equivalent to Matisse's *facility*, we must look for it among musicians. Bach, to make the point clear. There is nothing Beethovenish about Matisse.

He remarked of a great contemporary writer,* one of those whom everyone admires unquestioningly and who attain for a while the stature of a Goethe in our world: 'He thinks that all this' – pointing to his drawings – 'is just a knack!' What a mistake, and the painter may perhaps despise him for it, although he never shows it. I find this remark highly illuminating. Moreover it clearly defines the writer in question, who thinks that everything can be reduced to tricks of the trade, to cleverness, and that you can write verse as you ride horseback, through the development and exercise of certain sets of muscles.

Of course there is mastery, as well, in Matisse's drawings. But only *as well*. What this writer does not understand is that there are some men who deliberately tackle the inexpressible, I repeat, the inexpressible. Not out of mischief, nor to show their skill. From all that I have already said you will readily infer that for me Matisse is one of these. And on reflection you will perhaps realize that for me the aforesaid great writer, on the other hand, has nothing to do with the inexpressible. He has quite enough to do making what has already been expressed seem elusive.†

MICHELANGELO'S POINT OF VIEW

Good painting is noble and pious in itself,‡ since for wise men there is nothing more elevating to the soul, more conducive to piety than the difficult quest for perfection, which leads it

* Paul Valéry was alive at the time. I mention him by name today so that there may be no misunderstanding. (*1968*)

† I wrote this in 1942, because there were some things, such as the speech on his reception to the Academy, for which I could not forgive Valéry. But today, as in my twenties, I think of him only as the author of *La Soirée avec Monsieur Teste* and *the Cantique des Colonnes*. (*1970*)

‡ Having practically finished this book, I feel bound to urge the reader to return to this quotation from Michelangelo when he has read the later chapter, *Que l'un fût de la chapelle* . . . Then study Michelangelo's *piety* in his sculptures . . . (*1969*)

near to God and unites it with Him: now good painting is no other than a copy of His perfections, a shadow of His painting, in fact a music and a melody, and only a very keen intelligence can be aware of its difficulty; that is why few people can attain it or know how to produce it.

I had declared over-hastily that what Michelangelo may have said to Francisco de Hollanda did not concern me. For now I wonder what Matisse would think of this definition of good painting. It must be understood that Michelangelo had just been condemning Flemish painting because it chose to represent,

. . . in order to deceive the outward eye, either objects that delight it or objects of which no ill can be spoken, such as saints and prophets. They usually depict fabrics, bricks and mortar, green fields shaded by trees, with rivers and bridges, what are called landscapes with many figures scattered here and there.

And if, in the first quotation, everyone is free to understand 'God' in his own way, whatever is God for him, perhaps that quest for perfection that goes beyond the execution of *what are called landscapes* or, as I was saying, of portraiture, will bring us straight back to Henri Matisse and these late drawings of whose difficulty only a very keen intelligence can be aware. A music, in fact, a melody.

THE PALETTE OF OBJECTS

Matisse is not the only modern painter who has moved away from portraiture, from landscape as Michelangelo would call it; for these are obviously one and the same. But those who have done so have differed widely in their attitude to their subject-matter. There are some who profess not to draw or paint from nature. There are those who treat natural objects with contempt. There are those who invent objects as they paint or imagine they paint. None of these is Matisse's way. It's all too extravagantly Faustian.

Matisse never dispenses with nature. He chooses his model with particular care. Of one girl, he made as many drawings as there are stars in the sky,* and com-

* I exaggerate, but a hundred stars make a sky, just as in painting thirty leaves give the illusion of a tree. (*1969*)

mented regretfully that when she left he would be deprived of one whole source of inspiration. When one wanders through those rooms at Cimiez, amidst that profusion of objects, plants, sculptures and hangings which recur in the master's paintings, what is most striking is the choice he has made, on which we should need to ponder at length in order to discover what Matisse is seeking. They form his true palette, a palette of objects with which chance and the painter's thought and fancy play endlessly until he suddenly perceives a certain relation between a fruit and a table, a leaf and a woman, and then drops everything else in order to give it permanent shape.

Note omitted by the printer in 1943 and restored in 1961:

Matisse tells me: 'I have been looking for a new object for months. I don't know what . . . Something to provide a shock . . .' (*Conversation of March 18*[1])

The palette of objects is quite another thing from the palette of colours. It is closer to the poet's palette of words. It is not a technical thing. The mistake that is made in those general comparisons between poetry and painting which may be futile but are sometimes illuminating is to mix up the field of technique (by confusing words and colours) with that field of choice which is the great general mystery of art, of all arts: the mystery of man. Why do you like this and not that? A work of art is more than a portrait, it is a man's expression of himself,† of his tastes, his relations with the world, his understanding of the world.

(*There are no dictionaries for painters: how I pity them!*)

† Once again, *our subject is man.*

And if in the sixteenth century Michelangelo could say: *It is only to the works being created in Italy that the name of true painting can be given, and that is why good painting is known as Italian painting* . . . precisely because it expressed the understanding of the world, the perfections of God in a different language, could not Matisse claim as much for French painting if he should wish to assert its supremacy? But would he wish to? Not that this would be difficult or hazardous. It is really only to the works being created in France that the name of true painting can be given, etc.

But I do not know if Matisse is prepared to be unfair, as the Italian master was towards the Flemings. In one corner of the room where his drawings hang there are photographs of the Byzantine mosaics of

Here, with reference to the mention made of the mosaics of Santa Sophia, the painter has written in pencil, as though to explain, in the 1942 edition, the reason for his possession of these photographs, indicating with little crosses:

The Byzantine cross, imagination and reason.

(*Note made only in 1968*)

1. Notes in which no year is specified refer to 1942.

28 and 29. – Drawings O_3 and O_4 of *Thèmes et Variations* (pencil).

Santa Sophia, to which he often refers when speaking of whatever preoccupies him. Matisse has travelled. I am inclined to think that his culture is wider than that of Michelangelo, at any rate as regards painting. Michelangelo had little choice beyond Italy. Matisse has, moreover, an infinitely richer *palette* (in the sense I have already given to that word). An imperial palette. We should try to assess its range. And if it extends beyond the boundaries of France, this in no way invalidates what I am saying. As though French painting were a matter of frontiers. And while, with Henri Matisse, it looks beyond the dotted lines on maps for its *nature*, we learn from him better perhaps than from anyone else that French painting is, primarily, a radiance.

Genius has more space now than in former days; it is less narrowly confined within its own nation and time; by dint of patience and energy it can remove itself, live elsewhere, make for itself a shelter and a cloister. You would find here a man who for sixty years looked at no other sun but your own; in Rome or in Paris, absent or present, he saw it constantly, and he saw it with sixteenth-century eyes.

From the last words it will be clear that the subject is not Henri Matisse but Ingres, and that the preceding words are by Hippolyte Taine.

Brazil, Martinique, pencilled in margin by H.M. (*Noted in 1968*)

O8
à mon cher
A. Rouveyre Henri Matisse 2/42

POSTERITY IS OURSELVES

It is in his drawings that Matisse finally achieves that satisfaction that has something divine about it, that perfection in which the painter of the *Last Judgment* recognized God.* This does not make him unfair, as Michelangelo was, towards Flemish or Japanese painting: but perhaps, in my opinion, towards his own painting. When a great painter speaks, we must retain much of what he says. But also, when he judges himself, we must know how to close our ears to his words, firmly though respectfully. Surely we may thus take our revenge, seeing in him to some extent *our* nature, and to a very great extent our France.

* We shall see later how this, written in 1942, seems to echo the words spoken by H.M. six or seven years later about the Chapel at Vence. (*Note, 1968*)

A CINEMA OF SENSATIONS

I had been saying this to him, or something like it.† As a matter of fact, he was talking of something else; but the connection was evident. It was just as if we had moved on to the next drawing. And now I realize that I have left something essential unexplained. The essential thing is the *serial* character of the drawings I was looking at while we spoke. That is, in terms of a game of billiards, each drawing is in itself a cannon, but one which starts afresh from the situation left by the previous cannon. The model, that is, a certain arrangement *that takes hold of his heart*, or a woman's posture, inspires him, and the drawing issues from his hand with, no doubt, all that hand's acquired mastery but, as Matisse insists, without any intervention on the painter's part to correct the hand. I shall return to this point. The finished drawing undergoes no correction. It seems nevertheless that the hand has not said everything, has not exhausted the artist's emotion. It will make the second drawing in the same way, then the third, and so on. Suddenly the painter will discover that what he was seeking for has been expressed, or else the impetus is interrupted. Then he puts aside the sheets of paper. The series is complete

† First version: *I showed him this.* The change is due to a conversation on the following day, reverting to this passage which H.M. had misunderstood and which, moreover, I had corrected. (*1966*)

Here Henri Matisse pencilled approval in the margin, with two letters:

T.B. (*Très bien*)

A trail to be followed: animated cartoons . . . There'd be a protest if I tried to compare Matisse with Walt Disney . . . And yet the girl on his walls at Cimiez reminds one of Snow White.[1]

Note: *that takes hold of his heart* (*qui lui prend le cœur*) added in pencil by Matisse. (*1968*)

1. I am amused now (*1968*) by what seemed so daring in 1942. One would have to find the equivalent in the strip cartoons of today, Jodelle or Barbarella. Walt Disney is already a classic.

. . . the girl on his walls at Cimiez reminds one of Snow White . . .

30. – Drawing O_8 of *Thèmes et Variations*, dedicated to *my dear A. Rouveyre* and dated 2/42 (pencil).

(I put this very crudely so as to make the rest easier to understand).

Matisse, reading the manuscript, objected to *This is what comes of being . . .* and wrote in pencil: *Who is summary?*[1] *Not the drawings. One must never be summary.* Then, having read further on, crossed out his remark. (*1968*)

This is what comes of being summary! At this point Matisse intervenes. He explains to me what he wanted to say, and what I said too hastily; he explains it to me, taking into account that I am a professional writer, in terms a writer can understand. Each drawing is like a sentence; a writer would not leave a sentence incomplete, would not keep it so. The sentence must be finished. And in that sense each drawing is perfectly complete. A poem, if you prefer. Then the artist, painter or poet, enriched by the experience of the earlier sentence, poem, drawing, will re-make his poem, his drawing, his sentence into another poem or drawing having greater substance. Or if we take the example of an acrobat making a pirouette, the pirouette has really been made, but the acrobat feels there is something stiff or clumsy about it, a lack of harmony; he begins it again, and the second pirouette is not a corrected version of the first but an experiment following another experiment . . . Then Matisse drops the image of the acrobat, which might wrongly sug-

Yet he likes to repeat a remark of André Masson's, who had gone with some friends to the Cirque Médrano: on seeing Rastelli, they couldn't help thinking of Matisse . . . A juggler is not an acrobat, he is more like a pianist.

1. Not realizing that I was referring to myself.

31–36. – Drawings O_9–O_{14} of *Thèmes et Variations*, following the variation dedicated to André Rouveyre (pencil).

31. 32. 33.

gest some imperfection in the curve of the first drawing, no, it's not that, his curve is always perfect . . .

And at that point, without perhaps being aware of the synthesis he is achieving, the painter suddenly chooses, in preference to poet or acrobat, the metaphor of a pianist. Cortot, for instance. When Cortot is practising he plays the piece in a purely mechanical fashion. It is only before an audience that, having acquired technical experience, he will give the finer shades. Well then . . .

I see what matters to Matisse: the comparison with a pianist is also faulty, but it is the finished perfection of Cortot's technical performance that he wants to compare with the intrinsic value, the perfection, of each drawing. Matisse is anxious to prevent me from implying, through some clumsy use of words, that any one of his drawings could be something more or less right. The technical probity of the draughtsman equals that of the poet, the acrobat, the pianist. The question of artistic probity is present in the background of all Matisse's remarks. Let us not forget that he refers to himself as having less *désinvolture*, less unconstraint, than Michelangelo.

Here Matisse has pencilled in the margin:
Cortot
Chopin
this desert
(Copied out later, 1946)

I've worked for years, he said several times, *just to have people say: So that's all Matisse is . . . !*

As we shall see later, he made the same remark on another occasion. Here H.M. had just written in the margin, to remind me, the last words: *So that's all Matisse is.* Noted in 1967 from the 1942 copy.

35.

36.

O 15
Henri Matisse 42

Now Cortot suggests a new train of thought. And all that he says about Cortot reflects what he wants us to think about himself. Cortot's panic in front of his audience (or Casals', or Thibaud's). Because Matisse knows panic too, it seizes him in front of a blank canvas. Years have passed, fame has come; he has never shaken it off.

blanche (blank): word added in Matisse's own hand. (*Noted in 1968*)

I have put this here, because I had to bring out clearly what, in the preceding pages, disturbed Matisse. Oh, that's putting it too strongly. He is not disturbed. He wouldn't let it be seen for anything in the world. But still, let's be a bit mischievous about him. There's no lack of mischief in that blue eye watching me: you know the game, a little boy stands up against the wall and you have to reach him without his seeing you move, he turns round suddenly and you have to stop motionless, fixed in some incredible pose. Matisse's blue eye is like that small boy, and at every instant he catches the world out, catches it moving and makes it hold an impossible pose. I was saying, then, that what disturbed Henri Matisse about the preceding pages was not what was said there nor the fact that Michelangelo had said it, but the intrusion of Michelangelo into the whole thing. I tried to find out why, and it seems to me, to sum it all up, that Matisse is afraid of the misunderstanding to which such a name might give rise. Michelangelo is certainly not his sort of artist. I mean that he feels a certain mistrust of those Renaissance people, Michelangelo, Leonardo . . . those men who dissected secretly, who investigated anatomy, who were preoccupied not with catching the movement of a hand but with knowing about the tiny bones and tendons inside it. Needless to say, for Matisse – he has even told me so himself – the art of the Renaissance was something terribly decadent.[1]

1. An idea which seemed strange in 1942, but which has become a commonplace in 1970: one forgets where what one says has come from, as if one had picked it up out of the air.

Snow White has risen . . .

◀ 37. – Drawing O_{15} of the preceding series (pencil).

H. Matisse Juill. 47

(Not that Matisse, who says this, despises or has ever despised anatomy. He has worked at it. For instance, he once spent two years copying one of Barye's tigers in evening class at the municipal school on the Rue Étienne-Marcel, first with his eyes, with what he could see, then with his eyes closed, with the sensations of volume acquired by touch alone. To go further than this copy he had asked an assistant at the Beaux-Arts to procure a dissected cat for him, so that he could study its back and its paws. But the difference between the men of the Renaissance and Matisse is that, for them, this was the essential part of their work, their construction and composition were based upon anatomy; whereas with Matisse, once he has studied and understood anatomy, when he is at work, it's no longer a question of anatomy but of *feeling*.)

evening class, etc. – Matisse insists on this detail. I told him then that I knew the building well, having been on night duty there several times in 1917–18, in the army medical corps, in anticipation of air-raid warnings, and that I subsequently introduced this school into *Anicet* for a night scene. He wanted to see the relevant passage in the novel, but in 1942 it was even more impossible to find *Anicet* at Nice than to find Charles Cros! Moreover, later on, in the preface to this novel written for the *Œuvres romanesques croisées d'Elsa Triolet et Aragon*, a printer's error put Rue Saint-Marcel instead of Rue Étienne-Marcel, referring to the place which, in the novel, was in the Rue aux Ours. (*Note, 1968*)

39. – *The Tiger*, sculpture after Barye.

◀ 38. – *Self-portrait*, July 1947.

A SLAP[1]

It's not surprising that he should not agree with the great writer I spoke of, the man who knows all the tricks, the Ali Baba of poetry. And that brings me back to the question of knack, of mastery, and of the independence of the draughtsman's line. The writer had praised Matisse for the *decisiveness* of his line. The term made Matisse smile. Of course he was not dissatisfied with that *acquired mastery*[2] which is the starting-point of his drawing. He even remarked, with a certain pride, that his line was 'not bad for seventy-two!' But what he could not accept was the word 'decisiveness'. Decisiveness? Nothing of the sort. Conviction, that's what it is.

Re-reading this passage, Matisse specifies (*these words suppressed in the book*):
Mastery over one's hand, forcing it to forget acquired gestures . . . You know: the pencil stroke . . . as one says that So-and-So has a pretty pencil stroke! (Recopied in 1966)

The blue eye brightens: 'When you give someone a slap in the face, obviously you don't give it limply, irresolutely. No, there's an impetus behind your movement. And that impetus comes not from decisiveness but from conviction. You give someone a slap with conviction . . .'

Pencilled note by Matisse:
When I want to fill in a gap left by the pen-nib before the ink has reached it, however short it may be I can't do it without my hand shaking, without spoiling (the stroke crossed out) *the impetus of the line. (Added in 1968)*

His drawings are certainly finished slaps, one involving the next. What checks his hand is the certainty of having put his utmost conviction into the last. The impetus, once broken, cannot be resumed . . .

Matisse has pencilled across the margin here:
as for the portrait of the model afterwards . . . (Noted in 1968)

And that's just what induces Matisse to comment on my use of the phrase *Madame Bovary is myself.* This is so true, he says, that when he is interrupted[3] at work by some importunate visitor, even though he may find his model, his Madame Bovary, exactly as he had left her, he cannot do a thing. The impetus has been lost. This proves that what the drawing represented was within the painter. Now the moment has passed.

At the end of this line, pencilled and immediately crossed out: *to create so as to live.* (*Noted in 1968*)

1. Subtitle omitted by mistake in the book and restored in 1966.
2. Underlined in pencil by Matisse, thus referring to the marginal note (*1966*).
3. *Lets himself be interrupted,* Matisse prefers. (*Noted on the MS. in 1968*)

He would rather I spoke of caves than of Michelangelo. Surely prehistoric man, with his aurochs, is closer to Matisse than the men of the Renaissance. For he, too, let his hand take over. Without thinking, he set down what he saw; what he caught himself seeing. Without thinking. The technique is the same. But. That tiny 'but' which is the whole mystery of Matisse's blue eye; of all that the blue eye has seen, the world, the whole history of painting, the culture of all the centuries, the knowledge of man's experience under all skies. Here Matisse resorts to a comparison. A *like* is going to explain that *but* . . .

'You see, I'm like a seaplane. It has to become airborne. It can't do so because of the floats that carry it . . . Then it takes off. But not with the help of its floats. Once it's airborne it forgets its floats. They're no more use to it. The floats are whatever you like, the Louvre, the old masters, all that I've learned . . . The thing is to lose oneself.'

Here (in the margin by *You see, I'm . . .*), Matisse has written:
which distinguishes him from the caveman.
(*Noted in 1968*)

There's something in this vein in Apollinaire:

. . . Perdre
Mais perdre vraiment
Pour laisser place à la trouvaille

. . . to lose
Really to lose
So as to leave room for discovery

From his seaplane Matisse goes cannoning off into a whole shower of *likes* and *buts*. As you'd say of a poet, it pours out of him. A scent is only a scent (his hand sketches a kind of vapour). But. The whole series of processes that bring about the creation, the manufacture, the evaporation of the scent. For my part, I'm quite willing to consider only the scent, to say of Matisse's splendid drawings that they are that nothing, that scent. Such an image will serve me better than that earlier one of a slap in the face.

But when you think it over, what difference is there between a slap and a scent?[1]

1. Here I myself had crossed something out: I'd written, as far as I can see under the ink, *a slap like a scent*, then preferred *a scent like a slap*. But that's my own business. (*1968*)

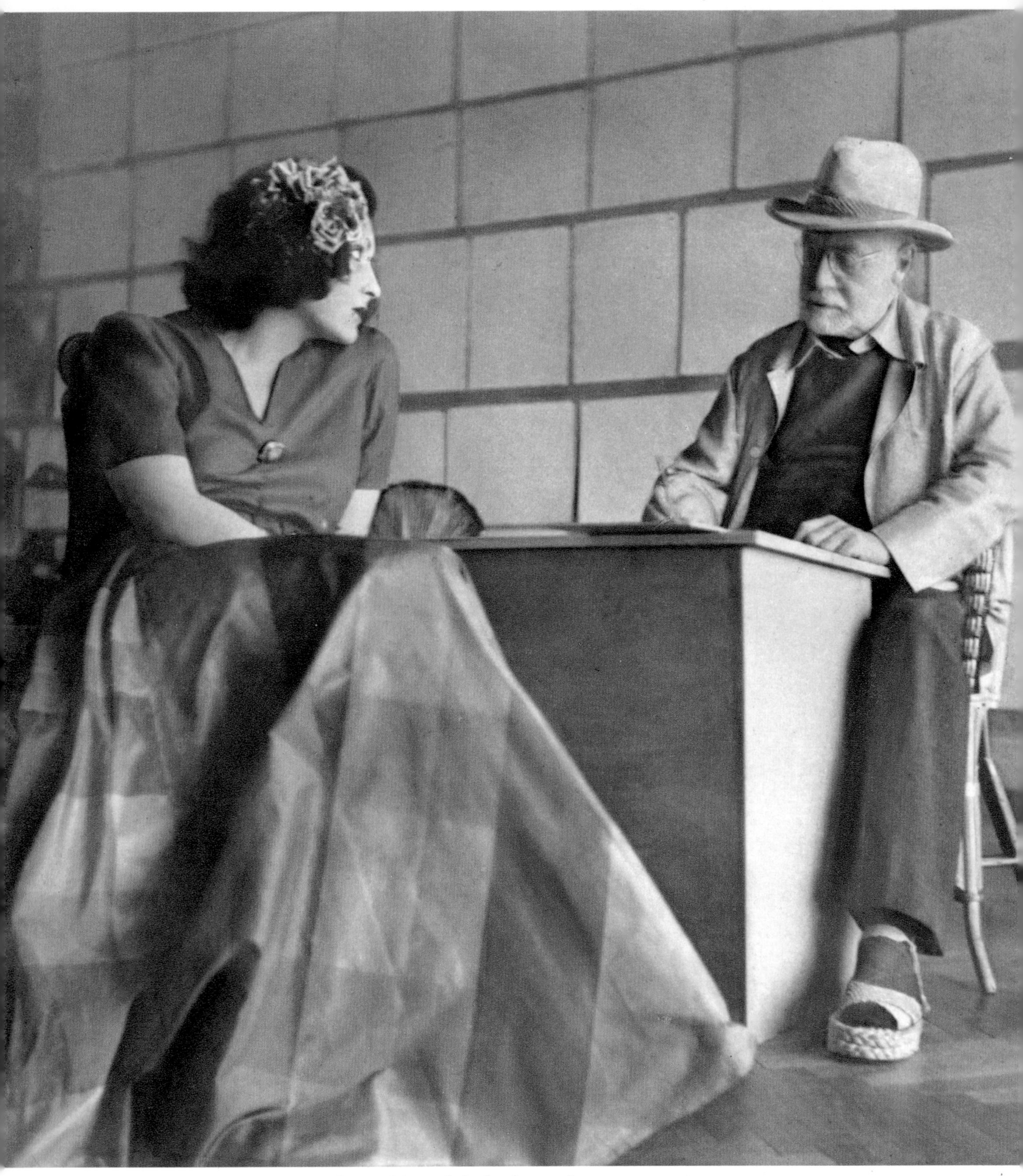

The model . . . 'It's the focus of my energy . . .'

40. – Henri Matisse in the 'bright room' drawing Nezy, the great-granddaughter of Abdul-Hamid.

EMMA BOVARY AGAIN

We spoke of Emma Bovary again; that is to say, of the model. Matisse had just been saying, by the way, that he had less unconstraint (*désinvolture*) than Michelangelo. What had brought him back to Madame Bovary? I think it was I who did so, simply because I had seen him fasten on the idea a short while before, and because I'm apt to think of Madame Bovary as the typical model, and that one could say something about the Madame Bovary aspect of every model, the way every model would like to be seen, ingenuously plotting to get Matisse (or Flaubert) to produce the desirably flattering image of herself. And then the big fellow's gruff assertion: *Madame Bovary is myself!* Matisse's blue eye says nothing. Matisse says something different.

'The model, for other people, is a source of information. For me, it's something that arrests me.'

It's the focus of my energy . . . (Conversation of March 18)

Another stone flung in Michelangelo's garden.

AN ORATORICAL PRECAUTION

Now Matisse is on the way to confession. I shan't betray him. I shall not imitate that inimitable tone of voice. I shall not try to pin him down or copy him. Matisse shall not be my model here, my Madame Bovary; I'd be too frightened. It's not my business to make him say what I myself think. Henri Matisse is not myself.

PORTRAIT OF THE PAINTER

The photographer who came a short while ago insisted on his wearing his beautiful dressing-gown, and also the hat that suits him so well, having been warned not to leave without photographing Matisse in his dressing-gown. People have come to form a special mental image of great painters. One must not depart from that. It would disconcert the public. So Matisse

The words *à regret* (reluctantly) added by H.M. (*1968*)

*I don't know if it was the dressing-gown seen in photographs taken at Vence after the war, or a camelhair lining sometimes worn by H.M. because of its lightness. But photographers visiting a great man always think of him as Honoré de Balzac. (*1967*)

had *reluctantly* to put on the 'dressing-gown'* and the felt hat. Luckily, the photographer didn't insist on the palette – you know, with the thumb showing through.

I myself am afraid of conforming to these mysterious and absurd rites. Of giving you, good people, the Matisse you expect with his moral dressing-gown, his hat of words, his palette, the certified setting for genius. Don't forget his blue eye. That's what saves me like a sort of talisman. That blue eye is something that had not been foreseen. You won't find it in magazine articles, nor in Vasari, *Lives of the Most Eminent Painters, Sculptors and Architects* . . . An eye like that isn't something you invent. There's humour and mystery in it.

The one does not preclude the other. Again, the fact that Matisse has less unconstraint than Michelangelo does not preclude an unconstrained gleam in that eye, mingled with undeniable mystery. I don't know what Michelangelo's eyes were like, Vasari does not say, and Francisco de Hollanda was too profoundly respectful to mention such a thing, but those eyes could scarcely have expressed more self-confident ease than Matisse's do at certain moments . . .

And what has Madame Bovary to do with all this?

THE COMEDY OF THE MODEL

One could write a play on the lines of *Six Characters in Search of an Author* about a painter in search of a model, assuming that the real model is himself. In the first act, the painter approaches a leading film agency: he needs a woman of such and such a type . . . his specifications are a bit of a worry, but with the endless string of supers we get here, it shouldn't be impossible . . . and those that come every day hoping to be taken on, and wait in the little bar next to the Théâtre Antoine . . . they really want a stage job, but failing that[1] . . . I see what you want . . . This act of the play offers the author the chance to display at least two types of psychology, face to face: the traditional type represented by the director of the agency with his cigar, his big gold ring and the bust of Napoleon on his desk; and the psychology of genius personified by the painter, who carries improbability to the point of visiting this office, stacked with green files, in the familiar dressing-gown* and the fine soft felt hat with a Tahitian wreath round it.

* Again! But it's more dramatic, more theatrical than the camelhair garment. (*1968*)

The second act takes place a few days later in the artist's studio. Of course he has a studio, but it's the sort that explains a lot to the spectator, a studio-cum-

1. Sentence omitted in *Matisse-en-France*, restored in 1968.

Matisse had *reluctantly* to put on the 'dressing-gown' and the felt hat.
41. – Photograph by Henri Cartier-Bresson (1945) taken at Vence, whereas the text was written at Cimiez in 1942. No cheating.

42. – This photograph (about 1920), showing Matisse painting the model Henriette, has been purposely chosen to take us back a little and serve as background to 'The Comedy of the Model'.

laboratory-cum-drawing-room, the extreme embodiment of the various concepts of the artist: as people imagined him at the time of Henry Bataille, the hero of *La Femme Nue*, or as Francis Carco pictures him, the *Lapin Agile* type, or as he is shown by . . . the name doesn't matter, the book is called *Les Montparnos*, as he was imagined by Dr Freud (not to be confused with Dr Faust) . . . in short, a setting which in itself comprises every sort of psychology of art, from Vasari's to Salvador Dali's. There's a ring at the bell and a model appears. She's not right. Another. Another. A whole string of them. This provides a splendid opportunity for stressing the psychology of models, the psychology of nature in all ages and all systems and for all painters. Rubens's model, and Greco's, and Van Dongen's. And a model for Descartes, or Spinoza, or Taine, or Nietzsche. In short, there's nothing doing. The painter abandons this kind of quest.

In the third act we are on the upper deck of an old-fashioned bus. Somewhere on the Left Bank, near the Carrefour Buci.

I wonder what that blue eye is going to think of my little Pirandello effort. But the play is not necessarily a comedy. It may turn into a drama. In any case a love story. Not one of the Romeo and Juliet kind, but a love story none the less. A different sort of love. The discovery of the model, as described by Matisse, is always love at first sight. In the case of the bus journey it was for a piece of stuff hanging in a junk shop. Matisse painted with that piece of stuff for years.[1] He falls in love at first sight with a flower, a green plant, a copper or a pewter jug.[2] And with women too, of course. There was one, once. In an antique shop. She had come to sell a few things. So she must have been in need of money. I kept her for five years.[3]

It's always love at first sight for his models. And there was an encounter in Martinique, where his boat had called for a few hours. The painter had jumped into a taxi for a quick trip to Mount Pelée. On the way back the driver had asked leave to stop at a certain house. A Negress came out and brought him a bunch of bananas. This woman was perfection. Not just beauty: perfection.

43 and 44. – Two other models of Matisse's: the copper pan and the little fluted pewter jug.

Pencil note, crossed out in red:

I could have worked for months with that Mad. de Senonnes.[1]

1. Ingres's *Madame de Senonnes* in the Musée des Beaux-Arts at Nantes. Always cited by Matisse, as we shall see, on account of her swelling throat, as the image of a certain beauty. Or perfection. (*1968*)

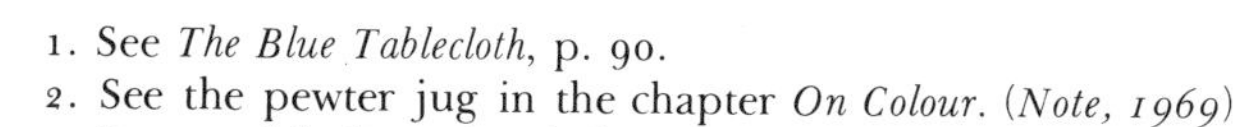

1. See *The Blue Tablecloth*, p. 90.
2. See the pewter jug in the chapter *On Colour*. (*Note, 1969*)
3. Presumably 'Henriette', but six years and not five (1921–7).

And again at Collioure: an ear of rye and three or four flowers. Something inexpressible. Useless to try and reproduce it. Quite hopeless. Two days, three days went by and then, click . . . Matisse actually said *tac* . . . he's got it, he does it . . . with such ease and zest.

And this defies any producer and all the Pirandellos on earth.

An ear of rye, three or four flowers: a living organism.

Madame Bovary or the Metamorphoses.

◀45. – *The ear of rye at Collioure* (pen and ink).

MADAME BOVARY AS AN ARMCHAIR

This time – was it at Ciboure, or am I dreaming? – Matisse was looking at a house. He didn't like it. He wouldn't have it, his face said. The person who was showing him over opened various doors. One glance. No, really, no. They had gone up and come down again. There's still one more room, but I won't show it you. It's not attractive. We may as well . . . I should like to convey Matisse's gestures as he told the story, wide-eyed, open-mouthed, his hand stroking his beard in perplexity, thumb and forefinger seeming to underline his lower lip, then his arm flung out, his whole body spinning round . . . Well, I saw Matisse; but I never saw the room, which was yellow, with a dark engraving on the wall, the red armchair (a Second Empire, Louis XV-style armchair[1]) and many other things which he enumerated very fast, a real country room, peaceful and charming . . . 'I don't know what it reminded me of, Eugénie Grandet maybe?' And then the window. It opened on to a garden on the slope of a hill, quite close, right up against the window, with a path leading up . . . No sky. Only the garden, the tree, the path. He described it all, with the colours. And a wave of his hand following the path uphill. The same hand, you know, that does those drawings on its own. I never saw the path, but I saw the hand fly up.

It was love at first sight for the yellow room. Matisse stopped there. The armchair. He drew that armchair endlessly. He felt at home in this room. Through the window he could sometimes see a woman in the garden, going up the path, or perched on a ladder picking fruit.[2] You'd have thought she was in the room. The path up. The tree. The flowers. Then Matisse made a painting of it. The State bought it, when there was that exhibition at the Albi Museum.

Through the window he could sometimes see a woman in the garden . . . perched on a ladder . . .
46. – Ciboure, 1940, pencil.

Actually, later on, returning to one of his sketchbooks, Matisse was to give me a closer description of the room and the landscape. There were two windows, which he had forgotten. And between the two windows a mirror, in which he saw himself drawing. One of the windows looked out over the wall, the open door, the steps leading up in the garden . . . That wasn't where he had seen the woman on the ladder in the trees . . .

In fact, this was how he came to remember the second window . . . (Sketch for The Room at Ciboure, *p. 224)*

He drew that armchair endlessly, 'patiently, so as to flirt with the room without seeming to do so and get close enough to it to discover its secret'. A stratagem. Compare this armchair with another in Matisse's life: that baroque rocking-chair which he had in his room in Tahiti and which he chose to draw instead of that incredible landscape and sky . . . Matisse was to say of that curious feint or flirtation that it was like a pickpocket's conversation with his victim, during the course of which he pinched his watch.

1. A detail insisted on by Matisse, who pencilled in the margin: 'Louis XV N. III' (*noted in 1967*). Reproduced here, pp. 28 and 224.
2. I had written *flowers*. Matisse corrected me. (*Note, 1967*)

VIII. – *The Blue Tablecloth* (1909) is the usual name given to this still life where, in fact, the subject, the model, is the material itself (which reappears in Matisse's painting throughout his life). The complete title of the picture is *Still Life – Blue Monochrome*: it will be noticed henceforward that I sometimes use the current description of a work instead of its 'official' title. The list of coloured plates, in both volumes, puts the matter right.

One must be careful not to ascribe more than their due importance to these explanations added subsequently by Matisse, and to consider them as a sign of his extreme modesty; and to remember that the important thing is that 'flirtation', a deliberate understatement, that *love affair* with the yellow room or with Tahiti.

I wanted to say that this is what always happens, in any household; the daughter or the room that seemed least promising is the one that dazzles the traveller, and the traveller stays on, the king's son marries Cinderella, Matisse settles down in the yellow room, and the next thing is the Court ball, the Albi Museum. I did not say anything, because of that blue eye and those hands silently waving, evoking something as though by magic . . . Can you picture Matisse standing there telling his story? A room such as you find only in remote country places, and an armchair . . . His hands sketch the armchair, cutting through the cotton wool of dream.

Madame Bovary as an armchair . . . That brings me back to Ovid, to the *Metamorphoses: Os homini sublime dedit* . . . Was he speaking of Matisse, of Matisse's face? I can still see that face turned towards the window, lifted, as Ovid's God required, towards the sky . . . *Cælumque tueri jussit* . . .[1] looking at the sky which does not exist.

CÆLUMQUE . . .

Stop-press: *I have at last found the object for which I've been longing for a whole year. It's a Venetian baroque chair, silver-gilt with tinted varnish, like a piece of enamel. You've probably seen something like it. When I found it in an antique shop, a few weeks ago, I was quite bowled over. It's splendid. I'm obsessed with it. I am going to bounce on it gently when I come back in the summer* . . .

Letter from Henri Matisse to the author, *April 20, 1942*, to be seen with the 'longed-for object' on p. 212.

(Thus, from one armchair to another, the strange romance is carried on. Our story continues . . .)

In the room we are in now, in Matisse's room at Cimiez, there is a sky, a strange potential sky, which is not on the ceiling but on the walls surrounding those women's faces which the God of this place has rendered sublime, often in the etymological sense of *uplifted*. It is a white sky, Matisse's sky. Against that sky the faces or the still lifes have been inscribed without blurring it, carefully preserving the uniform whiteness of the air. The line, the way it unfolds, the way it limits surfaces have all been calculated so as to respect that whiteness. Matisse is fully conscious of the whiteness thus maintained. He has repeatedly pointed it out to me, as also, in his book illustrations, his respect

1. Oddly enough, in 1968, for the Chagall exhibition at Pierre Matisse's in New York, I quoted the same passage, as though I were the Petit Larousse dictionary of my childhood, the one that had pink pages . . . (*Note, 1968*)

. . . the veil with which she . . . is playing, which *in reality* is a black veil, is here a blankness . . .
47, 48 and 49. – Variations marked 2, 3 and 4 in Series N of *Thèmes et Variations* (pen and ink).

for the lay-out of the page, the balance kept between text and drawing . . . One can't help remembering a line of Mallarmé's: *Le blanc souci*[1] . . . True, but the poet's cult of the empty page, that reverent dread of blackening it, is something the painter feels only to begin with, for he has – and he knows he has – the gift of not blackening the page, and I would readily assert that the sheet of paper on which he has traced a line is whiter than the virgin sheet it was. Whiter, because it is conscious of its whiteness.

Like women to whom love imparts a glow . . . (*1970*)

With a sweeping gesture of his hand, Matisse shows the walls covered with sets of drawings in close juxtaposition: 'You see,' he says, 'it's the same whiteness everywhere . . . I haven't removed it anywhere . . .'

Here Matisse has pencilled in the margin: *and yet there are ten shades on every sheet . . .* (*Noted in 1968*)

White everywhere. A strange game of dominoes. Between my visits these dominoes, changing their position with the majestic slowness of chessmen, finish their game with a few more moves, and other drawings are added to the incomplete set, wherever there's room, as it were blank/four, blank/one . . .

1. *Le blanc souci de notre toile* (Mallarmé, *Salut*). The white preoccupation with our canvas (the obsession of the blank canvas).

50, 51 and 52. – Continuation of the variations on the previous page, pen and ink (February 1942).

Actually, the latest series is built up round a veiled or half-veiled woman. Not that she's wearing a domino (to explain the odd 'actually' in my remark) . . . But the veil with which she, or rather Matisse, is playing, which in reality is a black veil, is here a white space enclosed by a swift elusive line, sometimes left open on the white paper, which itself becomes the veil, the *blackness*, the absence of drawing, black by dint of whiteness . . . The whole series of drawings of the veiled woman invites endless commentary.

WHERE COLOUR TAKES ITS REVENGE

(During the same period when these drawings appeared mysteriously, like some unexpected modulation of a theme already treated, a picture was painted, born of the same preoccupations with the same model, the same veil, by the same painter's meditative hand . . . And one can imagine nothing more unlike those drawings than that painting: a plump blonde with pretty pink flesh, a blend of freshness and maturity. The veil is there; but it's a veil bought in a shop. The mystery is no longer the same. I don't mean that there is no mystery. There is the mystery of the painting, of the painter. But not the mystery of the veil, nor of the woman. It is a magnificent picture. The red of the lips echoed in the background, on the wall . . . Matisse shows me the picture and asks with an anxious note that baffles me: 'Don't you think it's rather too straightforward? Rather Manet-ish?')

(*And I refer you to the frontispiece to* Matisse-en-France, *p.* 52.)

CORRESPONDENCES

The similarities that exist between Matisse and Manet . . . One is tempted, rather, to stress the dissimilarities. There's the period, for one thing, and a very different attitude. But the fact that Matisse should ask this question (*Don't you think* . . .) is as it should be. And in the same way that famous quatrain of Baudelaire's (*Le charme inattendu d'un bijou rose et noir*), written about a Manet, might just as well have referred to a Matisse, Perhaps even . . .

The unexpected charm of a pink and black jewel.

And so we find the meeting-point between all the myths rambling cat-like through this article: the Baudelairean note in that story of Anne of Avignon painted by King René, and the thing that impelled me to think of it immediately the first time I visited Matisse, that painter of a sunlit world. The contradiction is between periods, not between minds: *Luxe, calme et volupté* . . . there's more than one line of Baudelaire's that can be read in a demonic light, by Dr Faust's lamplight, or on the contrary, although it's the same line, in the bright modern sunlight of Matisse. To digress a little from my subject, his recent drawings, the feeling conveyed by certain paintings of Matisse, *Goldfish, The Painter and His Model, The Piano Lesson, Interior with Forget-me-nots*, is an extraordinary sense of seeing, at long last, and understanding the inside, the very inwards of our modern homes, in which we live unawares:[1] just as, probably, Chardin's contemporaries learned the mystery of their dwellings

A well-known painting by Matisse bears this title (see infra, p. 291).

1. I was to remember this in 1947, when writing the poem *Matisse Parle*. (*Note, 1968*)

IX. – *Goldfish* (1914–15), which André Bréton and I with some difficulty persuaded Jacques Doucet, that patron of the arts, to buy for his collection (now in the Museum of Modern Art, New York).

X. – *The Painter and His Model* (1917), in Matisse's apartment on the Quai Saint-Michel. The model is Laurette. The building visible on the other side of the bridge is the Sûreté.

XI. – *The Piano Lesson* (1916). Pierre Matisse, the painter's son, is at the piano; in the background, on the wall, the picture *Woman with Stool*, painted in 1914.

XII. – *The Window – Interior with Forget-me-nots* (1916). As with *The Piano Lesson*, the setting is the Matisse home at Issy-les-Moulineaux.

through seeing his pictures. Is this feeling so very remote from that other feeling, conveyed in a different style, the style of a different period, which we get from certain lines in *La Mort des Amants*, for instance (*Des divans profonds comme des tombeaux*)?

Divans as deep as tombs.

The relation between Manet and Baudelaire admits no question. And yet, speaking of divans, take a look at the one on which Olympia is lying. And those famous sheets of hers. It's obvious that Baudelaire would literally have adored Matisse. And I am surprised not to find a final verse in *Les Phares*, one about Matisse. That should be put right.

One should not forget Matisse's portrait of Baudelaire, illustrating Le Tombeau de Baudelaire *by Mallarmé. The only portrait which can stand comparison with Nadar's photographs.*

A THROW OF THE DICE

I attach the greatest importance to these relations between the mind and sensibility of a painter, a great painter, and the poets who touch our deepest feelings. Even though it may be a digression, I can't go on speaking about Matisse except in the light of these hallowed associations.

I spoke of Baudelaire . . . but about Mallarmé there is nothing to say, because Matisse has forestalled me with illustrations to his poems. The other day he was worrying over:

> *Quelle soie aux baumes de temps*
> *Où la chimère s'exténue*
> *Vaut la torse et native nue*
> *Que, hors de ton miroir, tu tends!*

And suddenly something obvious struck me: this quatrain is a Matisse. When you've thought of that, you cannot possibly see it any other way. In each line, in every word. In the syntax: I mean in that way of showing us first a piece of stuff, then the pattern of the stuff, and only afterwards the form of the woman, her hair, and at the end of it all we learn that it was not the woman herself but her reflection in the mirror.

THE CLOUDS

As Matisse pointed out to me, this quatrain (and,

53. – *Baudelaire*, etching from *Poésies de Stéphane Mallarmé* (Skira, Lausanne, 1932).

after all, why should it not be a case of two successive drawings in a series, in spite of the change of authorship from Gautier to Mallarmé?) is strangely like that other from *Émaux et Camées*:

A l'horizon monte une nue
Sculptant sa forme dans l'azur!
On dirait une vierge nue
Émergeant d'un lac au flot pur.

He thinks that Mallarmé must have known it. 'But,' he says, 'one's not an idiot, one can't repeat what someone has said earlier . . .' He means that one goes on from that point. Mallarmé would have been *an idiot* if he had reproduced in his own quatrain the sculptured *torso* rising from the mirror-like lake; no, he merely shows the *hair*. This cloud, a torso for Gautier and a woman's hair [*torse* = twisted] for Mallarmé, has led the painter's mind far afield. He shows me the series of drawings he made which conclude with one of a woman emerging from a pedestal of clouds and lifting up her hair, the meeting-point, so to speak, of two poetic ideas. A third idea has added something to these – the opposite of its weight, its impetus, that's the word – a personal contribution born of Matisse's own experience. He shows me a dark little amateur snapshot which sheds surprising light on the whole story.

Matisse is here seen to be punning on the word torse *which in Mallarmé's poem is an adjective (twisted) but whose substantival meaning, torso, is implied though not expressed in the Anadyomene of Gautier's lake. (On reflection I notice a double pun in the two meanings of* nue*: cloud, naked.)*

This commentary was suggested by a pencilled remark of H.M.'s: *why hair?* because in both cases he understood *torse* as a noun. (*Additional note, 1968*)

The photograph shows a place in some distant sea, Tahiti probably, with the islands scarcely outlined, but above them something looming amazingly close, a huge cloud, like the shaft of a pillar on its base, a crushing presence just above the waters. Not a distant, flat cloud like those you see in the sky: no, a presence, you could go round it, you feel as if you could touch it. As Matisse says, it was more like an airship than like a cloud. This cloud-formation irresistibly evokes the idea of a gigantic statue rising close by, a woman standing, something like the Victory of Samothrace on her ship. The memory of this sight occurred to Matisse when he began to illustrate Mallarmé. He found the

. . . *la torse et native nue* . . .
54. – Etching from the 1932 *Mallarmé.*

55. – *Cloud at Tahiti,* photograph by Henri Matisse.

photograph again and it was while looking at it, it was from the sight of this cloud, that his nude was born, that sweeping movement confined at the base in its matrix of storm.

And thus Matisse succeeded in going beyond Mallarmé, as Mallarmé had gone beyond Gautier.

RONSARD AND CROS

At the present moment, Henri Matisse is doing drawings for Ronsard. This had shocked me at first.* How foolish one is. I had said to Matisse (before he had ever expressed to me his criticism of Renaissance painting): 'Why are you concerned with all that Renais-

* I have left this and all that follows about both Cros and Ronsard as it was written in 1943, in spite of having had to reintroduce the story in an article inserted above, written in 1967 (*To Be Inserted – An explanatory note*). The sequel will be found further on, in *A Character Called Pain,* written in February 1968.

sance stuff, the cult of Classical antiquity?' He did not answer. He said: 'Is that what you think?' He showed me his first drawings. A woman. Another woman, or the same one. And then faces drawn with a single stroke, mascarons at the head of each poem, no more important than decorative initials – faces which are always the same face, incredibly graphic, an ornament . . . what a misleading word for the barest, least ornamented thing in the world! Matisse found his own road to Ronsard: the love poems, Hélène – perhaps we shall read Ronsard differently now, since Matisse, like that *soie aux baumes de temps* . . .

In the margin of this whole paragraph Matisse pencilled ornate capital E's. (*Note, 1968*)

I told him: 'I have always thought there was a close connection between you and the poetry of Charles Cros: why don't you illustrate Charles Cros?' Matisse had never read Cros. And I hunted in vain in the bookshops of Nice for *Le Collier de Griffes* and *Le Coffret de Santal*. Nowhere to be found. How unfair! Cros not to be found, and Matisse here, alive, able to read him! Few poets stand apart from their setting as much as Charles Cros. If I had his works by me I should only have to open them: I'd show you Matisse everywhere. Nowadays one can't find Cros when one wants to. I used never to be understood when I said that the finest line in French poetry was Charles Cros's:

Amie éclatante et brune . . .

I can date this incident approximately. Among Matisse's letters to Mme Marie Dormoy which are in the Doucet Library, and which she allowed me to consult, I find a letter dated March 16, 1942, which says, after referring to the Skira *Ronsard*: *Can you have sent to me, or rather to Mr Fabiani, Av. Matignon Ancienne Gal^ie Weil, 2 vols. of Charles Cros's poetry which are unobtainable here. Published by Stock: Collier de Griffes, Coffret de Santal – he will pay for them for me* . . .

On May 16 of the same year M. writes to the same correspondent:

I shall not go to Paris for a few months because I've got to go to Switzerland in July and August to see to the publication of my Ronsard . . . I have not yet seen Cros's books. Didn't I ask you to have them sent to Fabiani's? He may not have had an opportunity. Perhaps the post will be better.

And finally in a note of June 2:

I have just received the 2 Cros and a catalogue of the next sale. Many thanks . . . (Note, 1968)

But let's get back to Henri Matisse. Really, it's not a matter of getting back: it's of him that I have been speaking all along.

FROM NATURE

One of the most mysterious things about Matisse, I mean one of those mysteries to which the painter himself draws attention, is that dual attitude towards the model: on the one hand he cannot do without a model, and on the other the model inspires something so detached from itself that, for example, a window opening on to a blue luminous sky produces in the picture a

Close to the model – within it – eyes less than a metre away from the model and knees within reach of its knees – as in the room at Ciboure where I seemed not to exist. (Note by Matisse re-copied 1968)

broad black band, or a piece of green and white marble becomes a red network on a black background, and so on. Not to mention the dark girl who becomes, in one particular painting, a mature redhead, and, in one of his drawings, herself in twenty years' time. You will find ten interpretations of the same Arab tapestry hanging here by the window, bearing witness to the painter's faithfulness and unfaithfulness.

Or a little girl, in a different light . . . adds Matisse in the margin, in pencil. (*Noted in 1968*)

And this is surely how he takes us beyond portraiture, in this room of his decked out with differing likenesses of the same face, of the same model. Just as I might repeat some hundred times my favourite line:

Amie éclatante et brune

so Matisse has returned some hundred times to that same face, which is always alike and yet always different. When I tell him humbly what I find disturbing about this apparent contradiction, his need for a model and his detachment from the model, Matisse always insists (I have noticed it repeatedly) on the constant factor in these apparently diverse drawings. In those of this particular model, for instance, the mouth is always the same. Matisse evidently prized the mouth above anything else in this model; it must have been a decisive factor in his choice of her. He points out that it is a perfect mouth, that it corresponds closely to one's idea of a mouth, how wonderfully it is joined to the face with that slight pout of the lower lip, how the two lips not only lie against one another but are pressed against one another, how they curve, how . . . In short, he is inexhaustible on the subject.

No, but it is more obviously significant . . . pencilled correction by Matisse in the margin, in 1942. (*Noted by me in 1968*)

Matisse once more pencils in the margin: *Mad^e de Senonnes . . .* See supra: this reference, not in this case to the fullness of the throat but to the slightly pouting lip, shows Matisse's awareness of the attraction that a certain type of woman had for him. (*Noted and commented on, 1968*)

'In my time, you see, we used always to refer to nature, we painted from nature . . .'

This explanation, which makes education responsible, is of doubtful validity, and Matisse, that free spirit, is well aware of it. He goes on:

'When I draw a mouth it's got to be a real mouth . . . an eye, a real eye . . . Look, look here . . . and this one, and that one . . . is it an eye, yes or no? It is an eye . . .'

'Nature accompanies me and uplifts me,' he says further. And he tries to explain that the contradiction between contemplation and action is thus solved for him: 'Contemplative action, active contemplation . . . how shall I put it.'

This is probably just as much a criticism of certain painters whom he has in mind as a defence of what he does himself, or his need for a model. Some painters draw a face: but look at the eye, it's anything you like but not an eye . . . in the face, it's where the eye should be, and that's all.[1] Nothing of the sort with Matisse. He could put the eye wherever he liked, it would still be an eye. Like this young woman's breast. It is a breast. In the drawing it is not where it is on the young woman. Matisse has drawn it very low. He needed that for the balance of his drawing, one of the series with the veil that I referred to. It's quite true that the breast was needed there. Cover it with your hand and you'll see. It's impossible to leave it out. But it is a breast, not just a line to help out the composition.

THE SIGN-FOR-A-MOUTH

I am almost inclined to see in this contradiction the motive power of Matisse's genius, his fire (to speak like Heraclitus), his war. Perpetually animated by this pair of opposing forces, imitation and invention – when they balance one another a drawing is born and the hand stops. And then Matisse has the twofold feeling that the woman in front of him has dictated the drawing and yet (just as the seaplane forgets its floats) that it has issued from himself and not from her.

This contradiction recurs here in many forms. For instance in the way imitation leads in the end to that which is furthest from portraiture: to a sign. It was in connection with what I said much earlier about signs, and also about the caveman drawings, that Matisse began to speak of his model's mouth and of what he discovered every day about that mouth, to such an extent that now it always came out the same. So well imi-

In the margin of this passage on the sign-for-a-mouth, Matisse illustrates his point with other feminine signs, and I am sorry not to be able even to summarize this conversation here, all that remains of it being a single sign repeated and then crossed out in pencil, and the inscription: *Toulon, red-light district.* (*1968*)

1. The *sign* for an eye has no meaning of its own here, it is only significant in its context. (*Note, 1968*)

tated. So lifelike. Like the mouth, and like his drawings, the other drawings he had made of it. He'd got that mouth at his fingertips . . . d'you see, d'you see? It's always the same mouth. And the result of this knowledge, this skill in reproducing and imitating, is a sign. For he has come to know it so well that now he *writes* it rather than drawing it. The mouth, this particular mouth, has become a hieroglyph. Like the Chinese character that means man, bird, or even mouth. And yet it's still the same mouth we studied so closely, with its slightly pouting lower lip, the lips pressed together in the same way, joined to the face in the same way, the same curve down to the chin . . . But here we have reached a higher stage of knowledge of this mouth, its sign . . .

Matisse takes me into the other room to show me something: the drawings for his Ronsard, the mascarons, you know, the same face which is never the same, drawn with a single line. 'I hadn't noticed it,' he assures me, 'somebody pointed it out to me . . .' And it's true: all the mouths in these faces are drawn in the same way, with no more difference than between different versions of a letter drawn by the same hand, sometimes bigger, sometimes smaller, with certain slight variations which would not mislead a graphologist, a *y* is always a *y*. Here the mouth is somewhat like a 3 on its side, or a sort of complicated *S*. And it has all the characteristics of the direct drawings, patiently imitated, of the mouth of the model, of one particular model, Mlle X . . .

'Well,' the painter says triumphantly, 'just look . . . isn't this a mouth?'

Exactly in the same tone in which he had said a short while before: 'It's an eye!'

56. – Sketches of the sign-for-a-mouth, taken from a letter from Henri Matisse to the author, February 16, 1942, reproduced in this volume on p. 150.

57. – Mascaron for the *Ronsard*, chosen by Matisse himself to explain the preceding sketches.

(...*Quand sa lèvre est l'M où*
Renaît le mois de mai dès la première moue
if I may be allowed to quote myself here; I won't make a habit of it.)

(When her lip is the M that gives birth to the month of May with its first pout . . .)

In the margin a dozen or more pencilled signs for mouths, drawn with a single stroke, like a kind of flattened Z. (*Noted in 1968*)

THE CHINESE

This sign business cannot be exhausted in a handful of words.* Matisse returns to it by various paths, as mysterious as those forest tracks which are all unlike but which all lead to the same clearing. Shall I follow him through this bracken, or these bushes, or that moss? Mallarmé, once again, most aptly provides the pretext he is seeking. The famous passage:

Imiter le Chinois au cœur limpide et fin
De qui l'extase pure est de peindre la fin
Sur des tasses de neige à la lune ravie
D'une bizarre fleur qui parfume sa vie
Transparente, la fleur qu'il a sentie enfant
Au filigrane bleu de l'âme se greffant

is quoted more than once by Matisse, and from these six lines, moreover, he goes off in at least two directions. He slips along one path by way of *the flower he smelled as a child*. The other is the way we were already following.

* Hence the next chapter in this book, *Signs*, p. 145.

MATISSE CONFESSES

'To imitate the Chinese . . .' Matisse says. Here follows the painter's confession, which was not made all at once. I should like to retain the essence of it, I'm afraid of breaking its branches. If he admits that he laboured for long years in quest of a theme, or rather of a formula, a sign for each thing, this can be connected with that other admission, the most disturbing one: 'I have been working at my craft for a long time, and it's just as if up till now I had only been learning things, elaborating my means of expression.'

Once again, what amazing modesty, what scrupulous conscientiousness he shows: that immense lifelong labour, those fifty years of work were merely the preparation of his craft. What is he trying to do? Matisse continues:

Training day after day, writes H.M. in the margin after reading this paragraph. (*Noted in 1967*)

58 and 59. – *Studies of a Tree* seen through the painter's window, drawings numbered *7* and *8* and dated August 25, 1941 (pen and ink).

'I have shown you, haven't I, the drawings I have been doing lately, learning to represent a tree, or trees? As if I'd never seen or drawn a tree. I can see one from my window. I have to learn, patiently, how the mass of the tree is made, then the tree itself, the trunk, the branches, the leaves. First the symmetrical way the branches are disposed on a single plane. Then the way they turn and cross in front of the trunk[1] . . . Don't misunderstand me: I don't mean that, seeing the tree through my window, I work at copying it. The tree is also the sum total of its effects upon me. There's no question of my drawing a tree that I see. I have before

Hitherto my passionate attention had been concentrated on the trunk and the main branches . . . The rest existed, of course . . . the leaves . . . but only as related masses and colour. In my latest research I began with the leaves . . . (Conversation of March 18)

1. We shall see this recurring in 1951, with reference to the plane trees of Villeneuve-Loubet, when the tree is represented by a woman or vice versa. (*Note, 1969*)

dans le langage courant. These four words added by H.M. (*1968*)

me an object that affects my mind not only as a tree but also in relation to all sorts of other feelings . . . I shan't get free of my emotion by copying the tree faithfully, or by drawing its leaves one by one *in the common language*, but only after identifying myself with it. I have to create an object which resembles the tree. The sign for the tree, and not the sign that other artists may have found for the tree: those painters, for instance, who learned to represent foliage by drawing 33, 33, 33, just as a doctor who's sounding you makes you repeat 99 . . . This is only the residuum of the expression of other artists. These others have invented their own sign . . . to reproduce that means reproducing something dead, the last stage of their own emotion . . .'

As he spoke to me I was thinking of Matisse's followers, of all those who imitate him clumsily or too cleverly, but who can see only his superficial gestures: they think they are starting from *his signs*, but they are in fact bound to fail because one can imitate a man's voice but not his emotion.

'. . . and the residuum of another's expression can never be related to one's own feeling. For instance: Claude Lorrain and Poussin have ways of their own of drawing the leaves of a tree, they have invented their own way of expressing those leaves. So cleverly that people say they have drawn their trees leaf by leaf. It's just a manner of speaking: in fact they may have represented fifty leaves out of a total two thousand. But the way they place the sign that represents a leaf multiplies the leaves in the spectator's mind so that he sees two thousand of them . . . They had their personal language. Other people have learned that language since then, so that I have to find signs that are related to the quality of my own invention. These will be new plastic signs which in their turn will be absorbed into the common language, if what I say by their means has any importance for other people . . .'

And very quickly Matisse adds a truth, his own truth, which sums it all up:

'The importance of an artist is to be measured by

the number of new signs he has introduced into the language of art . . .'[1]

THE CONFESSION CONTINUED

It was after confiding this concept of signs that he made a remark which takes us a long way from the trees: 'It's just as if I were someone who is preparing to tackle large-scale composition.'

'I don't understand . . .'

Those blue eyes. Matisse stretches out his arms, holding his hands in a curious position with the wrists half bent and the fingers slightly turned in as though illustrating a foreshortened effect, which was to be the subject of his next sentence. 'Look, look . . . why do they say Delacroix never painted hands . . . that he only painted claws . . . like this? Because Delacroix composed his paintings on the grand scale. He had to finish off, at a certain place, the movement, the line, the curve, the arabesque that ran through his picture. He carried it to the end of his figure's arm and there he bent it over, he finished it off with a sign, don't you see? A sign! Always the same sign, the hand, made in the same way, not a particular hand but *his* hand, the claw . . . The painter who composes on the grand scale, carried away by the movement of his picture, cannot stop over details, paint each detail *as if it were a portrait*, portray a different hand each time . . .'

'You said that you were going to . . . that it's just as if you . . .'

'As if I were going to tackle large scale composition: it's odd, isn't it? As if I had all my life ahead of me, or rather a whole other life . . . I don't know, but the quest for signs – I felt absolutely obliged to go on searching for signs in preparation for a new development in my life as painter . . . Perhaps after all I have

1. This idea, expressed in the same terms, recurs five years later in another text by Henri Matisse.

Here H.M. had noted:
it's the play of the arm in the composition that indicates the expression. (1966)

This note was combined with (or explained by) a few pencilled lines, crossed out and barely decipherable, because in fact Matisse was correcting himself and had not eliminated the superfluous words: he seems to say that the arm makes use of the hand, *turns it in different directions, that the hand implying supplication* (or anything else) *is always the same hand. It's the direction of the arm leading up to it that gives the expression. (Attempted reading, March 1968)*

Everyone knows the charming fable about the invention of the Corinthian capital by Callimachus: the artist was roaming through the countryside, musing over his various ideas; he paused, moved with pity, before the tomb of a child – just a stone on which a pious mother had laid a basketful of fruit – but lest the birds of the air should come and devour the provisions offered to the dear departed spirit, a tile had been placed over the top of the basket; an acanthus had taken root and grown there; its supple stems, checked in their growth by the unyielding terra cotta, had curved over spirally. This was all he needed. The tile became the abacus of the capital; the acanthus leaves surrounded its base with a carved wreath; the stems with their sheaths became scrolls and tendrils, and the most elegant constituents of Greek architecture had been discovered.

A. JACQUEMART
Les Merveilles de la céramique

60. – Drawing made to explain the Burmese hand to me (1944).

an unconscious belief in a future life . . . some paradise where I shall paint frescoes . . .'

There's more laughter than ever in those blue eyes. On another occasion Matisse starts off once more from the Chinese artist with the transparent and delicate heart to consider signs. This time his own hand describes not the claws in a Delacroix but a Burmese hand . . . 'You know those Burmese statues with very long, flexible arms, rather like this . . . and ending in a hand that looks like a flower at the end of its stalk . . .' That's the Burmese sign-for-a-hand. The sign may have a religious, priestly, liturgical character or simply an artistic one. Each thing has its own sign. This marks the artist's progress in the knowledge and expression of the world, a saving of time, the briefest possible indication of the character of a thing. The sign. 'There are two sorts of artist,' Matisse says, 'some who on each occasion paint the portrait of a hand, a new hand each time, Corot for instance, and the others who paint the sign-for-a-hand, like Delacroix. With signs you can compose freely and ornamentally . . .'

Thereupon he returns to his own example, the mouth shaped like a 3. He draws the series of hieroglyphs based on a specific model, whose mouth has a slightly pouting lower lip, both lips being fleshy and pressed close together: I see the figure 3 gradually appearing under his hand as a profile of that mouth, although it is seen from the front. 'Why a 3 and not an 8? Because the mind can always imagine a line cutting the two parts of the 8 in the middle, whereas the 3 has to remain a whole . . .' On reflection, he adds: 'There's also the fact that I have grown used to seeing objects in a certain light, like all the painters of my time. So in the 3 of the mouth there's one part in shadow and the other, the part that disappears, is swallowed up by the light.'

At this point in his explanation I reproach myself for having, even for an instant, given a passing thought earlier on to Matisse's followers, those who ape him (it must have made me miss a few words of his). The distance between himself and them is as vast as those African deserts that lie between the bazaar on the city outskirts and the distant town where craftsmen create the masks that the traders copy. In their case, a sign is a mass-produced imitation, like a typographical sign. In the case of Matisse it is the invention itself, the word. What a gulf between the typographical sign and the word! And that's just as regards their means; there is also an abyss between their aims. For Matisse's imitators, the sign is a way of producing and selling more pictures. For the Master of Cimiez, it is a path towards composition on the grand scale, towards something which eludes our loftiest speculation.[1]

APOLLINAIRE AND MATISSE

It is rather curious: Apollinaire, who was associated with so many painters of his time, whose poems actually *copy* pictures – by Chagall or Picasso – had very little to do with Matisse. They are on different registers. He devoted a page of *La Phalange* to Matisse in 1907; and there is nothing else so sensible, so fair, and so completely unenthusiastic in all Apollinaire's writings, even in his most trifling notes or in the scholarly works he wrote for a livelihood. For Apollinaire understood the genius of Matisse and paid tribute to it, but he felt remote from it. There is no extravagance of language here, not a shadow of the playfulness he always introduced when speaking about painters, even those for whom he cared less (*Léger, j'aime vos couleurs légères . . .* Léger, I love your light colours). He would not venture to impose his own poetry on the painting of Matisse. He was aware that it could in no wise explain Matisse.

The page in *La Phalange* was entitled *Connaissance de soi-même* – Self-knowledge. Apollinaire is here trying to single out one of Matisse's qualities, but even more he is using Matisse in order to point out to himself what

1. Discovery. (*Note of 1968*)

Je juge cette longue querelle de la tradition et de l'invention
De l'Ordre et de l'Aventure

. . . .

Soyez indulgents quand vous nous comparez
A ceux qui furent la perfection de l'ordre
Nous qui quêtons partout l'aventure

. . . .

Voici que vient l'été la saison violente,
Et ma jeunesse est morte ainsi que le printemps
O soleil c'est le temps de la Raison ardente...

GUILLAUME APOLLINAIRE
La Jolie Rousse

it was that he admired in Matisse because he recognized it in himself: curiosity. Every point in this short article is as applicable to Apollinaire as to Matisse (Madame Bovary again). Of all that Henri Matisse may have said to him he notes one single remark, about imitation and personality (*I have never avoided the influence of other people. I should have considered that as cowardice and a lack of sincerity towards myself . . .*) from which he draws the conclusion that 'any kind of plastic handwriting . . . can interest an artist and help him to develop his personality'. Is he really thinking of Matisse or of himself, and of which of the two, when he asserts that Matisse's curiosity is directed chiefly towards the beauty of Europe, which is, to say the least, no longer true? Matisse is not restricted by this narrow concept, narrower and more artificial than that of nationhood, and when Apollinaire goes on: 'We are Europeans, and our heritage stretches from the gardens bathed by the Mediterranean to the frozen seas of the Far North. We find there the nourishment that we love, and the aromatic plants of the rest of the world merely provide us with spices . . .' of whom is he speaking, if not of Guillaume Apollinaire?

And whom is he defending, in the heyday of the Fauvist movement, when he declares: 'This is no extravagant venture; the essence of Matisse's art is its reasonableness'? Is not this the tone he assumes every time he speaks *pro domo*, as for example in the preface to *Les Mamelles de Tirésias*? Of course the art of Matisse is reasonable. It can be discussed rationally, like everything that's human. But this is not characteristic of it. And if one took Matisse's confidences literally, one might even say that a drawing by him is unreasonable, in the sense that it is never the result of rational thought, never, since it issues from an uncontrolled impulse, from the painter's hand rather than from his brain. And it is in this respect, no doubt, that he feels himself so profoundly different from the 'decadent' painters of the Renaissance, whose works are deep-laid plots, anatomical constructions.

No, reasonableness is not the characteristic of Matisse's art.

Nor, indeed, is it that of Apollinaire's.

There was an element of Faust in Apollinaire.

Not in Matisse. I shall speak of this later.

THE THREE ASPECTS OF THE PAINTER

Matisse is more and at the same time less than a European. His culture extends far beyond Flanders, where he was born, or that Mediterranean on whose shores he lives. Tahiti, the Arab world, the archaic civilizations of Asia Minor, all contribute to feed his mysterious and insatiable hunger for knowledge. There are birds from the whole world in his aviary.

And yet the unforgettable thing is that Matisse is a Frenchman. One of those Northern Frenchmen in whom all the diverse elements that make up France are most fully united. He is a man from Cambrésis, a French painter, a citizen of the world. A theme to be unfolded.

'MY GALLIC ANCESTORS'

The man from Cambrésis. *Cameracensis pagus.* The region through which runs the main road to the North, the road from Cologne to Paris. The highway of invading armies. The people of these parts, during the course of centuries, have seen all sorts go by. They have learned to put up with them.

Where does Matisse get his blue eyes from? I like to think that these are Celtic eyes, and that Matisse is like his remotest ancestors, the Nervii who dwelt in the region of Cambrésis and kept out two sorts of people: traders and Germans. They were the best foot-soldiers in Gaul; unconquerable men, to whom even the Romans had to allow the title of *free people.* Caesar speaks of their courage and their spirit of independence. They were said to be barbarians; but that is

From my Gallic ancestors I get my pale blue eyes, my narrow skull, and my lack of skill in fighting. My dress seems to me as barbarous as theirs. But I don't butter my hair.

ARTHUR RIMBAUD
Une Saison en Enfer

how an invader always considers those who refuse to bow to him. There's a certain similarity about it all; the name *fauve*, invented by Matisse in the first place, implies what the academics thought of as barbaric. Matisse is a good illustration of liberty. I mean of that French liberty which is like no other.

Note that the Ardennes, at least between the Sambre and the Meuse, was inhabited by the Nervii, and that we may therefore consider Rimbaud as a Nervian as well as Matisse.

I imagine what Matisse is going to say about my fancies: 'So now I'm a Nervian?' One particular feature of this tribe was their aversion to horses, in which they differed notably from other Gallic peoples. I must ask Matisse what he thinks about horses. In point of fact I have never seen any horses in Matisse's paintings or drawings.[1]

One cannot picture Rimbaud on horseback. 'A foot-slogger', as Péguy said of himself. And Rimbaud: 'I throw myself at the feet of horses!'

Alas!
I've never been able to become a real horseman. My legs are too short for me to be at ease on horseback. The riding-school in the Rue Lhomond.
Such spills!

Manuscript note by Matisse, after reading the copy of 1942. (*Transcribed in 1968*)

The battles that determined the birth of France – divided up to that time between the Neustrians and the Austrasians – were waged somewhere in Cambrésis. The victory that made France was won by the Austrasian Charles Martel, in a place named Vincy, near the town of Crèvecœur . . .

Matisse's blue gaze checks my wanderings along this path.

FROM THE NORTH TO THE SOUTH

Out of fifty years of life as a painter, Henri Matisse of Le Cateau-Cambrésis spent twenty-five at Nice. And it's true that there is in his painting, in the whole of his art, something Mediterranean – the light, to begin with. And so without the help of Charles Martel he embodies the synthesis of France, North and South. Reason and unreason. Imitation and invention. Sunlight and mist. Inspiration and reality. But these contrasts are in the man, in his attitude, in what he says: his work has achieved a balance of opposites, it is France.

And that is how Matisse from Cambrésis has become the Master of Cimiez.

1. He read this without making any immediate comment. He referred to it again next day or the day after, whence the later paragraph *Matisse and Horses*. (*Note, 1968*)

When, towards evening, I take my leave of Henri Matisse, I go down through that huge Régina where he lives, where the public rooms are plunged in darkness in accordance with the regulations of that wartime winter (1941–42), I pass through that hall/peristyle/verandah with its tree-like columns, and I go out, slithering on the cold dark road at the foot of Cimiez, I take a turning and go uphill a little, then stand waiting in that deserted spot under the high walls of some property, where the bus to Nice stops. It's a sort of crossroads, the road divides there and runs round a strange and sombre mass, round and yet broken: the ruins of the arena of Cimiez. Beside that parcelled-out Grand Hotel, the Régina, what a strange reminder of History. I have ample time to ponder over it while waiting for the bus.

. . . .

The arena was built for the occupying troops: the victors' leisure hours had to be filled, and Cimiez, hill town of the ancient Cemenelum, had a considerable garrison because it had been the capital of the Vediantii, a long-haired Ligurian tribe, and the centre of their resistance, opposite Antibes. The Ligurians of this region, like the Nervii, were the infantrymen of the Gallic armies. After all, Matisse is still on familiar ground. The Vediantii, although less cruel than the Nervii, who cut off people's heads (is that why I am always a little afraid of Matisse?), were also considered extremely wild, precisely because of their unwillingness to submit either to the armies of Rome or to those of Carthage. And all good authors, who, needless to say, are either Roman or Carthaginian, tell us with shocked horror how savagely they attacked Caesar's troops or those of Hannibal.

Is it by a pure verbal coincidence that the Ligurian tribes akin to the Vediantii include one called the Ceutrones, while among those subject to the Nervii, in the Belgian Brabant, there is one that bears the same name?

61. – *Les Ponchettes*, at Nice. The house at the top, on the left, is where Matisse lived before he moved to Cimiez. In 1942, Elsa Triolet and I lived in the row of small houses on the Quai des États-Unis which can be seen at the foot of Matisse's house. It was only after our departure (November 1942) that the Italians camouflaged the buildings, supposedly in order to protect this part of the town from American bombings.

Like Matisse's Cambrésis, this region has suffered: after the Romans came the Visigoths, then the Lombards, then the Saracens . . . until at last in the tenth century the first of those Grimaldi who, through the ages, were the French party, from Fréjus to Genoa, Guelphs or Garibaldians, came to free the old land of the Ligurians and to give his name to the Gulf of Grimaud. It so happened that he was descended from Grimoald, son of Pepin of Herstal and brother of Charles Martel. Another coincidence! And here comes my bus.

THE CARNIVAL AT NICE

Nice, where he first lived in the Ponchettes district and then on the heights of Cimiez, is closely associated with the fame of Matisse. This relationship is just as important as any links the painter may have with Mallarmé or Ronsard. It is not a matter of indifference that a great painter should have worked in some particular place; and above all this is true of Matisse.

The reason is this artist's honesty. As I write the word I feel surprise at not having used it before. Honesty is something far more characteristic of Matisse's work than reasonableness. Honesty is often unreasonable.

Beside this paragraph Matisse had written in pencil: *I worked for some time to show that 'that's all Matisse is'.* Then he crossed it out.

As will be remembered, I have quoted this remark elsewhere. (*1968*)

I can already picture people shrugging their shoulders. The word 'honesty' is usually interpreted as foolishness in a world where illusionism reigns supreme. Too bad; let them drop their shoulders and their illusions. There's no cheating here. The Casino is further down, on the right.

Matisse's windows open on to Nice. In his pictures, I mean. Those marvellous open windows, behind which the sky is as blue as Matisse's eyes behind his spectacles. Here is a dialogue between mirrors. Nice looks at her painter and is imaged in his eyes. A funny sort of Madame Bovary!

62 and 63. – Those marvellous open windows, behind which the sky is as blue as Matisse's eyes behind his spectacles. Here is a dialogue between mirrors . . .

If I could only make Matisse say: *'Nice is myself!'* He is too proud for that (I thought *too modest* at first, then I wrote *proud*) and too honest. After all, Flaubert maligned himself: Emma Bovary was not himself. Flaubert was too honest. And not in the least modest.

'Shall I tell you? Nice . . . why Nice? In my art I have tried to create a setting that will be crystal-clear to the mind; I have found that necessary limpidity in several places in the world, in New York, in Oceania and at Nice. If I had gone on painting up north, as I did thirty years ago, my painting would have been different; there would have been cloudiness, greys, colours shading off in the distance. Whereas in New York, the painters tell you: One can't paint here, with this metallic sky! And actually it's wonderful! Everything becomes clear, *crystalline*, precise, limpid. Nice helped me in this respect. Understand, the things I paint are objects conceived with plastic means: if I close my eyes I can see the things better than with my eyes open, I see them stripped of their accidental qualities, and that's what I paint . . .'

Crystalline is an adjective added at Matisse's own request. (*1968*)

At the end of this paragraph H.M. had added: *the search for the cause of emotion in front of the subject,* then had crossed it out. (*1968*)

Moreover, Nice offered the painter, besides its light and its tropical vegetation, another source of inspiration: no town in France, not even Paris, is more cosmopolitan than Nice, and not only because of the tourists. People have come to Nice from the four corners of the earth, bringing with them the dust of their homeland, their customs and traditions. Thus the town provided Matisse with a choice of models, types of women that he could have found nowhere else, a breath from the wide world outside: the East, Russia, primitive countries, even the South Seas. The powerful lure is felt throughout his work: a world reconstituted.

Sur les bords de la Riviéra
Où murmure une brise embaumée
Chaque femme a rêvé là-bas
D'être belle et toujours adorée

(On the shores of the Riviera
Where the scented breezes whisper
Every woman dreams there
Of being lovely and always beloved)

Song of my young days

This world contains not only women. There are chosen objects in it, green plants like those that form a forest in his *winter* studio. Fabrics. Here we recognize the truth of that statement reiterated by Matisse, that he looks in the same way at the living model and the elements of a still life. Just as he says: 'I marry objects,' here is a series of drawings that marry a plant and a

Winter added by H.M. (*1968*)

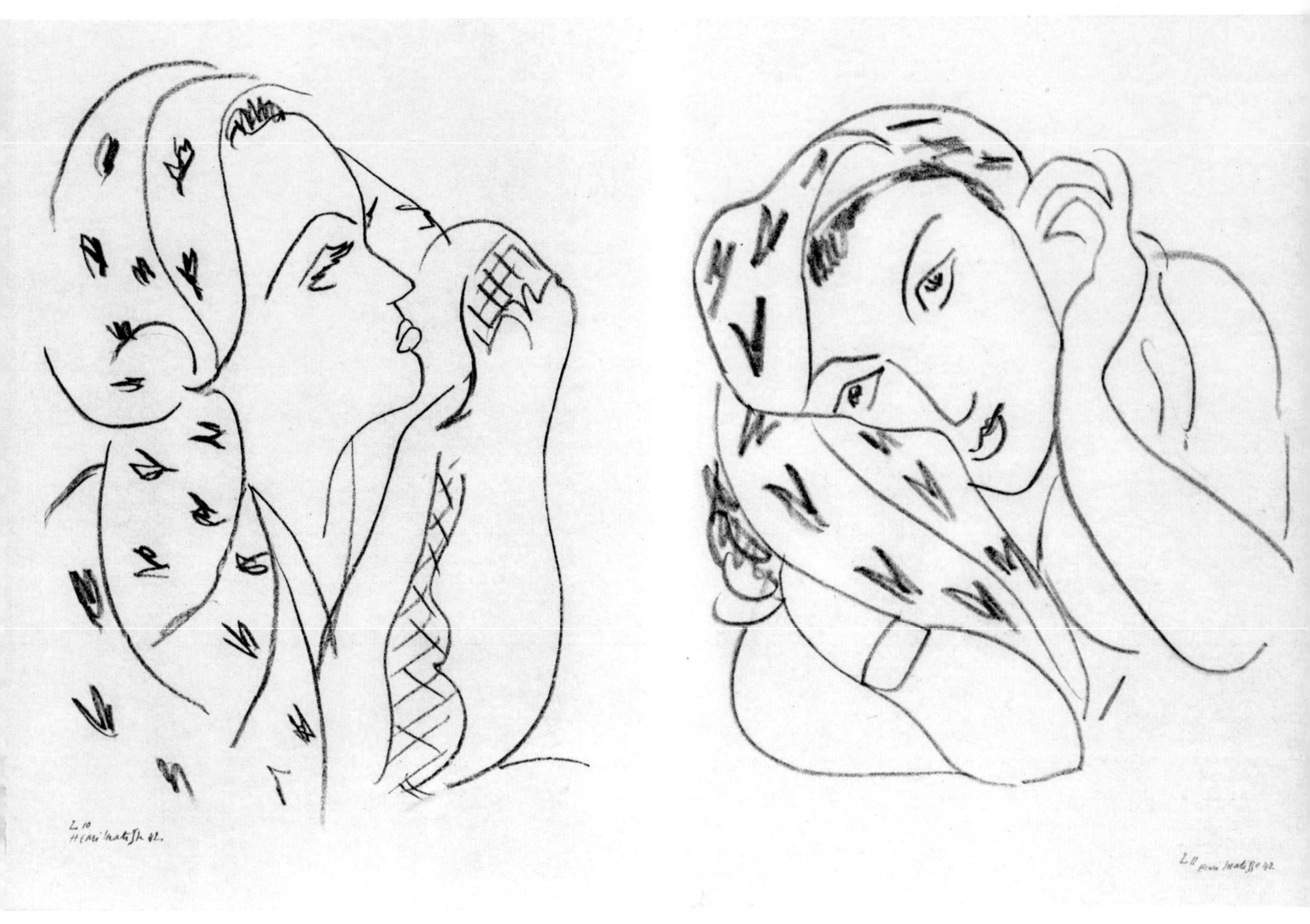

64. – (65, 66.) – Variations of Series L: L_{10}, L_{11}, L_{12}. *The Spotted Veil (64 and 65, pencil).*

Une surtout, un ange, une jeune Espagnole
(One above all, an angel, a young Spanish girl)

This line occurs to me by the way, and I suddenly begin to trace the relation between Matisse and Hugo: who but Matisse could ever have illustrated the line *Elle aimait trop le bal...*? Not Manet, nor Ingres, nor Renoir . . .

(I am suddenly struck by the physical resemblance between Hugo and Matisse, between the Matisse of today and the Hugo of after 1870 . . .)

flow. Oh, if Madame Bovary had been able to discuss Flaubert!

I know that Matisse takes an interest in the lives of his models, in their family history (as hospital records say), in what happens to them. But Flaubert, I am sure, must have mourned the death of Madame Bovary. At any rate I should have done so in his place. Matisse has more humanity than either Flaubert or myself: he would not have allowed her to die. At least in so far as that depended on Flaubert.

I don't know whether anything has been written about Matisse's humanism. It exists. It is very great, and deserves more than respect. A great painter can also be a great man. This is the case here.

woman, the woman's arms curved in her pose, the plant curving towards the sun (a great deal might be said about heliotropism in the work of Matisse). The exoticism of the objects (meaning, he would say, freedom for the mind, for the imagination, for invention) presupposes the same concern in his choice of these objects as that which governs his choice of female models.[1]

'The eloquence of curved lines . . .' Matisse said. (He added, without clarifying his remark, *plumb-line*: see the explanation of this in *Jazz*, 1947.) (*Parenthesis of 1968*)

HUMAN, ALL TOO HUMAN

And yet the difference that exists between a human figure and a still life, which has often been denied, is obvious just from hearing Matisse talk about his models. His curiosity about them is too great for it to be otherwise. He talks to this woman. He is interested in her life and about what she thinks. He lets her chatter while he draws. Perhaps he even takes it into account, in his own way, of course. Thus . . .

In pencil: *but if she asks him the time, he's lost.* Adding, on reflection: *see if this has been mentioned earlier.*

It had indeed, and was to be mentioned again later; for I shall return to this point in *La Grande Songerie*. But today I find a virtue in repetition. When Matisse repeats a remark, it's not the same as if it had occurred to him on one single occasion. And besides, who would dare to claim that any particular remark had been made to him alone by Matisse! He repeated himself. This is one of the characteristics of his conversation. Only in 1942 I was the only person to whom he could really talk. What he said, he was merely lending to me. It was not my property. The same remark may be quoted later by other authors who think it belongs to them because Matisse had made it to them too. But it belonged only to him. Listeners should be modest.

(*This note was transcribed only in 1968, when the commentary was added*)

Thus in this flock of drawings which have sprung up between two of my visits: it's still the same woman,[2] with a veil on her head, but this time the veil is patterned, with biggish spots. The model pointed out to him that he always set about it in the same way, drawing the outline first, the veil, and when it was finished putting in the spots. This set Matisse thinking: he tried doing the opposite, putting in the spots first . . . and it was as a result of this experiment that he eliminated them and reverted to the veil pure and simple, so to speak. And it was this, too, that led him to the drawings I have already referred to, those mysterious drawings in which the material of the veil is the most insubstantial and yet the most tangible, where white becomes black and disappears in a swift unbroken

1. See *infra*, remarks on Matisse's taste for models of marked hypothyroid tendency (Mme de Senonnes). The curves of certain objects have the same sensuous effect for him. (*Note, 1967*)

2. In *Thèmes et Variations*, the model in the series B, C, D, E, F and K, L, N. A Turkish princess, great-granddaughter of Abdul-Hamid. (*1968*)

66. – Charcoal drawing.

CHARDIN SEEN BY GAUTIER

Sub-title omitted from the book, I don't know why. I have restored it. (*1968*)

I found in Théophile Gautier a sentence which I shall have to show to Matisse:[1]

Chardin began by painting still lifes, inanimate objects (wrongly called natures mortes, *since there is nothing dead in nature). The closeness of his imitation, the strength of his colour, the solidity of his impasto, make him the equal of Dutch and Flemish painters. In the midst of all this prettily mannered, charmingly untruthful art* [Gautier has just been speaking of Greuze and of Boucher] *he represents absolute truth; he is a realist in the best sense of the word. Velazquez began in the same way and for a long time painted fruit, vegetables,*

1. Because of a remark he made about the earlier quotation from Gautier he had read in my text. (*1968*)

Where white becomes black . . .
67. – Variation 13 of Series L (charcoal).

game, fish, vases, jars, table and kitchen utensils, and it was by studying these that he acquired that admirable knowledge of local colour which characterizes his painting. After this preparation, when Chardin ventured to paint figures his attempts were completely successful. He displays the same honesty, the same care, the same conscientiousness. He excels in rendering the wholesome orderly bourgeois life of the period, when there were other people besides marquises and opera girls . . .

THE BLUE WATERMARK

In all this, we have lost sight of the *Chinese with the transparent and delicate heart*, and I had asked you to remind me of it.

The meaning of this passage from Mallarmé becomes luminous in the light of Matisse. The painter speaks to me, once more, about something which has never ceased to worry him: when he first outlined the composition of his drawing for Mallarmé's *Les Fleurs*, he did it with lilies, but when he came to the final work he unconsciously substituted for these an equal number of different flowers, recognized by him as white clematis, and certainly a ten-year-old memory of a hedge of *white* clematis he had seen for several successive summers and which at the time had seemed to him inimitable.[1] And now they suddenly blossomed in the etching, quite perfect, with something about them of the utmost elusive delicacy, as if they had dropped from the stars . . .

white, for the second time, insisted on by Matisse; I had omitted it in 1942. (*Note, 1968*)

Isn't that what Mallarmé meant: *the flower he had smelled as a child . . . engrafted in the blue watermark of the soul?* This is what Matisse asks in somewhat different terms: 'Isn't a drawing the synthesis, the climax, of a series of sensations which the brain has retained and

Des avalanches d'or du vieil azur, au jour
Premier, et de la neige éternelle des astres
Jadis tu détachas les grands calices pour
La terre jeune encore et vierge de désastres...

(From the golden avalanches of the ancient azure, on the first day, and from the eternal snow of the stars you once took the huge calyxes for the earth which was still young and innocent of disasters . . .)

(Transl. Anthony Hartley)

◀ 68. – *Clematis.* Etching for the *Poésies de Stéphane Mallarmé* (1932).

gathered together, and which one final sensation triggers off, so that I execute the drawing almost as irresponsibly as a medium?'

1. The story of the clematis is often told, as though for the first time; in Father Couturier's book, for instance (1962). This reflects the importance Matisse attached to it. (*1968*)

He stresses the impossibility of this final swift *thunderbolt* containing all the manifold and varied sensations which the drawing presupposes. The image that seems to guide his hand as it draws must, he declares, represent many such remembered sensations, probably from a distant past (once again, he insists that it's his hand that draws; but this time he explains the phenomenon differently, for fear I might have misunderstood him the other day and implied that he was casual or unconscientious: what he does unconsciously is a different matter).

Matisse likes to compare this 'thunderbolt' with the classic experiment of that physiologist who arranged to have a metal cord fastened round his neck while he was asleep, and to be suddenly wakened by having it pulled: in that flash of time he dreamed a whole long story at the end of which his head was cut off.

MATISSE AND HORSES

'No,' he said at first, 'I don't remember ever draw-

69. – From left to right: Marguerite, Pierre, Henri and Jean Matisse. *At the age of fifty,* H.M. says. Mme Duthuit corrects this: 'at forty, rather', that is to say about 1909. Matisse's memory for dates was always rather vague.

70. – *Page of studies: horse and cab-drivers,* probably at the time he was preoccupied with the preface to *Pierre et Jean.* Matisse ▶ seems to have forgotten a whole series of drawings made probably at the same time as this one, which I choose at random.

Henri-Matisse

'I tried to learn to ride at fifty, at the riding-school in the Rue Lhomond: what a lot of spills!'
(*Conversation of March 18*)

This sentence was left in the 1942 text in spite of Matisse and in spite of a previous marginal note which it repeats . . . Some sentences are obsessions. (*1968*)

ing horses. But I'd have liked to be a jockey. I never managed to ride on horseback.'

And later the same day he said, quite naturally, that horses were rather stupid animals, although they did have memory. I was overjoyed. What did I tell you? A true Nervian!

But next day he sent me a note to tell me he remembered having drawn cab-horses and their drivers standing waiting.* Theories are as short-lived as roses. Actually, Matisse was not thinking of what I had told him when he sent me this note, but of something quite different. After all, your keen horseman isn't concerned with waiting cab-horses.

* *It's odd*, L.D. said to me in 1969, *that he did not tell you about his sculpture 'The Horse', which, after all, can't have been made in a day.* Odd, indeed, but he did not tell me about it then.

This cab-horse business . . .

He said to me: When you pass in front of a grocer sitting on his doorstep, or a concierge smoking his pipe, or a cab-rank, show me this grocer and this concierge, their attitude and their whole physical appearance, conveying by the skill of your portrayal their whole moral nature, so that I cannot confuse them with any other grocer or any other concierge, and show me, by a single word, how one cab-horse differs from the fifty others behind it or in front of it.

GUY DE MAUPASSANT
Preface to *Pierre et Jean*

A LESSON FROM MAUPASSANT

Matisse was referring to a number of preoccupations which certain remarks or anecdotes had suggested to him or at least crystallized in his mind.

This cab-horse business was an illustration of the thoughts evoked by Maupassant's preface to *Pierre et Jean*. He remembered Maupassant speaking of *the briefest possible indication of the character of a thing*; he wanted to find the context. It should be easier than for Cros's poetry.†

† Actually, no: because that preface does not contain the idea of *the briefest possible indication* . . . etc. Matisse must have attributed to Maupassant a thought that occurred to himself while pondering over the preface to *Pierre et Jean*; or in some other fashion. The expression *the briefest possible indication* . . . etc. is probably a development of Maupassant's *show me with a single word*, and no doubt the same is true in the case of Vuillard's *defining touch*. (*1967*)

'How that made me work!' Matisse told me. But what strikes me here is that the speaker is not Maupassant but Flaubert, whose words are being repeated.

And this other advice of Flaubert's, also according to Maupassant:

To describe a blazing fire or a tree in a plain, we must stand in front of that fire and that tree until they have become for us unlike any other tree or any other fire.

Such phrases and anecdotes sent his mind ranging, because they appealed to him, because they moved him, but not necessarily because they were true or well founded. Perhaps, to begin with, he had even felt them to be mistaken. But for the sake of the man, the artist who had uttered them, Matisse refused to follow his feeling straight forward. He would give the words a chance to act on him. He would accept them provisionally as being true and well founded, he would submit to the consequences of this acceptance. He always practises the rules of what I might call the *'fair play' of genius*. It is yet another sign of that conscientiousness, that scrupulous honesty that cannot be stressed too often.

A remark overheard . . .

Thus he remembered from a conversation with Vuillard the expression *the defining touch*

II. – *The Painter's Family* (1911). Back left, Mme Matisse, right foreground Marguerite, and playing in the middle Pierre and Jean.

(one should use the defining touch, or something of the sort). And so Matisse, launched in this direction, tried never to go back on a stroke of colour once laid down, putting a second beside it and harmonizing them by means of a third; confining himself, in fact, to the fact, to the relation established, instead of pursuing local colour.

This idea of the defining touch is one which, he admits, proved very useful to him.

Well, when later on he spoke of it to Bonnard, who must have known what Vuillard thought, Bonnard told him he didn't know what it meant, he did not understand . . .

When do we first find that obsession with the preface to *Pierre et Jean*, to which Matisse so often reverted? And whence did it spring? I only noticed lately that these two names are those of the painter's two sons. Now they often appeared together, as children, in their father's paintings. To cite only one, *The Painter's Family*, painted at Issy-les-Moulineaux in the spring of 1911, shows Pierre and Jean playing draughts, Mme Matisse in the background and Marguerite in the foreground, on the right. In 1917 *The Music Lesson* shows the same four figures, still at Issy, Mme Matisse in the background, seen in the garden through the window, working at her embroidery as in the earlier picture; Jean, who has already been conscripted, in an armchair; Marguerite beside the younger boy Pierre at the piano, on the right. Now in 1923 at Nice Matisse apparently reconstructs the same family atmosphere in two compositions, each with three figures, two boys and a young woman, the latter at the piano in the background, thus replacing both Mme Matisse and Marguerite: we recognize the model Henriette. The two boys are Henriette's brothers playing draughts in one version, a painting, and reading a book together in the other, a charcoal drawing in which the age difference is more marked. *Pierre et Jean* thus means for Matisse not merely a preface by Maupassant but a theme of his personal life. (*Note, 1969*)

71. – *The Music Lesson* (1917), painted slightly earlier than *The Piano Lesson* (p. 98). Mme Matisse is seen in the garden, Marguerite and Pierre at the piano, Jean on the left in the foreground (about to leave for the army). This picture is shown in black and white (exceptionally in the present book) since the Barnes Foundation will not allow it to be reproduced in colour. ▶

XIV. – *Henriette and Her Brothers* (1923)

COURBET

A true masterpiece should be repeatable by the artist in order to prove to himself that he is not the plaything of his nerves or of chance.

Of this remark, attributed to Courbet, Matisse says that it made him very exacting, that it made him work very hard. Matisse does not dispute it. It is easy to see that today he considers it mistaken. But I suspect him (Matisse) of feeling a certain gratitude towards Courbet for that very mistake, and the help he got from the efforts it impelled him to make.

A saying of Rude's: 'What is beyond my compass shall be my personality.' *Matisse applied this to the plumb-line, the strict discipline which he imposed upon himself, for instance, in that experiment in sculpture which lasted three years, with about two thousand sittings, and which resulted in the well-known statue* The Slave.

See infra what he says of this in *Jazz.* (*1969*)

'We know only one remark of Rembrandt's: "I do portraits!" In the storm I have often clung to this saying.'

PHOTOGRAPHS

This concern with showing the character of a thing in the briefest possible form, which Matisse found* in Maupassant, can be connected not only with the actual development of his sign-language but with a number of his past experiments. That he should have sought (in his own words) *to get away from the individuality of the artist who in his works relegates to the background the specific intimate character of the thing in question, as do Raphael, Renoir etc. . . . who seem always to have been painting the same women*, is probably a step in that direction, but what method did he use for it?

He told me: 'I copied photographs, trying to achieve the greatest possible likeness.[1] I thus restricted the field of error, but what a lot of things this made me understand!'

* . . . *imagined he had found, rather.* While copying out this remark, crossed out in 1942, which seemed to me worth more than crossing out, I suddenly recognized that this mental process not only explains the Maupassant business but is also the logical sequel to what Courbet's remark implies. And of course I also recognized in it things which have nothing to do with Matisse or with painting. Bitter things. But doubtless *mistakes* have been useful in my own life too. Just as proverbs, a nation's folly, can be useful. You go forward, thinking you're accepting ready-made ideas. Then one day these ready-made ideas are seen for what they really are. And you tell yourself that the things that helped you to advance were really maintained with your help, and perhaps that was in fact what you were trying to move away from. You only realize this afterwards . . . do you follow me? You see, when you're pulling up briars you don't notice that the thorns pierce your skin here and there, and it's only later on, when they've gone in deep, that you feel them hurting you. And then you need scissors or a knife to dig them out. But what am I talking about? (*Note, 1967*)

1. A remark I quote later to justify my own idea, that before a new model – woman or object – his first drawing or painting photographed it. Later he 'got away from it', using the model as a spring-board. This is equally true of the pewter coffee pot and of the model for *Blue Eyes* or the one he nicknamed 'the Plane Tree'. (*1969*)

◀ 72. – *Henriette at the Piano, Her Brothers Reading.* Charcoal.

Again, he quotes the remark of another painter, a member of the *avant-garde* of twenty years ago:[1] 'We must not make autographs.' I like the modesty with which Matisse is willing to profit morally from something he has heard, wherever it comes from; and the way he admits that this remark aroused an echo within him and made him realize that each picture had to be something important, indispensable to his progress, to the development of his painting.

Matisse told me this because there had been a picture which I had greatly admired and still think worthy of admiration, which he had finished a week before, but at my next visit there was nothing left of it on the canvas, which he had painted over almost entirely with red, leaving only the barest sketch of the woman's figure which had been there the other day . . . I cried out in dismay that I could never bear to associate with a man capable of creating things of such beauty and then calmly destroying them, it would give me heart attacks. Then Matisse said: 'We must not make autographs.' And then, thinking it over: 'One always keeps too many paintings . . . A painter has no real enemy but his own bad paintings.'

This was what he said at Nice in 1942, avoiding certain topics of conversation. But suddenly, when I least expected it, having spoken of his son the sculptor without saying anything very specific about him, he added just as I was leaving: 'And don't *you* do too many either . . . that's what bad painters do . . .' As he then looked away, I felt entitled to interpret his words as I pleased, to suit the pale blue sky above Cimiez and the wind that cuts like a knife and the bus that keeps you waiting . . . And so he said to me: *'A painter has no real enemy but his own bad paintings . . .'*

1. This, don't forget, was said and noted in 1942.

73. – Wall of the studio with five windows (see note below).

Note of 1968. I have nowhere altered the text of *Matisse-en-France*; apart from the corrections, which I had been unable to make because of our flight from Nice, it remains what it was in *Thèmes et Variations.*

However, I have ventured to add a paragraph here, at the end of *His Worst Enemy* (*This was what he said . . .* etc.), having found a first version of it among my papers.

My observation could have been made only on our return to Nice at the beginning of October 1942: the paintings made that September (*Girl at the Window, White Dress and Black Belt, The Purple Dress, Girl in a Pink Dress, The Window Open and the Shutters Closed, The Black Door*) all represent a *female figure* in front of the window. A fifth painting which hung beside these on Matisse's wall, the biggest in the accompanying photograph, has never been reproduced anywhere. It is included in *Anthology II*; one of its sister pictures is shown on p. 180. This was what I had remembered. The picture, presumably destroyed or painted over, must have been done at the beginning of October.

Moreover, at this period there were things that could never have been written down. What H.M. had said about his son Jean was that he was very worried about him, knowing that Jean had dynamite hidden under his sculptures. Whence the significance of 'don't *you* . . . either', and perhaps a bitter kind of smile when he said that a painter has no real *enemy* but his own bad paintings, in the autumn of 1942.

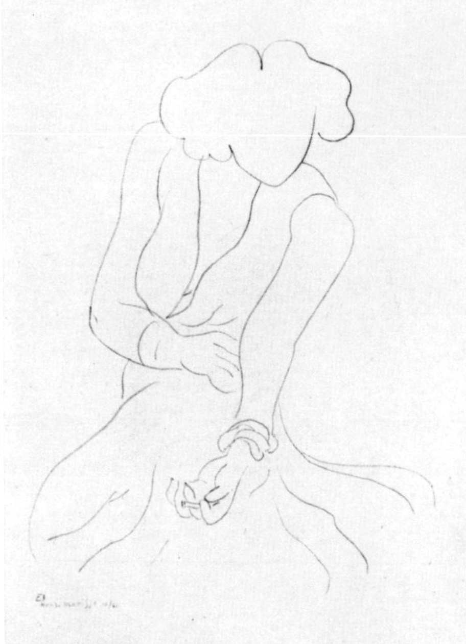

74, 75 and 76. – Variations 2, 3 and 4 of Series E (October 1941), pencil.

. . . partitioning:

Matisse said to me on another occasion: *'Often, when I felt at the end of my resources, I thought of Rembrandt . . .' Rembrandt intervenes here for the second time, and in a note. It must be mentioned that Matisse very often refers to Rembrandt, his neighbour, that he was concerned with Rembrandt for a long time. '. . . I said to myself that Rembrandt does not need to touch his paper to give it a certain quality: the first states of Rembrandt's etchings are very interesting in this respect, with their indications of certain areas of paper enclosed and marked out . . .' Then Matisse went on to speak of one of his own paintings, the little girl in red, done at Collioure:*[1] *the same red is used for the child's dress and elsewhere in the picture, well,* you cannot see *that it's the same red shown in light and in shadow, and that the difference between them is a matter of relationships.*

He brought me back to his drawings. Of what I was saying about the white sky in his drawings. (*Le blanc souci . . .*)

'Notice that every page of my drawings has kept . . . that no page has lost . . . the touching whiteness of the paper, even when a stroke divides them into sections of varying quality.'

He explains: that part of the paper which represents the dress has acquired a different quality from that of the background, which is slightly more bluish or greyish, more ethereal than the flesh, which is a creamy white . . . or simply more insubstantial than the other parts of the drawing, than the flesh, for instance, etc.

(Don't get this wrong: there is no difference of colour in the paper, where a simple line is traced, and where the draughtsman has introduced no tint to differentiate this from that; the diversity of the whites, the difference of quality between the whites, is due solely to partitioning, and one must recognize this as real when one looks, with Matisse, at this or that drawing . . . Yes, the flesh is more solid, the fabric of a different

1. The painting in question is *The Siesta* (Collioure, 1906), *private collection, Ascona.* The little girl is outside the room, on the balcony seen through the open window, and in the room on the left, three chairs in

XV. – *The Siesta* (Collioure, 1906).

77. – Photograph of the landscape seen through the window in *The Siesta.*

disarray under the window, on the right the slippers lying by the bed on which a woman is resting, wearing a dark green slip. Note that red is not the only colour that light and shade have in common. The green on the woman, which appears as back-lighting on the far wall and under the window, is the same that makes the distant trees outside, the pinkish mauve of the sunlit window-recess recurs on the bed (where it presumably represents the white bed-clothes) and the upper edge of the far wall, in the room, like a sort of reflection (*described subsequently*, in 1956, from a reproduction, but I have just lately [1968] discovered in the margin of the copy I submitted to Matisse a little explanatory drawing which I shall try to get reproduced here).

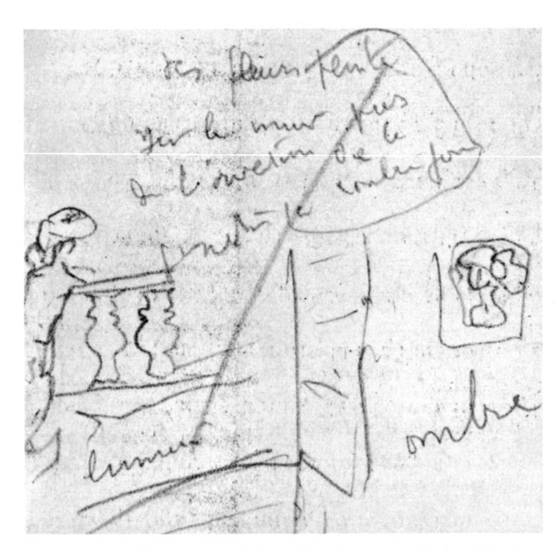

78. – Drawing to explain *The Siesta*, made by Matisse in the margin of a typed copy of my text, which I had shown him.

79. – Photograph of another window at Collioure overlooking the jetty, the landscape glimpsed in Plate XVI.

substance, the background is bluer . . . This is creation through relationships: *I don't paint things, I only paint differences between things.*)

He goes on: 'In a single set of drawings, consider for instance the dress or the fabrics . . . You'll find that they have the same quality in each drawing throughout the series . . . And this is the case with all the other elements in the drawing. Thus throughout these series there is something, the descriptive factor, which remains unchanged from one drawing to another . . . Even if the fancy takes me to add a few little grace-notes! Only the expression of the model has changed.'

He is well aware of what is disturbing about his drawings, and he can formulate that uneasiness. I had said two or three things to this effect, but without going to the heart of the mystery. Matisse concludes that only the emotive factor varies in his drawings, expanding throughout the series in the same direction, in accordance with the growing excitement of his mind. The blue eyes gaze at me from behind the spectacles, the tone of voice alters: 'But am I clear?' he asks. It's his favourite question. It, too, is like a sign, the point at which the conversation takes a new turn, the invisible hook over which a fold of the drapery hangs in that great composition which I shall not venture to discuss, the fresco of the living Matisse, his past, his achievement, his thought, and that future life of the second Matisse who at seventy-two declares that he has finished studying and is now going to start painting.

Yesterday I was trying to convey to someone the splendid and touching aspect of this fresh start, someone who does not know what I am writing here and who exclaimed: 'But look here, wasn't it Michelangelo who, after finishing the *Last Judgment*, said something like: *Now I am beginning to know how to draw'?*

I'm not responsible for this sudden intrusive reappearance of Michelangelo's. And there's something of Matisse, too, in Hokusai's remark, right at the end of his life: *If I were to live longer I might be able to paint.**

* Note by Matisse, *forgotten in 1942* because it was almost rubbed out, which, however, I am re-reading today, March 2, 1968:
or else: I no longer know how to draw –

XVI. – *Window at Collioure* (1905).

When Matisse studied in Gustave Moreau's studio he never did anything but still lifes: '*I thought I should never do figures, then I put figures into my still lifes . . . My figures are alive through the same causes that gave life to my still lifes . . . a unifying affection, a feeling in my objects that gave them their quality . . .*'

(Conversation of March 18)

As for the passage from Gautier about Chardin and Velazquez, Matisse remarked that it surprised him coming from Gautier. But for my part I wanted to move on from there to something else. In conversation, Matisse, as has been repeatedly noted here, assumes the indifference of the painter towards the nature of his model, inanimate object or living being. He uses the term 'portrait' for a pewter jug just as readily as for a woman. He treats a woman's arm like the stem of a plant. And in the Gautier passage he may have been most impressed by that criticism of the term *nature morte* (since *there is nothing dead in nature*). And yet what we chiefly learn from Gautier is that both Chardin and Velazquez considered that their art must develop gradually from the representation of inanimate objects to that of the human figure, which they tackled only at a late stage and with a certain respect and awe. On this theme I cannot resist making one observation.

The evolution of great painters like Chardin and Velazquez seems to reproduce, for certain artistic reasons which so far remain obscure, an evolution which is that of the human mind itself, the feelings which, under a very different aspect and with different pretexts, we recognize in the history of nations. There are many peoples who, on religious grounds (and this is true both of the Hebrews and of the Gauls), were for a long while unwilling to depict living beings, and confined themselves to an ornamental art in which reality could be glimpsed only through elusive references. Gradually they passed on from pure ornament to emblematic ornament, in which familiar objects were represented, then animals. In Gaul, it was not until the time of Caesar or thereabouts that, in imitation of the Greeks and Romans, gods, men, chieftains were depicted on coins. The first French portrait is surely that of Vercingetorix.

80. – *It is practically certain that the effigy (on Gaulish coins) . . . offers a true portrait of Vercingetorix. We can therefore assert that Caesar was right in describing him as a young man: that he wore no moustaches, that he had short curly hair and a rather heavy lower jaw.*

DE SAULCY

(The strange thing, moreover, is that the image of the hero which has been handed down to us bears not the slightest resemblance to that precious portrait, as though the popular imagination had rebelled against reality and had re-introduced an unreal representation of that earliest of our country's symbols.[1])

In this respect Matisse has not retained the superstition which must have been that of his Nervian forebears. Once he had left Moreau's studio, the distinction between objects and human figures does not seem to have played the same part in his work as, according to Gautier, it did with Velazquez and Chardin. If the ontogenesis of these painters reproduces the phylogenesis of peoples, nature, as is well known, is liable to sudden economies, and, while carrying on the evolution of a species, after a certain point reproduces roughly the evolution of the individual with certain stages left out. Between Chardin and Matisse a hundred and fifty years have elapsed; the process is speeding up. I am almost inclined to think that (since here the stage that reflects the old ancestral superstitions about the representation of the human form tends to disappear between Chardin and Matisse) it is precisely within these hundred and fifty years that we must place the birth of modern painting, and the end of the first stage of painting, the one which began with Giotto in the cave of Vespignano, on which I was reflecting the other day in Matisse's studio.

Is mankind ready yet, as that great painter is, to attempt 'large-scale composition', and is it on the threshold of its second life, as he is at seventy-two? This is a hope which, in the present year 1942, one would like to see fulfilled in other fields than painting.

I don't know what awaits us. But I am assuredly proud of having spoken at length here about Henri

Matisse, impatiently, ticks me off in a marginal note:

See above

See what? where? This is probably explained in the following note, which was omitted; I shall explain why:

I thought for a number of years that I should paint nothing but still lifes. It was after representing still-life objects that I was able to represent the human figure.

Matisse had pencilled this note in the margin of the text I had shown him, and had later crossed it out, thinking he had interfered too much already with my text; I obeyed him and did not transcribe this note in *Thèmes et Variations* in 1942.

But on re-reading it in 1968 I have changed my mind: it is well worth overloading my text in order not to lose one moment of the painter's thought, one change of mind: after all, I am merely commenting, while he speaks. (So then, *1968*)

1. Re-read in March 1953, with some bitterness.

Matisse. In those days, people will say, they did at least have Matisse, in France . . .

Matisse-en-France: it rings like Le Puy-en-Velay, Marcq-en-Barœul, Crépy-en-Valois . . . Matisse-en-France.

At the darkest point in our night, they will say, he made those luminous drawings . . .

Sister Anne, sister Anne, do you see anyone coming? I see only the sun shining, the sun shining and the dust rising . . .

The knights came riding along the road. And in the bright sunshine they saw Matisse-en-France, and the fair Lady Anne was restored to life.

And they said: What a fair country!

◄81. – *The Slave*, bronze.

Signs

(1968)

afterthoughts
(unpublished)

In hoc signo vinces

If I consider a picture as a sentence, that is to say an assemblage of expressive elements which acquires from the relation between its elements a meaning different from that of these elements taken separately, it seems to me evident that this meaning results from the way they have been assembled, in other words, from the syntax of the picture.

Yet this is something very different from a *sentence* in the usual sense of the term, and I only use the word 'sentence' by analogy. A sentence (written or spoken) has in fact a beginning and an end, it follows from certain premises; I do not hear it and still less see it at a single glance. What the painted 'sentence' says is not the story which is taking place on the canvas, that is to say the particular moment of the story from which I can imagine what happened before and what is to come later, for instance that Roger, mounted on an eagle-hippogryph, has come down from the sky and with one thrust of his lance has struck the nostrils of the sea-monster guarding Angelica, as he passes before that naked beauty chained by the wrists to a rock, and in that single moment conveys the whole story of these lovers as told by Ariosto in Canto X of *Orlando furioso*. As I look at Ingres's painting I think of something Matisse once said to me: we had been talking about contemporary painters, and I had asked him whom, apart from Picasso, he considered a true painter. He mentioned Bonnard . . . then corrected himself without correcting himself and said: 'Miró . . . yes, Miró . . . because it doesn't matter what he represents on his canvas, but if, in a certain place, he has put a red spot, you can be sure that it had to be there and not elsewhere . . . take it away and the painting collapses.' I remember that, and I believe indeed that Ingres could have represented anything he pleased, for instance some episode from

82. – Crayon.

Orlando furioso, but that what was needed here, a little to the right of centre, was the whiteness of Angelica's nude body towards which the light and the sea-foam converged . . . The essential thing is the situation of the word, colour or sign, in the sentence, just as in writing. Try and shift one word in something written by a genuine writer, prose or verse, and you kill it.

It was many years ago that Matisse said this to me. It occurred to me to look at his own paintings from this point of view, that is, as a balance (and whatever the weight and counter-weight, the important thing is that these should balance one another). I looked through some books of reproductions. And it was then that it struck me that Angelica in Ingres's picture was in fact none other than the sign representing woman, with that fullness of the throat and mouth, that thyroid character which was both for him and for Matisse a mark of beauty, the sign representing feminine beauty for them.[1]

It goes without saying that Ingres's sign is inevitably of a different nature from Matisse's, because the sign is an element in the representation, which cannot be considered as an unalterable datum, established once and for all. Ingres's sign is characteristic of his period and of his own personality. Matisse's sign differs from it by all the length of human history that lies between them, and by the special genius of Henri Matisse.

And furthermore, just as the sensibility of one period cannot be likened to that of a different period, we must bear in mind that its art is the art of a particular time and consequently has to *invent* on the basis of everything that came before that time, just as science itself *changes*. The concept of a sign in painting is not the same as the use of a sign in language, but we cannot define it without taking into account the evolution of the concept in modern linguistic science.

I mean that it is only by analogy, and with very distinct reservations, that we can describe 'the language of painting' (and the expression itself is valid only as an analogy) in the words of a language strictly so called, the language of language. I have caught myself, in my effort to fix my thoughts, making use three or four times in these two pages of the word *sign*, which is part of Matisse's vocabulary, but which if I dwell on it leads to confusion, because a *sign* in semantics is not the same as the painter's sign. And yet we might, if we follow Matisse, speak of a semantic of representation. This is because in spite of the enormous recent proliferation of neologisms in linguistics, French is still very poor in that field that lies between signification and signalization, and because amid the shifting sands of a science still in its infancy, linguists tend to cling, as one clings to a plank in a storm, to etymology, which they

1. See infra, Vol. II, *Marie Marcoz and Her Lovers* (1968–69).

think the only reliable plank where words are concerned. Whence their constant efforts to connect the words of their own system – whose contents may be different, divergent, mutually contradictory, and sometimes even hostile – with their common Greek root which means *a sign*, *σημεῖον*, the seed of the entire vocabulary of human communications.

One of the most ancient cuttings in French soil of the Greek *semeion*, the word *sémion*, originates with Quintilian, for whom *semeion* meant the value of the breve as a prosodic unit, or the unit of song in a line of verse. This word has been lost in most fields, from music to speech, and replaced by the word *sign*: this denotes what I might call the outward aspect of the meaning, and when used in the field of writing it forms a kind of bridge between representation and statement, so that a letter is commonly called a sign, which, all things considered, is a kind of catachrestic pun, for since the sign carries a meaning and the letter does not, the equivalent of the sign should at least be the word (I say *at least*, because not all words by themselves have a meaning, and we should thus consider the sign as a kind of abbreviated pro-verb, for instance if we envisage it as the means of communication of semeiology, which was originally, we tend to forget, in the art of war, the science of commanding by means of gestures* – also called signs, as in the expression *to make signs* – rather than by voice). Strictly speaking, the hieroglyph is closer to a sign than is the letter, and by its means we pass from writing to painting. There really is a hieroglyph for the hand or mouth in the art of Matisse, the painter merely called them signs. But in all this what I want to stress is the existence of the sign (to adapt my vocabulary to Matisse's) as a unit of sound, so that, passing from the field of prosody to that of drawing, I may better understand what the *semeion*, the pictorial sign, really is in the art of Matisse.

Because, in the long run, the use of *signs* in painting, the importance attached to this by a painter like Matisse, inevitably entails several sorts of obscurity. And one cannot leave this practice unexplained, when one considers what Matisse said to me, I believe on March 18, 1942: *The importance of an artist can be measured by the quantity of new signs he introduces into the plastic language.* Particularly in view of the context where, referring to the sign-for-a-tree, the sign-for-a-leaf, used by such great painters as Claude Lorrain or Nicolas Poussin, he says: *They had their personal language* (that is, *their signs*). *Other people have learned that language since then, and I have to find signs that are related to the quality of my own invention.* I stress these comments lest the reader should miss them in their context. Matisse's *new signs* are units of visual significance, in the sense that the *semeion* is a prosodic unit or the *tone* a musical one (the spatial value of the latter would have gained had the word *diatone*

* The development of linguistics with its various branches and kindred sciences has brought about, among various authors, a diversity and proliferation of vocabulary which actually could be reduced to a series of catachreses in which abstract words are the 'leaves', not of a tree or a book, but of the mind.

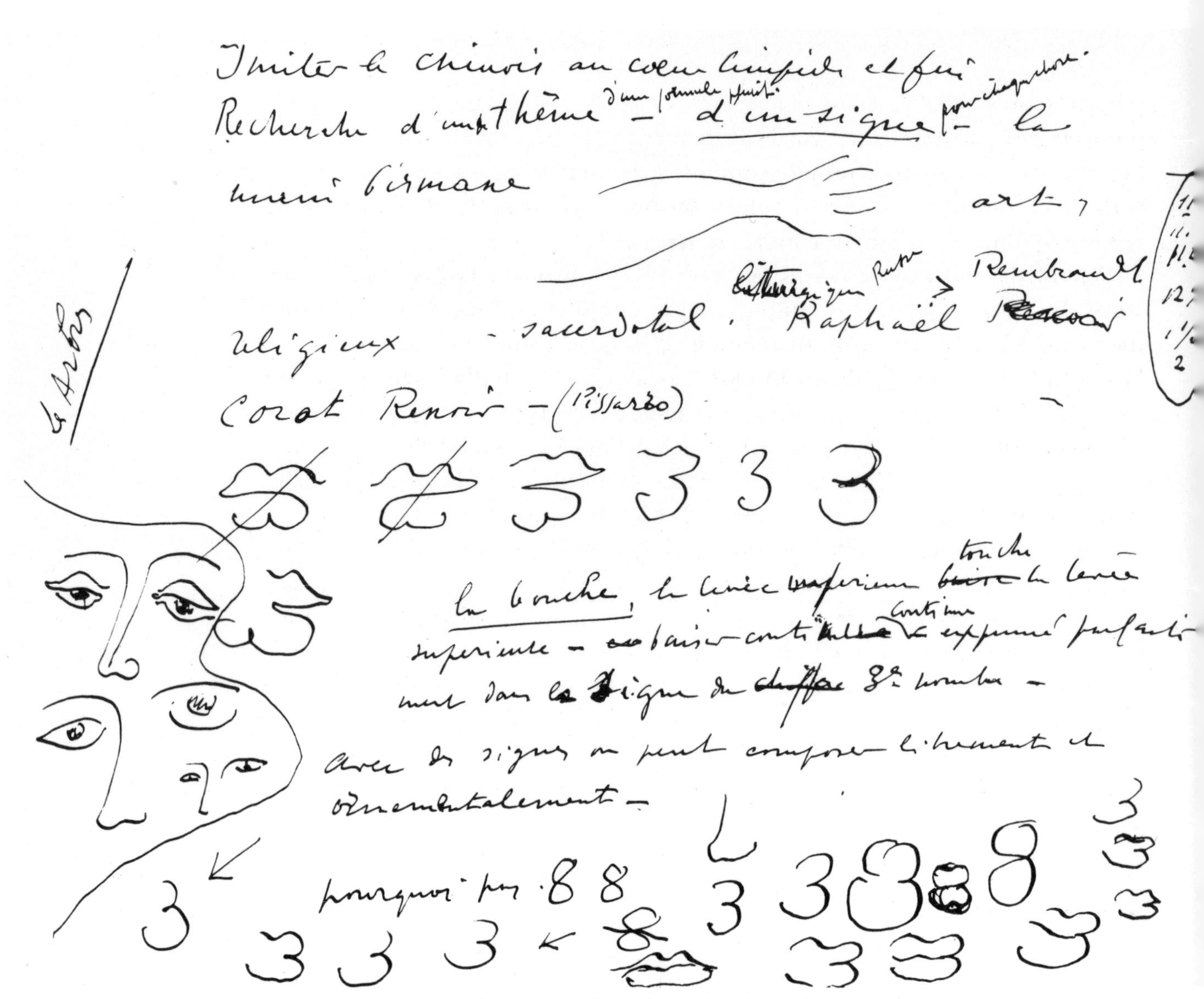

Imiter le chinois au coeur limpide et fin

Recherche d'un thème d'une formule stricte — d'un signe pour chaque chose — la

art ?

religieux — sacerdotal. Raphaël Rembrandt

Corot Renoir — (Pissarro)

la bouche, la lèvre inférieure touche la lèvre supérieure — un baiser continu exprimé parfaitement dans le signe du 3e nombre —

Avec des signes on peut composer librement et ornementalement —

pourquoi pas 8 8

83. – Letter from Henri Matisse to the author (Feb. 16, 1942).

replaced it, as proposed by Choron). But drawing and painting are not music or versification. When the word 'sign' refers to space drawn on or painted, it is neither a unit of scansion nor an interval between sounds, it becomes the thing that furnishes that space, so that where it is, for instance, the sign-for-an-eye or the sign-for-a-mouth, a space surrounded by a line is transformed from a kind of balloon into a face, ceases to be a flat surface and acquires relief, enabling one to understand the apparently meaningless partitioning of the white paper or the expanse of colour. Matisse means that what makes the greatness (or, as he says, the importance) of an artist is the invention of signs peculiar to himself, which the eye will read like a printed paper. These signs denote, at the same time, an eye or a mouth and its, or their, position on the space that has been drawn or painted on; they are at the same time the direction that one's eye follows and the path to something beyond, towards which one's gaze leads. For the outline which had been merely the place of a face has become a face through the presence of the sign-for-a-mouth or the sign-for-an-eye, and thereby moreover leads us further on.

People may say that I am trying to extract from Matisse's remarks more than they contain. Let them say so! But the whole of this passage about signs, which Matisse himself corrected, commented on and annotated on the rough draft of *Matisse-en-France*, ends with the admission:

It's just as if I were someone who is preparing to tackle large-scale composition . . .

In 1942, and even a little later, these words only conveyed to me the astonishing modesty of Henri Matisse, aged seventy-two years and three months. Today, on re-reading my words, *his* words, I find myself wondering not so much about the painter's psychology as about what he was trying to say. Perhaps I was led to this by the notes which I have, this year, restored in the margin of the published text: *it's the play of the arm in the composition which indicates the expression*; and in the second note, *it's the direction of the arm leading up to it*[1] *that gives the expression.* These are marginal notes on the passage about Delacroix, who *composed his paintings on the grand scale*, and of whom Henri Matisse says: *He had to finish off, at a certain place, the movement, the line, the arabesque that ran through his picture. He brought it to the end of his figure's arm and there he bent it over, he finished it with a sign, d'you understand, a sign . . .*

I'll allow you to take breath . . . *a sign, always the same sign, the hand, made in the same way, not a particular hand but His hand, the claw . . .*

The point being not to take breath but to read, I suggest a practical exercise: in the light of this, study a familiar painting, *The Death of Sardanapalus*, since Delacroix, who is here quoted as an example, is actually far closer to Matisse than is Ingres. Over the width of 4.95 metres it is easy to follow the painter's thought directly, moving upwards from the black man pulling the red bridle of a horse on the left, by way of the suppliant hands of the weeping woman and the outstretched arms of the auburn-haired concubine prostrate on the royal couch, turning past the background figures of the queens awaiting death and then moving downwards to the right to the executioner who is thrusting his sword into the female figure that closes the circle, directly, from hand to hand, from claw to claw, to complete the scene played out before the indifferent gaze of the King.

1. *The hand.*

84. – Charcoal drawing after Grünewald (1949).

85. – Study for the hand of St Dominic, pencil (1949). ▶

And this is indeed how Matisse interprets the sign-for-a-hand in the work of Delacroix, the painter of large-scale compositions: the ending *at a certain place of the movement* (the line) *that runs through the picture*, but also the point from which it rebounds. This point in Matisse's thought must be connected with the comment made immediately afterwards about the Burmese hand, *a hand that looks like a flower at the end of its stalk*, and his assertion: *The sign may have a religious, priestly, liturgical character or simply an artistic one. Each thing has its own sign. This marks the artist's progress in the knowledge and expression of the world, a saving of time, the briefest possible indication of the character of a thing. The sign . . .*

Whether it's Delacroix's claw or the Burmese flower, the hand (and Matisse goes on immediately afterwards to discuss the sign-for-a-mouth), or rather the sign-for-a-hand given individuality not through the hand itself that is represented but by the way the painter depicts it, deriving its character from the painter and not from the model or landscape, the sign-for-a-hand thus appears in Matisse's language, as do all other signs, first as a way of approach and then as a means to large-scale composition. It is the nodal point to which the line clings before starting off again, the true story.

And if only for the fun of it we might study, instead of the dance of doomed women before the couch of Sardanapalus, the *Lion Hunt* by the same painter in the Museum at Bordeaux. Here the sign-for-a-hand assumes, both in the hunters and in their quarry, the same resolutely claw-like character, and thus we can trace, from the lion's claws tearing the man on the left to the hands of the dead man on the right, whose body the lioness has dropped as she pounces on the dapple-grey horse, a ballet of cruelty in which the similarity of the sign-for-a-hand or a claw in man and beast is further emphasized by the rearing or bent hooves of the horses at the top and at the bottom of the scene. It is as though these innocent subordinates aroused the pity of the painter, in whose eyes man and lion are akin in bestiality (and I might equally well refer you to the tournament between angels, horseman, guards and the prostrate man in the lower half of *Heliodorus Driven from the Temple*, if I wanted to send you into Saint-Sulpice for a sadistic rather than a genuinely ritual spectacle).

But speaking of ballets, I shall instead bring you back to Matisse with the great *Dance* which is in the Hermitage in Leningrad, and which, dated 1909–1910, repeats and amplifies a theme from the *Joie de vivre* of 1906, now owned by the Barnes Foundation (Merion, Pennsylvania). What this second version brings out is in fact the dancing ring of figures, linked by the hands or signs-for-hands, and emphasized by the fact that between the figure on the left and

XVII. – *The Dance* (final version), now in the Hermitage in Leningrad (1910).

HENRY-MATISSE

XVIII. – *La Joie de vivre* (autumn 1905), study for the painting of that name, which cannot be reproduced in colour owing to the regulations of the Barnes Foundation. This study does not yet contain the ring of dancers, prefiguring *The Dance*, in the background.

that in the central foreground the ring, the chain, is broken between two of the hands, which the movement seems to have separated, so that the message of the hands is really movement.[1]

Matisse's hands, not Delacroix's claw. The hands of *The Dance*, which recur throughout the long trail of years, clasping each other, letting go, now pressed against a leaning forehead, now laid on the arms of a chair, now folded as in the long series of studies for *The Rumanian Blouse*, and then Matisse seems to lose self-confidence when, seeking to express a feeling that

1. Which might pass unnoticed in the distance in the *Joie de vivre*.

86. – Henri Matisse's hand holding a branch of medlar (1944).

is alien to him, that of prayer, he copies hands from Matthias Grünewald, but eventually his own hands provide the great hand of St Dominic in the Chapel at Vence. And St Dominic's hand is not a praying hand, Grünewald has been cast aside, the hand simply holds a book, a missal. Matisse does not know how to pray (I mean as a painter, for I would not venture to interpret his inward vision, what goes on behind closed eyelids, but must confine myself to the realm of things seen, to which the picture invites me, beckons me on to explore and, if I know how to look or to read, guides me) . . .

None of this would have any meaning if it did not help to explain those words let slip in 1942, to which I have returned yet again (*it's just as if . . .*) and from which I seem, this time, to have been diverted by Delacroix. But you must take it as it comes, like a step on a staircase, having no meaning in itself but leading us up whither the staircase *goes*: and perhaps you can already see that this is whither all this book, this staircase, is leading.

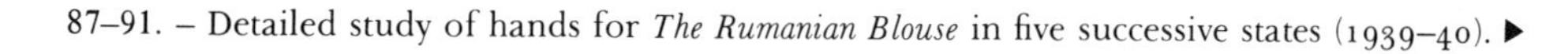

87–91. – Detailed study of hands for *The Rumanian Blouse* in five successive states (1939–40). ▶

Matisse

2/4 ep d'art

Preamble to a Lecture Given in the Large Amphitheatre of the Sorbonne

Evening organized by 'Tourisme et Culture'
and 'Tourisme et Travail'
(December 6, 1946)

I have skipped four years. I apologize for my failure to follow the chronological order of my writing or of my story; I have to accept confusion as I accept this life, which I never chose.

92. – *Self-portrait* (1949). Lithograph; 25 copies and 4 artist's proofs printed.

Ladies and Gentlemen,

At the end of the nineteenth century there was a painter who represented exactly that tendency in French painting which is furthest from what, in the middle of the twentieth, is commonly called modern art. Gustave Moreau was a painter of mysterious mythological scenes, which he treated with a miniaturist's skill. He carried meticulous draughtsmanship to its highest pitch. Now he was a teacher as well as a painter, and his pupils included such young men as Derain, Rouault, Marquet, Matisse . . . the very artists who introduced into French painting the opposite of all that their master stood for.

After fifty years spent in the practise of his art, however, Henri Matisse, in whom the whole world recognizes the finished expression of French painting, still speaks with the greatest respect of his old master, Gustave Moreau, who guided the first steps of men so different from himself, instructing them without ever thwarting them. But the undeniable gulf that lies between master and pupil, between Gustave Moreau and Henri Matisse, both in their attitudes and in their techniques, reveals better, perhaps, than anything else the evolution of French painting in our day, the transformation of the whole concept of painting between the end of the nineteenth and the middle of the twentieth century. Today young men throughout the world who are seized with a passion for painting look, first of all, towards Matisse. He is above all the man whose presence makes France the land of painters, and Paris the capital of living painting. The prestige we owe to him is almost immeasurable. During the most difficult hours of our national life, yesterday when we suffered shame, today when we are still surrounded by ruins, we are indebted to

◀ XIX. – *Le Luxe* (1907–8).

Matisse for having maintained, for still maintaining the radiant image of France. At the darkest point in our history, when so many people were irresolute and bewildered, or based their art on a delight in their own sufferings, on contemplation of their misfortunes, Henri Matisse, conversely, without rhetoric or lamentation, without apparent effort, preserved better than anyone else, to the world's amazement, the calm, wise and wonderful light of our country, that heritage of poise and beauty which has survived centuries of fury and destruction, and despite storms, sickness and old age his work sums up, as an unalterable hope, the perpetual declaration of trust in life which is the true message of France.[1]

We can say that for nearly forty years, ever since the time when the pupil of Gustave Moreau became the master of what was known as Fauvism, there have been throughout the world painters who cannot help painting like him, or at least who endeavour to do so – ever since the period when his pictures and those of his friends caused a scandal at the Salon des Indépendants, because they meant primarily the open abandonment of the Impressionist techniques to which painters and the public had so slowly become accustomed, and at the same time the whole of that tradition of painting which makes use of modelling, chiaroscuro and the gradation of colours, and which began in the sixteenth century. And people did not see at the time that, overleaping three centuries of painting, the true tradition of the great medieval painters was here reborn, enriched with all that men have learned since then through that exploration of the world and that confluence of cultures which was unknown to our forebears, and having moreover a keen awareness of modern life and the pulse of contemporary reality. For nearly forty years now, from all parts of the world, people have given up everything to come to Paris, to see Matisses and to see Matisse, and to learn from his example.

Even before the 1914 war, Pan-Germanists inveighed against those young Germans who preferred this Frenchman's lessons to those of any other teacher. The whole of Central European art, because of him, has ever since glowed with the reflected light of France. American millionaires have Matisses in their skyscrapers, and Moscow has thrown open to the Soviet people the museum which contains the largest collection of Matisse's works.* Italy, which apart from France has the greatest pictorial tradition of the world, reproduced Matisses even when she was at war with us, and in Brazil, that new land of painting, when France seemed an unattainable land, the painters of a friendly nation dreamed of Matisse as they might dream of a song.

* In the early 1930's I visited the Shchukin Museum in Moscow, the home of the collector, a rather remote place beyond the Pushkin Museum. It was almost always empty and one walked about alone among marvellous things. When I wrote this Preamble, in spite of a few days' visit to Moscow (to which I had not returned since 1936, that is, since the arrest of my brother-in-law Vitaly Primakov), I thought this museum had simply not been reopened because of the war. I could not imagine how long it was going to take for the Matisses, the Picassos, the Cézannes and the Van Goghs to see the light of day again.

1. See infra: *A Character Called Pain.*

93. – Matisse in Moscow in 1911, at the home of the collector Shchukin (on his wall, *Girl in Green*, reproduced in Vol. II of this book, p. 97).

This is a tremendous fact, whose wing-span overspreads all we can think of to say about a painter, all the inadequate praise we give him and the pleasure he gives us. It is a fact beyond art criticism, and for this reason, when one speaks of Matisse at this time, when conferences are being held to arrange the peace of the world and the fate of our country, one cannot approach this great painter without first recognizing the position to which the world's admiration entitles him, and in which, with all the power of his unparalleled gifts and his genius, he contributes to that which lies at the very heart of the debate, the dominant position of France in the realm of art and of thought.

This is the reason, furthermore, why I propose to approach the problem of Matisse from one angle only: not with trivial descriptions, not with a history of his paintings and his successive *manners*, not with a discussion of an art that defies discussion, but directly, like an established fact, an achievement that has taken its place in the history of mankind, and that attains perfection before our eyes. And so you will not be surprised if I speak of Henri Matisse as I would speak of Raphael, Chardin or Renoir.

But bear with me now if I take a devious route which will better enable me to reach my dazzling objective . . .

This Preamble was followed by a greatly shortened version of the following pages, which were written for publication and not for the lecture hall. Even thus abridged, the text aroused the impatience of my student audience, at least half of whom interrupted my speech, uproariously chanting: Get to the point! Get to the point! *Which I don't intend to conceal from the readers of this book.* All this was happening at the time when André Malraux, at Nice, was offering French youth a future that consisted only of tragedy and death, and when the young men of the day were bitterly intoxicated with his words. What was I doing talking about Fauvism or whatever? Get to the point! – which is not Matisse, but what's going to become of us, what they're going to do to us, young people, with our fresh lips and pure unlined foreheads, our wonder and our longings, our calendar the abyss, and our newly discovered bodies cast away somewhere into the mud . . . *Au sujet!* Get to the point!

But isn't it essential, here, to break off my speech and return to my novel, I mean to that story told in solitude, addressed to no audience, free from the need to consider the ears of listeners assembled by chance in an amphitheatre, their probable weariness or inattention . . . and by this very interruption to transform the reader from a critical spectator into a listener, not so much to my text as to Henri Matisse, that is, to a man to whom, by that time, he will no longer have access, in the context through which I approach him, save through me, through my story, this story?

(The interrupted speech will not be resumed until p. 199 : you may, if you choose, skip what follows to pick up the story again . . . it depends on what sort of reader you are.)

A Character Called Pain

(February 1968)

Interruption to the speech
(unpublished)

XX. – *The Windshield* (1917).

For readers of today and tomorrow: there were no longer any cars, even for great painters, in those days. I was thinking of this with some bitterness, at Nice in 1942, in that topsy-turvy existence, reminded of the earlier war by this picture, the first ever to show the world as it is seen from the inside of a car, going along a road.

I apologize.

But for my concern with completeness, I might well have left out the preceding pages, that *Preamble* to a lecture the original text of which follows hereafter.* Except that on re-reading it I realize that I wrote it essentially for the sake of one passage: *despite storms, sickness and old age*, with the words that precede and follow this. While Matisse was alive, I could not speak of that figure that dwelt in his shadow and whose presence was almost never betrayed in front of me, except when the painter, during my visits, had sometimes for a brief moment been unable to conceal from me the pain that haunted him. H.M. rarely revealed what was going on within him. Have you noticed that among all the human figures he depicted, all his life long, there is not one that betrays pain? And the same thing is true of himself. As for the few surprise attacks that he suffered in my presence, so fleeting, so quickly disguised, I had to behave as though I had not guessed at them from a contraction of his facial muscles. I don't know, I probably felt it was indiscreet of me to have seen them. I tried to forget them. I succeeded. I forgot them. Of course, it was understood that Matisse had to rest, that he was accessible only at certain times, that he seldom went into Nice . . . That was all.

. . . Seldom into Nice. Towards the end of 1941 he wanted to take us out to a restaurant. I think it was to La Coquille, in the Rue Masséna. It was more for Elsa's sake than for mine; he had just met her (about a week after me). He had taken us driving through Nice in a hired victoria, in the bright sunshine of the last day of the year. At that time we were unaccustomed to eating as we did that day. Matisse watched us with a kindly, regal smile. The ghostly figure was absent: it was not spying on us from a corner of the restaurant or the cloakroom. During the whole of that January I was not even aware of its existence, any more than on a pleasure boat one can hear the panting of the

*This was written in 1968. Since then, in 1969, yet another text has been inserted, further postponing *La Grande Songerie*, which would take us to 1945–46. I seem to be getting lost in this labyrinth of time. If only I could! (*1970*)

stokers within the bowels of the vessel. It may have been stupid of me, in my eagerness to listen, to ask questions, to note down what the painter said to me. I had been visiting Matisse almost daily, and my 'preface' was not progressing fast enough for his liking. I therefore got down to work, and my visits to Cimiez became less frequent.

On Friday, February 14, Matisse wrote to me after reading an article that annoyed him in the latest number of the *Nouvelle Revue française*. We had made an appointment for the following Tuesday. But he suddenly became afraid I might finish the 'preface' before that date without having seen the article that had vexed him:

. . . there is a criticism of my drawings which you ought to see . . . for it would be advisable to stress certain points in the study you are now writing. I should be glad to send you the magazine, but I should like to give you a brief preliminary explanation, before going through the article, of certain things in the past which to my mind give it its significance. Please let me know as soon as you have an hour or two to spare so that I can do this. I mean when you have finished the preface you are working on – if that should be before the meeting we have already arranged.

I must just ask you not to write anything more about me before you have seen me . . .

I had not finished, in fact, and Matisse obviously had not the patience to wait till our meeting on Tuesday. But it so happened that we had just been sent half a goose liver by our friend Jeanne Moussinac, in Lot, who had been fattening a goose for us, and for Léon and herself, for the past six or eight months. You cannot imagine what a godsend this was at Nice in February 1942, during those days of famine. And besides, Elsa felt indebted to Matisse for our meal at La Coquille. The goose liver gave us an opportunity. Over the telephone, Matisse accepted our invitation to lunch that Sunday. Neither Elsa nor I had any idea, I must confess, how to prepare *foie gras*; fortunately, the landlord of 16 Cité du Parc, where we were living, who kept the restaurant La Pergola on the quayside, was a former chef from Larue's. But I see that Elsa has told the story in her *Préface à la Clandestinité*, which precedes *Le Cheval blanc* in our *Œuvres romanesques croisées*:

This master of the art of cookery [she writes] *had advised me to sew up the liver in a cloth and boil it in salted water, while as for details about the addition of port wine, etc. . . . he would give me these next day. But that very night we were awakened by the sound of motor-cars and voices under our windows . . . we were convinced they were coming to arrest us. Actually it was the first-aid service of the police taking away the cook and his wife, who had been asphyxiated by a sawdust-burning stove. They did not die, but I never learned how to cook* foie gras *with port. We ate it for lunch none the less with Matisse and his secretary Lydia, and for dinner with Carco and his wife. A* foie gras, *in those days, was something unforgettable . . .*

Matisse had not brought me the article, but since I was to see him on Tuesday . . . I had noticed him looking rather pale. But above all, he was almost voiceless. He joked about it. That very evening he sent us a note, part of which I reproduce:

Dear friends. I have recovered my voice! I just had an hour's siesta. I was very tired when I was with you at two o'clock and I never thought of telling you.

I got up this morning at eight instead of twelve, my usual time, without having been able to make up for a poor night with a little sleep. Just to go to the Savoy for the preview of a sale, at which there was nothing interesting. It doesn't suit me, at my age, to get up early. I must remember that . . .

. . . Thank you for your delightful lunch, it was good to be with you and I was sorry to have to leave you.

I only realized much later the full significance of 'without having been able to make up for a poor night with a little sleep'. And yet I seemed to feel that day the breath of that invisible being whom Matisse was obliged to obey. The letter of Friday, February 14, also contained one sentence which I have not quoted, towards the end: *I hope you have reassuring news of your mother's health, and that you and Madame Aragon are enjoying peace of mind . . .*

This was by no means the case, and during the end of February and the beginning of March when Matisse started my portrait, or more precisely portraits, I had my own spectres too. Matisse seemed to be well, and I seemed to have no worries. My mother died on March 2, 1942, at Cahors. That's another story, a long and bitter one. I had twice been to Cahors at brief intervals. But let's talk of something else.

It did seem, however, that I could see the spectre more clearly than I had done, behind the painter, and that I could hear in the old man's voice something I had hitherto not noticed. It was at the end of March that Matisse made the charcoal sketch, *the theme*, that is the usually accepted version of my portrait (there are four of them in existence, plus some thirty *variations*, if he has kept them all). I have repeatedly referred to this portrait elsewhere;* I have exactly my mother's mouth in it, rather than my own, although Matisse had never seen my mother. A few more drawings were made in April; apparently several bear the date March 1943, but this was added a long time afterwards, when Matisse noticed that he had forgotten to date his drawings, possibly in

* Notably in *Appearances Fixed*. But should one be afraid of repeating oneself, and of doing so as an afterthought? All this may be considered as just a caption to that portrait where the mouth is *exactly my mother's mouth* and which can be seen by turning to the next page.

'45 or '46: it was just a mistake, for all the drawings had been made within the space of a few days, and I had sat for them. And in 1943 I did not see Henri Matisse at all, for a number of reasons that don't concern us here.

My dear friend, I am still where you left me on your last visit – namely, in bed.

Yesterday the thing I was coming down with broke out, a hidden pleurisy – I didn't hear the doctor well for I'm getting muddle-headed, and I have an incipient otitis in the right ear which prevents me from hearing distinctly. I had a temperature of 38.5 last night, 37.5 this morning. I have dizzy spells that make the ceiling turn round (reminding me of after the Carnival when I was sixteen). That's why you have had no news of me.

I have a little 'volumetto' *that I want to send to Elsa Triolet; I should like to decorate it with a little dedicatory drawing, but I'm too exhausted at the moment. However, I cannot resist sending it to her – if she'll accept it as a wild rose, i.e. a pretty-coloured flower with no scent.**

I have enjoyed reading her books,[1] *and found them most interesting. With kindest regards to both of you. – H.M.*

* The *volumetto* had a beautiful red cover. It was one of the little books published in Milan *'all'insegna del Pesce d'Oro'*, and dated February 28, 1942, a date which is moving for me not because it was the third anniversary of our wedding but because it was the day of my first visit to my mother at Cahors. It has the French title *Notes d'un peintre*, and is described as the celebrated article by Matisse in *La Grande Revue* (December 1908) republished in French; 250 copies were printed. The Italian publishers seem to have made a mistake, for there is not a word of this text in *La Grande Revue*. I have identified it, however: it appeared in the special issue, devoted to Matisse, of *Point*, Vol. 4, No. XXI, then unpublished.

And in the margin, running vertically: *If you have a moment . . . what's happening to your preface? Aren't you afraid of doing too much to it?*

On Sunday, April 19, when he sent back my text, he wrote that there was not much to be changed in it, but he had just received Fabiani's typographical sample, which apparently disregarded my 'most precise' instructions. If I would just make certain slight alterations, so that Fabiani could take it back, etc. . . . No mention of his health. He was glad to hear *Mille Regrets* had been a success . . . But the very same day as this letter he sent me a telegram, and the following morning I received a note from him at my flat, while I was still in bed:

My dear friend, are you unwell? or away, perhaps, or busy? I sent you a telegram yesterday afternoon, asking you to ring me up as soon as you could, and you haven't done so . . .

This letter can be found in full in *La Grande Songerie*, it's the one referring to the discovery of the rococo armchair. I had been to see the armchair and it was then that I talked to him about what I really had in mind, over and above *Thèmes et Variations*, without mentioning the word 'novel' of course – well, about the book which would give an account of the extraordinary menagerie with which he has always surrounded himself and which recurs throughout his painting. That day, I saw the star-shaped pucker in his cheek

1. *Bonsoir Thérèse* and *Mille Regrets.*

94. – *Aragon.* Charcoal portrait, providing the theme for the variations to be seen in the chapter *On Likeness* (Vol. II, pp. 50–5

à Louis Aragon
Henri Matisse 3/42

95. – Drawing on the opening pages of the *volumetto* given to Elsa Triolet (Nice, May 25, 1942).

hommage
à Elsa Triolet Aragon
Henri Matisse
Nice 25/5 42

of which I spoke earlier, a star of ill omen. Some time after – there's no date on his letter, it may have been early in May – I received a note written in a firmer hand, asking me to come and talk to him about this project: *since I am not working, it would be a good opportunity*, thus marking the end of that period of ill-health when he had not felt capable of decorating the *volumetto* for Elsa. *If you agree, when will you come? At the same time, will you also bring Elsa Triolet's little Italian book so that I can embellish it, if I may say so, with a small drawing – now that I'm recovering my taste for life.**

It was not to last very long. I had been back to see him several times, and he had never looked well since that 'hidden pleurisy'. Towards the end of May we left for Villeneuve-lès-Avignon.

For some time past (see his letter of March 16, '42, to Mme Marie Dormoy, in the margin of *Matisse-en-France*), Matisse had been planning to visit Switzerland in the summer to supervise the printing of his *Ronsard*. On the eve of our departure, he was still talking about this. But I felt uneasy. The stranger was sneering in the shadows.

And, in fact, on June 2 H.M. wrote to Marie Dormoy in the letter acknowledging the receipt of two books by Cros, of which he had as yet said nothing to me:

I have just had another bad attack of hepatitis and it looks as if the unwelcome object has been expelled – though no one saw it . . . repeating none the less his intention of spending July and August in Geneva (still *Ronsard*). I myself had the following letter from him on June 13:

My dear friend, I am glad to know you have arrived safely and are feeling quite at home already: that's so easy in lovely country and among kind friends.

As far as I'm concerned nothing is changed except for a fresh attack of hepatitis that seized me from 10 p.m. last Sunday till 10 a.m. next morning – it was less painful than the previous one, a fortnight ago,[1] *so that my journey to Switzerland has had to be postponed a couple of weeks, till about July 15, provided I don't have a fresh attack in the meanwhile, in which case I shall not go at all. I can't go unless I've had no attack for a month. I'm very vexed about it, but what can I do? . . .*

Then he asks for some typographical advice about the *Ronsard*, adding:

I can't write to you at greater length, for my attack, which ended only yesterday morning, has left me with a headache, in addition to which I have to endure the tiring effects of morphine.

A visit from Fabiani was the pretext for another letter, on June 26 (Fabiani wanted me to sign with a pseudonym). He says *I feel as if I were with you*, on

1. Of which he had not told me.

* And the *volumetto*, that wild rose, became a red rose scented by the dedication and the drawing, spread over two pages, for Elsa. Which gives a different meaning, for me, through that very scent (as one might say through that music) to this passage which I cannot resist copying out, which I had not re-read since Nice, particularly as, with our packings and unpackings over the course of years, Elsa thought it was lost, and found it again, to her surprise, only two or three months ago:

My models, human figures, are never 'extras' in an interior. They are the principal theme of my work. I am absolutely dependent on my model, I watch her moving freely, and then settle on the pose that seems most natural to her. When I take a new model, it's from her relaxed attitude while at rest that I guess at the pose that suits her best, and then follow it slavishly. I often keep these girls several years until I have exhausted their interest. My plastic signs probably express their psychological state (their état d'âme, *a term that I don't like), in which (or in what else?) I take an unconscious interest. Their forms are not always perfect, but they are always expressive. The emotional interest they inspire in me is not shown specifically in my representation of their bodies, but often in special lines of values which are scattered over the whole canvas or paper and form its orchestration, its architecture. But not everyone notices this. It may perhaps be sublimated eroticism, which is not generally perceptible . . .*

reading my poem *Absent de Paris* in *Poésie 42*. He was at last reading Cros, as I had suggested in December '41. But this letter is chiefly important as regards his health:

I'm still here, in bed. I get up for half an hour in the evening to have my bed made. In a few days it'll be the end of the month – that's the fatal moment when I shall get another attack if my little trouble hasn't cleared up – and so I'm waiting with a certain anxiety. I have another injection every two days, a very deep one, 6 to 7 cm. at least, of extract of pancreatic juice. I feel much the better for this.

I should be glad to know you are nicely settled in at last, and look forward to seeing you again in the autumn . . .

No attack on the 1st. Everything was being got ready for his Swiss visit. But we had reckoned without the Shadow.

On July 15, sending me for Seghers the photo of a drawing to illustrate one of Cros's poems, he wrote:

I was caught out by a half-attack on July 13 after going scot-free on the 1st. My general condition is better and there's no more thought of an operation.

But my Swiss journey, which was planned for August 1, is postponed for at least a month. So I'm still closeted with Ronsard, whose book is the gainer by my illness . . . For my own part I don't know what to ask for – my periodical attacks have become less acute, by dint of great precautions, I diet, I stay in bed – if things go on improving thus I'm on the road to recovery – but if an operation becomes necessary I don't know what to think because there are great risks involved . . .

We were, in fact, 'nicely settled in', at the far end of Villeneuve, opposite the hospital that houses Nicolas Froment's *Triumph of the Virgin*, in the house next to the doctor's, the ground floor back, three high, dark, cool rooms, opening on to a secret garden, all stones and walls, with one fig tree. Except that, out for a walk in Avignon, I'd been recognized by somebody I'd known before the war at the *Maison de la Culture*, who had become one of Ferdonnet's assistants on Radio Stuttgart. Each of us had his shadow.

On July 30, more about Cros. A letter to Marie Dormoy:

. . . Have you the address of Cros's son? I have approached Seghers, editor of Poésie 42*, through Aragon, suggesting that he should publish a poem from Cros's* Collier de Griffes*, p. 128, 'Tableau de Sainteté' . . . mother and child . . . with a drawing of the subject by myself. They are delighted. They need his address to write about royalties. Seghers's address is Montée du Fort, Villeneuve-lès-Avignon (Gard), same address for Aragon as Seghers looks after his mail.* If you should see young Cros let him know, he can write directly, that will save time. I am still in bed, but with Ronsard, and I'm not*

*It was rather rash of Matisse to write this in a letter to Paris . . .

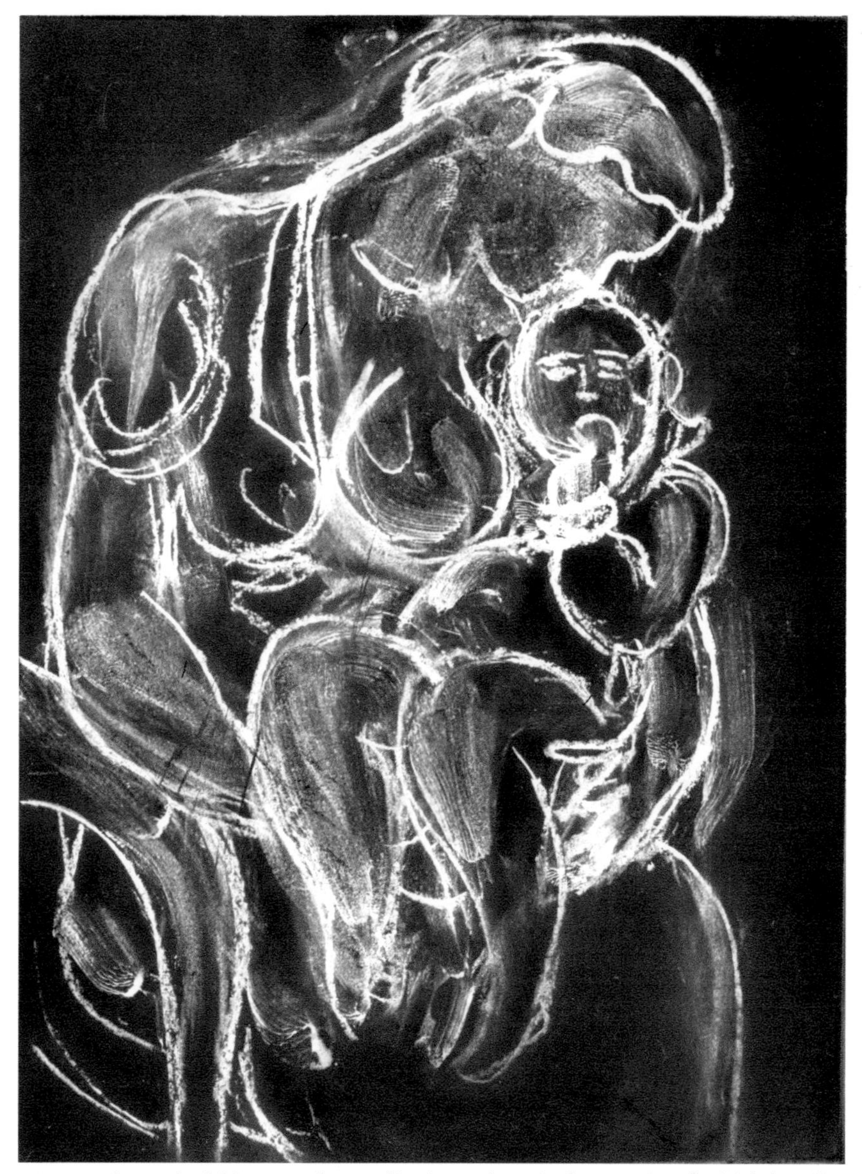

96. – *Mother and Child.* Gouache on linoleum (1939), the matrix of which has disappeared, and of which there only remains the photograph reproduced in *Poésie 42* to illustrate the poem by Charles Cros: *Tableau de sainteté.*

bored. It's still the gall bladder. I had an important consultation recently which will make my future somewhat clearer . . .

The Shadow was still in the background, yawning. He had no Ronsard to read while Matisse was drawing. But he showed some patience, having perhaps overheard the doctors talking in the next room. At all events, on August 2 Matisse wrote to me:

Dear Louis Aragon – I shan't go to Switzerland this summer: I am too much taken up with illness and doctors – I have two teams of them. (1) One wants me to be operated on. (2) The other doesn't – the one that doesn't is presided over by a surgeon – *my own surgeon from Lyons, who knows what risks I ran and is not anxious to expose me to the same risks again, unless the case makes it imperative. Particularly as those who want to operate aren't even sure whether I have a stone to be removed – But it's an orthodox solution, indicated by three slight attacks of jaundice. The surgeon says that if I have a stone it is not embedded, and that without undue optimism we may assume that it will be expelled naturally.*

Wednesday, a grand consultation with (1) – Prof. Wertheimer of Lyons, now on holiday near Aix-les-Bains; (2) – Prof. Gutmann, of the Paris hospitals, now retired in the neighbourhood of Nîmes;

(3/4) – my own Dr Augier and his pal Rivoire.

I don't go to the Casino, I have no expensive vices, so why not have some fun.

There's yet a fifth at the consultation, Dr Stephan Chauvet, who blames everything on intestinal infection, which fosters and creates all diseases. He didn't make up this theory specially for me.

Why aren't you here to protect me? * *I keep on working none the less and I've only a few drawings still to do for Ronsard. Lucky Ronsard, who needn't worry about doctors. I remember a song from the* Kapellmeister *or from* Le Sourd ou l'Auberge pleine*: 'You'd think, to hear him, that all doctors . . . are murderers . . .' Forgive me!*

* Matisse mistakenly believed that I was both a typographical expert and a real doctor.

Surely I've the right to protect my own skin, I don't want an operation – so why let myself be invaded? The fact is I've no strength of will – I'd rather have an attack from time to time and not have to expose myself to the shock of an operation which would leave me the worse – as I've no great reserves, I shouldn't be able to stand it.

This Professor Wertheimer was an old acquaintance of Pain. It was he who, at Lyons, when Matisse left hospital, used to visit him at his hotel to keep an eye on the Shadow's victim. On one occasion the consultation grew tumultuous, and from behind the closed doors of the room where the doctors were, Professor Wertheimer's angry voice rang out, reaching the sick man and his nurses, saying that the heart would not stand the operation . . . *and have you inserted a tube? I forbid you . . .*

In the aviary the birds were fluttering. I think the Stranger was there, watching or provoking their panic-stricken flight.

All that month, discussions with Fabiani, who had agreed to let my name appear; Matisse's fear of being over-praised (in my book and in *Poésie 42*); arguments about the price of the book; repeated requests to a Swiss publisher to send him *Les Yeux d'Elsa*. He could not finish *Ronsard* for lack of ten sheets of transfer paper, etc. On August 17 he wrote to me:

. . . and I've started painting again at last – on August 15 with great delight. I'm settling down as a valetudinarian old fogey!'

97. – In the aviary the birds were fluttering . . .

The letter of August 24 begins rather oddly:

My dear friend, I've found your kind letter again, I had certainly read it, but at a moment when I was in pain, and what it said, although of great interest, had been 'shelved' somewhere. It is most interesting for me to know that you are subject to calculi too, and that you refused to be operated on ten years ago[1] *– but I'm sorry your bile is so capricious, for you must suffer too. Perhaps you don't get the* paroxysmal *symptoms that my four doctors' report mentions . . .*

Later on in the same long letter: *I am getting better. I even had a painting session from 2 to 6.30 – I shouldn't have spent five hours at it, but it was going so well that I didn't want to stop! – and I was none the worse afterwards. I had an undisturbed night, but I don't think I shall be very enterprising. I keep near the coast during these*

1. Not quite: in 1934.

sessions. I hope I shall eventually get beyond my depth and then I shall have to have recourse to the unknown.

On the night of August 31, at Villeneuve, there was a great round-up of Jews, about which I wrote *Le Médecin de Villeneuve* in honour of our neighbour:

> *Dans ce pays de fenêtres étranges*
> *Il fait trop nuit pour qu'un sanglot dérange*
> *Les jardins clos qui sont des cœurs murés*
> *Tout est de pierre et tout démesuré*
> *Dans ce pays de fenêtres étranges*

And on September 1 Matisse wrote to us: *My dear friends, how glad I am that you've decided to come back to Nice on October 1. I think you'll be better off spending the winter here than at Villeneuve. There's an unpleasant wind that blows through the streets of Villeneuve, and the temperature is often freezing. Our Nice is kindlier . . . but not for everyone these days. It's too horrible!*

That is how we learned that Villeneuve was not the only place where such things had happened. And in the same letter there occurs the passage: *I have at last begun to grapple seriously with Painting . . .* which I quoted at the beginning of *La Grande Songerie.*[1] But there I stopped at the point where he says:

Since I started painting I have treated myself to two small attacks of inflammation of the bile-duct, which suggest, according to the doctors I think most reliable, that my only trouble is a small stone or even some sediment which a spoonful of olive oil taken every morning will eventually clear up.

The postscript to a note on September 4 says: *I am well and I'm working . . . but . . . who knows –*

And here, after all, we must include the letter dated September 1, to Marie Dormoy, since, as a note at the end of it says, it was *by mistake sent only on the 6th*:

I am still kept in bed nearly all day to immobilize a little something that I've got in the bile-duct. I shan't go to Switzerland before the spring. I shall stay in Nice – far from Nice, fortunately. Just as you are far from Paris if you don't go out of your house –[2]

And while the Shadow triumphs in silence, Matisse turns to the question of Cros:

What have I told you about G. Ch. Cros? Perhaps I didn't mention that having found among the drawings I had in reserve something that might fit in with a poem of his father's, I had asked Seghers, editor of Poésie 42, *to publish these with a note by*

1. In the present book, the next chapter in the novel (no, the one after that – *1970*).
2. Compare with the *too horrible!* of our letter of September 1.

Aragon who has the greatest admiration for Cros. There was no more to it than that. Did G. Ch. Cros think we had a book in mind? I believe he did, for he wrote to Seghers to ask what he would get in the way of royalties. I think he should just have said thank you – now that somebody wants to honour his father.

My work is getting on, between attacks.

His work . . . in September '42 it was the *Dancer and Armchair, Black Background* (the *fauteuil rocaille* of *Matisse-en-France* had in its turn become a character in the story, taking tea with the dancing girl). And all those 'Girls in front of the window', one in a white dress with a black belt, a second in a violet dress, a third in a pink dress (the window open, the shutters closed) and the one simply called *The Black Door*, who is merely an adjunct to what is going on behind that door . . . For all this, what price did he have to pay to Pain, that sinister pimp or recruiting-sergeant, one of those figures from the underworld such as we find in *Manon Lescaut?* What did it cost Matisse, still procreative at seventy-three, how much did he have to pay to go on enjoying the world and loving it in this way?

Note, 1969. – I mentioned only four girls here . . . because until this year I had not made the acquaintance of the fifth, although she was painted at the same time. She raises questions that can be better dealt with in the second volume, where she can be seen in *Anthology II* (p. 323 of Vol. II). This picture has a bearing on several of the secrets of the painter's art, and to my mind it is more important than the other four put together.

There was only one more letter before our return to Nice at the beginning of October, asking me to make sure, if my portrait was used in *Brocéliande* (to appear in Switzerland) that it was not spoiled in reproduction as Montherlant's was in his latest book. In October my visits to Cimiez were resumed; just one small note:

It's such a bother for you to come and see me that I daren't press it, and yet . . . I shall always be at your disposal . . .

History was going to decide otherwise.

From November 11, 1942, until the autumn of 1945 we were to see no more of Henri Matisse. We were difficult to reach. I got three letters in 1943.

The first, written on January 20, reached us at Lyons, from where we had found it easier to send news than from the mountain hide-out where we had spent the end of 1942:

I am quite pleased with myself: my trouble seems to be clearing up. By tomorrow morning I shall have gone 70 days without pain, or fever, or jaundice, if all goes well.

And so I have taken advantage of this respite from my torments to work at Painting, *and I've produced things which allow me to hope for progress in my development.*

XXII. – *The Idol* (December 1942).

Ronsard is finished except for two or three drawings – and I've become close friends with Charles d'Orléans, who stays by my side. I get constant new delight from him, as when you find violets under the grass. If I were to illustrate him, it would be fascinating to seek for a graphic expression worthy of his music. I can see myself reading him early each morning, as one takes a deep breath of fresh air on rising. That's what I did with Mallarmé.

I hope that you will spend pleasant evenings in front of a good blazing fire and that your work will be linked with the gay dancing life of the flames. Mme Lydia asks to be remembered to you. Affectionately. H.M.

This letter ought to have reached me in the place we called The Sky, where, oh yes, there were big wood fires, but other reasons for unhappiness. It had to travel by way of Villeneuve, where Seghers had not yet got our new address, after we had left that mountain retreat. Finally, in our attic in a suburb of Lyons, I read it, among those drawings which we took with us everywhere so that any wall would be our home, thanks to Matisse, thanks to that feminine beauty expressed in a single line, as one tosses off a glass. The seventy days' respite covered almost exactly the period from the Italians' entry into Nice to the day on which that letter was sent us. In December, H.M. had painted

XXI. – *The Black Door* (1942).

XXIII. – *The Idol* of the Fauve period (1906).

XXIV. – *Michaëla* (January 1943).

the big picture called *The Idol*, which has two peculiar features: the first, that it bears that title, already conferred on a painting of the Fauve period (1906) which bears no resemblance to it, and the second, that it is the portrait of a young woman who had been his nurse and whom we meet later as Sœur Jacques-Marie of the Dominican Convent at Vence. In January he had painted *Michaëla.*

Actually Matisse had spent one year, the whole time I was seeing him at Nice and a short period afterwards, in an alarming condition, with attacks of jaundice every two weeks more or less regularly, with pain and bouts of fever. This had gone on altogether for a year and a half since his return to Nice. And it meant that he had to have a night nurse. The sick man showed astonishing powers of dissimulation; all the time that he was producing those inspired drawings, and the great paintings he did that September, he was suffering, without ever betraying it except at home, to those who were nursing him. Every night, three or four times a night, he was seized with anguish, he called for help. Night belonged to Pain, which then reigned at the Cimiez hotel. Pain was always there, ready to bite. The painter was condemned to lie in bed. *All right, I won't budge!* he said. Pain laughed silently, baring yellowed teeth, knowing that it was not enough for its victim to keep still. He was sentenced to a diet: 'What sort of diet?' Matisse asked. And he stared at Pain, he defied Pain. For a whole year. At the outset of 1943 he was considered cured. A new period of his painting began. And so: *I have taken advantage of this respite from my torments to work at Painting*, he wrote, as I have said, in January 1943. And again in February, telling us: *You're in the best possible position to do important work. An artist once said to me: 'Genius is the power of standing up to one damn thing after another.' This is obviously an incomplete definition, but it's true for me. But haven't you the support of Hope and the approach of Spring?**

As for me, I am still here in bed except for one hour a day when I get up. I don't enjoy that much, for I've lost the habit – I'm always glad to be back in bed. I work there regularly. Painting in the afternoon, in the morning illustrating Ch. d'O. (what do you think of him? A fortunate writer who has just scored a triumph in one of our leading theatres[1] *tells me he thinks the ballades a bit silly). I myself think of them as crystalline music which, because of a certain ambiguity that surrounds it, leaves room for the artist's line.*[2]

*I think, not that Matisse had no idea of the conditions under which we lived illegally in 1943, but that he *did not want* to show that he could imagine them.

1. Presumably *La Reine Morte* by Montherlant, which had just been produced with resounding success.

2. It was after his death that I replied to Matisse, quoting at the close of my *Roman inachevé* the words of Charles d'Orléans: *Amoureux ont parolles peintes* (Lovers have painted words).

Pain is a patient character in the play, able to wait endlessly for its cue to appear on the stage with all the gestures of tragedy, wringing of hands and loud cries. Pain, temporarily, had withdrawn a little into the shadows, knowing that after all, if for the moment it could no longer rely on gall-stones, the least carelessness would enable it to resume its sway, in some part or other of the victim's body. Pain had its eye on him. And meanwhile he spent the mornings drawing for the *Charles d'Orléans*, the afternoon painting . . . in February *The Lute*, in March *Le Tabac royal** and the *Lemons against Fleur-de-Lis Background*, of which I speak elsewhere, three of the most splendid pictures he ever painted, the calm and powerful expression of pain overcome.

* Here again, the future Dominican nun. I don't know why this character in my story, whom we shall meet again when Matisse decides to build and decorate the Chapel of the Rosary, habitually declared that H.M. only made drawings of her. As though there were something about painting and its colours unsuited to the past history of a nun. In fact, she sat for *The Idol*, *Le Tabac royal* and the *Girl in a Pale Green Dress*. She ought rather to have rejoiced at this. Was she afraid that having been *painted* would add to the somewhat confused ideas that pious people may have about artists' models? In any case, as regards *Le Tabac royal*, the fact that the picture is so called gives the leading role to the china jar, behind which everything in the room fades into unimportance beside the vividness of the written words, and the young woman who is seen side view, in a long, very chaste dress, is merely an accessory to the still life in the centre, having not even the value of the musical instrument on the blue armchair on the other side, in the foreground, whose silence echoes in this muffled, curtained place.

Pain, reduced to playing a minor role, was waiting in the wings. What was it waiting for?

That still life I referred to just now, the *Lemons against Fleur-de-Lis Background*,[1] to give it its official title, painted in March 1943, marks the end of the *Charles d'Orléans* series, which gave rise to it. His *Ronsard* being finished, Matisse set to work to give shape to a project previously set aside.

It was in 1937, probably at the time when his *Mallarmé*, published by Skira in 1930, had at last begun to arouse interest after a long period of neglect, that the publisher of Henry de Montherlant, Bernard Grasset I believe or someone like that, took it into his head that Matisse ought to illustrate Montherlant's works, complete or otherwise. That was why the author of *Les Jeunes Filles* came to Ponchettes, where the painter was then living, and Matisse did a series of portraits of him, one of which, as H.M. told me in 1942, had been so badly reproduced for a book cover. But as for the Works, whether complete, selected or whatever, the thing was pointless. Matisse considered that this writer had said in his prose all that he had to say and therefore left no room for the artist's drawing. This, in fact, was what he repeated in a letter of February '43 and what he had told me a year earlier. But in '41 Montherlant happened to be at Nice, having found it difficult to get back to Paris. Matisse had seen him then, and had gone back to one of his portraits to make a linoleum cut of it. He also told Montherlant that of all his books only one, *Pasiphaé*, might give his imagination scope. The whole thing displeased Jean Matisse, the sculptor, who, as H.M. told me a little later, would rather have seen his father working with me, for instance. Everyone to his taste. In March '43, happening on a few studies he had attempted, Matisse decided to spend his mornings illustrating *Pasiphaé*, essentially with linoleum cuts, for which

1. This picture is reproduced infra, in *La Grande Songerie*, p. 241.

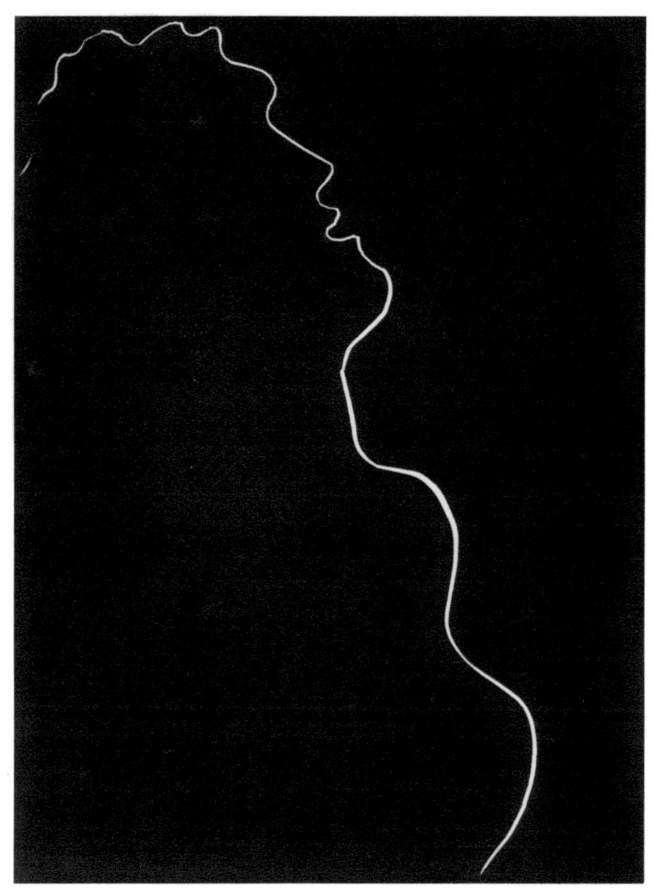

98. – *L'angoisse qui s'amasse . . .* (The gathering anguish . . .)

the Turkish girl I have mentioned and Lydia D. posed. The result was a very fine book, the only one of Matisse's* which has a tragic character and in which one image at least contradicts what I said earlier, that in all this painter's work there is no face expressing pain; and yet, seeing this woman's head flung back, a single white stroke against the black background like a jagged flash of lightning, one cannot be sure, in spite of the caption:

> . . . *L'angoisse qui s'amasse en frappant sous ta gorge . . .*[1]

whether she has been struck by the thunderbolt of pain or that of pleasure.† Perhaps he thus pacified for a while his cruel guest, who was proud (and very ready to believe) that his presence had sufficed to call forth the tragic sense so long rejected by the painter. Perhaps, too, it was an awareness of other *sufferings* outside his home that to us, at least, made this ancient story seem like a cry echoing the thing that was never talked about in Matisse's presence.

Pasiphaé altogether occupied the painter from March to August 1943. It is not absurd to believe that the decisive technique of the draughtsmanship here

* I say *the only one* because Matisse never counted Joyce's *Ulysses*, for which he did six engravings, as one of *his* books. I discuss this later.

† In Montherlant's text the reference is in fact to sexual pleasure. But is there any difference in the picture between the expression of extreme pleasure and that of extreme pain?

1. 'The gathering anguish strikes beneath your throat . . .' *Chant de Minos*, prologue to *Pasiphaé* (printing finished on May 28, 1944, but this probably cut by Matisse in 1941 or '42).

resulted from his practice in the *Variations*, the skill of the *Variations*. By a dialectic process, the white page with its sparse pen-lines is replaced by the black Cretan sky where the white line stands out dazzlingly bright against night, or rather against insomnia. This is the book of a man who cannot sleep.

Since July 15 Matisse had been away from Cimiez and was living at Vence, in a far more sheltered place, the Villa Le Rêve. In July '43, it must be remembered, the rumour was current of a possible bombardment of Nice by the Allies. This was no doubt owing to the illusions we had in France about the opening of a second front, as a result of the American landing in Sicily on July 10. It was said that the occupying forces would evacuate children and old people from the town. In view of the state of his health, H.M. chose to leave Nice before being forced to. I had written to him twice at his new address and we were anxious at having received no reply. At last, after some delay, because Georges Sadoul had to go and pick up our mail at Pierre Seghers's and bring it to us at Saint-Donat, in the Drôme, where we had our point of contact, we received a letter from Vence dated August 22, 1943:

*My dear friends, I have been very slow in answering your letter of July 28 and that of August 15. Why? Because, although I thought of you, I was absorbed in finishing a job which has been going on for four or even five months. I had to perfect it: at my age, one never knows if the work in hand is not the last of one's life – one has to strengthen it as much as one can; one can't put off the completion of one's idea to a later occasion. Living with all the linoleum cuts to illustrate your old school-fellow's** Pasiphaé, *I have worked over one or two which did not seem to have as much tension as the rest. Now I am satisfied, and I've sent the lot to Fabiani. I'm expecting the dummy any day now, to give it a final going over. Now I've got that off my mind. Since our* T. et V. *is really finished, I should like to send you an ordinary copy, for the time being, until you receive . . .*

* Montherlant and I had both been at the École Saint-Pierre, Rue Louis-Philippe, Neuilly-sur-Seine, from 1908 to 1911, I believe, but in different classes.

Then followed endless details about the number printed, the price, the copies for Elsa and myself, the distribution, not to the press but to museums and libraries, seven long pages, then he continues:

So much for your child. I have read Elsa's book,[1] which the publisher sent me, and so has Mme Lydia. It is a fascinating book, I read it straight through and I liked it very much, and so did my secretary. Congratulations. I am not at all surprised at its great success. You see that life always has something good for those who serve its cause.

From your letter, you seem to be planning some work in which I am to have a share; I wonder what this may be?

1. *Le Chevat blanc*

I have been at Vence for a month and a half – everything very satisfactory. A lovely view along the road to Saint-Jeannet, the village that always makes me think of Baudelaire's Giantess:

. . . Dormir nonchalamment à l'ombre de ses seins
Comme un hameau paisible au pied d'une montagne

(To sleep nonchalantly in the shadow of her breasts like a peaceful hamlet at the foot of a mountain)

99. – Extract from the letter to the author written August 22, 1943, with a tiny drawing at the bottom representing the position of Vence at the foot of the Saint-Jeannet hill.

A beautiful villa, I mean with nothing fanciful or fussy about it. Thick walls and glazed doors and windows up to the ceiling – so there's plenty of light – this villa was built by a British admiral in his country's colonial style.

A fine terrace with a balustrade abundantly covered with variegated ivy and beautiful geraniums of a warm colour that I didn't know – my windows full of fine palm-tree fronds – the whole thing seems to me so far from Nice, a long journey which I did in less than an hour, that I can put all my memories of Tahiti in this setting. This morning, as I walk about in front of my house and see all the girls and men and women hurrying towards the market place on their bicycles, I can fancy myself at Tahiti at market time.

100. – The Villa Le Rêve, at Vence.

When the breeze brings me a smell of burnt wood I can smell the wood of the islands – and then, I am an elephant, feeling, in my present frame of mind, that I am the master of my fate, and capable of thinking that nothing matters for me except the conclusion of all these years of work, for which I feel myself so well equipped . . .

It was at Lyons that I read this letter, which had pursued me in Georges's pocket. I had just finished writing *Le Musée Grévin* and was about to leave for Paris with Elsa. It was on that very day, I remember, that we learned at the same time that Laurent Casanova had escaped from Germany and was back in France, and that Danielle Casanova and Maïe Politzer had both died in Auschwitz.

(What had I written to Matisse about the work that I 'seemed to be planning' and which could only be that poem over which I had brooded so long, that *Musée Grévin** in which, actually, Matisse could hardly have had a share?)

* (Unless it could have been *Aurélien* . . .)

In the train, carrying the manuscript which I thought I had finished, together with Elsa's *Les Amants d'Avignon*, to give them to Vercors for the clandestine *Éditions de Minuit*, I wrote on my knee a dozen lines for our two dead friends, which I inserted into the last pages of the poem.

Over there, on the road to Saint-Jeannet, the character called Pain had withdrawn for a while from the Villa Le Rêve; it had work to do elsewhere.

Written in 1969

I am correcting these proofs at the end of July 1970, and the Shadow *has come to dwell with me, like a knife in my heart, not to be withdrawn as long as I live. And I don't care if these words upset the typography of the book. Here, strange as the place may seem, I dedicate this whole book to the one who inhabits it entirely, to Elsa, now that my only wish is to join her under the beech trees where she lies, not yet asleep. – A.*

Je n'ai jamais appris à écrire ou les Incipit, Skira, 1969 (fragment)

101. – Henri Matisse working on the illustrations for *Ulysses* (1935).

What follows next is taken from a little book which is still unfinished but which, in all probability, will appear two or three months before the present book. It has as yet no title, but, together with a new book of Elsa's, will inaugurate a series called* Les Sentiers de la création et de l'invention, *to be published by Albert Skira, who nearly produced my* Matisse. *I had happened to mention Joyce's* Ulysses. *And what I said there seems to fall naturally into place here:*

* In fact, *Je n'ai jamais appris à écrire* appeared about November 15, 1969, a year or so before this book, which will have taken twenty-nine years to assume form and substance.

. . . .

While I was writing this I was just finishing a meditation on Henri Matisse, with which I had been concerned for twenty-seven years, with gaps of course. Now it happened that my thoughts about these two projects coincided over Joyce and *Ulysses*, in connection with certain details I had had to seek out regarding a singular episode in my 'hero's' life.

I had read here and there of illustrations made by Matisse for *Ulysses*; I had seen two or three of these reproduced in books, but it was only lately that for a few hours I held the book in my hands. I had always found it strange, far more than in the case of Ronsard, that Matisse should have illustrated a book so remote and so different from himself. Particularly as it appeared that in his interpretation of *Ulysses* he had confined himself to the Homeric themes, illustrating the *Odyssey* rather than Joyce.

Apparently the suggestion had been made to the painter towards the end of 1934 by the New York publisher George Macy, for his Club of some fifteen hundred subscribers, offering a considerable sum of money and asking how many engravings H.M. could produce in exchange. This was done by telephone from Paris to Nice. Matisse unexpectedly replied that he must think it over, not having read *Ulysses*, but that he would give his answer next morning. George Macy rang up again next day, without great hopes.

That Matisse should then have accepted the offer, saying he had spent the night looking through the French translation of *Ulysses* and undertaking to make six engravings, based not on Joyce but on Homer, that is, on six of the episodes of the *Odyssey* which he had recognized in *Ulysses*, surprised the publisher as much as it surprised me. Who can read, or even seriously skim through, *Ulysses* in a single sleepless night? And above all, who, not being acquainted with Joyce's work, could recognize in it the episodes of the *Odyssey* on which it seems that the book is constructed, but which in fact most readers have never discerned? This was to remain an enigma.

I confess that I myself was incapable of understanding it, but someone put forward in my presence the hypothesis that the solution of the problem might lie with the person who, at Nice, before nightfall, had procured for H.M. a copy of Auguste Morel's translation; a person who no doubt knew *Ulysses* well and shared Valery Larbaud's point of view about this novel and its relation to the Homeric episodes. But who?

There was probably only one person in Nice at the time capable of disclosing the secret character of the novel, its kinship with the journeys of Ulysses and Telemachus. It must have been someone of the painter's immediate circle who so promptly lent him *Ulysses* in French, and who probably suggested the Odyssean solution, which Matisse offered Macy as his own. Who could it be? As far as one knows, for H.M. seems not to have spoken of this to anyone, it might have been, and I'd be inclined to say it was, Mme Simon Bussy, who translated Gide into English (she was a member of the great Strachey clan and was later to publish a rather remarkable novel which Roger Martin du Gard translated, *Olivia*, under the pseudonym Olivia).

In Richard Ellmann's *James Joyce*, published in 1959 (and in a French translation in 1962), I find a passage about the matter which shows how Matisse's acceptance must have been presented to the author of *Ulysses*:

[Joyce] *wished to make sure that Henri Matisse, who had agreed to illustrate Ulysses for a special American edition by the Limited Editions Club, would have his Irish details right. So he wrote to T. W. Pugh, that knowledgeable Dubliner, asking him to find some illustrated weekly published in Dublin about 1904.* Matisse, *he told Pugh,* knows the French translation very well but has never been in Ireland.

This was clearly far from the truth and when the book appeared Joyce must have suffered some disappointment. Richard Ellmann adds:

But Pugh's researches were in vain: Matisse, after consulting briefly with Eugene Jolas, went his own way, in the late summer and early fall of 1934; when asked why his drawings bore so little relation to the book, he said frankly, 'Je ne l'ai pas lu.' He had based them on the Odyssey.

102. – *Ulysses piercing the single eye of Polyphemus.* Etching for Joyce's *Ulysses.*

The mention of Jolas made me doubt somewhat the part played by Mme Simon Bussy, but the *Je ne l'ai pas lu*, quoted in a letter from Mrs Jolas to Ellmann in 1959 as though it were a confession made to her, makes me set aside this alternative hypothesis; he would not have needed to confess any such thing to Mme Bussy, if indeed it were she who lent him the translation of *Ulysses* for a night. Moreover, Mrs Jolas has told me that it was not from her husband that the painter borrowed *Ulysses*. The discussion mentioned in Ellmann's book took place much later, in the summer of 1935, when Matisse went to lunch with the Jolases in the mountains above Nice.

A little further on Ellmann informs us that Joyce believed the initial letters in the Macy edition were by Matisse. Had he been told this to make up for his disappointment at not having 'documented' illustrations of Dublin life? It's possible. But the *lettrines* in question did not satisfy him, and he preferred those that his daughter Lucia had made for the Albatros Press *Ulysses*, but which had been mislaid there.

In fact Macy's *Ulysses* is *not* 'one of Matisse's books', and he never considered it as such, never mentioned it among *his* books. The whole appearance of the book is out of keeping with the style of Matisse's books. It was a commercial undertaking in the glossy style of the best American houses, in which by way of *lettrines* there was an ornament repeated here and there which would have gone just as well in a book by Kipling. This is not meant as an adverse criticism.

But what interests me in all this is the process of inspiration, and the different way it works in a writer like Joyce and a painter like Matisse. To draw a shameless parallel, I imagine what Fénelon might have thought of my own little *Aventures de Télémaque*, taking an interest in my knowledge of the court of Louis XIV. Or suppose Homer had sent that noble prelate photographs of the Trojan war or documents about contemporary navigation among the Cyclades.

For if the book was alien to him and his drawings for it were merely undertaken on commission, Matisse is known to have liked having themes suggested for his work, and he did in fact like commissions, as we shall see with the Chapel at Vence.

On this occasion George Macy's suggestion resulted in something which is surely unique in Matisse's art, since it impelled the painter to introduce into his work, with the image of Ulysses piercing the eye of Polyphemus, the theme of violence and, at the same time, the *suffering* of the Cyclops.

He was thinking not of Joyce, but of Homer. Yet Joyce, like the Cyclops, had been cruelly wounded in the eyes.

. . . .

Ulysses contains eighteen episodes borrowed from the *Odyssey*.[1] They do not follow the same sequence as in Homer. In the *Odyssey*, the episode of the Cyclops is followed by that of Aeolus, then the Lestrygonians, and it is immediately after this that Odysseus and his companions reach the island of Aiaie where Circe lives, in Book X of the twenty-four that comprise the Homeric poem. The Circe episode, or at least its equivalent in *Ulysses*, the huge Nighttown chapter, appears on p. 425 of the Penguin edition and ends on p. 532. This is more than mere disproportion; the Dublin Circe, followed by Eumaeus, Ithaca and Penelope, concludes Bloom's Odyssey, even if the three final episodes, the return of Bloom-Ulysses, take up another hundred and seventy pages. In the *Odyssey*, the Nausicaa episode appears in Book VI, three books before that of the Cyclops. In Joyce's book, Nausicaa follows the Cyclops. This means that Joyce has not followed the Homeric time-sequence or the Odyssean chronology but has subordinated his analogies to the development of Bloom-Ulysses's story instead of the converse.

We see thus that Matisse not only preferred the aspect of *Ulysses* that is connected with antiquity, choosing to illustrate the mythology underlying the Irish novel, but in fact kept strictly to the *Odyssey*, leaving the future reader to disentangle things for himself. Also, as we know, H.M. decided to do only six drawings corresponding to six Homeric episodes: Joyce's first three (Telemachus, Nestor, Proteus) being omitted, the first drawing corresponds to the episode of Aeolus in the *Odyssey* and the newspaper office in *Ulysses*. Nothing was provided for the Lestrygonians, Scylla and Charybdis, the Wandering Rocks or the Sirens . . . The third drawing represents the close of the Cyclops episode, the blinding of Polyphemus. As we have seen, the fourth drawing is devoted to Nausicaa (which reverses the Homeric sequence of godlike Odysseus's wanderings), immediately after the Cyclops; Odysseus issues from the thicket, having broken off a leafy branch to hide his naked manhood, and so advances towards Nausicaa and her companions, who have come to the river to wash the linen of the royal palace of Phaeacia . . . Matisse's fifth drawing* represents the Circe episode. And of the three books that tell of the traveller's return, only the second (Ithaca) is illustrated with the sixth and final drawing.

Note, here, that this drawing of Ithaca is the landscape towards Montboron, where the path leading through the forest towards a house (which we must therefore identify with Penelope's royal palace) passes between rocks whose phallic shapes Matisse somewhat mischievously stresses, I suppose as an allusion to the Suitors.

* It is worth noting that Matisse's 'illustration' of Circe, that is, of that sort of apocalypse of Leopold Bloom and his companions in the sexual confusion of the brothel, was made with, or from, or after (as you please) photographs of acrobats. As though the disorder of these bodies represented a profound disturbance of the laws of nature, a challenge to gravity for instance, a gymnastic exercise flouting society. An opportunity, in any case, to show that nothing is forbidden to the painter.

1. The following pages do not appear in *Je n'ai jamais appris à écrire*, the little book I have mentioned. But I was impelled to write them by what came before.

103. – *Ulysses meeting Nausicaa*, etching (1935).

104. – *Ithaca, the road to Penelope's palace*, etching (1935).

This enumeration of texts and images, these comparisons may seem otiose. And yet it is perhaps the first time since man began to write or paint that such an interplay of reflections has taken place, complicating the journey to and fro across the centuries that thus links Matisse to Joyce and to Homer. Dublin's novelist could not grasp, nor had Matisse imagined, how much *reality* the painter brought to Mr Leopold Bloom, that Irish Jew who (as Joyce tells us the first time his name appears) 'ate with relish the inner organs of beasts and fowls'.

If on finishing his book, in September 1920, Joyce explained himself by saying: 'It is an epic of two races (Israelite – Irish) and at the same time the cycle of the human body as well as a little story of a day (life) . . .' adding: 'My intention is to transpose the myth *sub specie temporis nostri*,' he could certainly not be satisfied by the way Matisse was to reverse the process, moving back from contemporary reality to Homeric myth. But for us, when we consider not Bloom's day alone but Joyce's lasting fame, Matisse's 'gloss' contributes far more than any laborious, well-documented illustrations could have done, had T. W. Pugh sent him from Dublin the illustrated magazine of 1904, enabling him to turn *Ulysses* into a sort of Jules Verne story. We have good reason to be grateful for George Macy's strange idea for his Limited Editions Club.

And in fact this gloss of mine has no *raison d'être* except in the Blinding of Polyphemus, about which I postponed speaking when I wrote *A Character Called Pain*. The only true image of pain in all Matisse's work, if we deny that characteristic to the *pain of love* shown by the woman in the throes of sexual pleasure in the prologue to *Pasiphaé*. And where does Homer himself display as much ferocity against man, monster or god as in this thrusting of the olive stake into the eye of Polyphemus, who 'gave a dreadful shriek . . . while he pulled the stake from his eye, streaming with blood, and hurled it away from him with frenzied hands . . .' As though on purpose to give the painter, long centuries after, the unique opportunity to prove that the magic of the world, the happiness of man, and all that of which Matisse was to create his universe of splendour, did not imply ignorance of that shriek, of darkness and of horror.

April 1969

La Grande Songerie, or the Return from Thule

(1945–46)

Unpublished text, except for a few pages, of the interrupted speech

XXV. – *Dancer and Armchair, Black Background* (1942).

Countless writers have argued and contended over Petrarch's life, work and love. They have appealed to the evidence of his contemporaries and successors, to tombstones, to the poet's ambiguities, to his Latin verses and his letters. They have ascribed bastards to him and discovered Lauras without end. Few men have known such posthumous persecution.

And yet there is, in the poet's life, one period to which biographers seem to have paid only brief and casual attention: in 1337, during the month of January when the Tyrrhenian Sea is rough, leaving Rome as though, still in flight from Avignon where his beloved dwelt, he could only hope to allay his frenzy by distance, he went by sea, not towards Marseilles, whence the Rhône would have brought him back to the enclosed valley, but towards the coast of Spain, along which he sailed, passing through the Pillars of Hercules, entering the Atlantic, skirting the coast of France and then reaching England, where we know nothing of what places he visited. What had suggested this singular voyage, a dangerous one in view of the conditions of navigation at that time? It was to last eight months, and the end of August found him back at Avignon.

All we know of this strange adventure comes to us from a letter to Tommaso de Calaria, in which Petrarch describes himself as searching for the Thule of antiquity. This assertion has generally been interpreted as an alibi for his flight from the loved one. Thule was beyond the commentators' imagining. Thule must have been a poor excuse. I admit, myself, that nothing seems to me more natural than Petrarch's desire to discover this legendary island, whose name has the sort of power that sets poets travelling. I imagine Petrarch on the deck of the sailing ship, impatient with the long and complicated journey which was to bring him to that Arthurian Britain which he knew from so many manuscripts, the cradle of the loves of Guinevere, who so closely resembled Laura, though lacking Laura's virtue, and all the philosophy of the world could not stop Petrarch at times from thinking how tender she must have been to Lancelot. But when at last he reached that dreamed-of land, it was of Thule that he was in quest: Thule, of which all trace had been lost, as if the island had been engulfed with the cup of gold which its legendary king flung into the sea. It is thought, commonly, to lie somewhere in the Orkneys, north of Scotland. It might be Hoy or Rousay, Flotta, Sanday or Pomona . . . The chief industry of these islands, apart from fishing, was the weaving of straw hats. Did Petrarch and his Roman ship get so far? Did he follow the coast of Britain up to that remote north, or was he diverted from his quest by London and the major cities of England and Scotland, where libraries and manuscripts might well have played the part of the magnetic mountain in luring this traveller off course? Nobody tells us. In a verse letter to his friend Giacomo Colonna, written on his return, in which there is no mention of Thule, Petrarch merely says of this English journey: *I went alone on the steep shores which are fretted by the dark, restless waves of the British sea; the soil, in these lands, repels the ploughshare, vines are unknown, and wheat grows with difficulty in these inhospitable furrows.* He does not speak of the Orkneys, of Pomona, or of Thule, and nobody at Kirkwall has heard it said that an Italian poet travelling in a red-sailed coaster, who, knowing no single word of English, expressed himself in Latin, principally by quotations from Virgil, had left in those regions any deep trace or even a puzzled recollection. And yet I like to imagine Petrarch landing on those windy islands (it must have been in mid-springtime), on the fishermen's wharfs, making contact with the basket-workers who were weaving their straw hats, buying one which must have suited his head, as yet uncrowned with laurel, and on a tiny boat, accompanied by the barbaric natives of this northern archipelago, sailing off in search of other islands, and meeting a monk who could speak Norman-French mingled with dubious Latin and who told of earlier inhabitants drinking in goblets strange drinks unknown in Rome or Avignon. The poet must have found it awkward jumping ashore in that long, cumbersome Italian robe he wore, looking almost like Dante in the Inferno, you remember, standing in Charon's boat while at his feet, in the dark waters, the lost souls . . . but here the hair was only seaweed and the heads were pink and yellow shells that hurt your feet if you took off your shoes . . . In the hollows of the rocks, when summer came, he could fish for shrimps and crabs in clear water where weeds were floating.

A strange summer holiday, in 1337 . . . In vain might Laura's lover display

105. – *The Straw Hat*, pen and ink (1944).

an erudition equalled only by his superhuman memory, and without access to any library compare all the texts ever written about Thule, all attempts to identify its position, he was never to discover it; from some small Scottish port, in one of those traditional inns with an old branch of holly over the door, his Orcadian straw hat flung down in one corner of the room, with a disillusioned pen and ink even worse than the yellowish mud in which he had copied out Cicero at Liège in Flanders, while from the tavern below rose the music of bagpipes, so uncongenial to Florentine ears, he wrote to Tommaso de Calaria: *What matter if the North or the South hide Thule from me! May God grant us only to know that virtue always equidistant from the opposite poles, and that path in our brief existence along which almost all men advance in dread and hesitation towards an uncertain fate!*

If it has not been granted me to discover the secrets of Nature, I shall rest content with knowing myself. This study shall absorb me henceforth.

Thus ended the voyage to Thule.

And I shall explain that Orcadian straw hat.*

* Did the hat that Matisse is wearing on p. 253 of this book come from Scotland? That doesn't matter, nor whether or not it came from Tahiti. But at any rate here is the drawing of it, made two years earlier . . .

106. – The Tahitian landscape seen through Matisse's window, photograph by Henri Matisse (1931).

It was not of Petrarch that I meant to speak today, but of Henri Matisse, and to my knowledge he never visited the Orkneys. But in the life of every man there is always some Thule lying dormant, some latent dream which one day impels him to go journeying. And Matisse's Thule was another island, where they made straw hats too but where they wore wreaths of flowers and shells. The ukulele sounded there more sweetly than the bagpipes, the tiari grew there instead of heather, and Tahiti replaced Thule.

It is easy to understand what decided the painter to visit the islands: what complex, shifting mirages, what miraculous signs, what earlier adventures. Not so much the story of Gauguin as all that he had heard about the supernatural beauty of nature and of human beings in that lingering paradise: corals, transparent water, and above all the light. I think it was chiefly the snare of that incomparable light that attracted Matisse in the 'thirties to the waters of the Pacific. It's no use asking him: there was surely an intermingling of many temptations, even those of which he was unaware, all those modern legends which account for the success, at that time, of the film

107. – *The Windows*, etching for *Poésies de Stéphane Mallarmé* (Skira, Lausanne, 1932). The painter had neglected to reverse th name of the boat (*Papeete*) before the engraving of the Tahitian landscape, where the balcony belongs to Nice.

White Shadows, and that longing to escape which always, in some measure, suggests Rimbaud. Those were the last years in which the islands still had their mysterious remoteness, there were no airlines and the war had not yet changed the quiet ocean into a suburb of Chicago. But we can safely assert that among so many dreams only a reason connected with painting could have determined his departure. For Matisse, the Chinese artist with the transparent and delicate heart, painting is far more than an art, it is a feeling, I might say the only feeling, to judge by the little room it leaves for anything else in his life. When Matisse goes walking, when he sees someone, when he reads, painting invariably intervenes and asks: What is there for me in all this? Of course he loves flowers, women, birds. But not as you or I do. Not for their own sake. Whatever sets others dreaming is for him an essential and implacable element in the ordering of his thought.

This autumn* I went back to Villeneuve-lès-Avignon, where towards the end of 1941 I had begun writing about Henri Matisse. I saw the same picture through my window, the same things set my mind wandering or held my attention, interwoven in the same way, as when I had first mingled in my writing Matisse and Petrarch. I reopened the boxes, hidden somewhere in the neighbourhood, in which I had left my exile's library when the illusory demarcation-line was shattered. The Germans or the militia, visiting the little house where these things lay, had taken off one new case containing a manuscript of *Aurélien*, but had not bothered about the papers in the wooden box I'd had made at Carcassonne when nothing else was available. And so I found once more Henri Matisse's letters of 1941 and 1942. I re-read them slowly, letting my mind wander. Of course they are for the most part connected with the work I had undertaken, with what I was then writing about the painter. But also with the daily round of his life, of our life. With what he had read, whom he had met, the ups and downs of his health, unwelcome visitors, an article in some paper that annoyed him . . . At the time, as I received them one by one, sometimes a brief note sent from Cimiez to Nice after a conversation, the same evening or early next morning, like an afterthought, a correction to something said . . . I did not see then what is so striking when they are read all together, that the man was a prisoner to his painting. I had certainly said this somewhere, but indirectly and casually. I had not understood it deeply until I re-read those letters. They are surely the starting-point of what I am writing now.

It will be remembered that at this time, I mean in the summer of 1942, Matisse, having finished the great experiment in draughtsmanship which is summed up in his book *Thèmes et Variations*, for which I had written an introduction entitled *Matisse-en-France*, had begun painting again, meaning to

*In 1945, on our return from Moscow. I mention this because in July 1945 Matisse returned to Paris, but we had just *flown away* (as he says in a letter the following year). As I had been ill during the winter of 1944–45, I had not seen him again. I thus met him again for the first time since our experience as outlaws (November '42) by means of those letters hidden in packing-cases on the ground floor of a house quite close to Seghers's place, at the foot of the Montée du Fort, which in 1942 belonged to two old ladies whom we irreverently called 'the nanny-goats', but which Pierre subsequently bought back. Our real reunion must have taken place a few weeks later, when we visited Matisse at his house in Vence, Le Rêve, for the first time. It was here that I showed him the beginning of *La Grande Songerie*.

A first version of this text, typed on faded paper, contains a variant in the tense of the narrative which convinces me that it was at Villeneuve-lès-Avignon that I first began to write *La Grande Songerie*. This paragraph began as follows: *I am now back at Villeneuve-lès-Avignon, where towards the end of 1941 I began writing about Henri Matisse. I see the same picture through my window, the same things*, etc. . . . Which proves that in 1945 I was again living at Seghers's. But the interesting thing is that it was this Villeneuve version that I showed Matisse the following month; for on looking through the manuscript I find, further on, marginal comments by H.M. which I shall note as they occur.

profit by the lessons learned through that experiment. In a letter from Nice, dated September 1, 1942, he wrote to me:

. . . I have at last begun to grapple seriously with Painting – deliberately, without preliminary over-excitement – My first sessions were not very significant from the point of view of the campaign I am planning, but the latest, yesterday's, marked a real step forward – For a long time now I have been involved with a certain colour of ideas – though it suppresses much of myself as regards delicacy and refinement, it is full of fresh air. In short, I am breaking new ground. The essential thing is that my position in this struggle is satisfactory. I am the passive Spaniard or Roman looking down from his raised platform, with calm indifference, at a cockfight – the champions are one Matisse whom he has known and observed for so long, and a very dissimilar figure, very perverse, who behaves differently with each of those from whom she demands everything, and who is called Painting. I seem to be writing like a young art student who doesn't know what he is talking about . . .

And a little later:

. . . I'm sending you this funny letter because I'm incapable of writing any other. My attention is entirely absorbed by my work and I have to write to you about the manuscript[1] *. . .*

I have copied this out, of course, because it shows that monopolizing power of painting which *demands everything* . . . and the painter's obsession. But if this were all, the passage would be a weak expression of what I am trying to make objective, and would suggest a sudden attack, an episodic absorption of the painter in his work, whereas in fact it is the substance of his days, his nights, his very brief slumbers. No, it was rather for the sake of the phrase: *For a long time now I have been involved with a certain colour of ideas . . .* and what follows. For I was speaking of Tahiti, of Henri Matisse's departure for Tahiti.

I was saying that it was useless to ask him what on earth he had gone to look for there. He would only have given one his pretexts. Neither the beauty of Tahiti nor its strangeness nor escapism à la Rimbaud would explain things: I myself am convinced that he was in search of that 'colour of ideas'. Of himself. But let us not anticipate, as Jules Verne says, being an expert on strange voyages although he never left home.

After all, when a painter goes off, taking with him his paintbox, palette, brushes, mixing-pans, camp-stool, a clean rag and a dirty rag, you assume that he's going to settle down in front of the landscape and get on with it. If Corot goes off to Rome or Gauguin to Tahiti, you can be sure they go in

1. About *Matisse-en-France.*

search of renewal, they paint.* But when Matisse, visiting Tahiti, finds Thule, an inverted Thule so absolutely lacking in mist, in any shading-off or indecisiveness of colour that it seems to correspond to the kind of painting he had been doing for thirty years at least, for the first time in his life he does not paint. Why? At any rate, he does not paint what he finds there. The strange fact must be noted: at Tahiti, the thing he chose to draw over and over again was a baroque rocking-chair that he had in his room.†

* A very long note written by Matisse in the margin of the Villeneuve manuscript, running down the margins of two pages, with two half-sheets pinned over erased passages at the end, bears witness to his concern with *fixing ideas* as well as with their colour. Was it for fear of interrupting the development of what I was saying that I failed to retain this, or did Matisse himself prevent me from doing so, considering that it was for my guidance and not for the reader? I don't know. But today I have the feeling that I have no right to keep this note for myself alone. Here it is, then, it belongs where the reference mark is, except that there's a shift to the first person, with no capital letter to begin with:

for a very long time now I have been conscious of expressing myself through light or in light, which seems to me like a block of crystal in which something is happening – it was only after enjoying the sunlight for a long time that I tried to express myself through the light of the mind. At the same time I began to simplify things greatly and to move away from what Maurice Denis wrote to me forty years ago: 'Don't forget that painting is primarily an art of imitation.'

Being captured by light, I often wondered, while mentally escaping from the narrow space surrounding my motif, *consciousness of a similar space having apparently been sufficient for painters in the past – while I thus escaped from the space which was in the background to the* motif *of my picture, I was mentally aware that above me, above any* motif, *above the studio, even above the house there was a cosmic space in which I was as unconscious of any walls as a fish in the sea – immediately values (differences from Black to White) grow lighter and the shadows are no longer 'deep as tombs' – Painting becomes airy and even aerial. So at the same time that my 'picture space' was expanding I often wondered as I worked what the quality of light must be like in the Tropics. It was to see this that I went to Tahiti. Tahiti? At first I had settled on the first port of call after Panama, the Galápagos, to which a German baroness had recently called our attention – But since no boat called there, I had to go to Tahiti, the first stop of the MM. boat. It was thus only the light that interested me. I never thought of Gauguin; and when I thought I found, in an out-of-the-way spot, a hut with its inhabitants in front of it, wearing grass skirts, I quickly rejected as old-fashioned this thing which I only loved in painting – and through Gauguin.*

The note, which at first stopped here, is carried on over the next page of the manuscript:

In order really to know our Western light I had to be able to judge it by comparison. Already, on the way to Tahiti, I recognized the crystalline light of New York (my first port of call). And then there was the light of the Pacific – The different sorts of light I experienced have made me more exacting about imagining the spiritual light of which I am speaking, born of all the lights I have absorbed.

This note suggests to me a few comments on his writing: had you noticed, for instance, that H.M. rarely uses a full stop at the end of his sentences, but puts a dash instead? As though he were drawing a silence. I have not described here, as elsewhere in this book, H.M.'s *deletions,* whether they be corrections or afterthought: as when he says he has *tried to express himself through the light of the mind,* he hesitated, thought at first of writing *through a light* rather than *the light,* then crossed out the words a second time and reverted to his original expression, and as for *of the mind (de l'esprit)* he had begun by writing, or rather begun to write *the spiritual light,* stopping halfway, *lumière spi . . .,* then writing on the left *de,* on the right *l'esprit . . .* More curious is the reflection on Gauguin, about the group of Tahitian natives in front of a hut; he had been writing *I quickly rejected this as old-fashioned . . . (une vieillerie),* then, crossing out *this (cela),* he corrects himself: *this thing which I had often seen in painting* in the first draft, then crossing out *I had often seen* he writes above it *I only loved (cette chose que je n'aimais qu'en peinture –)* with the dash, you notice, and as an afterthought adding below it *and through Gauguin.* Note: a full stop.

And again, in the latter part of the note, having written: *In order really to know light . . .* he changes his mind and instead of *light* makes it *our Western light.*

† *It was so different that it took me three months to assimilate.* As far as painting is concerned Matisse confined himself to one small landscape of 15 by 26 cm. I found this phrase among my notes. Note that what I showed Matisse of *La Grande Songerie* in the autumn of 1945, at Vence, stopped short after the two following paragraphs. (*1967*)

And yet the obsession with Tahiti did not leave him, when he came home to his dreams. Whoever knows Matisse is constantly aware of the influence of that distant island on his thoughts and even on his drawings and paintings. But like a surprising mirror in which he has seen himself more clearly than ever before. He tells of the light of Tahiti, the lagoon, the transparent water, the fish and the corals in that undersea light which is like a second sky. And I seem to see the goldfish swimming round in that picture he painted long before his journey, I seem to see all things bathed in that shocking light which offended visitors to the *Indépendants* in the days of Fauvism. If he did not find Thule at Tahiti, at any rate Matisse encountered there that *colour of ideas* with which he had become involved so long ago. And he might say, like Petrarch returning from the Orkneys: *If it has not been granted me to discover the secrets of Nature, I will rest content with knowing myself.*

Knowing myself: in the room the rocking-chair is swinging. Knowing myself? The rocking-chair and myself. A yellow rocking-chair.

108. – The Tahitian *Rocking-chair*, pen and ink (1931).

I must also speak about (*the Villeneuve MS. runs:* I have spoken about . . .) Matisse's craze for armchairs, the importance of armchairs in the story of his painting.* There was the one at Ciboure which appears in a painting in the Albi Museum, there was the Tahitian rocking-chair, there have been many

* I published the few pages that follow in *Les Lettres françaises* of December 31, 1964 (from *I must also speak about* . . . to . . . *in dark places and in late hours!* and it was probably there that I substituted *I must also speak* for *I have spoken*) under the title *The Venetian Armchair.* I introduced this with these remarks:

. . . The following passage was written in 1946. It is a fragment of the book on Henri Matisse which I have been promising to Claude Gallimard for the past seventeen years, but whose publication has been delayed by various circumstances and my mania for writing other things. It will get finished eventually, when I can find a little leisure to read over what I have written and add to what I 'then' considered complete the few pages which will convey the distance, the terrible distance that has intervened between ourselves and a living man whom I cannot bring myself to think of except as alive. – A.

It will be seen that I then ascribed the date 1946 to the text begun in 1945 . . . I don't know at what point the transition occurred from one year to the other.

XXVI. – *Landscape Painted at Tahiti* (1931), 0.14 by 0.18 m. Reproduced for the first time.

109. – *Forest at Tahiti*, drawing (1931).

others. I witnessed one of these infatuations, just as I was finishing *Matisse-en-France*, and I pointed it out in a marginal note entitled *Stop-press*, added at the last minute on the typescript. I quoted part of a letter from Matisse received on April 20, 1942, and I added: *Thus, from one armchair to another, the strange romance is carried on. Our story continues . . .*

But today I have more leisure to return to the matter and I want to reproduce the letter of April 20 *in extenso* for the sake of something in it that cannot be conveyed, the Matissian atmosphere we breathe in it. I have just found it again among my Villeneuve papers. It was brought by hand, the envelope addressed to *Monsieur Aragon*, underlined, with a full stop. The letter is on two separate sheets, written on both sides, on paper of small format, used widthwise; each sheet being twice as long as an ordinary envelope. The two sheets have each been subsequently folded down the middle, across the lines of writing. I transcribe them, page by page:

First sheet, recto:

My dear friend, *Monday 20/4/42*

Are you unwell? or perhaps just away from home, or busy? I sent you a telegram yesterday afternoon asking you to ring me when you could – and although it was not a long time ago I am surprised you have not done so.

I wanted to tell you that I have received from Paris the proofs of the book of drawings. That they are satisfactory. That I have not quite decided about their dimensions on the page, and as an old publisher you could perhaps see to it with me. This book interests you

Verso:

I'm sure of it. I have also decided to send the drawings to Paris to speed up production. I think it would be as well to send your text at the same time. I like it very much and there is little you need to do to it I think – Perhaps you might say in a marginal note that I have at last found the object for which I've been longing for a whole year. It's a Venetian baroque chair, silver gilt with tinted varnish, like a piece of enamel. You've

Second sheet, recto:

probably seen something like it. When I found it in an antique shop, a few weeks ago, I was quite bowled over. It's splendid. I'm obsessed with it. I am going to bounce on it gently when I come back in the summer from Switzerland.

(On the front of this sheet, except for the first line, which runs across the whole width of the paper, the writing begins on the central fold, on the right-hand side of the sheet. The left half is filled by the sketch of the armchair.)

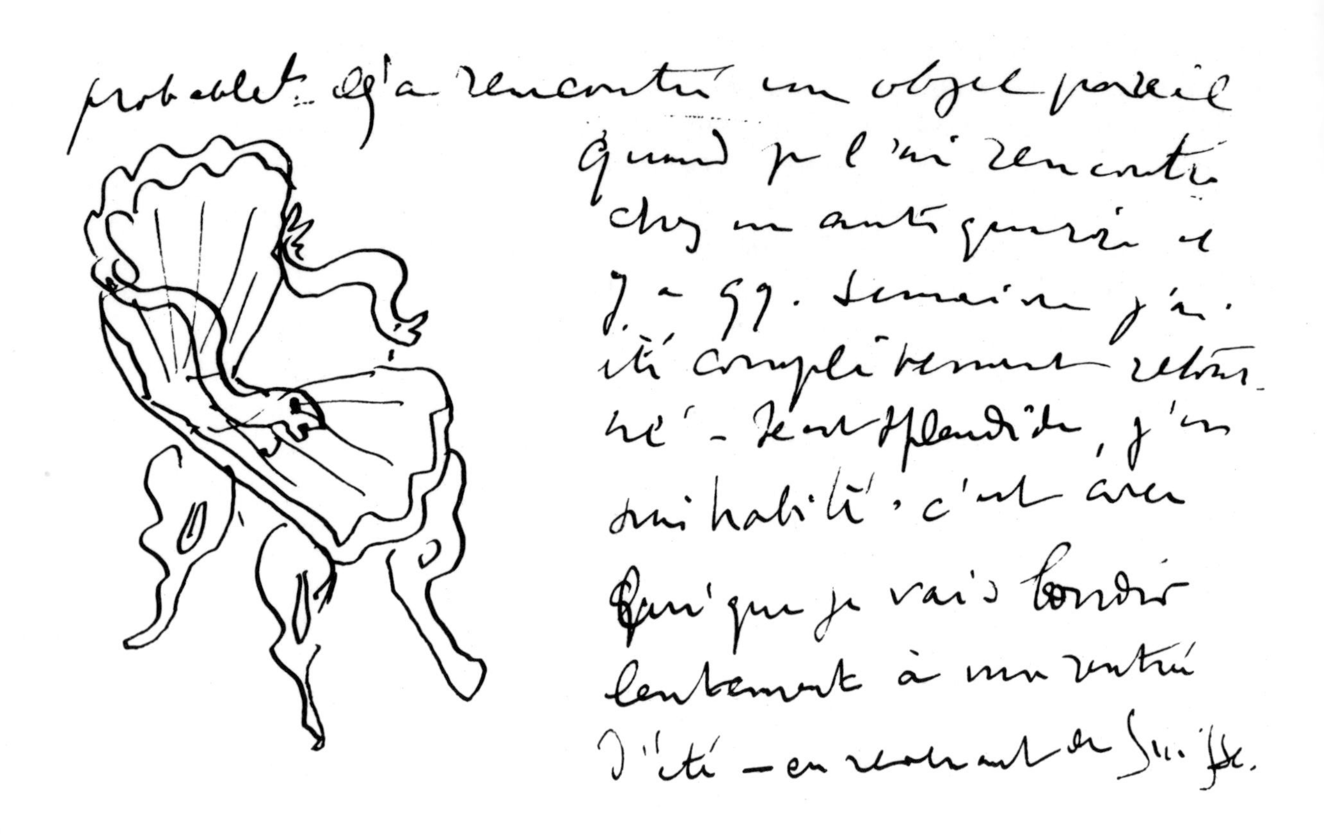
probablt. qu'a rencontré un objet pareil
quand je l'ai rencontré
chez un antiquaire il
y a qq. semaines j'ai
été complètement retourné - Il est splendide, j'en
suis habité. C'est avec
lui que je vais [illegible]
lentement à ma rentrée
d'été - en revenant de Suisse.

110. – Extract from letter from Henri Matisse to the author (20/4/42) with first sketch of the rococo armchair.

(Verso written only on the left half, the first line spreading a little beyond the fold. The blank right half allows the chair to show through):

If you think you'd like to say something about it, it would be as well for you to see it first. Whenever you like! Forgive this scribble. I got up for a moment today – I'm better for the first time, but tired.

Affectionate regards to you both.

H. Matisse

A sketch of the armchair accompanies the letter.

Any commentary would weaken this text. As may well be imagined, I rushed off to Cimiez. Actually, I knew the chair, having seen it at Nice in the window of an antique shop in the Rue Paradis, I think. It had caught my attention, because I had seen its double in Paris, at Lise Deharme's. But how can I describe with what precautions, with what theatrical preparations, Matisse showed me the armchair by which he had been 'quite bowled over'. And four years later, to help me to do this part of my book, Matisse gave me no less than eight photographs of this chair, not to mention one of an oil sketch, in ochre, 1942, for the painting which is the portrait of this armchair (spring 1946) and which shows it entirely filling the canvas with a small bunch of flowers in a glass standing on the seat. Clearly the romance was of long standing. The picture I saw recently at Matisse's home in the Boulevard Montparnasse* is for me one of the most mysterious paintings in the world, together with Uccello's *Battles*, La Tour's *Prisoner*, Watteau's *Gersaint's Shop Sign* and Renoir's *White Clown*. Almost the only painting I should like to live with (there are finer Matisses, perhaps, ones I like better, but I'm as happy looking at them in reproduction – the armchair is a different matter . . .)

*Matisse arrived in Paris on June 3, 1946. Which shows that this text, begun at Villeneuve in late September 1945, was written with interruptions and alterations.

The back and the seat of this armchair are shaped like big cockleshells joined at the sides by absolutely reptilian arms. In the lower left-hand corner of the picture you can see the tip of the front right leg of the chair, and the beginning of the front left leg. There is only a little space behind the armchair (lower right-hand corner) and above the right-hand reptile (at the top, on the left).

The creature is seen from above, and is placed in a somewhat feline attitude, complacently displaying the lower cockleshell on which the white flower stands in its vase. It is placed obliquely, as though on a slightly sloping plane following the diagonal that runs from the top left-hand corner to the lower right-hand corner of the canvas. I was going to say that its face is hidden, in other words that the top of the chair is outside the canvas, is cut off, if you like. It is extremely interesting to compare the portrait and its original, that is the creature interpreted by Matisse and the creature seen by the camera.

I have it in front of me, caught by the photographer in all sorts of familiar scenes: against a large patterned screen, seen full face between a bouquet of tall calla lilies in a metal pot standing on the ground and a hassock with a few flowers strewn in front of it on the tiled floor. Or else seen in profile, with its white rose in its bosom, in the glass, as in the picture, but somewhat lost in the same corner of the room between a small Oriental table on which there are some eggs and a cut glass on a tray, and a sculptor's stool with flowers in a pewter jug and a small tea-cup, in front of a marble table with metal legs on which you see some Venetian glass, a porcelain vase of fanciful style with three or four sprays of blossom, a Persian pot, and two large gourds: the whole thing underneath a Matisse painting, in front of a window, not far

XXVII. – Above: *Portrait of the Armchair* (oil, 1946): *It is extremely interesting to compare the portrait and its original . . .*

◀ 111. – The rococo armchair photographed at Vence in 1946.

XXVIII. – *The Armchair*, sketch (oil, 1942).

from the white marble mantelpiece. I have three more variations on this interior scene. In one of the photographs the armchair is closer to the screen, somewhat hidden by the calla lilies, and the foreground is taken up by the china pot *Le Tabac royal* which recurs in many of Matisse's drawings, standing on a piece of stuff. And the marble table is much more crowded, and the suspended picture, of which only a bit is seen, is a different Matisse. In another photograph the leading part is played by a Venetian table which is even more

112–118. – Photographs of the armchair in various poses (Vence, 1946). ▶

baroque than the chair, and which has robbed it of its glass and flowers; so that the chair seems to withdraw in some annoyance, as though embarrassed by the somewhat provincial exhibitionism of a member of its family. Elsewhere, we have a three-quarters view of the armchair, with nothing else but the Oriental table, the mantelpiece and the fabric of the screen; its flower in its lap. Here the chair is consciously posing, and wears a misleading air of discretion and distinction, which it drops completely on the next print, where the Venetian table, the bunch of calla lilies and itself are shown in a row in the same setting, like three acrobats taking a bow. And its true nature is revealed most clearly against the background of a quite different material patterned with stripes and flowers, forming a mural panel and spreading like a carpet under the chair-legs, between two reproduction antique chairs covered with Louis XV brocade, showing very little wood. We discover that our protagonist is smallish, which Matisse had unfairly concealed from us, and not

The Comedy of the Rococo Armchair (domestic scenes).

112.

113.

114.

115.

116.

at all as lyrical as we might have supposed. Between its two stalwart companions, it looks like a gigolo who has been caught by the cops. It's almost vulgar.

All this may seem futile, but I must explain myself: this armchair is Don Juan or at least Casanova de Seingalt. We have no photographs of these heroes of the imagination. I'll wager that if we could compare the disappointing reality with our romantic mental image of them, we should be

118. – Between its two stalwart companions, it looks like a gigolo who has been caught by the cops.

sadly shocked. Some little Mediterranean toughs, foppish and plump, with frizzed hair and swaggering walk; what a come-down after Byron or Musset:

Il est l'homme du siècle et l'étoile polaire . . .[1]

to this over-elaborate courtesan's chair. May Matisse forgive me! But one never appreciates one's friends' women, how should one fall in love with the same armchairs as they do?

What endures is the picture, the crazily dramatic quality of that picture, which is just an armchair, that particular armchair. And it's not because of the white rose in its buttonhole or at the corner of its lip . . . There were painters, some twenty-five or thirty years ago, who tried to convey metaphysical anguish through objects, and whose dangerous example has been followed. Let them look at this armchair, and admit defeat!

. . . One never appreciates one's friends' women . . . Laura, for instance: how eagerly men have sought for pictures of *Madonna Laura*, and look what they found! Not even charming, an irregular face, a colourless complexion, nothing to explain that sudden passion, that revelation at dawn in a church of a love such as only a young man of twenty-two can feel, in early spring . . .

I imagine this is the chief reason why some people have so doggedly refused to believe that Laure de Noves was the poet's Laura. Particularly one Velutello, who in 1520, a century and a half after Petrarch's death, travelled twice in the same year from Italy to Avignon to dethrone Laure de Noves and discover evidence to convict her of imposture and usurpation. Velutello insisted that the manuscript notes found in a copy of Virgil and other books belonging to Petrarch were forgeries, because they clearly indicated Laura's identity. The violence with which he accuses of senile incompetence the witnesses consulted at Avignon, the subtle arguments he brings to bear against any evidence in favour of Hugues de Sade's wife, to denounce her, but not to explain her, to explain that frenzy, that passion, those journeys. I myself see therein a certain physical resentment, the need to invent for himself a Laura (thirteen years old, as she was when she first met Petrarch. he must have been inclined that way) who did not thwart his fantasies, a Laura about whom he could, on his own account, whisper Petrarch's lines:

Ch'i non son forte ad aspettar la luce
Di questa donna, e non so fare schermi
Di luoghi tenebrosi, e d'ore tarde.[1]

Henri Matisse has told me in confidence that whenever an instinctive wish – unexplainable by any objective beauty – seized him to draw or paint a woman, it can be said that she always had one physical characteristic common to all the others that had similarly affected him: an exaggerated development of the base of the throat, a swelling in the thyroid region often accompanied by a certain degree of exophthalmia. As though an uncertainty of mood, a readiness to laugh and weep, were the specific factor in that characteristic which after all must be considered as a form of beauty, being beautiful to Matisse.* I don't know, since Petrarch has not told us, what it was in Laura that did not appeal to Velutello but that set her, for himself, above all other women. But it must have been some secret charm of the same kind, which eludes us.

* 'What complicates things,' Matisse says, 'is the attraction I've always felt towards Ingres's Mme de Senonnes . . . you know the *Mme de Senonnes* in the Nantes Museum? She, too, is . . . she's got rather . . .' And Matisse points to his throat, spreading his fingers to indicate enlargement. (*Note of 1946, omitted, reinserted in 1966*)

(This admission can be compared with a note in *Matisse-en-France*, p. 89, stressing the painter's predilection for thyroid curves in objects as well as in women. – *Addendum of 1968*)

If we consider the women Matisse has painted, they are not all of equally convincing beauty but they have a certain family likeness: as though the painter sought in them, as in Tahiti or Thule, merely the reflection of a certain thought that obsessed him, a certain colour of ideas, pursuing self-knowledge through them. I must confess that I find more variety among Matisse's armchairs than among his women, although in their case, too, there is a likeness which probably lies in the almost thyroid character of their curves. This is true in any case of the Venetian armchair, of the one at Ciboure (Second Empire–Louis XV) and of several others.

There's a contradiction here, however, that I cannot resolve: the baroque, twisted, reptilian elements in the model, which should correspond to something in Matisse, give rise to an art as remote as possible from the baroque, from any complication or distortion of line. As though Matisse chose his models from a feminine type which corresponds to himself, but which he controls and delights to control, to enslave. At least, this is how things seem to be. What a far-fetched idea, he will say to me. And yet this is the question suggested by the purest, the clearest, least turbid art ever born in France. And so much the worse for those who, seeing the photographs of the subjects of Matisse's reveries, grumble disappointedly: why can't they be content with the incomparable beauty the painter has extracted from them, like Laura's

1. I have not the strength to look at the light
Of this lady, nor can I shelter from it
In dark places and in late hours.

The Villeneuve MS. did not include the translation of these three lines.

119. – Sketch for *The Room at Ciboure* (drawing, 1940).

120.– Photograph of the Second Empire–Louis XV armchair (Ciboure).

beauty, like the sun that no one has the strength to look at or the skill to shelter from in dark places and in late hours!

The Room at Ciboure, in the Albi Museum, one of the paintings Matisse most frequently talked to me about,[1] is unquestionably the portrait of an armchair. This armchair had been one of the decisive factors that had won over the painter when, on opening the door, he had seen that room. The other factor was the landscape seen through the window, the garden of his neighbour, M. Masson. I have before me a sketch, a drawing for that picture. The Second Empire–Louis XV armchair stands in the foreground, under the open window, against the wall, and, as a note by Matisse at the bottom of the drawing points out, *on the right, the looking-glass in which I can be seen painting.*

1. See above, in *To be inserted*, p. 28, the reproduction of this painting.

This first grouping shows what had fascinated the painter (as for the garden, there is another sketch showing only the open window, with the caption: *Ciboure – my window opening on to Masson's garden, Mme Masson on the ladder*). In the Albi picture, the window is on the left, the armchair seen almost full face, its back against the far wall, between the open window and the corner of the mantelpiece with its vase of flowers, and a picture hanging above it. In the foreground (like the *Tabac royal* in the other photograph) the dark surface of a pedestal table. The armchair, thus placed, in *its* room, looks out at the garden, *its* landscape. This sums up, by the most disconcertingly simple means, what surprised Matisse when he first visited the Ciboure house: the atmosphere of the room, the links between the room and the Massons' garden, *a certain light of ideas*,* human life present and yet absent (the armchair). Not so much a way of living as a way of dreaming, perhaps . . . and yet a way of living, that takes shape here. Nothing strange, and yet strangeness pervades the picture: the strangeness of choice, the passionate interest taken by Matisse in this room, this window, this armchair. Only some deep-seated correspondence between himself and this place can explain the enthusiasm that seized and held him when he opened the door and caught the room, the armchair, *unawares*. He rented the house, he lived here, he worked here in order to *say* this: the Albi painting. A secret, given permanence. Exactly what that secret consists in, words cannot express. But the picture can. It's Thule, yet again. By means which are those of painting, Matisse expresses a feeling which could not be expressed otherwise; and since he is a painter, this is a step forward in the knowledge of himself, of what he is searching for. In brief, it is a door opening on to Matisse's world.

* Matisse said *a certain colour* . . .

I look at the photograph of the Second Empire–Louis XV armchair at Ciboure. Yes, that's it, one is tempted to say that it's a lifelike portrait. But in the photograph, this armchair which is Baudelaire's contemporary has the look of a portrait by Nadar, which it loses in the painting (owing not only to the gilt nails and the play of light on the turned wood of the legs and arms, which Matisse spares us, but to the armchair's posture in the photograph: here it is an object in a catalogue, in the painting it is a chair involved with the life of someone who has only just left it, still at the angle given it by the man as he got up, and it exists in terms of all the rest, room, mantelpiece, window, garden). The armchair poses, watching the black cloth over the camera. It might have been placed differently. It is like a man being measured by an anthropometrist. In the painting, on the contrary, it could not possibly be swung round, it's in its place, and if you imagine it for one instant facing a different way everything collapses, everything becomes dislocated in this composition where, from the mantelpiece to the window and from the table to the hanging picture, everything implies that the armchair is the node of forces that balance one another, the point of intersection of the architectural lines of this peace.

I have, too, photographs of a Voltaire-style seat, à la Balzac, two Louis XV easy chairs, broad and low, one striped, the other in plain velvet, and some armchairs, one of wood, the other of wood and stretched leather, on either side of their little sister, a small sixteenth-century chair; all these have appeared somewhere or other in Matisse's drawings or paintings. In the

. . . a Voltaire-style seat, à la Balzac . . .
◀ 121. – Photograph of the second armchair, in the room where Matisse worked at Ciboure.

It is this easy chair that appears in the drawing that takes up two pages of the catalogue of the exhibition of drawings shown Nov. 10–30, 1941, at the Galerie Louis Carré. ▼

122. – Two Louis XV easy chairs . . . (Vence, 1946).

123. – Matisse's 'antique chairs' . . . (Vence, 1946).

photographs they are no more than actors who have forgotten the lines of the play. I am not quite sure that they were all chosen for their own sakes; perhaps their virtue lay in forcing the woman who sat down there to keep very upright in some cases, to lean back in others. These photographs are quite recent, they were taken at Vence (I recognize the floor-tiles), they bear witness not to Matisse's awareness of what armchairs mean to him but to his willingness to join in a game of labelling and enumerating which he had not invented . . .

We should study the contents of his warehouse of props.* We should question the painter as to the accidents that brought them together, the reveries that led to their selection. I don't mean only the armchairs. It requires no great subtlety, nor any outstanding faculty of observation, to perceive a certain unity in that world of Matisse's of which I spoke. A unity within the mind that convened these disparate objects, whose kinship is more mysterious than any of them taken separately. The key to this world is what I am searching for. And I stand here, turning over and over a whole treasury of pictures,

*This remark dates the writing of this page: it must correspond to a letter of mine to H.M., asking for photographs which would include the chief article in the 'palette of objects', to which he replied from Vence, 4/5/46:

My dear friend, I am collecting the various photos asked for in the list you made four years ago, referring to the palette of objects . . .

. . . I am leaving Vence in a few weeks, so please answer me as soon as possible, since anything left here will be out of reach from Paris . . .

On May 16 he added:

Dear Louis Aragon, I have made a complete collection of the 'palette of objects' for you. You'll be satisfied . . .

those created by Matisse and those that correspond to them in the real world, index cards in a strange system of identification, photographs which are all that I can know about these objects without Matisse: let's compare them, and try to understand, in his absence, the nature of this man, this light, this *colour of ideas* which he sheds on things as they are.

When Rinaldo, who has not heard his own story countless times as we have, goes forward into the enchanted gardens, he is overwhelmed by the beauty of the flowers which are, perhaps, persicaria, amaranth, cinnamon, artemisia, amaryllis, and of the trees, apricot, buckthorn, cypress, laburnum, dwarf oak or vanilla plant, but he cannot recognize them, or that harmonious wandering voice that precedes him and leads him on: and who is to tell him that his joy and his misfortune are called Armida?

He would be arriving, he told me, on June 3. Further details in a note of July 12, brought by L.D. with a packet of photographs:

Dear Louis Aragon, I am sending you 136 different photos for the book you are doing for Skira. If you need it I could get the photo of a painting I did in 1915, 'The Pewter Jug'. You can choose photos of the aviary full of birds from Brassaï. I could not find all the photos on your list. I am writing for one from Nice which I should have in a few days.

This is, I believe, the first mention of the book provisionally commissioned by Skira, and which, after twenty-two years, has become this book. The result of what he had sent me was those parts of *La Grande Songerie* which deal with the palette of objects, and the marginal notes to the drawings of 'that very beautiful black woman' at Vence, and also of two other coloured women, one Madagascan and one of mixed blood from the Congo, probably in Paris. Consequently it must have been in the summer of 1946 that I finished *La Grande Songerie*, i.e. when Matisse was in Paris. (*Note of 1968*)

The Garden of Armida.
125. – The perforated blinds.

124. – The aviary . . .

As he wanders through these gardens, the hero is first of all amazed at their solitude, at the delicious wilderness where no footstep seems ever to have trod the soft sands, no breath disturbed the shady shelter of the branches. This world opens up before Rinaldo, he does not know how nor why. He had performed the most commonplace of actions: he had merely pressed the doorbell, and had found himself in Henri Matisse's home at Cimiez. Armida is invisible, and he goes through rooms where each object, each piece of furniture, every hanging corresponds to a dream. He finds himself in a room entirely overrun by green plants whose Greek or Saracen names I should like to tell: the very sunlight is filtered through the leaves as though the mysterious patterning of the latticed blinds hanging in the next room were repeated in front of these windows. He finds himself amidst huge cages of fluttering birds, of doves, of ferns as delicate as a shiver, of grasses more wayward than thought; and in earthenware pots of assorted sizes, plants that look

126. – Matisse in Armida's garden . . . only we are in Vence, where nothing has changed (1946).

like those we know well but, examined closely, prove different; and on the marble flagging where all these stand among tables, rulers, squares, sheets of blank paper, a few terra-cotta objects, gourds with crackled rinds and flavourless fruits of various sorts, Rinaldo has the feeling that he alone is out of place here, like one who penetrates another man's consciousness and, without grasping its laws, guesses at its singular coherence. Armida or Matisse. For nearly five years now I have been wandering through these enchanted gardens.

Scarcely anything changes when he moves house. At Vence, in a dwelling far less stately than the Régina at Cimiez,[1] his world took shape once more through the accumulation of objects, fresh flowers and cooing birds, and it gave on to a real garden, a garden like any other. I recognize over this window the perforated Arabian blind that sheds over these diverse accessories the light of an Eastern harem. For indeed this is a harem of forms and colours, and Matisse, pale-skinned and neat-bearded, in his light-coloured hat and whitish clothes, with nothing dark about him but the shadows of the flowers, is the sultan of this world full of fluttering pigeons. On a wide table there stands a tray crowded with vases and glasses, each seeming the suggestion of a still life, filled with a bewildering diversity of flowers: on what will he fix his gaze, this solitary man who shows by the pictures hanging on the walls that he is the master, here, of order and wisdom?

The choice and assembling of all this is the work of a single mind. If I try to enumerate the perfect things brought together by his will, I feel a little dizzy. One expects to find in a painter's home the combined elements of one, or two, or ten pictures, with the possible combinations they suggest: one does not expect to find the crowded figures from a thousand operas, a whole forest of props, wonders accumulated through the years and grouped haphazard, in case the wise man in his pale clothes – alone and unsmiling – should mentally reach out for this glass, that piece of pottery. Here I suddenly understood the infinite complexity of the painter's temptations. For one moment, I seem to glimpse a vast novel* peopled by more characters than any Odyssey, in the life of this solitary man, in a silence broken only by the cooing of birds and the flutter of their wings.

* Now my secret is out! The word 'novel' was written here in all innocence, before I had any intention of presenting this incomplete book as a work of the imagination – not my own but the painter's. (*1970*)

Yes, here I surprise Henri Matisse in his dream world, his *grande songerie*, where however everything is real, everything is tangible and visible like the mystery of being. A day-dream whose stages are here before me, standing on saucers, on the edge of the mantelpiece or on chairs. A materialized

1. It was in June 1943 that H.M. rented the house at Vence, where he came to live. Obviously, this piece cannot have been written all at one go with the beginning, which I showed the painter on my first visit to the Villa Le Rêve in 1945.

day-dream, where suddenly Matisse lifts those eyelids that had seemed so heavy and turns transparent eyes on me, or maybe on some Chinese jar.

(When you look at a man's photograph it is sometimes like seeing yourself in a glass with an unfamiliar face: the strange thing, sometimes, is that one does not see one's own eyes.)

La Grande Songerie (The Storehouse of Dreams) . . . I should like to explain this expression, which cannot be confined to the usual sense of the words. The word *songerie*, which means merely a drifting series of thoughts, may have been finally included in the Dictionary of the Academy, but although it is to be found in ancient texts, it did not appear in 1862 in the *Vocabulaire de la langue française extrait de la sixième et dernière édition du Dictionnaire de l'Académie* by Charles Nodier and Ackermann.* The word has been formed on the analogy of *rêverie*, which has long had its letters-patent, and which was then defined by Nodier as: *the state of mind preoccupied by vague ideas and the pleasant or unhappy thoughts indulged in by the imagination – an extravagant or chimerical idea. – Delirium due to illness or the effect of such delirium.* Note that he also defines *rêve* by the word *songe*, and we are thus entitled to consider *rêverie* and *songerie* as synonymous. But in the latter word we hear the echo of a whole series of other French words, *tuilerie*, *orangerie*, which mean the places where orange trees are kept or tiles made, *menuiserie* which is at once the art of the *menuisier* or joiner, the product of that art and the place where it is practised, *gendarmerie* both the company of *gendarmes* and their quarters, and so forth: why should not *songerie* mean both the place where the *songe*, the dream, takes place and the materials it uses? I mean Cimiez or Vence, when I say that I surprised Matisse in his *grande songerie*. You can gather from this that I ascribe to dreams a material character which they would lack if they were only 'a state of mind preoccupied with vague ideas', pleasant or unhappy thoughts, chimerical ideas, delirium or its products. For tiles are stacked in the *tuilerie* and orange trees kept in the *orangerie*, and in the *songerie* I am speaking of, dreams are very far from being chimerical, they are the objects amidst which the dreamer walks about, touching and seeing them, and which moreover you and I, having entered the realm of this new Armida, can touch and see, real dreams, not those of a poet or a novelist but a painter's, to which, when the painter's invisible dream has taken shape as a drawing or a picture, we can compare that invisible dream. As I do when I compare the thing in the painting with the thing in the photograph.

And in this way, by this comparison, we can go forward in the discovery of man's nature, as Petrarch did on his return from Thule; or into the gardens of Armida, surprised at last at her task of fashioning dreams . . .

* It did not appear, either, in the original *Littré*. It was not until 1877 that it was defined there as: *s.f. State of one who indulges in day-dreams* . . . (illustrated by an example from the *Revue des Deux-Mondes* of October 1869, signed André Theuriet: *Cette musique berçait si bien ma songerie* (this music lulled my day-dreams so aptly . . .). Even today the word is only defined, in French and as far as I know in foreign dictionaries, in the sense of day-dream, vague reverie (the English *brown study*). (*Note of 1967*)

Sunday April '42 (4.30 a.m.)*
My dear friend,

You sat for me like an angel, and yet you were forever eluding me. Behind the screen formed by your interest in my doings I could only guess at you. May I ask you next time to withdraw into yourself, so that I can watch a private Aragon.

You need only let your thoughts dwell on some favourable subject. In hopes of gaining access to an Aragon who is alone at last.

Affectionately yours, *Henri Matisse*

* Sunday the 5th? In that case the sitting referred to must have been on April 4.

127. – *Aragon*, pen-and-ink drawing (1942, mistakenly dated 1943 by the artist, like the whole series of portraits of the author). This drawing was made on Monday, April 6 (see next page, commentary on drawings made that day).

And in the margin of the letter he had added:

> *The heart's passion is revealed in the face.*
> *The face does not lie: it is the heart's mirror.*

So it was my turn now. If I had tried to catch Matisse in his *songerie*, he had wanted to see me in mine. The fact is that each of us was at grips with the portrait of the other. So that on the April Monday that followed this note, the result of his night thoughts, Henri Matisse asked me to think *about politics*, which was of all things the remotest from himself. There were terrible reasons at that time which made this easy for me. I was expecting a friend who was never to come again. What strikes me about the drawings that Matisse did that day is the youthful look, my youth restored to me. The heart's passion . . .

I was an object then, like those green plants, shells, armchairs, gourds and vases in his *songerie*. An object with a terrible longing to watch the draughtsman's hand. Sitting alarmingly close, an arm's length away, I saw Matisse's pencil start off, take flight and pounce, the drawing completed at one sweep. I have found a paper on which he had scribbled after reading the manuscript of *Matisse-en-France*, and which is headed:

Continuation of the marginal note on p. 23 – do what you like with it.

I'll copy it out:

When I make my drawings – 'Variations' – the path traced by my pencil on the sheet of paper is, to some extent, analogous to the gesture of a man groping his way in the darkness. I mean that there is nothing foreseen about my path: I am led. I do not lead.[1] *I go from one point in the thing which is my model to another point which I always see in isolation, independent of the other points towards which my pen will subsequently move. I am simply guided by an interior impulse which I translate as it takes shape, rather than by the exterior on which my eyes are fixed yet which has no more importance for me than a feeble*[2] *glimmer in the darkness, towards which I have to make my way first – and then, having reached it, I perceive another gleam towards which I shall move, constantly inventing my way thither. The way is so interesting, isn't it the most interesting part of the performance?*

Just as the spider[3] *throws out (or fastens?) its thread to some convenient protuberance and thence to another that it perceives, and from one point to another weaves its web.*

As for the way I draw my studies, my 'Themes', my action has not yet appeared so clearly to me, because it is far more complex and very deliberate. This 'deliberateness' is a serious obstacle to the perception of what is most important – because it prevents instinct from emerging unmistakably.

We must leave the responsibility for his concept to Matisse. Apart from any comparative value judgment as to what is 'very' deliberate and what is less so, it implies the existence of two procedures in drawing, and thus of two cate-

1. Here a deletion, the words *Just as the spider* . . . crossed out.
2. Matisse had written *vague* but had crossed it out.
3. *Ronsard calls it arachnée*, crossed out.

gories of drawing. My portrait as frontispiece to *Brocéliande*[1] belongs indubitably to the second category, those 'Themes' in which the action is 'very deliberate'. Several 'very deliberate' drawings, one made at each sitting, have thus given rise to other drawings where the line is simple, drawings of the 'Variations' type where instinct takes precedence over will. It is a strange experience to feel oneself of no more importance to the man in front of you, with his eyes fixed on you, than a feeble glimmer in the darkness towards which . . . etc. I have yet another note in Matisse's hand, slightly earlier than the previous one (bearing in the corner the date 17–18/3/42), which says:

Sheltering behind my irresponsibility, I love these drawings, I study them; I seek from them revelations about myself. I consider them as materializations of my feeling.

After *materializations*, Matisse had inserted *for the creation of myself*, deleting it again and substituting *to shed light on my path.*

Here again, as ever, we see the return from Thule. What did Petrarch remember of it, what did he learn there, having seen nothing of England but steep cliffs, dark waves, a soil where nothing grows and where vines are unknown . . . What did he get from it save what he discovered about himself in the Orkneys? What does Matisse hope to retain from this unimportant *exterior* which may be the tobacco jar or your servant? *I seek from them revelations about myself* . . . And Petrarch: *I shall rest content with knowing myself.*

On the same sheet of paper (March 17–18, 1942) there is a separate note:

People never believe me when I say I have made some slight progress – they laugh. My progress, I consider I have made some progress when I note in my work an increasingly evident independence from the support of the model. I should like to do without it completely one day – I don't expect to, because I haven't adequately trained myself to remember forms. Shall I still need forms? It's more a question of triumphing over one's dizziness during flight. I know well enough how a human body is made. A flower – if I don't find it† in my memory I shall make it up.*

* *a man*, crossed out.

† Matisse had written *trouve*, in the present. He added above it the future ending: *trouverai*.

This text has a twofold value. For one thing, it reveals the hope contained in Matisse's great experiment in draughtsmanship in 1942, which produced *Thèmes et Variations*: the hope of doing without the support of the model. Note that Matisse does not say 'doing without a model'; the model as starting-point is a principle which he never calls in question. But starting from the model, he considers it a sign of progress to do without its *support*, and to triumph over dizziness during flight (that is, while he is drawing).‡

‡ In the margin of this and the following paragraph H.M. adds a note to my text: *The model is a springboard for me – it's a door which I must break down to reach the garden in which I am alone and so happy – even the model exists only for the use I can make of it.*

The second thing which is here implied seems to contradict the first: Matisse admits that he cannot do without a model because he has not adequately trained himself to remember forms, and if he speaks of making up

1. Reproduced on p. 171 of this volume.

a flower he does not mean a fantastic flower but one such as memory shows him.

Thus that *exterior* which is for him merely a faint glimmer in the darkness, and yet a starting-point and a guide while he is drawing, none the less supplies the painter with the object as he remembers it, the real object, which he has studied (*I know well enough how a human body is made*), which he rediscovers, so to speak, while he draws. We are far from that instinctive drawing which, from an isolated phrase, one might suppose to be the ideal aimed at by Matisse. What is involved is the means of expression (*it's a question of triumphing over one's dizziness during flight*), not the thing expressed. What Matisse expresses is a part of nature, of nature and of himself, the painter, of course, nature as seen by him: the purpose of his invention is not to forget nature but to see it.

There is a third passage in that letter of 17–18/3/42, separated by a dash from the preceding one:

While I am working at my inspired[1] *drawings, if my model asks me the time and I pay attention, I'm done for, the drawing is done for. When I am working differently, at my studies, I can carry on a conversation on a more or less cloudy level which is unconnected with the work I'm doing – But here, if I am asked the time I come out of a different world.*[2]

The distinction is clearly made: for Matisse there are study-drawings and inspired drawings. Themes and Variations. And we can deduce from this, taking into account his admission that he does not expect to do without the support of the model* because *I have not adequately trained myself to remember forms,*† that the *theme* is a study the aim of which is to cultivate the memory of a particular model's form, so as to allow Henri Matisse, when he then turns to inspired drawing, in a series of *variations*, without interrupting his line by constant reference to the model, to provide an image of that model in which memory, being still fresh, precludes any fumbling. Here, clearly, we are dealing with an entirely different sort of inspiration, of instinct, from the instinct and inspiration extolled by recent poetic schools which base their discoveries on the processes of the subconscious, on the unity of dream and reality, of reason and madness. And it must be obvious why I have intentionally given a wholly material sense to the word *songerie*, why I stress the existence of that jug of flowers, that armchair, that pan or tobacco jar about which Matisse is going to tell us. This is why, side by side with a painting, I want to show the photograph of its elements.

* Pencil note by H.M. in the margin beside *to do without the model* (rubbed out and rewritten in ink by himself): *the presence of the model [which] counts not as a potential source of information about its make-up, but to keep me in an emotional state, like a kind of flirtation which ends in a rape. Rape of what? Of myself, of a certain emotional involvement with the object that appeals to me.*

† Another pencil note by H.M., traced over in ink, in the margin above the previous one: *what an illusion I should have written – I have not, in order to do without the support of the model, meditated recently in front of similar objects – objects of the same order – what I call doing the theme.*

1. *Instantaneous*, crossed out.

2. In the margin of his own text H.M. has put a question mark before *I come out of a different world*, underlined in pencil

XXIX. – *Le Tabac royal* (1943).

128. – Photograph of the elements of *Le Tabac royal* (taken in 1946 at Vence, at my request. A.). ▶

And to be sure, some of Petrarch's contemporaries and even some of his friends, reading his poems, cast doubt on the very existence of Laura. Giacomo Colonna, Bishop of Lombez, accuses the poet of having invented her as a pretext for verses which would win him the laurels. Petrarch answers him: *What are you insinuating? That I have made up this specious name of Laura so that I might have someone of whom to speak, and on whose account many would speak of me; but that in fact I know no other Laura but the poet's laurel wreath, to which I aspire, as my long and untiring studies bear witness; that the living Laura whose beauty seems to have seduced me is my own creation, like these feigned verses, these simulated signs. Would to heaven that your mockery were justified on this point, and that my frenzy were feigned and not real.'* [1] . . .

Even when Matisse is absorbed in his inspired drawings, his inspiration is never derived from a purely imaginative, abstract thought, detached from the world and from memory. There is always a Laura. There is always something real in his heart. And although he may go to the ends of the earth, to Tahiti, to seek oblivion of reality, he will return from this quest for Thule knowing that even in those Islands* one can only draw an armchair, encountering afresh that perpetual Laura, the model, theme and study, without which there would be no variations, no inspired drawings.

*Note by H.M. written directly in ink, probably on a second reading, after going over in ink the previous notes which had first been made in pencil: after my words *knowing that even in those Islands*, Matisse adds: *one may need to collect oneself in front of an armchair since one cannot do so directly – the superabundance – the vast scale and total newness of the natural scene – it is one's loving admiration transferred to a familiar object that makes this object interesting enough to take the overflow of a heart.* (For *overflow* (*trop-plein*) Matisse had first written *impulse* (*élan*), but crossed this out, then after *of a heart* had crossed out *brimming over* (*débordant*), possibly added between the first draft and the final version, as well as the words *full of emotion, with emotion*, omitted from his sentence.)

And yet what if Laura had never existed? What if she were only the fruit of an imagination which can do without the support of the model, a sheer invention of Petrarch's, the Dulcinea of another Don Quixote? But after all there was an original for Dulcinea, a peasant girl whom the fanciful Hidalgo saw with different eyes from other men, beautifying and ennobling her. Don Quixote had this springboard, this starting-point in a model, and he was the very type of the mind that triumphs over dizziness during flight. They seek to deny even this to Petrarch, making him out to be the author of a lifelong hoax. They disregard the letter to Giacomo Colonna that I quoted above, where he says, furthermore: . . . *but believe me, nobody can sham all day without taking immense pains. And to take such pains gratuitously, in order to be held mad, would be supreme madness. Added to which, we can imitate sickness by cunningly calculated attitudes, but not true pallor. You, however, know my pallor and my pain . . .*

If Laura never existed, Petrarch was certainly the most vicious impostor mankind has ever produced; and nothing entitles us to imagine that abyss formed by the absence, worse than absence, the non-existence, of the beloved. Serious historians reject the hypothesis of such perversity, and it must be con-

1. December 1334.

sidered as a calumny of human nature, the fantasy of unbalanced minds always ready to ascribe to genius their own stagnant impotence. I ask you, what would Petrarch's loveliest verse be if Laura had not existed, if Laura were not its *circumstance?* Pure poetry, as they say nowadays to excuse a lie: no, revolting affectation! I'll say more: it would no longer be beautiful, it would be *impure*.

And perhaps if we had the photograph of Laure de Noves, we might find that Petrarch's image of that lady is not a good likeness; that, starting from this model, the song bird has flown off very deliberately, and that within the usual meaning of realism he suffered very little dizziness . . . none the less he sings of an authentic love, a real Laura, and therein lies the value of his song. He has explained himself, once and for all, regarding his picture of her, which you may have criticized:[1]

Ivi è'l mio cor, e quella chè'l m'involа:
Qui veder puoi l'imagine mia sola.

(*Yonder is my heart, and she who stole it from me: here I can see only my own image of her.*)

Of course, it is Matisse speaking: and it is a Venetian armchair, or a branch of ivy with its roots, or a little pewter jug, or a piece of flowered material that has stolen his heart.

Since we are in Armida's garden, in Matisse's world, the time has come to note a fact and make a comparison: this world is peopled with elements deliberately chosen for their individual beauty, for their shape above all, like that curve of a woman's throat, and with objects which already bear the mark of man's workmanship and his desire to attain beauty.*

There are two sorts of painters: some make beauty out of anything, they pick up common, shapeless, humble things and transform them, ensuring for them acceptance into that higher life of art and poetry. They are those who first thought of making an apple, or later a packet of tobacco, into the hero of a picture. But the others . . . the others choose, from among all glasses, one that is perfect, or cut like a diamond, a goblet of purer shape . . . they surround themselves with key-objects from that higher world, they re-create that higher world starting from the results of other men's dreams, they carry on that upward effort of mankind's . . .

1. Canzone 17.

* The curve of a woman's throat . . . All his life Matisse chose as models women with this swelling curve to the throat. In this choice, yet again, where we recognize the obsession with Mme de Senonnes as Ingres saw her, woman is not a simple, natural object but one already elaborated by man.

I leave these successive notes incomplete, intending to return to them in a separate article. (*1967*)

I have waited until 1969 to say something which, owing to Matisse as well as to myself, echoes throughout this book like some imperious (and to me irritating) reminder. I repeat myself, no doubt, cf. text and note supra (p. 223), but I beg to be allowed to do in writing what is quite usual for musicians. (*1970*)

Let who will give preference to one or the other sort, I make no choice. The means differ but not the goal. Matisse has brought the second method to a dizzy pitch of perfection. This is why the exclusive supporters of the first method, those who change mud into gold, those whom I might call the alchemists of modern beauty, tend to accuse Matisse of being a painter of luxury in a world where poverty exists. And this indeed he is.* And of well-being in a world where suffering exists. And of light in a world corroded by darkness. He is all this. One must accept the notion that Matisse paints to make things more beautiful. I don't say that this is the only reason for painting. But it is one reason for painting. I noted this remark of his, as I was observing that the older he grew and the more his health declined, the more luminous and happy his painting became: *It's in self-defence.* I repeat this, and also that nobody could be further from existentialism than Henri Matisse. This cannot and must not be understood as a hostile attitude to realism, which I have never shown. But I prefer those who make things more beautiful to those who make them uglier (this does not refer to painters of the first sort, who also confer beauty, or rather nobility, on what they paint), that's all. And I find it thrilling that Matisse should have been, and should remain, at the apex of his life's work, the painter of perpetual hope.†

To make myself understood I would refer the reader to a painting of Matisse's which illustrates and illuminates in a special way what I am saying. It is that very simple still life, a vase of flowers and some fruit, on the edge of a fireplace of rose-coloured bricks,[1] against a background of the same pink as the table but decorated with great fleurs-de-lis that seem drawn in Indian ink. I was discussing the mystery of the picture based on the Venetian armchair.[2] Here is a second example of that sort of mystery. It is almost impossible to say in words what makes the beauty of such a composition. One of the most extraordinarily successful achievements of painting, the most elusive and yet assured. There are three stages in this story: Jean Fouquet's *Procès de Vendôme en 1458*, Chardin's white-on-white *Still Life*, and Henri Matisse's *Still Life with Fleurs-de-lis.*[3] This is the history of French painting, I might almost say the history of France.

There's no doubt that this picture resulted from the preoccupations that haunted Matisse when he was thinking of illustrating the poetry of Charles

*I find here a note by Matisse, pencilled in as he read and then gone over in ink. If the reader refers to *In Defence of Luxury*, infra, which I had given H.M. to read as soon as I had written it, I think in January '46, he will see that Matisse actually forestalls Mr Barr's criticism by some eight years, writing this, for my benefit, on the idea of luxury:

My luxury? Is it not communicable, being something more precious than wealth, within everyone's reach – a certain quality of love is what gives it, it means dressing or undressing the woman one loves in all the purity of one's love, without affectation or exaggeration.

The reader must forgive me: this note should perhaps have been inserted, not here, but as a postcript to *In Defence of Luxury*. True; only it was here that Matisse wrote it. I apologize for the back and forth that this implies, but this book cannot be read like other books: you have to keep interrupting yourself, turning the pages, seeking as it were a reflection of what you have read somewhere else.

† The foregoing must not be taken for a defence of what the Russians call *lakirovka*, the varnishing or lacquering of reality. I wrote it in perfect innocence: I only saw that what Matisse painted was beautiful, not to please those in power, subserviently, but for himself, with that profound goodness which chooses where to shed its light for posterity. Matisse does not flatter: he sees beauty. In that sense, it is real. (*Note of 1967*)

1. With a mantelpiece of beige marble. The fireplace was designed by Matisse himself. The rose-coloured background is burlap. This is the picture known as *Lemons against a Fleur-de-Lis Background* (1943).

2. See supra, *Matisse-en-France* (p. 92), in a last-minute marginal note, and in the present article pp. 233–44.

3. March 1943. I only saw this painting at Vence in the autumn of 1945.

. . . France in the days of her humiliation, when Matisse was painting that French marvel . . .

XXX. – *Lemons against a Fleur-de-Lis Background* (1943).

d'Orléans. He had not yet finished his Ronsard, he was about to undertake a Baudelaire, and he let himself be seduced by Charles d'Orléans. I saw him during this period. He worked at it with his customary frenzy, and only the inadequacy of modern technique still debars us, today, from knowing this experiment of Matisse's.

(*I had written, at first* – he worked at it with his customary frenzy and then gave it up, it was a failure . . . *Henri Matisse, when he read my typescript, crossed out the words* 'gave it up' *in pencil, and wrote above them in ink:* simply postponed, *referring to the word* 'experiment', *adding this note in the margin to explain the painting I love so much:* it is the happy interpretation of a feeling of love, a hallucination in front of certain objects. This hallucination, obviously, is love itself – its eloquence springs from the sincerity with which the emotion is expressed – from the bringing together of the object, its reflection, and the painter's abilities (see Maupassant's Preface to *Pierre et Jean*).

And beside the words 'it was a failure', *in pencil:*

The illustrations have been completely finished for a long time. Draeger has already done a lot of work on the reproduction of them. But the various proofs have been unsatisfactory, for the colours needed and their relationships are too subtle. I am looking for a method to convey them without too much loss.

I have therefore corrected my text in view of these remarks. The Charles d'Orléans *was to appear later – that book which had given rise to the picture I have described, which sums up and yet goes beyond the whole tradition of French painting.*)

It takes great boldness to introduce into painting any object which has never before been depicted, if it's a common one, as for instance the pear was to Hugo's predecessors, who would never have admitted it into poetry save as 'a long golden fruit'. It takes an equal boldness nowadays to scatter great fleurs-de-lis on the background of a still life. The fleur-de-lys* is a conventional sign, the idealization of those spear heads which the Kings of the Second Dynasty bore on their standards to indicate the troops under their command: by some devious verbal transition, from *fers de lance* they became *fleurs de lis* or *lys*, making of one of nature's purest floral inventions the symbol of France. Royalty, nowadays, has no more to do with it than with the rest of the things that made us dream of France, in the days of her humiliation, when Matisse was painting that French marvel. It isn't possible to look at this

* Here's a spelling problem. I had written, correctly, *fleur de lis*, then a *y* intervened. There's a tendency nowadays to Hellenize this flower's name, both for heraldry and for botany. Is it ignorance, error or snobbery? The Greek letter appears in some ancient texts, and there's no proof that the copyist was responsible. Myself, I prefer the simpler form *lis* in its original purity, like a well-washed face. *Lys* flourished, however, in Symbolist poetry, where it took on and retained the descriptive aspect which the likeness of the typographical sign bestowed on it. I therefore leave, here, its Pre-Raphaelitish spelling, which undoubtedly future reformers (whose axing of French writing I somewhat dread) will strip of those drooping petals. It strikes me that the dual use of *lis* and *lys*, none the less, with skilful handling, allows one to say different things. I can't help it; I consider the signs made by Matisse[1] in Indian ink on the pink wall as *y*'s on wallpaper. This may contravene taste and reason. But dreamers don't care about taste or reason!

1. Matisse had, moreover, written: *Nature-morte aux citrons, fond fleurdelysé* . . . with a *y*.

129. – *Portrait of Charles d'Orléans*, sepia

Henri Matisse 3/43

picture without remembering the date when it was painted, without understanding how, in his own way, through the medium of painting, Matisse uttered his own protest, or rather his assertion of French hopes. Moreover, did not Charles d'Orléans signify primarily poetry's captivity, France's exile, a whole set of associated feelings which several of us, at Nice at that time, felt in different but analogous ways? I don't know how far Matisse was conscious of this when he chose to illustrate Charles d'Orléans: the result has been this painting, this magnificent thing, this calm assertion of French principles.*

There is so much we could find in Armida's garden!

Voltaire's poetry has been unfairly condemned: and although the boy Musset, yielding to fashion and the prevalent social taste, showered abuse on him in *Rolla*, I doubt whether *Les Nuits* would have been written without Voltaire:

> . . . *Ainsi le dieu des bois enflait ses chalumeaux:*
> *Quand le voleur Cacus enlevait nos troupeaux,*
> *Il n'interrompit point sa douce mélodie.*
> *Heureux qui, jusqu'au temps du terme de sa vie,*
> *Des beaux-arts amoureux, peut cultiver leurs fruits.*
> *Il brave l'injustice, il calme ses ennuis,*
> *Il pardonne aux humains, il rit de leur délire,*
> *Et de sa main mourante il touche encor sa lyre* . . .

But to tell the truth (that last line will serve to explain the hidden kinship I suggested) I am not the man to rehabilitate Voltaire. What recalled the passage to me was the distich:

> . . . *Quand le voleur Cacus enlevait nos troupeaux,*
> *Il n'interrompit point sa douce mélodie* . . .

which seems a natural commentary on the *Lemons against a Fleur-de-Lis Background*. And also that youthful serenity of old age here described, never better exemplified than in Henri Matisse.

The chief impression made by this extraordinary man on anyone seeing him at Cimiez, at Vence, or last year in Paris, is astonishment and admiration at that ceaseless flow of ideas, of varied interests, of passionate themes into which he flings himself.† This man does nothing by halves: I have seen him, for instance, spend his nights drawing letters, re-learning the alphabet at

* I had originally written: *But there is no illustrated Charles d'Orléans: the result has been this painting* . . . I corrected this, as is seen here. Matisse had commented in the margin of the last lines of the paragraph: *Very good. But this is based on a mistake, as the previous marginal note shows. I'm sorry!*

And I hardly dare explain by a personal recollection my fondness for this painting; but it's a fact that at the age of eleven I had written a play in five acts, in verse, entitled *L'Otage* (1908, mind you!) whose hero was Charles, hostage in the hands of the English during their occupation of France. Perhaps I recognized a childhood dream, a fantasy, a myth. (*1969*)

† The present tense, which I shall not alter, shows that this was written while Matisse was alive; I cannot leave it today (in the long night after he has gone) without a kind of shudder, as though one had had a knife stuck in one's heart, and had come to forget about it, and then someone brushed (brushes) against it, passing by . . . It will be clear from this sentence (and that year in Paris) that from this point at any rate we are in the summer or autumn of 1946. I think that was when I started to complete the article which had been broken off where the space is, just before the words: *Voltaire's poetry* . . . I wrote the end more or less at one go.

130. – *Faun and Nymph*, charcoal study for the painting *La Verdure*.

seventy-six, I have seen him fill notebooks with foliage, I have seen him literally obsessed by Baudelaire or Ronsard, or absorbed by hyacinths, which had been so hard to procure that year because none had been grown in France, and it had been almost impossible to get them from Holland . . . I have seen him invent a new game of paper cut-outs, which resulted in the series of cut-and-pasted paper about the circus . . . I have seen him adapt this pastime to the decoration of his room, covering the wall with birds, jellyfish, floating seaweed . . . I have seen him passing on from this ploy of his sleepless nights to find a new use for his cut-outs, planning a pattern for a Gobelin tapestry . . . And passing, too, from one poet to another . . . loving verse as he loves objects, as the starting-point for a day-dream, the support of the model: the problem being to take flight, and then to triumph over dizziness.

I think I can generalize from the suggestions made in the preceding paragraph: Matisse's art never does without nature, it starts from nature. This is why I can say not only that a poet's lines may be the source of a drawing or painting as much as any given object, a flower, or a woman, but that the converse is also true, that Matisse reacts towards a woman, a flower, an object as to a poem. And to make myself clearly understood I would say, contrariwise, that Matisse illustrates an object, a flower, a woman, and that he *paints* poems (not *illustrates* them).

Which makes it easier to understand Matisse's world. As I said earlier, distinguishing and comparing two sorts of painters, Matisse surrounds himself with key-objects, from which he starts off to conquer the higher world of art and poetry, with the help of material often elaborated by other men's dreams and of his long acquaintance with them . . . he starts off from objects beautiful in themselves, meticulously chosen, or from chosen poets or poems. His painting goes beyond them. They are particular objects or poems, but it's Matisse himself who takes flight from these objects or poems; from the Turkish girl who was, for a long time, his model at Cimiez, or from Baudelaire or Charles d'Orléans or Ronsard.

Here one scruple occurs to me: in so far as much of what I have said is based on Matisse's immediate or inspired drawings, his 'Variations', one might think, in spite of the clear distinction he had himself made between 'Variations' and 'Themes', that this experiment provides the key to Matisse's art. In fact it is only one extension of it, but one in which the process of the draughtsman's thought is revealed. And to put things in order I might quote from a letter written me in February 1942, one day when he had been annoyed by a critical article in some magazine. Referring to a painter he dislikes, he wrote: *Unlike those of the Scrounger,* my immediate drawings are not my most important production. They are simply a cinema film of a series of visions that occur to me constantly while I'm working on something fundamental, some picture which is only the result of a series of precise reconceptions which quietly acquire increased intensity, one providing the impetus for the next. I suddenly think of the morning lark – yet if I begin with a trill, I should like to end with an organ peal.*

And I'll assert that in the world of Matisse's models, skylarks greet the dawn, but that the bird-charmer surpasses their morning song with a daylight symphony.

. . . The world of Matisse's models . . . Matisse himself let me into it: I have found the photograph he sent me while I was writing *La Grande Songerie*; it appears here on pages 248 and 249.

* Why not come out with it today? He meant Raoul Dufy. Unjust, perhaps. But he complained that as soon as he, Matisse, had chosen a house somewhere, in all secrecy, to work there in solitude, Dufy would turn up in the neighbourhood and rent the house next door so as to see from his own window the same landscape that Matisse painted from his. (*1967*)

On the back of the photograph Matisse has written for me: *Objects which have been of use to me nearly all my life.**

This is a group of faithful servants, shown as in a school photograph, three rows in front, and behind them, standing, or on steps, the seniors who would have hidden the small boys if they had been put in front.

Fruit dishes, jugs with handles, vases, glasses, a butter-dish with a cover, vessels of pewter, porcelain, opaline, earthenware, a little box, a Persian pedestal table supporting a Chinese vase . . . the white vase that held the sprig of ivy in *Thèmes et Variations* is capped with narcissi, there are big leaves in two pots, one of the dishes holds an apple, the little teacup decorated in red and blue looks tiny in the front row between a cut-glass tumbler and a candy dish, and at the end of the row the *Tabac royal*, the tobacco jar, in front of the opaline bowl with the white and gold frill, enhances the elegance of the hookah-shaped vase with a single spidery leaf in it, next to a bottle encased in straw.

Thirty-nine pieces in all, including the little table and the figurine in ochre earthenware[1] (a woman seated, with her right foot on her left knee and her left hand against her right temple) which is in the back row, as though on a shelf, between the narcissi and the foliage. All this company, from the wooden-handled coffee-pot to the small pewter jug to which I have often referred and shall refer again, from the humble ribbed glass tumbler at the opposite end from the tobacco jar to the slightly chipped porcelain pot with its floral design beside the footed fruit dish, wear the stiff look of sixth-formers interrupted in their game of football by the master on duty who has summoned them in front of the camera: Don't move, now!

*Except where the contrary is specified, what follows took place at Vence, that is, necessarily after June 1943, most likely in 1945 or '46. But it was written in 1946; besides, the photograph mentioned here was in the bundle that came with the letter of July 12, '46.

Objects which have been of use to me nearly all my life.

There's something nostalgic about it. Still, they have their reward: here they are, assembled in an appealing group. Later on, someone will say of the piece of Bohemian glass that stands in the middle, or of the lacquer box: you see that glass, that box, well, they were of use to Matisse nearly all his life . . . They are mostly breakable objects, which Matisse looked after carefully, he was a good master, it was a pleasure to work for him. When there was a gap in some arrangement or other, something not quite right, they vied with one another to complete the still life, to form a contrast, to set off the flowers. This is not quite what I meant by the *palette of objects*: or at any rate it is just *one*, far from complete, palette of objects. Matisse's brief comment

1. A statuette by the sculptor Laurens. Bought by Matisse (in '39 or '40) supposedly for a connoisseur. The sculptor was then in financial straits. (*Note of 1969*)

on the back of the photograph tells us plenty about something which cannot be described: the reverie that preceded the painting, the way a choice was made in front of what I have called his harem.

They stand there primly in front of the camera: but when the painter gives them leave, when the group breaks up and re-forms casually for a game of marbles, tag, prisoner's base or leapfrog, then new harmonies are born, the world of props comes to life, organized only in terms of the power that brought them together.

On seeing them thus I understand what is lacking in the term *palette*. Can one call a chessboard a *palette*? And yet I seem to see Matisse's hand poised, as he moves forward the Rook (the *Tabac royal*) or the Queen (the statuette),

Objects which have been of use to me nearly all my life . . .

◀ 131. – A palette of objects, photograph taken at my request and sent by Matisse with his letter of July 12, 1946.

the White Bishop (with the narcissi) or the Black (the little pewter jug with spiral markings). Chessmen are not colours with which to decorate a game, but rather the words that make up a sentence, or the arguments that lead to a discovery. I've got it: we should call this a vocabulary of objects.*

Poets, too, have that sort of vocabulary: night, the sky, the stars, a rose, blood, the heart, scents . . .

> *Prends mon deuil: un pavot, une feuille d'absinthe,*
> *Quelques lilas d'avril dont j'aimais tant la fleur;*
> *Durant tout un printemps qu'ils sèchent sur ton cœur*
> *Je t'en prie: un printemps! cette espérance est sainte.* †

* And a painting, a game of chess.

† Madame Desbordes-Valmore, *Élégies*: surely what was needed here was a quotation from Pierre Reverdy, the most *painterly* poet of our day, whose poetic invention also starts from a palette of words, the wind, the window, the table, the Venetian blind, the night . . . but this would entail all kinds of developments, a study of Reverdy's poetry, and here I'm sticking to Matisse. (*Added in 1959*)

I imagine that this bouquet was determined according to laws akin to those that were to bring together the great shell (not seen in this photograph), the pewter jug and the cauldron in the *Still Life with Magnolias* (eventually to hang in the Louvre). And who is to say which Mme Valmore chose first, the poppy, the April lilac or the leaf of wormwood?

The day on which the group of old retainers was taken, several photographs which I have before me reveal the painter's private thoughts about his servants: there is one corner of a table, in front of the pigeons' cages, the Louis XV mantelpiece and the bookshelves, where we see that the glasses and pots had at first been set out full of flowers.* On the mantelpiece and on the shelves, the big shell from the *Still Life with Magnolias* and some pine cones have been set aside; they lack the requisite seniority. On the wall, a number of paintings . . . but the secret of his preparations is betrayed even better by another print, taken from a little further off and more to the left, spreading out left of the fireplace to the mirror, which shows the chest of drawers against the side wall, with, lined up on the marble top, the pot of narcissi, the pot with spidery leaves, a small Chinese vase, a fruit dish . . . a set piece subsequently broken up to leave just the table and the chest of drawers. In the mirror, at the back of the room, through an open door . . . but this is even clearer in this third photograph taken facing the mirror which now shows neither the table nor the chest of drawers, just the edge of the mantelpiece with three pictures on the wall above it: here, it's in the mirror that we see the corner of the table loaded with vases and flowers, and beyond it part of the room with the camera set up, and on the wall a drawing, and some first attempts at cut-outs (this is interesting to note, as showing that it was not during sleepless nights in the Boulevard Montparnasse in Paris but earlier, at Vence, that those cut-out corals and foliage made their first appearance, recurring later on the walls of his Paris studio and in the blue-and-white Gobelin tapestry of autumn 1946: it was thus clearly an old-established obsession, probably originating in his work for *Jazz*, for which this may be an unused cut-out).

* They were always filled with whatever flowers were in season. They were emptied only for the photograph, as Lydia said: *to let you see their individual personalities.*

The interesting thing about this picture is that at the far end of the room, beyond the familiar low striped easy chair above which some garments, including a white overall, are hanging from a peg, we catch a glimpse into the next room, where Matisse (with his back to us, in a dark jacket and wearing a hat) is drawing the portrait of that lovely black woman who appears in countless drawings made at Vence, a woman from Haiti,† and who can herself be seen, posing at a suitable distance at the foot of the wall where there are several Matisse pictures, including *The Cloak.* A bunch of mistletoe is hanging above.

† At Vence . . . *Haiti* – noted in 1967. She was one of his 'Mme de Senonnes'.

132. – Interior at Vence, in 1946: in the background Matisse can be seen painting the Haitian woman . . .

I call *The Cloak* (*Le Manteau*)* that painting of a dark woman leaning back in an armchair on that cloak lined with white Tibetan tiger-skin, which is perhaps the high point of Matisse's choice. It reappears in several of his paintings, and deserves a book to itself.

* *The Cloak* was painted in 1946, therefore at Vence. The woman in it is the Congolese girl who also appears in the *Girl in the White Gown* and *Asia* of the same year. The 1946 *Cloak* reappears in the film of which we shall speak later.

XXXI. – *The Cloak* (1946).

I cannot fly in one leap through the looking-glass into the room where the portrait scene is being played; I have no less than twenty-two photographs of this scene.

On the first set, seven different views, Matisse is wearing a light coat and his hat. All twenty-two photographs show the same drawing being made. On one single print, the model is on the right, the painter on the left; this is our first picture: the beautiful black woman's face, barely sketched in the drawing, was smiling. Next, the photographer has moved around, the model has resumed an expression of nostalgia for Africa, and we see her on the left, the painter on the right . . . actually, in the first view, Matisse was drawing with his left hand! It was an inverted photograph, taken in the mirror (or printed in reverse, which comes to the same thing). Next we follow the draughtsman's hand directly as the charcoal moves upward to form the forehead and then over to the right eye . . . This time, what has he been saying to her? The model is smiling, Matisse starts on her blouse . . . the model is laughing outright, and the little frill at the throat of the blouse appears . . . then the

133. – First photograph in *The Comedy of the Model*, Vence 1946 – Act I.

134–139. – Act I.

135.

136.

137.

138.

139. – End of Act I.

140–146. – Act II. ▶

model becomes sad again, and Matisse considers the finished drawing. Six other pictures can be identified as forming a single series by the clothes Matisse is wearing and by the drawing in progress at some later sitting. We are in the room where, close to the window, the round table is standing, with much the same still life as that described above, beside the Venetian armchair (no more flowers now in the fanciful vase). I cannot see the armchair in front of the flower-patterned drapery, but the calla lilies show above the painter's arm, between the model and himself. The model has a dreamy look. The painter, seen from the other side, holds up his charcoal to draw the right eye, and beyond him are the striped easy chair, the hanging garments, the chest of drawers with its gleaming array of faithful servants.

141

142.

The sitting over, Matisse considers his work: he looks interested, then amused, then absent, then he turns round, looks elsewhere, and, perhaps at

143.

144.

the photographer's request, poses: three-quarter view, leaning on his elbow, and behind him I guess at the Venetian armchair . . . I see the calla lilies, the edge of the shell that forms the back of the chair.

145. – End of Act II.

Third series: Matisse has shed his coat (*pace* Charles d'Orléans, in this case it's his dressing-gown) and put on a long white coat; he is seen close up, from the back, his head and shoulders bent over the drawing, which is almost obliterated, there's just one eye to be seen, the hand holding the charcoal is tracing the neck (I forgot to say that this drawing belongs to the 'theme' rather than the 'variations' type*). Seen beyond Matisse's hat, the woman with her blouse, her necklace, her gaze, looks like the pattern on a piece of stuff. One's attention is focused on the draughtsman's hand: already the right eye in the drawing has grown wider, the charcoal underlines the lower lip. Then three poses: Matisse is correcting something in the hollow of the right shoulder in the drawing, is measuring the proportion between the two shoulders. At first we saw the model, now we see Matisse alone, in profile, going over the line of the chin. The drawing is finished, down to the necklace. We notice particularly the Tahitian straw band which the painter wears round his felt hat.

* The 'variations' here are actually a series of etchings made in preparation for the frontispiece to Baudelaire, to be seen later. It was impossible to take photographs while Matisse was engaged on his real 'variations': the least movement of the photographer would have disturbed him, infuriated him, and everything would have been ruined. For an engraving, the study representing a 'theme' was sometimes made in white gouache on the plate itself.

146–152. – Act III.

147.

148.

149.

150.

151.

152. – End of Act III.

*from here on, there follows a series of details concerning Matisse's models, added in 1967.

† This was taken in Paris, where H.M. was working on a study for his illustrations to the poems of John-Antoine Nau, for which he used several exotic models from Montparnasse.

I have one more picture, certainly* taken on another day: Matisse, in a dark jacket, is wearing a check cap.† We are in a different room, to judge by the drawings on the wall, the table is in the foreground, the drawing in progress is of quite a different character, it seems to be of another woman, slender, almost European . . . The fact is that we are in Montparnasse, and the woman is a Madagascan: the mistake we almost made was due to her wearing the same blouse with a little frill, the short sleeve fastened on her arm with a lace, tied in a bow. In fact the blouse belonged to L.D., who lent it to all the models: the vaguely frilled neckline appealed to H.M.

Another black woman, looking almost white in the bright daylight, in side-view, with a round forehead, utterly different both in reality and in the drawing from all the other pictures we have seen. Almost ugly. She, too, is wearing the familiar blouse we saw on the Haitian girl.

153–156. – Act IV.

154. ▼

155.

They filmed Henri Matisse, not that day, but another day. He is seen drawing a different model, who might easily be mistaken for this one: but this time it is the mulatto girl from the Belgian Congo, the one in the 1946 *Cloak*. He is shown painting a picture, actually that very *Cloak*, at normal speed, his own speed, and then the same gestures in slow motion . . . Slow motion reveals what words do not: thought photographed, the dance of the brush, its revisions and corrections, the process of association of ideas. Prose cannot compete with film. And here, also, a demonstration is repeated and perfected which was made at an exhibition this year: a painting was shown flanked by enlarged photographs of its cancelled stages (each one cancelling out the rest, since Henri Matisse repaints over the same canvas). The film has this advantage over the exhibition, that it can superimpose images and make them seem to issue from one another, but its disadvantage is that each image vanishes and that we can only compare from memory. Each method of expression has

156. – End of Act IV and of *The Comedy of the Model.*

its limits, its virtues and its failings. Nothing is more arbitrary than to try to substitute the written word for painting or drawing. That is called art criticism, and I am not aware of being guilty of it here. The need to transpose from one plane to another the lesson we learn from Henri Matisse has led me to perform a sort of verbal dance around him. There is something more serious in this than may be supposed, and a deeper sense of the inexpressible.

I, too, have been to Thule. A Thule which is neither in the cold Scottish islands nor amid the coral reefs of the peaceful ocean. A mental Thule that may perhaps be represented by the spacious rooms of Cimiez and Vence, or the apartment in the Boulevard Montparnasse, but whose essence, whose visionary power, lies elsewhere. Thither I have followed the Enchanter, who gives these places their meaning and their magic. And like those hashish addicts who believe in their dreams, I have thought myself in contact with precious and elusive realities. Have I brought back anything at all of Matisse? Almost nothing. A certain colour of ideas perhaps. The certainty that I can learn more about myself, and nothing else? I don't know. Coming back from Thule is always sad; it's like the fall of the red-and-gold curtain at the theatre, when the house empties and the ushers put on their coats, and there's the cloakroom and the crowd and it's still daylight outside (for of course I'm talking about a Thursday matinée at the Châtelet, *Les Cinq sous de Lavarède* or *Les Quatre cent coups du diable*).

And yet, before the lights go out and the covers are put back on the seats in the stalls, I remember something which passed through my mind a little while ago: these cut-outs, these algae and jellyfish, these corals and birds on the walls of Matisse's room in Paris in the summer of 1946, and the couple of designs for Gobelin tapestry made from them that autumn, these cut-outs which I traced back, last spring, to the Vence photographs (*Durant tout un printemps qu'ils sèchent sur ton cœur* . . . Let them wither against your heart a whole springtide), these cut-outs, suddenly emerging for no apparent reason, during a sleepless night, a wakeful reverie, isn't it obvious? They come from Thule, I mean Tahiti, Tahiti or Thule taking its revenge, Thule which he had never left, which is ever present, and which has found its way into our hearts.*

* It may be objected, with regard to certain passages in this text, that today Thule is a port in Greenland. Yes, I'll reply, just as there are European towns in the United States, even a Paris in Texas. The Thule in Greenland has existed only since 1910, thanks to Rasmussen. And the effect has not been that foretold by Seneca, that the last lands known in his day would cease to be the last: though we may no longer know with certainty the position of the Thule of antiquity, it remains, poetically, that which tempted Petrarch. Moreover, anyone who thus displays his up-to-date geographical knowledge I suspect of having learned this merely from an incident that occurred this year, when an American aircraft dropped bombs in the sea off the coast of this new Thule . . . Neither Seneca nor Petrarch had read this in the newspaper which was brought me this morning with a carton of milk. (*Note of 1968*)

The Day Before Afterwards

(February 28 and 29, 1968)

Unpublished, in Leap Year

XXXII. – *Girl in Pink* (1942).

I retrace my steps, I count them and lose my way. I retrace my steps . . .

If I'm wearying you, go fishing. Do you think it's easy to pass from those terrible years to the din of peace? To find one's bearings, after that dark realm where neither people nor things had their right name, in the noisy world that came after it, where one races from one end of the earth to the other; to jump straight into post-war ceremonies, the return of the deported, the Nuremberg trials and the atomic stockpile and all the rest of it? Just as Henri Matisse in 1941, and later, goes over his thoughts, not following the newspapers' calendar but referring to a moment that was his alone, Tahiti, his Tahiti of 1930, thus in occupied France restoring order within himself by a return to Tahiti . . . so before I come to the period which I touched on in *La Grande Songerie* I have to go back into the heart of darkness. Whence the following pages. A strange sort of Thule, you'll say, if you've caught my way of thinking as a child catches whooping-cough. That inner Thule of mine emerges from the waters at different moments of my life, and there is no science, still less any chronology, that can foresee or locate these stirrings of the depths. So I come back from post-war Vence to Nice at that moment when it stood between being and not being. And there we were, a whole nation, holding poor Yorick's skull in our hands . . .

I retrace my steps, I count them and I lose my way. How can one get one's bearings, to what branch can one cling . . . There are days which are not mine alone. Objective days, marked with a cross or a stone. The others are before or after them. It's from such days that we reckon. One leans one's head on the shoulder of time, and one starts dreaming. Drifting.

Perhaps, instead, one should go back a little further, to when the thing that was as yet nameless was brewing, to the hiatus between yesterday and afterwards. A sort of waste space, there are districts like that in certain uncertain towns, and for all one's efforts to get out of them one keeps going round in a circle. Perhaps we should . . . We had got to the end of I don't know what I don't know where I don't know how, and that was that. I remember a lane, it had forgotten to go anywhere. We came back along it, and what if, behind it, a fall of rubble had blocked the way out? No, of course not, that doesn't happen.

In October, things weren't too bad yet. Not too cold, I mean when the sun was shining. I blinked a little, looking for signs on the houses. And even if I had seen them, should I have known what those signs meant? There's no alphabet for them. Nice was heavy and vacant, like a woman trying to remember her shopping list. There was no reason why anything should change. Or should not change. What wouldn't I give to smell coffee all of a sudden, in some little square? Not the slightest chance. How big is the slightest chance? A dead leaf in your hand, which crumbles when you clutch it. Your good health, says the practical joker. Actually, behind the Casino, well, down there, somewhere towards the south, where there are steps running both ways, leading down towards the Préfecture, you can picture it . . . Actually, here's that singer going past with his dog, what's his name, Georges Ulmer . . . funny name for a Mexican, apparently he's a Mexican nowadays. And a huge bank official in a blue coat with gilt buttons. You'll always meet the dog with M. Georges Ulmer unless you happen to miss him. The only new thing, these days, is the increase in Italian tradesmen in Nice, had you noticed? Bars, greengrocers' shops. Groups in cafés, talking with their hands. They're from Piedmont, you remember the cleaning woman used to say. A Piedmontese girl took that son of hers away from her. Now he lives somewhere outside, they sell something or other, she never sees him. The last carnations are lying on the ground in the covered market. Neither white nor pink, and the green of the leaves isn't green any longer. Torn newspapers. Anyhow, who reads them? November is coming on stealthily. On the banks of the Paillon, where they're pulling down houses.

When it was broad daylight one could still believe in something . . .

O great amphitheatre of plasterwork, with pink roofs!

Around here walked the woman in white from *Mille Regrets* who became a Christian Bérard, or rather the woman in whites, in the plural, every shade of white from yellow to grey, as if Matisse had outlined parts of her dress with that stroke that changes the value of whites . . . and Célimène, going down to the sand with her camp-stool, a little rococo pumpkin, accompanied by her young lover, tawny as autumn sunlight . . . the weather, too, one stroke would change the value of that . . . Doriot's arrival at the station a few days before . . . a few days before . . . suddenly the raging sea covers the Promenade des Anglais with countless omens, pebbles and sand . . . It was all just fiction – a novel.

Just fiction . . . What sort of fiction? All these characters in need of dusting, they're pretending, pretending what? Just pretending. Old gentlemen in panamas, carrying plaid rugs. And little loafing swindlers. Ladies at a loose end, humming Viennese waltzes in vain. What sort of fiction? The palm trees are bored. While daylight lasts . . .

Or perhaps it was November already, who knows? It turns chilly at four o'clock, on the dot. There are great empty spaces in the town, and nobody goes into the philatelists' shops, everyone has given up hope of a two-headed 48 or a Mauritius 20 centimes. Yes, maybe it was November already, who knows? We liked the lingering dusk. Even if the air was chilly, it was bliss no longer to see the photos of the Marshal. There were people in the gardens who were still young enough for adventures, and whose eyes asked questions. At all events the cinema . . . Sometimes benches must have looked pink in the sunset. They still seemed surprised at it. Someone happened to get up and move away. The cold, or a sudden thought? The quality of silence. And the white shiver of shoulders.

All this means nothing to you. November 1942. And what next? We never thought about that. We'd see, for better or worse. There was no particular reason for anything. We waited, without awaiting. Ration cards, or what? When night fell, a little way beyond the *Ruhl*, a night-club had opened in a street down that way, the ground floor of something or other, there must have been a balcony on the first floor, one of those buildings of the turn of the century, quite new-looking still, with carved garlands. Perhaps I'm inventing the garlands, perhaps not. You went down a couple of steps or more. An ordinary sort of room, they'd taken pains to make it look nice, with green plants, little tables, buckets of ice. Like a woman in a corset displaying her bosom. The place was not very crowded, but what with the announcer, the performers, the professional dancing couples, it never looked quite empty. It had just opened. In November '42. Rather odd, opening such a place, like a tin of sardines for guests who aren't going to come. What were they hoping for? Nothing, probably. To subsist. Besides, it's not only the public that want something to do in the evenings. The performers too, surely; the piano and its pianist. I wonder what we drank there. I can't remember. A saxophone sometimes. I mean when . . . no, probably too tired. And all this swept along, as by a woman's skirt, by the voice of the announcer, a tall, lumbering fellow, podgy, pale, too fair-haired for the times. His job was to blend us all, like a sauce. There was more than one number. But only one that counted: I've forgotten what went on between the piano pieces. This was what people came for. At least we did. Not only. But.

A woman. Not young. Not good-looking. A great gawk with hair dyed black, curls, a ribbon round them, her pitiful shoulders past their best, another ribbon round her neck, a lot of scarves; as soon as she got up everyone clapped, the bellboy, the waiters, the announcer, even the pianist, the cloakroom lady. She came on as if proclaiming an event. Arch little smiles, and an air of knowing what was due to her. Because she, after all, was Woman. In the midst of the fair man's phony hubbub. Her words tongue in cheek. There she was in the midst of it, sure of herself, of her royalty. She ought to have worn spangles, but she didn't. A bit dusty, perhaps, but. When she was announced: 'And here is' – pause – 'L'ÉTRANGE FARCY!' She sang. I remember nothing of what she sang, except the song she took so much pressing to get started on, her great international success, the fellow said, we never discovered why. It was called *Je suis biaiseuse** . . . Spare me the rest.

* Literally 'devious', from '*biaiser*', to use evasions; but there is an inevitable double-entendre, a pun on the broader sense of *baiser*. (*Translator's note*)

In the end, after all, there were four or five customers who pretended to toss off champagne. Like everyone else, we encored *La Biaiseuse*. We wanted our money's worth. The star turn of the evening was when the announcer overdid things so obviously that The Strange Farcy couldn't go on pretending not to notice. Then she'd begin to scream till her voice cracked, tugging at her fake pearls till she nearly broke the string, gathered up all her draperies and took herself off to a corner, thumping the table, with her eyes full of tears: 'I've had enough of it! I won't be insulted by a pansy!' Now she was overdoing it herself, the fair fellow thus challenged appealed to the audience, that's what women are like! Come on, sing it again, your *Biaiseuse*, and let's not hear any more about it. Ladies and gentlemen, once again, in her popular number, L'Étrange Farcy . . .

Eventually we went home to bed.

I was writing this, following the whims of memory, and then suddenly it occurred to me that Elsa must have said something somewhere about those days and that night-club. I puzzled, it's neither in the *Préface à la contrebande* nor in the *Préface à la clandestinité*, which, in our *Œuvres croisées*, introduced *Mille Regrets* and *Le Premier Accroc* respectively . . . and then I picked up *Le Cheval blanc* and in the *Préface à une 'Vie de Michel Vigaud'* I found this paragraph, which sums up Nice in 1942:

Those long afternoons and evenings to be spent. Michel Eymer was at the height of his glory, we used to listen to his band in a crowded café, thick with smoke. Mégarée *was being performed, and we relished the sense of complicity conveyed by the young playwright Maurice Druon's anti-Vichyssois Greece. We strolled about among the acetylene flares and the bright lights of a fair with enormous roundabouts adorned with female caryatids glittering with paint and gilt, dangerous entertainments attracted idlers, and the popping of guns in shooting-booths was infinitely depressing. Georges Ulmer was starting his career in a night-club where his success was rivalled by that of The Strange Farcy, a creature who sent the house into fits of laughter and nauseous pity when she repeated her* Biaiseuse . . . *And everywhere one heard the tune:* La fille de joie est triste. *Every day I read you a chapter from* Le Cheval blanc. *That made you happy. You began to write* Aurélien.

My forgetting and then rediscovering this passage explains a lot, my whole life as well as the story of *La Biaiseuse.* Do you see now why I copy out Matisse's letters so conscientiously? Matisse himself made mistakes about the date of my portraits! Anyhow, all this is only fiction.* But, speaking of fiction, it's true that while my inward eye was fixed on the painter I forgot to describe the facts that conditioned the lives of the secondary characters, Elsa and myself; because if I did not actually begin *Aurélien* until I had finished *Matisse-en-France*, that is in April '42, we had visited Matisse for the first time in late December '41, Elsa had been working at *Le Cheval blanc* for just under two months, and there is this background to my thoughts, my astonishment at finding it possible to write a novel at such a time, and what seemed at first a diversion, the appearance of Matisse. Perhaps this is the explanation of that crazy notion of mine, the idea I never expressed at the time, of writing a novel about Matisse. And of how *Matisse-en-France*, which had been a sort of digression in those dark days, launched me into novel-writing, and I undertook *Aurélien* like another Michel Vigaud.

* *Is only fiction*, a concession to the scientifico-commercial mentality? (*last-minute note*).

In the morning we went to market, queuing for unlikely foodstuffs. The short days, the sea. Going up there to silent Cimiez. By day there was Matisse, or if he was unwell . . . then what did we do with our days? Wrote, sitting by the sawdust-burning stove, waited. In the daytime we waited for evening. In the evening, for night. And then you could always go back to that show, after all, rather shamefacedly, not too early, you'd be the only one . . . ones there.

The fact is that we were fascinated by the queerness of the show. Somewhat ashamed, we visited it two nights running, and on the third, as Pierre Seghers had turned up in Nice, we took him to see *La Biaiseuse.* The more the merrier. Because it was Pierre's first time it was a little while before he laughed. Then he got started.

It was next morning that I went off to the other end of nowhere to hunt for unrationed offal, no matter what, and on my way back, what was happening? People were staring, with their backs to me, a crowd, and I could hear noises, the sound of footsteps, wheels, voices, that sort of thing . . . You look, and you take a little time to understand. This endless horde marching past from left to right, mountebanks from a travelling circus, with their blue and green cocks' feathers, and suddenly it became clear: the Italians were invading France. Nobody was allowed past. They were thin, aggressive little bastards. Finally, by dint of signs and my rudimentary Italian, I managed to. Back in the Cité du Parc, Elsa hadn't heard. She thought it was just the market. Come on, we must leave. At once. But how can we? I won't. Find out. What? In any case there are no more trains to Marseilles. Suppose we took the Digne line? And go where? Well, first to Villeneuve with Pierre . . . then . . . Anyhow, there was no choice and no time to think, just to pack and pay for the room . . . We rang up Matisse to warn him. Lydia answered the phone.

We'd prepared a hide-out in case of any kind of emergency. In the Drôme mountains, above Dieulefit. That was our own affair. But first we had to take our stuff to Villeneuve, to find out how Jean and Jo had managed. It would probably be the last train to Digne; afterwards, the occupying authorities . . . for there were such things already . . . yes, and the people in the bar across the street, on the other side of the Flower Market, were triumphant. They hung out their flag over the door. Lydia had turned up. She brought us a lot of stuff, all she had been able to, from Henri Matisse, and an envelope with proofs of the *Thèmes et Variations* drawings, the series with the spotted kerchief on the Turkish girl's head, and some others, I didn't see exactly what. So we shouldn't quite be going away and leaving him. The Digne station is on the other side of the main line, where I had been to get the offal. Others had had the same idea. The train was full. People seeing people off, a special sort of luggage, overcrowding.

We were leaving behind us almost two years of our life, and what years! The room overlooking sky and sea where we had been happy in spite of everything. And above all, in my case, that extraordinary man through whom I had in a way been able to go on being myself; that man who had come into my life so late, and who had come to represent its intellectual continuity, all that linked me with my childhood, and more, beyond it, with that world I had entered about 1917 and which I sometimes felt had been shattered. This man who helped me to believe in myself again, because he believed in me. And because he was part of my country to me . . . Something that was still standing.

Men classify one another, according to their feelings, whether reciprocally or not, in different generations. 1917 was the time when, I think, both André Breton and I became aware that we formed part (through each other's influence) of a new generation, not a sort of class of recruits, but what will eventually appear to posterity as a generation, that is to say, a small number of minds characteristic of their time as Keats and Shelley, or Hegel and Hölderlin, may represent the youth of their own day, the genesis of a temporal grouping of minds. The terrible rift which occurred between us at the beginning of the 'thirties had been completed by the shattering of a whole world that happened, for Frenchmen, in 1940. In that mute, humiliated country, where we were left singularly alone, Elsa and myself, our meeting with Henri Matisse, that kind of adoption which made him closer than anyone else to the two of us, seemed a sort of miracle. Now, abruptly, we were separated from Henri Matisse by an event whose import we could not measure, as from the windows of the train we watched the Bersaglieri on their motorcycles speeding past along the Alpine roads. And I tried to imagine, as if on a map, the reality of a world which, for me, comprised Henri Matisse and ourselves.

First of all, in time. I was just forty-five, but somehow I still thought of myself as a very young man. Except for my hair, it was almost true, and the gap between Matisse and myself seemed larger than in fact it was. For after all Matisse, born in 1869, was only four years older than my mother, and yet I'd have said he belonged to the generation before hers. Because of that artificial break, the war years 1870–71, between them? Possibly. I found it hard to imagine that Matisse might well have been my father, with the same woman for my mother, rather than my real father, who was born in 1841. This further disturbed the time-scheme. And if I had remembered that only two years separated Matisse and Romain Rolland, it would have surprised me even more. Romain Rolland was for me someone from before my time; I respected him as a historical figure. I did not imagine any real communication possible between us. And, in any event, I never did more than visit Romain Rolland: part of him belonged to a past inaccessible to me, his time in Rome, Malwida von Maysenburg, the strange time when Péguy acclaimed *Jean-Christophe*, and so on . . . The same is true of Maxim Gorky. All the more extraordinary that Matisse should be 'of my time', мой современник, as they say in your country, Elsa, remembering Lermontov. Had this train journey alongside the motorized Bersaglieri suddenly restored the perspective of time between us? But who was that handsome, tragically handsome man over there, a familiar face . . . From his seat, he greeted me: the actor Samson Fainsilber . . . A strange accident of our journey that we should be strangers for everyone except for Samson Fainsilber, and vice versa. Where was he going? And where were we going, tell me that?

At nightfall we left the train for an icy hotel, with clammy sheets, at the foot of the Basses-Alpes, where we had to change trains. Seghers went on, we . . . What a night in that hotel, with its clay walls. At dawn we were to move on towards Digne, and from there by bus to Pierre's place by the Fort Saint-André, where we might find sunshine. Or the mistral.

I had opened the envelope with the proofs of the drawings. There, in that inn. All the beauty of the world, somehow. Among them a woman's figure, twining her arms about her head, I don't think I had ever seen arms drawn like that, the way a woman's arms twine round a man, in bed. There was no man, there were the arms . . .

Just before we left I'd had a note from Matisse. He wanted to show me his menagerie, the troupe, so to speak, the company of objects he had in some fashion brought together for me and which had performed in all his plays for years and years, some dating from the first war; he had summoned me, you understand, before the characters in his novel, a story that begins in Gustave Moreau's studio and first fed on shadows and then one fine day flared up in every sort of colour, inventing the flat colour of the baroque *Desserte** (*Harmony in Red*) or the first *Dance*, then gradually, with maturity and a growing curiosity about the way creatures are, evolving into a great calm, dazzling fiesta, a sort of challenge to things as they are, flinging them into the brazier of colour, into those vast flaming canvases, sometimes quite small but always vast, where nothing is of its own colour but always of Matisse's colour, seen with his eye. Precisely on the eve of our departure he had wanted to introduce me to his company, to the characters in his novel. I had been thinking about it in the morning, while I went in search of off-ration foodstuffs. I'm going to be presented at Court soon. I was day-dreaming about it. And then those mountebanks came along with mules and trucks and wretched little guns, all clattering along the pavement among the trampled carnations from the flower market . . . No longer possible.

* The first *Desserte* was painted in 1897, the second (known as *Harmony in Red*) in 1908, the first *Dance* in 1909 (it is in the Philadelphia Museum, it's the sketch for the 1910 painting in Moscow). The *Harmony in Red* (1908) had originally been blue. It was painted over the blue version, as traces of colour reveal in the Hermitage picture reproduced here.

This book had been interrupted once again. Or once before the other times. Chaos, chaos! And besides that's not how history will be told. God, how cold our feet were! Day had dawned quite grey, over the frozen, colourless, glittering earth. You weren't at all interested in my stories about

XXXIII. – *Harmony in Red* (1908)

my childhood in the Basses-Alpes, or my father's electoral campaigns. Nor was I. When Gorky was born, my father used to ride on horseback from Paris to Dieppe on a Sunday to pay his court to Isabella II, the daughter of Queen Maria-Christina, both exiled. Later he was jailed as Republican when the war came, and set free on September 4. Who is interested in that today, Thursday, November 12, 1942, if I'm correct?

Or in the fact that my father, who died with a great crucifix on his breast, had his own romance, which was Isabella, and that later the Republic, that hussy who plays tricks on men in corners, had thought it clever to send my father as French Ambassador to Madrid, whither Isabella had never returned. I ask you, who's interested in that? Today, 12/11/42. Nobody, nobody. I

myself have only one desire, and that is to look at my pictures. The star-spangled veil on the Turkish girl's head . . . To start from those few words . . . and write a whole novel, where the day-stars are black . . . the lips dead . . .

The star-spangled veil on the Turkish girl's head . . .
157. – Drawing L_4 of *Thèmes et Variations* (crayon).

In Defence of Luxury

(Apologie du Luxe)

(January 1946)
with a second postscript 1968

Les Trésors de la Peinture française:
Matisse – *Albert Skira – May 1946*

XXXIV. – *Girl in White, Red Background* (1944).

I had an appointment with Henri Matisse: in his home up at Cimiez, we were going to look through the photographs which would enable me to write what I wanted to. I was going to make an inventory of all the armchairs featured in his paintings, comparing the photographs of these chairs with his representation of them. In fact I was not going to confine myself to armchairs. That was just the beginning. I hoped from the study of a *palette of objects* to deduce a few facts hitherto neglected in our knowledge of Henri Matisse and indeed of painters in general.

It was on that very day[1] that the Italians entered Nice, with the sort of turn-out that made one long regretfully for the armchairs. I left the town in something of a hurry, and although since then, both in Paris and at Vence, I have had the opportunity to see and talk to Henri Matisse, I never found time to undertake this experiment, which someone else may perhaps tackle. I remain convinced that there is much to be learnt from an inventory of the objects in a painter's work, and particularly in the work of Matisse.

If I consider what I have thought about Matisse's painting and what I have written about it, I am amazed at how little I have said. And at the same time, may I add, how little others have said about it. One can gauge through such comparisons how much is lost between mind and pen, between vision and expression. This is true not only of Matisse's painting, of course, and I am not the first to challenge La Bruyère's *tout est dit*. But let us stick to Matisse's painting.

I realize that my thoughts about it have repeatedly led me along ways where I discovered, or thought I had discovered, an entry into new realms, glimpses of unfamiliar landscapes. You know how it is when one tries to note down

1. I apologize for this repetition . . . the previous article did not exist when this was written: I am leaving it as it was published in 1946. (*1968*)

one's dreams accurately. And waking thoughts entail the same dishonest subterfuge. You hook a series of ideas on to some expression that provides a formula, some image, and from that you move on to reconstruct elusive thoughts, like a lost melody. I put more trust, myself, in the poetic association of ideas than in any process of logic. Logic, in this field, seems to explain things by hindsight. Well then . . .

I was talking about Matisse's painting and what I had said of it. Several times I naturally came up against those Baudelairean echoes that we find in Matisse, and I found myself involved in an explanation which is immediately illuminating, once one has associated these two names and has been irresistibly led to think over certain lines of Baudelaire in terms of Matisse. For instance:

Là, tout n'est qu'ordre et beauté,
Luxe, calme et volupté . . .

which seems written about Matisse, which seems to foresee, to foreshadow Matisse . . . and I even wrote something about that, twice if I remember rightly, twice I started off from that distich, that *Invitation au voyage*, that Baudelairean vision of Holland. I haven't my exact words by me at the moment. But I know that this starting-point is still valid for me, as if I had never used it before, that I can launch out again on the same reverie, still start off from the same landing-stage, without risk of repeating myself and, I fear, still without reaching by my words those shores towards which, from these two lines, if I let myself go, Matisse will once more carry me.

Là, tout n'est qu'ordre et beauté . . .

In January 1946, I thus pick up the thread of the interrupted dream. I am at Vence in the painter's studio, in front of a sort of rectangular box with two shutters which open to reveal a painted panel, it's like the conjuror's magic trunk from which a lady vanishes after being stabbed through and through with swords before our eyes. In fact it is the model of a door painted by Matisse for some rich South Americans. It is to be in their bedroom, hidden behind an ordinary double door. When these fortunate people decide to go into their bathroom, they will open the ordinary door and there they'll see Matisse's panel, framed between the two leaves of the outer door, which are painted too. Red and blue.[1] On the panels of the outer door, foliage is painted. I have seen on Matisse's table one or two dry leaves, such as he used to pick up every evening to study the way a leaf curls up as it shrivels, and which he must have copied countless times until it came naturally to him and in one inspired afternoon or evening he could paint from bottom to top, as in a motionless flight, the whole of those two folding panels that open on to Leda visited by the swan. For the door itself showed Leda and the swan, which our South Americans, after a slight pause each time I hope, will leave behind them when they open it to go into their bathroom.

Là, tout n'est qu'ordre et beauté . . .

I am writing this in a Paris which is a paradoxical Holland. Today, March 1, 1946, it is snowing harder than I have ever seen it snow in Paris. And the cloak of snow is like painting. It simplifies everything, it makes the foulest things dazzling, the most sordid clean and luxurious. And yet, coming so late in the year, it can only be disastrous. Two nights ago I was speaking to the students of the École Normale, and as I exclaimed that poetry consists only of what is lofty and beautiful, one of them asked me what I made of such a poem as *Le vin de l'assassin,* for instance. I have been reconsidering this false objection in reverse, as though, for Baudelaire, to write:

Là, tout n'est qu'ordre et beauté . . .

did not imply having first been horribly aware of ugliness and disorder, did not imply . . . The painter's longing plays as large a part as what we guess of the poet's . . .

. . . *Luxe, calme et volupté* . . .

But don't open the door: Madame is in her bath. I shall day-dream in front of Leda.

A paradoxical Holland . . . Matisse's Holland, though not a country of polders, has none the less its lands below sea-level, where tiaris or corals grow instead of tulips . . . Although it was only a short while ago, almost on the eve of the last war, that the painter visited Tahiti, long before that an unconscious nostalgia for the colours and the simplified life of those islands reigned in his painting. Had Baudelaire ever been to Holland? and if he had not, would this in any way alter *L'Invitation au Voyage*? Matisse loves to talk about

1. I leave the words *Red and blue* as they stood in the text printed on May 1, 1946, written in Paris on March 1 of that year, with merely a retinal memory of the colours. The accompanying reproduction will explain how I came to remember these two colours only. I had not checked up. Nor had Matisse, believe it or not! (*1969*)

the Pacific Islands. How could he not love to talk about those islands, where nature finally admits its likeness to his painting? where the colour knows nothing of the shadows and relief of pre-Fauve painting, where the light flouts local colour. Oceania or Low Countries, it's still the land of luxury. Of that magnificent thing about which nobody, to my knowledge, has spoken truly. Luxury is a shameful thing in a world where it is the monopoly of a few. But in Oceania it is the light, the colour, the supernatural way things are when men's eyes are pure. The luxury that now, at last, Matisse has restored to us: *Ivy, Flowers and Fruit*, *Still Life with Magnolia*, *Young Woman in a Pelisse*, *Lemons and Saxifrages* . . . a luxury beyond the reach of the rapacious, the true luxury which is the way two colours sing together, the harmony between an arm, a plant and an armchair . . . All that's needed is a pair of scissors cutting out a piece of paper, or a pencil stroke which, dividing and outlining the white paper, produces and separates off an absent colour, all that's needed is for Henri Matisse to be left alone to his uninterrupted reverie, and everything, the meanest things, commonplace substances will become, in his hands, objects of luxury, the essence of luxury.

(What happens to the object of luxury once out of its creator's hands is not my business here; I am concerned only with that strange process, never yet described, the birth of luxury, the light and patient hands touching canvas and paper, the skilful hands which after their long training can make out of that which was nothing something that has that virtue so little understood by men, the virtue of luxury, which only further great worldwide upheavals will enable us to understand . . . as Matisse has at last understood it by dint of measuring his strength against the beauty of dry leaves, the poetry of the way they crumple up, like the hands of children, beggars or country people hoping for rain . . .)

I saw Matisse at Vence a month or so ago: 'I know what a J is like now,' he told me proudly, 'and an A, the A is difficult . . . well, you shall see . . .' He spent his nights drawing letters. He could not sleep. He invented a terrible luxury for himself – to study and learn at the age of seventy-six. A dry leaf, a letter . . .

And on the wall there were pictures more beautiful than ever, younger and fresher, more luminous and gayer than ever, with ever greater confidence in light and life . . . 'In self-defence,' was Matisse's admirable comment.

Optimism* is the luxury of great men. Matisse's optimism is his gift to our sick world, the example he sets to those who revel in anguish. 'Self-defence,' he said. But in fact he is defending us.

Anger immediately cancels out any thought of luxury. It is just because I understand anger, the justification for a certain sort of anger, that when Madame has retired to her bathroom and closed the door I would gently remind these angry men, showing them Leda: 'It all depends on what is understood by the right to luxury, as Lafarge said of the right to idleness. There is a dialectical concept of luxury, in the name of which Baudelaire or Matisse, those who create that disarming thing beauty, cannot be on the side of those who would rob you of it, as they would rob its creators if they could. Luxury is something that cannot be paid for. It is that which is beyond payment. It's a luxury, as they say. It is just as much a gesture made for one's private enjoyment, unshared laughter, as it is a gift to all. It is the perpetual last cigarette of genius. Can you make of it something to be traded? . . .'

The door opens into the bedroom and the lady, in her peignoir, runs dripping wet past Leda, splashing the paint, amid the steam from the bathroom. 'My slippers!' she cries. 'Where are my slippers?' †

* Let it be understood what despair is implicit in my use of the word *optimism.* I admire the determination of the painter, with that hole in his inwards, to *bequeath to posterity* the story of a happy man. For a long time I tried to think that I myself was an optimist, I forced myself to believe it. I wanted it to be true. I sacrificed my life to asserting it. For other people. I have lived too long to 'hold the pose'. Forgive me. (*Note of 1969*)

† Actually, did she ever find them? The fact is that the lady very soon sold her *Leda*, and since then, somehow or other, has closed up her bathroom. Was it because, having read this 'apologia' of mine, or merely seen (in 1951) the commentary made on it by Alfred H. Barr, Jr, in his book *Matisse, His Art and His Public*, M. and Mme E. (whose name I discovered through that book) considered their Matisse compromising? In any case, this annoyed the painter. Today the work is in the Maeght Foundation at Saint-Paul-de-Vence. Home again.

XXXV. – *Still Life, Lemons and Saxifrages* (1943).

XXXVI. – *Leda*, triptych, oil painting on wood panel (1945–6).

Postscript, 1946

I thought I had written my apologia for luxury and now, on signing it, I feel impelled to add a postscript. A postscript which is no sort of luxury.

Out of deference, and in justice, to the man who is the pretext for my words. And those whom, willy-nilly, I have involved by my claim to write such an apologia.

If luxury implies the opposite of work, it's a crime to utter the word in connection with Matisse. That painter, for some fifty-six years, has done nothing else than work. He works as he breathes. He barely sleeps. Nothing in this world has meant anything to him except as it served his work. He doesn't know what it is to live as you or I do. He works. All his thoughts, even his wasted time, are devoted to work, to his work. You may call him a freak. He works fantastically hard, I'll admit.* His life is the negation of luxury, if by luxury one means something useless, if one implies idleness, if one implies the sort of luxury which is an insult to men who work.

*The common French expression for 'a glutton for work' is *un bourreau de travail.* Matisse was no *bourreau*, no torturer either of others or of himself: for him work was no self-flagellation, it was the highest form of pleasure. A fantastic pleasure, in fact. (*1968*)

In May 1940 there was an appalling storm, it must have been on the 23rd, in the midst of that implacable fine weather which was a *luxury* benefiting enemy aircraft (and we soldiers stared up into the blue sky from which those deadly winged creatures machine-gunned and bombed us so easily, and we resented its blue luxury). Then, we were incapable of distinguishing between thunder and the bursting of shells and bombs, and a heavy vapour like a sand-cloud filled the air between gusts of wind. Lightning flashes tore its dense texture like pale knives. The big slag-heap south-east of Carvin had been ablaze since the previous day. The roads, rocking with convoys and loud with the cries of the wounded, led to old deserted petrol stations. The British drove off in great coaches swaying from side to side of the narrow streets. The Moroccans were seized with panic because they thought the German troops included Moroccans like themselves, sent by Franco. There was a great slaughter of motor-cyclists. The town was suddenly empty amidst all these vehicles. The sand-storm darkened the air. It was clear that the end of the world was at hand. Then, from a street by the church, two children appeared. A girl and a boy, thirteen and twelve years old. They were holding hands and they were as beautiful as angels. All that day there was only one ray of sunlight shining down like one of those stage lights that always come from somewhere other than their supposed source. And that light, shining on the children's soft fair hair, seemed amidst the horror like all the beauty in the world. A house suddenly collapsed between them and myself.*

* I suddenly have the feeling that I have told this story before, and in connection with Matisse. This happens with certain dreams that recur throughout one's life, and it reveals the close association in my mind – as in some automatic mythology – between these Carvin children and the painting of Matisse. Let other people deduce what they like from it. Anyhow, I don't know where I can have written this.

What I mean is that for me, as I passed, those children, barely glimpsed, were luxury, the luxury that remains, even for those who have been despoiled of it, a reason for living and for loving, a reason for surviving.

And in our century of wars and revolutions Henri Matisse's painting is very like those two children at Carvin. Born of unremitting work. And by its example impelling me to effort, as a moral duty and as a justification.

Nothing in the least luxurious about such luxury.

Second postscript (1968)

This is in fact a postscript to the 1946 postscript. Because of that little note at the end: *I suddenly have the feeling that I have told this story before . . .* But when, where? I began hunting for the first draft of these Carvin children among all my available writings before, or contemporary with, my *Defence of Luxury*. Nothing. Not a trace. Neither in the many prefaces to my books of poetry, nor in *L'Homme communiste I*, which appeared in 1946, and parts of which were written in 1945. Nothing. I don't know my own books. Someone will find it for me[1] . . .

Note that it has often happened to me to describe in one form or another something that has happened to me or that I have chanced to witness, then to revert to it in a subsequent text. This habit grew more marked later with

1. I hunted for ten years without finding it. However, in 1966, when I re-wrote *Les Communistes*, which does not contain the story of the children, I corrected one wrong date: the storm at Carvin was not on May 23, 1940, but on the 25th (in 1970 I at last found this story in *La Mise à Mort*).

La Mise à Mort and *Blanche ou l'oubli*, but I had it before. Something might turn up in an article which had not yet been put into a novel, or vice versa. For one thing, this is understandable, because I often lend my characters my own eyes . . . And yet here, retrospectively, I was seized with strange misgivings. Not finding it. Perhaps I shall rediscover those Carvin children, somewhere else, later. It would be better to leave things as they are, and pretend that in fact . . . at any rate to say nothing, just in case they are rediscovered, by myself or somebody else . . . But, but, but, I've had a sort of idea. It's embarrassing, like a lock of hair falling into your eyes and you half-consciously throw it back, and it falls down again. And then, even if I'm wrong, it can't be helped, it had better be told. Here goes.

A sort of idea that in this particular note . . . that this note was a kind of guarantee taken by me against any possible criticism by the publisher, who might not have wanted any postscript, or by the reader, who might have considered the said postscript an irrelevance: are you talking about Matisse, yes or no? Keep to the point! Just fancy, in a book of reproductions. Talk about painting, please, and that's enough about the war, Monsieur A.'s war memories, you know what you can do with them. Because in 1946, at the time of the Nuremberg trials, war was already a political matter. And you're not going to mix up politics with Matisse's painting, I hope? Oh no, oh no, Heaven preserve us from that!

Particularly since that Carvin of mine – which took rather longer to present than an odalisque, because you've probably seen odalisques at Matisse's or in your own home, whereas Carvin is a provincial hole in which you never set foot, at any rate not that morning – had to be described, storm and all. And then I said to myself. I fancy I said to myself. I proba– presumably said to myself, people will think, and I pretended, I must have pretended to cross out the passage, and. Everything's in that *and*: one may happen to be fond of a certain bit of writing, one may think it successful; give up my Carvin children? So one lies. Whence the note. Since the story had automatically become associated with Matisse in my mind, since I'd got into the habit . . . Well, I'd smoothed things over, patched them up so as to conceal deficiencies. Seeing that . . . There must have been a reason . . . I was still keeping to the point. And so on.

You'll say: in these circumstances . . . Well, so what? You've caught me redhanded, lying. And what then? Apart from the fact that you've not noticed it for twenty-two years, this time you won't have been deceived for very long. I told you right away that I had never described the Carvin children before. And now manage as best you can.

Only why did I choose to admit a lie, and a futile one at that, rather than correct something written twenty-two years previously? Because it is to that early text that I am referring, and to what may have been said about it. You'll see later on.

In the meantime, isn't it obvious from that cheating note that already, in my *Defence of Luxury*, I was writing fiction about Henri Matisse? Writing a novel whose characters are the publisher, the reader (singular, out of modesty), the author and, of course, the painter. But for the time being the latter is at Cimiez, Alpes-Maritimes. Or rather he's already at Vence, in the Villa Le Rêve . . . In the background, you can just make him out through the window, in the room he used as a studio, painting a girl, nude or not, who has taken off the little gold cross she wore on a chain round her neck. Because for painting as well as in war, references to the Christian religion would here be out of place.

But here, precisely, politics intrude into the novel. In 1951 the Museum of Modern Art of New York published a very important book on Matisse by Alfred H. Barr, Jr, possibly the most complete at its time, entitled: *Matisse, His Art and His Public.* There are three references to my *Defence of Luxury*, on pp. 262, 264 and 270. Let's forget the final reference, which deals only with Mme Enchorrena's bathroom. The two earlier ones stress a personal detail about the present writer: p. 262: *Matisse's painting had even been defended by the Communist Aragon in 1946 in a poetic though somewhat specious essay entitled 'Apologie du Luxe'* . . .

'Specious' implies misleading, Jesuitical. The word 'even' refers to a mention in the previous sentence of 'a savage article against the decadent art of the West by Vladimir Kemenev', and in this case I won't dispute his terms, the article which appeared in *Voks* in 1947 can only be described as savage, and I must admit that there was an even more fiercely expressed article in a more important journal the *Bolshevik*, in 1947, under the same signature. That 'the Communist Aragon' should have defended Matisse (in 1946, in 1947 and at other times) seems to surprise A. H. Barr, Jr, but what surprises *me* is that all of a sudden I am referred to by him exclusively with this political attribute (page 264 more or less repeating page 262) and on a quite different subject, of which I shall speak later, and which seems thus to

XXXVII. – *Luxe, calme et volupté* (1904).

acquire a political slant. For the time being I shall confine myself to examining what might be called *specious* about my *Defence of Luxury*, apart from the political advantage to be gained from considering a few pages by a Communist as Jesuitical, or specious, or misleading.

It is a commentary not only on Matisse's painting but also on the Baudelaire of *L'Invitation au Voyage*, whence came the idea of luxury (*Luxe, calme et volupté*, words which seem expressly written for Matisse). My specious, or misleading, or Jesuitical defence seems to me for the most part to be a defence of Baudelaire at least as much as of Matisse. But it is not on account of its *luxurious* character that Kemenev attacks Matisse's painting so savagely.

In any case, when I wrote my *Defence*, I had not read in *Voks*, a monthly journal which is not my usual fare, an article which only appeared a year later. And moreover I was not writing a defence of Baudelaire or of Matisse, but of luxury, of the idea of luxury, which is usually interpreted in a restrictive, *specious* sense, I was in fact attacking, in this field, that demagogical, indeed Jesuitical restriction of the word to something which is an insult to our poor world. This, to an American, in the days of the Marshall Plan, seemed deceitful, specious, Jesuitical. What I should be interested to learn is *whom* I could be trying to deceive, for whom I was trying to confuse the issues, and for the sake of what Loyola? For lack of knowing the answer to these questions, I imagine that the author of *Matisse, His Art and His Public*, in the simplicity of his heart, slightly puzzled in his conception of a Communist by reading my *Defence*, interpreted the whole thing to himself as trickery and so forth on my part, rather than give up the stock political image so fashionable in his country. Besides, between ourselves, if a few pages about Matisse had forced him to reconsider his concept of Communism, where should we have got to, good heavens! Not to mention that he would also have had to wonder why I had failed to follow the aesthetic line of Vladimir Kemenev.[1] If one started thinking, there'd be no end to it, and that's how one ends up by killing generals and the President of the Republic (which the forms to be filled in before getting a visa for the U.S.A. ingenuously require you to state that you have no intention of doing). Oh, better stop at that point, things might become *somewhat specious*, I declare.

No doubt my novel is here wandering from its love story, the author is rambling, and it must be admitted that he enjoys that above all things, that he takes an irresistible delight, sometimes, in treating himself to that *luxury*, don't begrudge it him . . . the luxury of a *somewhat* what-d'you-call-it novel,[2] in which there appear, if not such characters as the Second Empire–Louis XV armchair, the little pewter jug or the sprig of ivy, at any rate figures that may be useful to me later on, such as Alfred H. Barr, Jr, Vladimir Kemenev or Mme Enchorrena (but this lady has got dressed again, and has lost all interest for us).

1. I only discovered the ferocious Mr Kemenev in the summer of 1947, in the *Bolshevik*, in an article where he did not mince his words and which sent me into a rage that I did not keep to myself.

2. I don't know whether it's an echo of that 'somewhat specious' or a personal opinion of M. Gaston Diehl's, but the latter, in his *Henri Matisse* (1954), writes this curious comment, apparently *in defence* of the painter:

If he chooses to lead a quiet, secluded life, buying pictures by Cézanne or Gauguin, surrounding himself with plants and birds, if he selects beautiful models and creates the setting he needs for his work, he is promptly condemned for his love of luxury, his bourgeois individualism . . . and note 319, to which the author refers us, shows *against whom* M. Diehl is defending Matisse. It runs: *Aragon as well as Alexander Romm, in* Matisse, *New York, Lear, 1947.*

A Final Correction

I don't know anything about *Matisse*, New York, Lear, 1947. Nor do I know what Alexander Romm may have written there or elsewhere. But the reader of the present book, having before his eyes *all* that I myself have written about Matisse (including the *Defence*), may observe that nowhere have I condemned Matisse, taken him to task for *his love of luxury*, *his bourgeois individualism*.

I can well understand that Mr Barr's 'Communist' Aragon was bound, in the eyes of M. Diehl, to speak like a Soviet author, bearing out the pronouncements (with which I am unacquainted) of Alexander Romm.* Only I should like to see the text where I have done so. If, according to Mr Barr, my defence of Matisse was *somewhat specious*, in M. Diehl's French version of the affair I no longer defend him, I condemn him. I condemn him to such an extent, it seems, that *Thèmes et Variations* by Henri Matisse, with a preface by myself, is not mentioned in M. Diehl's text but merely earns a bibliographical reference under my name. M. Diehl gives me credit for the *Henri Matisse* in the series *Trésors de la Peinture française*, which contains the *Apologie du Luxe*, but seems not to have read these pages any more than those of 1942, and is ready to believe (on whose authority? that of Lear, New York, 1947?) that like Alexander Romm (see marginal note) I condemn *Matisse's bourgeois individualism*, an expression for which I'll pay him good money if he can show it me anywhere, about anyone, under my signature, in French. This, however, is of little importance, I grant you; particularly in comparison with the fact that he ignores *Thèmes et Variations*, a strange omission (whatever the preface and its author) not so much of the work itself as of the great experiment it represents in the realm of drawing, to which Henri Matisse devoted himself in 1941 and 1942. And yet M. Diehl seems to have read the American book carefully before writing his own. It is a pity that he did not recognize from this that what had surprised A. H. Barr was not that I spoke like Alexander Romm but that (true, in a *somewhat specious* fashion in his view) I did just the opposite of another Soviet citizen, the ferocious Vladimir Kemenev, taking up the defence of Matisse instead of condemning him.

* These pronouncements were made, it seems, in 1934 and 1935. According to Mr Barr, Romm 'presented a generally sympathetic analysis of Matisse's art . . . but he saves his reputation-- and perhaps his skin – by references to Matisse's "bourgeois aestheticism" and "hedonistic outlook" in "the epoch of imperialism".' I confess I have never read the work, but in any case the expressions quoted have never been used by me in speaking of Matisse.

Addendum of 1969: *On re-reading my MS. as a whole, I feel the need to help the reader to connect the preceding article with* Que l'un fût de la Chapelle . . . *written early in this year, which follows later. If only to reflect on Mr Barr's use of adjectives, the* somewhat specious *we have noted about myself and the* far more conspicuous *applied to Picasso's Communism, compared (let's be quite fair) with that of Fernand Léger.*

XXXVIII. – *Girl in a Pelisse, Ochre Background* (1944).

Anthology I

158. – *Signac fishing, Derain swimming* (drawing, summer 1904, Saint-Tropez).

There is the *Novel about Matisse*, and there is the novel about the Novel . . . Little by little, like the silt left by passing time, chapters, parentheses, digressions have accumulated ever since the day when for the first time I entered the lofty cave-dwelling of the Master of Cimiez. Meetings, conversations, reveries, the events of history and those directly connected with the painter – books, experiments, exhibitions . . . the result of it all was that even with spoken flashbacks, when H.M. referred to his earlier works, those that I knew and those that I did not, my 'novel' about Matisse began at the onset of his seventy-second year, all that went before being fleetingly and incompletely recalled, and seeming indeed only to have been evoked in order to shed light on something else, on that which was taking place before my eyes.

Ever since it became customary to fix stories in writing, authors had formed the habit of catching the central character, at least, at his very beginnings, at his birth (sometimes even introducing us to his father and mother before him), so that we travelled along with him from year to year until he fell in love, the central point in the novel to which everything else led. From that the story went on to his marriage or death, and he might or might not reach old age.

But for the past hundred years or a little more, it has been usual to pick up the 'hero' at any point in time or place, by the arm or by the hair, so that we move forward knowing nothing, or little, about him. And so, flashbacks are needed to explain what may have happened before page 1, and indeed sometimes the 'anterior' novel (like the tense of a verb) became the essential part of the book, particularly during the Romantic period. This was not quite an invention, since, for secondary characters, such a device had always been necessary. Spanish fiction from *Don Quixote* onwards had diffused this retrospective technique outside the borders of Spain, and it had come into France with *Gil Blas*.

When I had already collected all that I'd written about Matisse over more than twenty-five years, I suddenly saw the weakness of this discursive method in the development of my subject. However, I was anxious not to give this dense thicket the appearance of a biography, to take on the role of *historian* to Matisse, and it seemed to me on the whole that, for the time being, it was enough to have placed my 'hero' by giving his date of birth, by stating that he had studied under Gustave Moreau and a few other details of that sort. Because the *Henri Matisse, a Novel* tells of a spiritual adventure, that of the man's work in painting, drawing and sculpture, and is not a series of anecdotes, of piquant facts about the young man I never knew or the old man, with a young look in his eyes, whom I met when he was the age I am now rapidly approaching. I'm not concerned with the women in his life or whether he was a good paterfamilias, nothing of that sort. This book is about a painter, and the expression of himself that he wanted to leave behind, that is, his paintings, his drawings, his sculptures and those paper cut-outs that he invented to crown his work. Every canvas, every sheet of paper over which his charcoal, his pencil or his pen wandered are Matisse's utterance about himself. The *Novel*, that novel that I am writing about him, is the story of those thoughts that contradict or continue one another, or suddenly recover a lost phase of themselves . . . It's through this that I have sought to reveal my protagonist.

When I examined my pages more attentively I discovered the weakness of what I had written: which was, chiefly, that it was nothing but my writing. It seems to me that I ought to go back to the old method of fiction and interrupt this flow of writing with a *narrative* which owes nothing to me, which involves Matisse alone, as when a character in the middle of a novel starts talking about his childhood, his youth or his middle age . . . And then, since quite different considerations impelled me, as I put this manuscript in order, to divide it into two equal halves, I accepted the idea that this *narrative* should come where the division occurred, namely, in the final pages of Volume I. I should thereby be enabled at this point in the novel to show, through Matisse's paintings, the unfolding of his true life, what is usually called *his art*, that is to say the successive stages of his thought, his imagination, his mastery.

It thus occurred to me to place at this point what I have for several years thought of as the *Anthology*, through which I could correct the ignorance in which I seem to have kept the reader of all that Matisse was, the Matisse whom I went to see in December 1941, and before that date the Matisse who had set me dreaming ever since the end of my childhood, when I did not yet know him.

Needless to say, having thought of putting this *Anthology* here, I immediately realized that, if only for the balance of the composition (mark you, I was not responsible for that, I had not composed anything at all), the second volume of the 'novel' should round it off with a second anthology, which would give one a *view* over all that Matisse did between the end of 1941 and his last days, that dazzling climax to his adventure, which he had forecast as early as 1942. Remember that!

It was, to be precise, on March 18, 1942, that Matisse had said to me:

'I have been studying my craft for a long time, it seems as if up till now I had done nothing but learn, elaborate my means of expression.'

This remark justifies, to my mind, placing the division here in the great painter's work. I had surprised him as he was beginning that experiment with *spontaneous drawings*, which is summed up in the book for which he made me write a preface (*Thèmes et Variations*). Thus my text, long as it is, becomes what H.M. in 1942 wanted it to be for that book, just a preface. And, of course, the break not being due to my arrival, I could not quite consider that day in December '41 as the *eventful* date. Should this first *Anthology* be carried on to March '42 so as to confirm, literally, the 'up till now' of H.M.'s comment? It seemed to me that for once the date had to depend on outside facts, because chronology – centuries, years, even days or weeks – is a matter affecting not the writer alone, nor his protagonist, but is something common to all men's lives.

Actually, shortly before my arrival at Cimiez, there was *one fact* which cut in half all our lives, whether artists or not, young or old: the war that broke out in the summer of 1939, from which date I had in fact begun my story. I therefore decided to leave a year and a half (a year and a half *before my time*, if I may make such a claim with a straight face) of Matisse's painting for the second *Anthology*, which might equally well have figured in the first. Would this in fact diminish the artificial effect of the division of what historians, in their barbaric jargon, call the system of periodicization? At all events it seemed to me to do so.

Anthology I, therefore, stops with the seeming peace that was the pause between the two great wars of our lifetime. In the dark days that followed, the artist's creative meditation seems entirely directed towards the future, thus shedding light on the remark he made in 1942 which I quoted in what I have called *Matisse Confesses*:

'It's just as if I were someone who is preparing to tackle large-scale composition . . .

But at the date when the present volume ends, we are only at the stage of anticipation.

Here, when the curtain falls between the acts, the reader must linger, as though granted a respite, over these Pythian words, these mingled ghosts of past and future, like an audience at *Macbeth* disturbed by the witches' words on the heath, but ignorant, as yet, of the play's ending.

I like to challenge and denounce *system*. And that goes for more than painting.

These two systematic *Anthologies* are not the novel I am writing. They complement and correct it. For in the texts of the two volumes, all the periods of Matisse's life are in fact present, for contrast or comparison, intermingled and mutually illuminating. Chronology plays only a secondary role in illustrating the text: up at Cimiez under the Occupation, we are free to come and go between the Fauve period, that of the Odalisques and the present moment. In contrast with this kaleidoscope, the *Anthology* puts things back in their right order. The two volumes differ, however, in that the first Anthology restores order within the past, the second within the future. But here is not the place to explain that.

Every book about Matisse rightly allots a certain place to his painting prior to 1900. In fact, from 1890 to 1900 this consists mainly of what one might call formative works: copies, imitations of Raphael, Poussin, Philippe de Champaigne, Dutch seventeenth-century painting and that of eighteenth-century France (Watteau, Fragonard, Boucher, Chardin) like the travels of the young Wilhelm Meister. But his original work in those early days gives no foretaste of the Matisse we know, of all that comprises his greatness: still lifes, interiors, dimly lit and low-toned. Open-air painting appears only towards 1895, and his landscapes reveal the evolution of his colour during his stay in Brittany (1896) and his visit to Corsica in 1898. A painting of 1897 which is constantly reproduced, *La Desserte* (*Harmony in Red*), which today, seventy years later, seems to differ little from the work of Matisse's contemporaries although it created a sensation at the time, is of great interest because of that other picture bearing the same title, and the extraordinary advance in the treatment of the same theme made in eleven or twelve years: we see here the transition from the pre-Matisse to the true, individual Matisse. This was no doubt what Gustave Moreau was dreading when he told his pupil: '*You're going to simplify painting.*' That remark has started many hares since then. Matisse liked to quote it, with a special smile. But that's his own business. Now, more than half a century after the remark was made in the early days of Matisse's painting, we find it impossible to understand what shocked Moreau, the critics and the public. And for my part, I think such language now belongs only to the academic tradition. Actually, in our eyes, this 'simplification' of painting, considered as a retrogression from accepted teaching, is far from being a simplifying process, quite the reverse. The abandonment of such teaching, the transition to a different sort of painting, is the mark of daring and inventiveness, which simplify nothing but reject the painstaking parrotry of those hacks who imitate (or think they imitate) their forerunners, who were themselves inventors. I am almost tempted to contradict

Gustave Moreau's formula and to say that Matisse has made the problem of painting more complex, he has *complicated painting*, confronting all future painters with that necessity for invention, for constant invention, which from the beginning of this century has opened up a new path for painting. Can we say that any one picture marks this fresh start? Any choice is arbitrary; at first there's an elusive period of meditation and then suddenly the thing breaks out like flame from a smouldering coal. And once again, I cannot take responsibility for the arbitrary decision to cut into a living work, into the physical evolution of a mind. If we're going to be arbitrary, I'd rather leave to human historians, to men's puerile habit of envisaging their own history as served up in neat hundred-year slices, the responsibility of asserting that Henri Matisse begins with the twentieth century.

And because the end of the preceding century was marked in his case by a sudden wish to study a different art, copying Barye's *Jaguar Devouring a Hare* and making his own version of it, because in the year 1900 he launched out on sculpture on his own account with *The Slave*, on which he worked until 1903 and which was exhibited in 1908 at the Salon d'Automne . . . I felt it right to make *Anthology I* start with the *Male Model*, which he painted in 1900 and which shows *The Slave* as seen with a painter's eyes (very unlike what the sculptor made of him), the true portrait of the model Bevilaqua, posing in the studio which is warmed by the stove visible in the background on his left, a picture in which blue predominates so much that it has also been called *Académie bleue* (*Anthology I*, p. 305).[1] Here, in what might then have been thought a mere study, the Fauve period is already foreshadowed (minus its violent colour), with the draughtsmanship we shall find in *The Dance* or *Music*. For my part I consider this work as the hinge between two periods in the history of painting. After that, Henri Matisse speaks with his own voice, and what he says soars high above our times, opens up the way of invention from which there is no going back, one of the greatest adventures of the human mind.

The scope of this adventure may perhaps be assessed by comparing the picture painted in Brittany during the summer of 1896, which is called *The Open Door*, with *The French Window* of 1914 (p. 331): for here mystery is added to the copy of the world, a mystery peculiar to Matisse which cannot be reduced to words, however ingeniously chosen and elaborated. The mystery through which painting says something that can only be shown, and that is related to no art save that which forced primitive man to draw bisons on the lightless walls of his caves.

It was during his so-called *dark* period, in the early years of this century, that those colours which were soon to invade his canvases made their first appearance, like flowers springing up on a forest floor. Needless to say, that other sort of 'periodicization', which forces the painter's hand as though a *period* must conform to the name given it, has little meaning in the case of Matisse. Even in 1897–98, a still life, *Dishes and Fruit*, which is in the Hermitage in Leningrad, and which *ought* to have been *dark*, is rich in colour, and, in the same museum, the *Still Life with Coffee Pot* might really be classified as already belonging to the *Fauve period*. The title *Académie bleue* sometimes applied to the painting of *The Slave* may perhaps refer to a sketch for that picture, on whose large canvas, in any case, the gamut of greens and blues is restricted to the shadowy studio background. The bearded figure of coarse type (the model Bevilaqua) is painted in light tones which stand out in contrast with the blues behind him. In the *Nude Study* from the Carrière Studio, probably of the same date, there are blue glints on the chest and biceps, the belly and left thigh of the bald model (who is certainly not Bevilaqua), but there are glowing reds on his left shoulder, right arm, knee-caps and right foot, spreading over his legs and thighs. It's not for any such pretty details that I have chosen another painting of the same time, *Interior with Harmonium*, but rather for its composition, a new kind of spatial perspective which foretells the future of Matisse's painting

1. From here onwards, references to the reproductions in *Anthology I* will merely indicate the page number in this volume.

better than any palmistry. I don't propose to trace from one canvas to another the choice made for this first *Anthology*. I shall merely say of the 1903 *Carmelina*, which reveals the painter's new-found daring in the division of lights and shadows, that this picture makes the light circulate round the model by means of a mirror, as in Ingres's *Mme de Senonnes*, that mirror with which H.M. was going to play all his life. Undoubtedly, the emphasis on the anatomy of both male and female models at this time is due to the painter's pre-occupation with sculpture.

But the artist's essential character is revealed by his contradictions. These appear clearly in the summer of 1904 at Saint-Tropez, where the influence of Seurat, and his friendship with Signac, led him to develop a style which is the opposite of *The Slave* or *Carmelina*, represented here by the *Woman with a Parasol* of 1905 (p. 308), less often reproduced than others of this period shown here among the illustrations to my text, such as *Luxe, calme et volupté* (see *In Defence of Luxury*, Vol. I, p. 291). But from 1905 onwards that division of light which is characteristic of Seurat's influence disappears from Matisse's painting, apparently under the influence of Gauguin (although I cannot consider as an effect of 'influence' Matisse's *meditation* on Gauguin or Van Gogh, Ingres or Delacroix, any more than Picasso's on Rembrandt, Velazquez or Cranach). This becomes evident with *Joie de Vivre* (see in *Signs*, p. 156) because the theme is akin to *Luxe, calme*... whereas the treatment seems to contradict it. These two pictures were painted each at the close of the year, *Luxe, calme*... from 1904 to 1905 and *Joie*... from 1905 to 1906. It is impossible to ignore the sequential relationship between these deliberately dissimilar works, in which the tendency to paganism or, as I should prefer to consider it, hedonism grows more marked.

It began at Collioure, I fancy, when he had abandoned Saint-Tropez and Signac, during that same summer of 1905. It is discernible in studies for the landscape to be used in *Joie de Vivre*. The Seurat period was merely a prelude to the dazzling event that took place at Collioure; with *The Siesta* (Vol. I, p. 139) and *Window at Collioure* (p. 141) and more markedly with *Woman with the Hat*, which is a portrait of Mme Matisse, and which was to serve as manifesto for what, by the time of the Salon d'Automne of that year, was known as *Fauvism*[1] (p. 309).

In this *Anthology*, Fauvism properly so called is represented by paintings of 1905, 1906 and 1907: after *Woman with the Hat* come *Marguerite Reading* (Matisse's daughter) (p. 310), two

1. I have pointed out that the *Fauve* character is already evident in earlier paintings, but less decisively, without prevailing there entirely or monopolizing them. As we shall see, Matisse's *Fauve period* never really ended even if it altered, and it did not preclude other experiments. It is somewhat far-fetched to trace Fauvist precedents to the Salon d'Automne of 1905 in the work of certain painters other than Matisse and those close friends, such as Derain, who were with him at Saint-Tropez and Collioure in the summer of 1905. Georges Duthuit justly points out: *As a collective phenomenon, Fauvism was as short-lived as it was violent. Most of those who slashed pure colours on to their canvases at that time soon gave it up, as though settling down after sowing their wild oats.* The Fauve period, in point of fact, lasted from 1904 to 1907, although pictures by a few painters can be so labelled as late as 1910. This *fashion* (to use the word without its usual pejorative implication) was later reflected, here and there, in the work of such epigoni as Raoul Dufy. By 1909–10 the new *fashion*, its masters being Braque, who had broken away from Fauvism by 1907, and Picasso, whose *blue period* is often, wrongly to my mind, compared with those paintings of Matisse which contain blues (generally in an attempt to show that Picasso derives from Matisse), was what became known as Cubism, a casual remark of Matisse's having been seized upon by journalists and systematized. Schools succeed one another and are alike in their ephemeral attraction for imitators. Masters invent, and are only happy inventing, and discard their followers. For Derain, his Fauve period was no more than an ordeal by fire; for Braque, a moment of his youth, a *physical painting* which suited him at the time. Matisse, whose Fauvism is often restricted by critics to the Moroccan paintings of 1912–13, was to remain profoundly faithful to the movement which made him the educator of the Fauves, and if he seemed to move away from Fauvism, it was never to go backwards but to transcend himself, retaining that fire from his youth and, in order to carry it further, altering its form of expression (as one's handwriting changes from childhood to manhood, acquiring other characteristics but remaining itself, while reflecting the stages of the psyche, the unforgettable imprint of existence).

versions of *The Young Sailor* painted in 1906 at Collioure, between which we trace a growing assertion of his individuality (in *Anthology I*, I reproduce only the one which, as I mentioned, André Breton and I had pinned up in 1917 in the Val-de-Grâce [p. 311] and which now belongs to Hans Seligmann of Basle; the earlier picture, somewhat less daring, may indeed be considered a study for the second), *The Hairdresser* and *The Bank* (*La Berge*) of 1907 (pp. 312 and 313), and *Red Madras Headdress* (Mme Matisse), also of 1907, which I do not reproduce here. I have reserved for Vol. II, p. 230, an earlier portrait of Mme Matisse (1905) known as *The Green Line* on account of the shadow that runs down from the forehead and divides the nose, marking off in fact the shadowed part of the face as well as the shadow in the room behind. But Fauvism is not confined to these years, it is merely modified in the work of the artist who was its master. A story told by Gertrude Stein, who owns the picture, made me introduce into *Matisse-en-France* the *Blue Nude* of 1907 which is subtitled *Souvenir of Biskra*. Two years later, a journey to Algeria brought a rebirth of violence, as it were, to Matisse's colour (see *Algerian Woman*, p. 316), and may have led to that search for violent light which took him twice, in 1911 and in 1912–13, to Morocco, to Tahiti in 1930, and a nostalgic yearning for which, in 1939, on the eve of the war, suggested a journey to Brazil. And although from 1908 onwards he began a new sort of painting, to my mind at any rate, with *Game of Bowls* (p. 314) and *Nymph and Satyr* (p. 315) painted in 1909, to which I shall return, works which only in a wider sense can be considered as Fauve, yet Fauvism persists throughout Matisse's work. Perhaps it was rekindled by a visit to Seville in 1911. Of the major works of this period I have chosen here the *Large Studio* and the *Interior with Eggplants*, while in *Matisse-en-France* will be found *The Painter's Family* (Issy-les-Moulineaux, 1911, now in Moscow: Vol. I, p. 133). But even if the admirable *Blue Window* (p. 322), painted the same year at Issy-les-Moulineaux, can be accounted for in terms of Fauvism, how can this be done with *Conversation* (p. 317), said to have been painted for Shchukin in 1911, which I include in *Anthology I*? It is absurd, of course, to look for any demarcation line for Fauvism in Matisse's painting. But it is impossible not to relate to that movement the works painted in Morocco in 1912, of which *Anthology I* includes *Window at Tangier, Zorah on the Terrace*, *Entrance to the Kasbah* (pp. 324, 325 and 326). *The Riffian, half length*, reproduced here (p. 327) and *The Riffian, seated*, were painted in 1913 during Matisse's second visit to Morocco; whereas *The Moroccans* of 1916 is composed from his memories, and its colour is no longer that of his travel paintings, owing far more to his subsequent experiments (pp. 335 and 336).

It is to these that we must return: I have already mentioned those paintings of 1908–09 which are in *Anthology I, Game of Bowls, Nymph and Satyr.* (Should we not also include the three *Female Nudes* of 1908 in the Hermitage? But they do not mark such an obvious break as the others I have cited, and they might here be considered as *studies*.) We must include the *Bathers with a Turtle*, of 1908, *The Bather* painted at Cavalière in 1909, the same year as the first version of *The Dance* which is in the Philadelphia Museum of Art. I have shown only the final version of that painting (1910, today in the Hermitage in Leningrad) in *Signs* (Vol. I, pp. 154 and 155). *Music*, shown in *Anthology I* (pp. 318 and 319), is also dated 1910. *The Dance* reappears as a picture on the wall in the two versions of *Nasturtiums and the 'Dance'*, of which I reproduce that from the Pushkin Museum in Moscow (p. 323). Barr dates these 1912, but Mme Duthuit corrects this to 1911.

Perhaps this *manner* of Matisse's, one of his most authoritative (and in which, for my own part, I see the origin of the wartime *Icarus* and the cut-outs of the final period, or at least a decisive step towards that development), can be attributed not only to a reaction against Fauvism but still more to an idea that had preoccupied him ever since he had attempted sculpture. This *sculptured* painting, like the *sculptured* self-portrait that serves as frontispiece to Vol. I, follows a return to statuary in 1905–07, and coincides with the time when Matisse sculpted *The Two Negresses* (1908), *La Serpentine* (1909) and the five busts entitled *Jeannette* which were made in 1910 and 1911. In any case, this sudden puritanism in the use of colour poses a problem to which Matisse gave no answer in his lifetime, and it would need great audacity to explain it now that he is no longer here. I will, however, refer the reader to Vol. II, the chapter *On Colour*, at any rate for one point (Vol. II, p. 249) which I have underlined with a note, Matisse's comment on the persistence of ultramarine in 1942 and 1943, as of a language invented thirty years earlier. I'm letting myself be carried away. In fact, reader, you need none of my commentaries, I shall simply guide you through the paintings of Matisse by setting them out, sending you from the *Anthology* to the reproductions in the text. If you are capable of understanding why, I need provide no further explanation. And if not, what use are my remarks to you, since in any case you'll be all at sea?

I must further mention, in this connection, certain paintings which appeared shortly before the war, in 1913. In the autumn of that year (if I leave out of account the *Still Life with a Bust* and the *Goldfish*, both painted in the summer of 1912 at Issy-les-Moulineaux), the *Mme Matisse*, of which I have spoken elsewhere because of its importance to myself at the age of twenty, where the top left-hand corner is of that same ultramarine, marks a leap forward in man's way of seeing things, with its deliberately *painted* face and the way the scarf slips, and the simplicity of the total effect contrasting with the *detail* in the hat (for the picture itself and my commentary, see *To Be Inserted*, p. 22 of this volume).

It is indeed the extreme simplicity and bareness of line (and for instance, in *Woman on a High Stool* [1914], the choice of the purely linear drawing-desk, the stool and the woman herself, to which we shall see Matisse return three years later as background to *The Piano Lesson*) (Vol. I, p. 98) as in the *View of Notre Dame* (also of 1914), possibly the most linear of all this artist's paintings, it is that simplicity, that spareness which characterize the pictures I am speaking of, where straight lines tend to prevail, as in the *Interior with Goldfish* of 1914 or the *Goldfish* of 1915 . . . the work which, in the 'twenties, my prayers and those of André Breton eventually persuaded Jacques Doucet to acquire. This tendency is carried to a challenging extreme in 1914 with *Head, White and Rose* (p. 333), constructed entirely from straight lines geometrically emphasized, with which we must compare the portrait, *Mme Greta Prozor* (1916), and the composition *Bathers by a River* (1916), where this rectilinear principle is combined with the introduction of curves (pp. 337 and 338).

For invariably, if H.M. takes one path, he provides himself with an alternative way out. And in the very same year of the *Head, White and Rose* (1914), the painter seems to have moved in entirely the opposite direction with a systematic play of curves (and indeed of straight lines too) in the portrait of *Mlle Yvonne Landsberg* (p. 330). The love of curves, indeed, was later to prevail with the *Odalisques*, and with everything connected with his feeling for 'Mme de Senonnes', in objects and in landscapes as well as in women's bodies, the appearance of the *arabesque* which was to lead him, thirty-three years after *Mlle Yvonne Landsberg*, to declare in *Jazz* (1947): *My curves are not crazy.* And this at the very time when he was providing his text with tailpieces which are pure curves without meaning, like those he had invented a year earlier for his *Fleurs du Mal.*

These, it would seem, are the paintings – and one might add to these *The Buff-coloured Curtain*, of 1915 (p. 334), on account of its curves, and *The Window: Interior*, of 1916, for its rectilinear character . . . and perhaps also, for its composition, the *Gourds*, a still life painted in the summer of 1916, and possibly also *The Painter and His Model*, the picture of that name painted in 1917[1] (people's minds work in their own way) . . . these are the paintings which critics have taken to calling Matisse's 'Cubist period', which is utterly absurd. I say this not in order to 'clear' Matisse from the imputed 'crime', but simply because these paintings have nothing in common with the art of Picasso and Braque. Time, at any rate, has clarified these

1. In which the model Laurette (Vol. I, p. 97) is seen sitting in an armchair in the background (and in the picture that has been begun) while through the window there can be seen (as also in *The Studio, Quai Saint-Michel*, where Laurette, nude, is on the sofa, in the absence of the painter, who has left his portfolio on a chair) the *new* landscape that is visible from the Quai Saint-Michel, that is, the recently completed white buildings of the Sûreté Nationale, which also appear in the *Interior with Goldfish* of the same year, whereas there had been a different view from the studio at 19 Quai Saint-Michel in earlier paintings, for instance the *Pont Saint-Michel* of 1900, where through the wide-open window can be seen, instead of these buildings, an irregular cluster of houses and a mass of trees. I mention this, if I may, for the sake of *historical* realism.

confusions. Inevitably, of course, *The Piano Lesson* provided a further excuse to invest Matisse with a title he had himself invented for an art as yet unnamed, which was not his own art. I have grouped the last-named picture along with *Goldfish* of 1915–16 and *The Painter and His Model* of 1917 as illustrating what, before 1900, had been called 'simplified' painting and what at the time, in 1916, was called Matisse's 'cubism'. Look at them (Vol. I, pp. 96 and 97 respectively); they form, as a group, one of the peaks of Matisse's achievement. I'll say the same, perhaps surprisingly but with profound conviction, of a picture here included in *Anthology I* (p. 331), *The French Window* of Issy-les-Moulineaux (1914), of which I spoke earlier, referring to the mystery still conveyed today (1969) by that door. I have discussed this in a small book from which I have already borrowed, for this 'novel', a passage on Joyce's *Ulysses* (*Je n'ai jamais appris à écrire ou les Incipit*, Skira, 1969, in the series *Les Sentiers de la création*). I quote my commentary on *The French Window* as it appears in that book, in the author's handwriting:

<u>La porte-fenêtre</u> de Matisse
(1914), le plus mystérieux
des tableaux jamais peints
semble s'ouvrir sur cet
"espace" d'un roman qui
commence et dont
l'auteur ignore tout encore
comme de cette vie,
dans la maison d'obscurité,
ses habitants, leur mémoire,
leurs rêves, leurs douleurs.

Matisse's *French Window* (1914), the most mysterious picture ever painted, seems to open on the 'space' of a novel just begun.

What makes *The French Window* so mysterious, to my mind, is first that, unlike all the *Open Windows* painted by Matisse and other contemporary or later artists, which give on to a luminous space outside, this french window opens on to a dark space, whether a garden or something we shall meet later in *Le silence habité des maisons*. But further, and I don't know if Matisse was aware of this or not, when one notes its date, 1914, and it must have been in summer, that mystery makes one shiver. Whether or not the painter intended it, and whatever that french window opens on to, it is still open. It was on to the war then, and it's still on to the black future, the 'inhabited silence' of the future, the event to come which will wreak havoc in the lives of men and women unseen in the darkness.

This commentary, disproportionate to the catalogue headings my *Anthology* requires, here deliberately cuts short the over-detailed account of the reasons that dictated my choice, and explains the presence of *Burst of Sunlight* (*Trivaux*), of 1917 (p. 340), which should be compared with the 1942 *Bars of Sunlight* (Vol. II, p. 323), one of those 'Girls in Front of the Window' which I discuss in the second volume. Apart from this, it will be seen that I have given cursory samples of the period that starts at Nice, when his models were Antoinette and then Henriette. The story of this period (and of Laurette) will be told later, seen in my own way, that is, through the 'window' opened on to it by Henri Matisse, in Volume II, in the chapter *Marie Marcoz and Her Lovers*. And whereas this inter-war period, 1918–39, is represented in *Anthology I* by five plates only (as against thirty-five for the period 1900–18), it provides a great many illustrations to the text, showing the development of the so-called 'Odalisque' period (represented here by two paintings only, of 1923 and 1927). It is in *Matisse-en-France* that the two studies of Henriette and her brothers (one painting of that name, and one drawing, *Henriette at the Piano, Her Brothers Reading*. both of 1923) provide a parallel to the pictures of his own family, *The Painter's Family* (1911) and *The Music Lesson* (1916). The paintings of Tahiti are in *La Grande Songerie*. Volume II will show the successive versions of *The Lady in Blue*, and the final painting (1937), while the series that concludes with *The Conservatory* (1938), shown in *Anthology I*, is also in the second volume.

Having given these explanations, lengthier than I had intended, I can now hand over to the only person who can *show* you what words cannot express. And at this point in the novel, Gil Blas, better than his author Lesage, will guide you through the tangle of facts. *My* Gil Blas, my protagonist, will *paint* for you, in his own incomparable way, the world he has travelled through, as so many episodes in a story which, in this first part, goes from the World Exhibition of 1900, looking back over past time, up till the moment when the threat of violence was on our threshold and that monstrous shadow had begun to spread over us, seeking to put out for ever the light of French art from Manet to Matisse and beyond . . . *degenerate art*, according to those who were already ruling over us when I came to Cimiez in quest of that blue gaze that restored my trust in a future after the storm. The gaze of the man who in 1914, at Issy-les-Moulineaux, had painted the french window opening on to the war, which I cannot get out of my mind.

XXXIX. – *Vase of Flowers* (1900[?], Picasso collection).

XL. – *The Slave* (1900).

XLI. – *Interior with Harmonium* (1900).

XLII. – *Carmelina* (1903).

XLIII. – *Woman with a Parasol* (1905).

XLIV. – *Woman with the Hat (Mme Matisse)* (1905).

XLV. – *Marguerite Reading* (1906).

XLVI. – *Young Sailor* (1906).

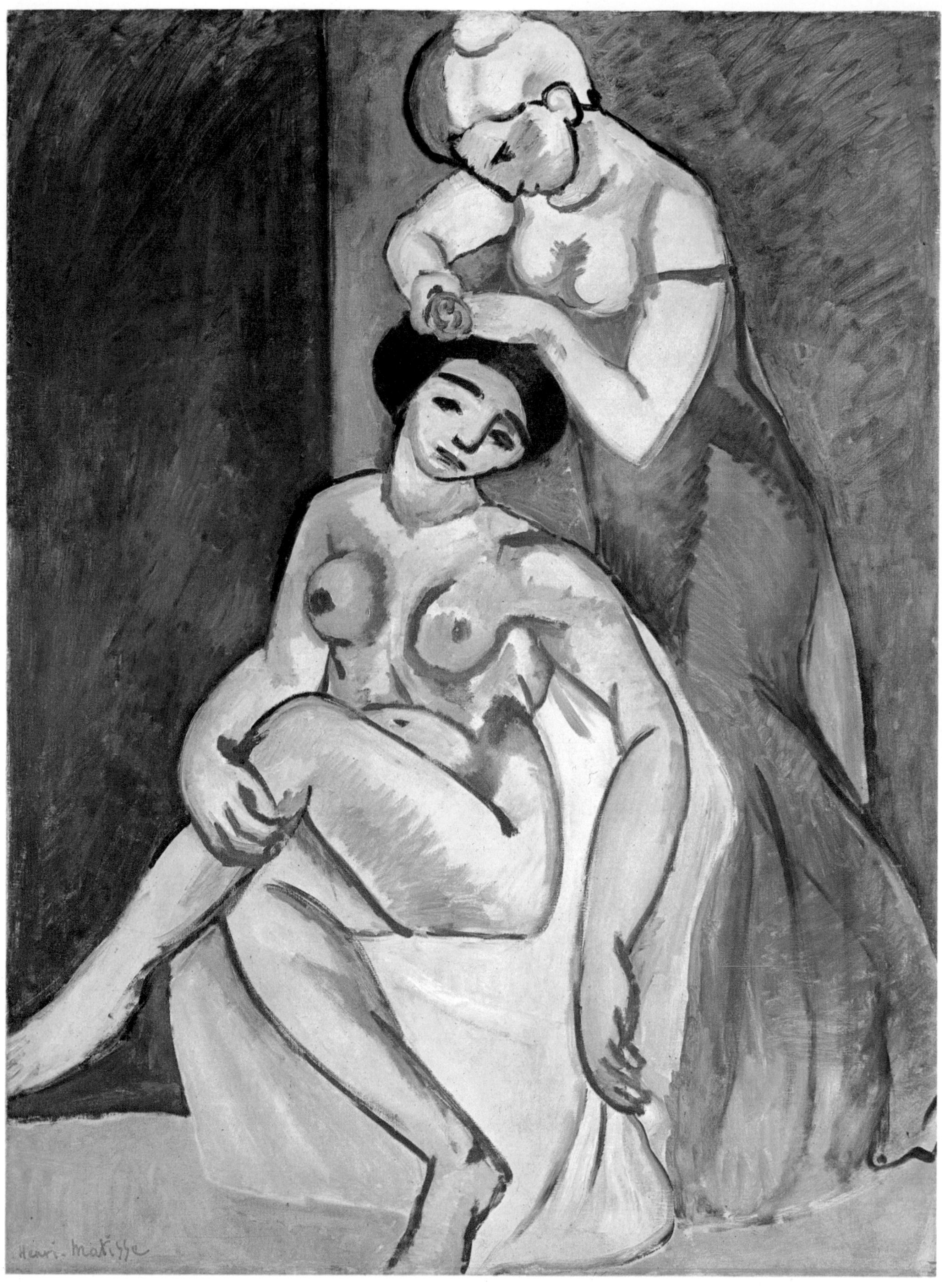

XLVII. – *The Hairdresser* (1907).

XLVIII. – *The Bank* (1907).

XLIX. – *Game of Bowls* (1908).

L. – *Nymph and Satyr* (1909).

LI. – *Algerian Woman* (1909).

LII. – *Conversation* (1911).

LIII. – *Music* (1910).

HENRI-MATISSE 1910

LIV. – *Large Studio* (Issy-les-Moulineaux, 1911).

LV. – *Interior with Eggplants* (Collioure, 1911).

LVI. – *The Blue Window* (1911).

LVII. – *Nasturtiums and the 'Dance'* (1911).

LVIII. – *Window at Tangier* (1912).

LXI. – *The Riffian, Half-length* (1913).

LX. – *Entrance to the Kasbah* (1912).

LIX. – *Zorah on the Terrace* (1912).
(The three paintings LVIII, LIX and LX form a triptych, set out here according to the wish expressed by Henri Matisse and shown together thus for the first time at the 1969 exhibition in the Pushkin Museum, Moscow, where they now are.)

LXII. – *Oranges* (1912).

LXIII. – *Flowers and Tambourines* (1913).

LXIV. – *Mlle Yvonne Landsberg* (1914).

LXV. – *The French Window* (1914).

LXVI. – *View of Notre Dame* (1914).

LXVII. – *Head, White and Rose* (1914).

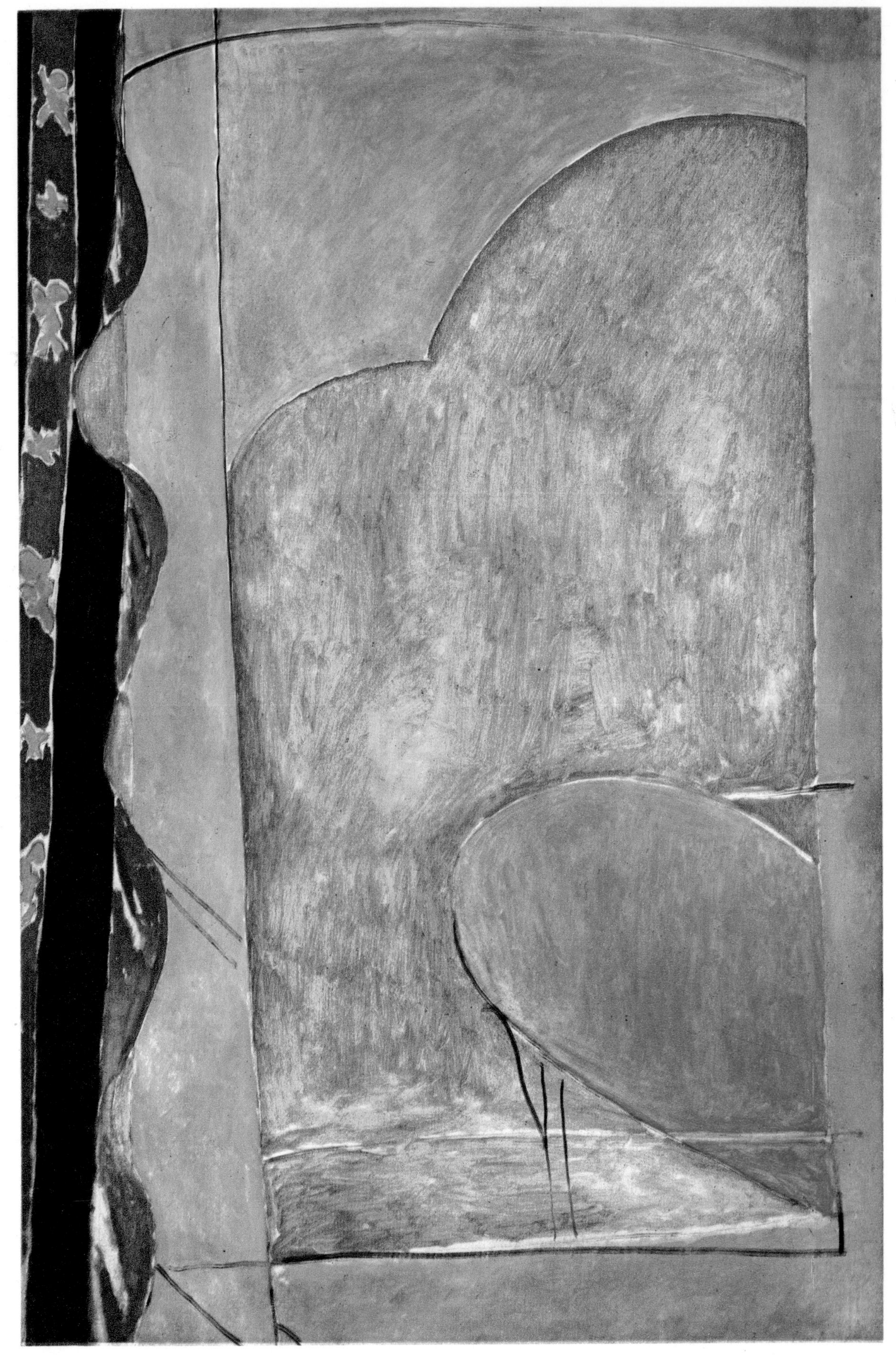

LXVIII. – *The Buff-coloured Curtain* (1915).

LXX. – *Bathers by a River* (1916).

Henri-Matisse

LXIX. – *The Moroccans* (1916).

LXXI. – *Mme Greta Prozor* (1916).

LXXII. – *Burst of Sunlight (Trivaux)* (1917).

.XXIII. – *The Hindu Pose* (1923).

LXXIV. – *Reclining Nude, Back View* (1927).

LXXV. – *Blue Eyes* (1935).

LXXVI. – *The Conservatory* (1938).

Sources of Illustrations

ILLUSTRATIONS IN COLOUR

1. The dimensions, height and width, are given in metres.

* Barr (p. 94) says Ellisen Collection, Paris.

ILLUSTRATIONS IN BLACK AND WHITE

The illustrations provided by the Author represent the selection made by Henri Matisse himself during his conversations with Aragon, which gave rise to the present book.

The publishers have furthermore received special permission to reproduce documents belonging to the family of Henri Matisse.

They wish to acknowledge the sources of the following photographs:

ADANT (HÉLÈNE), Paris. Nos. 12, 39, 43, 44, 61, 62, 73, 77, 79, 81, 97, 111, 112, 113, 114, 115, 116, 117, 118, 122, 123, 125, 126, 128, 131, 132, 133, 134, 135, 136, 137, 138, 139, 140, 141, 142, 143, 144, 145, 146, 147, 148, 149, 150, 151, 152, 153, 154, 155, 156.

BARNES FOUNDATION. No. 71 (copyright 1971, The Barnes Foundation).

BÉRARD, Nice. No. 23.

BIBLIOTHÈQUE NATIONALE (Cabinet des Médailles), Paris, No. 80.

BRASSAÏ, Paris. Nos. 6, 124.

BRAUN, Publishers, Paris. No. 109 (from the plate in *Matisse* by Jean Cassou in the series 'Couleurs des Maîtres', 1939).

CAHIERS D'ART, Paris. No. 108 (from the plate in *Dessins de Matisse*, published by Cahiers d'Art, 1936).

CARTIER-BRESSON (HENRI), Paris (Archives Magnum). No. 41.

CERCLE D'ART, Publishers, Paris. No. 158.

FABIANI, Publishers, Paris. No. 98 (from the plate in *Pasiphaé*, 1944). Nos. 18, 19, 20, 21, 22, 24, 25, 26, 28, 29, 30, 31, 32, 33, 34, 35, 36, 37, 47, 48, 49, 50, 51, 52, 64, 65, 66, 67, 74, 75, 76, 157 (from the plates in *Dessins, thèmes et variations*, 1943).

FRY (VARIAN). No. 17.

HERVÉ (LUCIEN), Paris. No. 63.

MACY (THE GEORGE MACY COMPANIES, INC.), New York. Nos. 102, 103, 104 (these three engravings, taken from *Ulysses*, form part of the series made by Henri Matisse for the Limited Editions Club, and are reproduced by kind permission of The George Macy Companies, Inc. (copyright 1935, © 1963).

MADONES, Le Cateau. No. 69.

MATISSE (PIERRE), Nos. 100, 101.

OSTIER (ANDRÉ), Paris. No. 40.

SKIRA, Publishers, Geneva. Nos. 53, 54, 68, 107 (from the plates in *Mallarmé*, 1932, reproduced by kind permission of Éditions d'Art Albert Skira, Geneva).

TÉRIADE, Publishers, Paris. No. 129 (from the plate in *Poèmes de Charles d'Orléans*, Éditions Verve, 1950).

Translations

Page 19 *You see marquises on bicycles.*
You see pimps in riding-habits
Snotty-nosed kids in little veils
You see firemen scorching along

Page 23 *Yes, since I have met my faithful friend once more . . .* (*Andromaque*, I. i)

My mind is made up, I must go, dear Theramenes,
And leave the delightful land of Troezen . . . (*Phèdre*, I. i)

Let us pause a moment: the splendour of these halls
Is strange to you, Arsaces, I can see.
In this splendid and secluded study
Titus often confides his secret thoughts.
He comes here sometimes, unknown to his court,
To tell the queen of his love . . . (*Bérénice*, I. i)

Page 35 *Alain, you who are held in suspense*
By snow seen in mid-August
Snow come from I know not where
Like wool spun from the sheep's back
And the spurt of water over the whale
You remind me of that poet whose name was
Bertrand de Born almost like your own
Almost like your own

Page 64 *O Time, suspend your flight . . .*

Page 101 *What silk with time's balms where the Chimera is emaciated is worth the twisted native cloud which you offer out of your mirror!*

(Transl. Anthony Hartley)

Page 102 *On the horizon, a sculptured cloud-shape rises up in the blue heaven, like a naked maiden emerging from the pure waters of a lake.*

Page 104 *My dazzling dark beloved . . .*

Page 114 *I am the judge in that long quarrel between tradition and invention.*

Be kindly when you make comparison
Of us and those who were ordered perfection,
While we go seeking adventure everywhere.

Now in comes summer, violent season,
And my youth lies dead together with the spring.
O Sun, now is the time of passionate Reason . . .

Page 108 *To imitate the Chinese artist with the clear and delicate heart who finds a pure ecstasy in painting, on snowy cups stolen from the moon, the finished perfection of a strange transparent flower, the flower which he smelled as a child and which has become engrafted into the blue watermark of the soul.*

Page 178 *In this land of strange windows*
Night is too dark for a sob to disturb
The enclosed gardens which are walled hearts
Everything is stony and inordinate
In this land of strange windows

Page 222 *He is the man of our century and our pole star . . .*

Page 244 *Thus the wood-god swelled his reeds:*
While the robber Cacus stole away our flocks
He did not interrupt his sweet piping.
Happy is he who, until the end of his days,
Enamoured of the arts, can cultivate their fruit.
He can defy injustice, allay his sorrows,
He forgives men and laughs at their folly,
And with his dying hand still plucks the lyre . . .

Page 249 *Wear mourning for me: a poppy, a leaf of wormwood,*
Some April lilac, the flower I loved so dearly,
Let them wither against your heart a whole springtide,
I beg you: one spring! a hallowed hope.

Page 282 *There, all is order and beauty,*
Luxury, calm and sensuous delight . . .

KING ALFRED'S COLLEGE
LIBRARY

HENRI MATISSE BY ARAGON, VOLUME I,
WAS DESIGNED BY THE AUTHOR,
WITH THE COLLABORATION OF ROGER PARRY AND MICHEL MUGUET,
ASSISTED BY SERGE ROMAIN

ENGLISH TEXT FILMSET BY
BUTLER & TANNER LTD, FROME AND LONDON
BLACK-AND-WHITE GRAVURE ILLUSTRATIONS PRINTED BY
ETS BRAUN & CIE, MULHOUSE-DORNACH
COLOUR AND OFFSET ILLUSTRATIONS PRINTED BY
DRAEGER FRÈRES, MONTROUGE
BOUND BY BABOUOT, GENTILLY